HARRIGAN

HARRIGAN

The referee in a league of his own

WITH DANIEL LANE

HODDER

A Hodder Book

First published in Australia and New Zealand in 2003
by Hodder Headline Australia Pty Limited
(A member of the Hodder Headline Group)
Level 17, 207 Kent Street, Sydney NSW 2000
Website: www.hha.com.au

This edition published in 2004

National Library of Australia
Cataloguing-in-Publication data

Harrigan, Bill.
  Harrigan.

  ISBN 0 7336 1888 X.

  1. Harrigan, Bill. 2. Rugby football referees - Australia -
  Biography. I. Lane, Daniel (Daniel Q.).

796.3333092

Text design and typesetting by Bookhouse, Sydney
Printed in Australia by Griffin Press, Adelaide

For Lesley's mum, Jean

contents

keeping my head

I am a firm believer in fate. To me, life is like a road map, you start at one point, travel down various paths and at some stage your road will finish off the page. When it finishes, that's your time—you die. Throughout the course of life you take left and right turns which will eventually deliver you to the edge of the page. You could say, 'But if I didn't take that turn I wouldn't have ended up here', but I believe you were meant to take that turn; if you changed your mind, you were meant to change it.

When I look at how I came to be a first grade referee, I can see a whole lot of turns that I nearly didn't take, but all of them were meant to be. One of those moments was in the '80s when I almost had my head blown off.

I was a member of the Tactical Response Group (TRG), an elite New South Wales police force group formed in 1981 to deal with high risk incidents such as riots and arresting dangerous criminals.

As a TRG officer I was involved in 'building entries' where trained officers, like myself, would go into a building to hunt out armed and dangerous criminals. I was always first or second man in and waiting outside the door with my shotgun ready was extremely nerve-racking. I'd try not to dwell on the numerous 'what ifs?' that would cross my mind because the answers were too damn frightening: 'What if this is *the* night? What if this is the last door I'm going to go through? What if I'm shot?'

I would focus on the skills I'd learnt in training— I knew what had to be done and, even though I couldn't control what was waiting on the other side of the door, I could control my thoughts and emotions. No matter what happened I wouldn't let my mates down. And— BANG!—with a nod we'd be through the front door and tearing through the joint yelling 'POLICE! POLICE! POLICE!' to identify ourselves.

The TRG could clear a house in seven seconds flat . . . but the uncertainty of what might happen made it feel like a lifetime.

My moment of truth occurred while filming a police training video at Skyville, an old army depot in Sydney's west where we'd practise our search and siege procedures.

My TRG mate Peter Gillam and I were demon-strating how we'd enter and clear a building while a cameraman filmed us. We were armed with shotguns and the criminals were represented by pop-up targets. Peter and I were dressed in our full kit with bulletproof vests, helmets and gas masks. But the vests we were wearing were old—a mistake that almost proved fatal.

One of the first things a TRG officer is taught about a building entry and search is that his gun barrel *always* follows his eyes; so if a criminal jumps out to take a pot shot, the officer can take immediate action. Instructors would tell us the split-second needed to adjust a weapon's line of fire could be the difference between a TRG member's life . . . and death.

At the time, I was nearly always the first man through the door out in the field, but on this occasion Peter went in first and I followed him in. Even though it was a demonstration, our guns were loaded with live ammo and we treated it like the real thing.

I was on the right side of the door frame, Peter on the left, facing the door. We nodded to each other, silently counted 1–2–3 and then Peter entered the door, raising his gun up and across his body as he moved.

BANG!

I heard a blast and felt this almighty force right near me. A solid round of ammunition slammed face-high into the door frame. Right next to my head. My gas mask protected me from the blast of sawdust and the barrage of wooden chunks that exploded in my face.

The door frame was absolutely hammered—it was just a shredded piece of wood dropping to the floor like confetti—and there was smoke and haze everywhere.

Peter and I stared at each other through our gas masks, *What the hell just happened?*

We staggered away from the building, ripped our gas masks off and, as the shock set in, we crumpled to the ground and lay there trying to regain our senses.

We figured out that the corner of Peter's old Kevlar vest had curled up and hooked onto his trigger. As soon as he made a sudden move to enter the door, his gun discharged. Almost right in my face.

He nearly blew my head off.

After about half an hour, Peter and I brushed ourselves off and finished filming the demonstration, as any good TRG officer would.

I'd come close to checking out, but obviously it wasn't the end of my road map. Other things were meant to be.

westie wonder

'm a 'Westie' through 'n' through and, what's more, I'm bloody proud of it.

For the uninitiated, a Westie is someone who lives in Sydney's working class western suburbs—a place I remember for its stinking hot summer days; fibro houses; tough footy teams; good friends; working at Target on a Thursday night and Saturday morning; KISS or AC/DC music blasting from our old turntable's speakers; Fairvale High; and *some* people working to better their lot in life. People, such as breakfast-radio star Alan Jones, call areas like Canley Heights 'Struggle Street' but I called 27 McIlvenie Street 'home' for most of my young life, and I couldn't have been happier.

I entered the world kicking and screaming on 24 May 1960; the firstborn child to Bill and Joy Harrigan. I was christened William James Harrigan and, as a kid, I only ever answered to 'Will' or 'William'. I refused to answer to Bill. You might as well have called me Peter or Mario.

When I was two we moved into a modest rented house on bustling Parramatta Road, Granville; before that we'd lived with relatives in Kirrawee and Chester Hill. In 1964, we dropped anchor smack-bang in the middle of Parramatta Eels territory in a three-bedroom Housing Commission place at Canley Heights. Back then the corner of Canley Vale Road and Humphries Road was the edge of the world, surrounded by bushland, and only the bravest of my gang would pedal their bike into the great unknown. The bush stretched for miles, and it would've been easy to get lost among the forest of gum and stringy-bark trees. The area is unrecognisable now; thanks to the great land grab, most of the trees have been cleared to build more houses for the growing population out west.

No one lived at Canley Heights because they were rich, most people struggled, but my mum and dad always worked hard. Before joining the Federal police force—the 'Feds'—Dad was a special constable with the state railways, while Mum worked a couple of jobs, ranging from book-keeping to operating a machine for optical products. After a few years, they ended up buying our house off the Housing Commission for $8000, which was a fair whack back then.

My parents met on a train while travelling from the Blue Mountains, where they both lived, to Sydney. My father's family had moved to the Mountains in 1941 after my grandfather had signed on with the army to fight in World War II. Pop was only in khaki for nine days before being diagnosed with tuberculosis. In those days doctors prescribed pure mountain air for that killer disease, so Dad's family packed up everything they owned and relocated to Wentworth Falls. Mum grew up in nearby Lawson. Her father was an electrician for the railways and a lot of her childhood was spent on a train nicknamed Fish (the other was Chips) travelling all the way to and from a private school in Strathfield. After a two-year courtship, Mum and Dad married amid the bushfires that engulfed the mountains in 1959.

Anyone who knows their footy would pick Dad as an old front rower—he played with Katoomba in the Group 10 competition and spent two years with the St George under-19s from 1955 to 1957. At nineteen, he was called up for National Service and, in between learning how to march and fire a .303 rifle, he won his unit's heavyweight boxing title. A no-nonsense type, Dad taught me not to be bullied by anyone.

One of my earliest lessons in Dad's university of hard knocks came when I was in primary school and he demanded I take a stand against a kid who was bullying me for my lunch. Dad wasn't impressed when he found out why I was going hungry at school and said the best way to put a stop to it was to whack him. When I looked scared at the thought of going the biff, Dad growled, 'Give that kid a flogging or you're no son of mine!' With those words ringing in my ears, I served the kid a knuckle sandwich the following lunchtime and, as well as gaining Dad's approval, I also gained a mate when the bully realised it was better to have me onside rather than against him.

It has always been important for me to have Dad's approval . . . my brother, Greg, reckons I crave it. While I know he and Mum love us, Dad is a tough taskmaster—even if I'd played a blinder in junior footy he'd tell me I could've done better. Although there have been occasions when Dad has told me I could have refereed better, he is full of praise for me now.

As the eldest boy in a family where both parents worked, it was my responsibility to look after Greg, four and a half years younger than me, and my sister Di, five and a half years my junior. I had to ensure our list of chores was done before Mum came home and that the little ones didn't get up to too much trouble—and that was a full-time job.

I was smarter than those big brothers who tried to rule their siblings with an iron fist though, because rather than bully Greg and Di, I'd reward them for a job well done with a gold star—the kind kindergarten teachers hand out for good artwork or neat handwriting. It was a great con because while they swept, mopped and did the wiping up to add to their collection of gold stars, I'd put my feet up, watch television and take it easy. When they collected a certain number of stars I'd reward them with a lolly or paddle-pop ice-cream. I forget exactly when it was Di and Greg realised they were being conned, but it was one hell of a rort while it lasted.

Greg, not me, was the tearaway in those days. He used to get into more fights than Mike Tyson—I lost count of the number of times when I had to help him finish a blue. Once he took on an entire family—the Punch boys from across the road—when one of the brothers yelled out an insult about our mum. Greg charged across the road screaming vengeance, flew up the stairs past the kid's mother, stormed onto the verandah and belted the kid who'd offended him. Greg then biffed another brother trying to escape through the house and then bolted around the front of the house and stopped to hammer the oldest boy who was about my age . . . it was savage, but that's how things were back then.

We Harrigan boys had a knack of getting into strife, even when we didn't mean to. We'd divide our school holidays between our grandparents' houses on the Central Coast and in the Blue Mountains where we'd go bushwalking, yabbying and swimming in crystal clear swimming holes.

Once when we were on holiday at our grandparents' place near the lake at Toukley on the Central Coast the granddaughter of the local storeowner was standing on the sand by the edge of the lake giving my siblings a gobful. I came wandering along looking for them, and I happened to be carrying a stick at the time. While she carried on yelling, I noticed a massive jellyfish lying in the sand a foot or two away from me.

Now, I still don't know why I did this but I yelled 'Why don't you just shut up!' and I stuck the stick under the blob of orange jelly and flicked it at her. It rocketed up in an arc from the sand and landed right on top of the girl's head.

Deadset, I can still see it now: a million to one shot. She ended up wearing it like a hat! The tentacles flopped down around her face, perfectly balancing the googly mess on her head. She just stood there with a look of absolute terror on her face.

Eventually she leaned forward and the jellyfish fell off, and we ran away laughing our heads off.

discipline

When we were growing up, Dad was working as a railway detective and would often work late or have to go away for days at a time. This left Mum in charge and on occasions, like any kids, we could be a handful. Mum didn't have the luxury we have these days with big four-wheel-drives and fancy prams to take us around in. When Greg and Di were small, Mum took them for their regular check-ups to Cabramatta, three kilometres away. No car meant walking. Mum would get out her hand-me-down stroller, load my brother and sister in and I would walk alongside holding onto the side of it. I was six years old. As well as these sojourns every fortnight, there were regular shopping trips. Walking three kilometres each way was certainly no picnic, but Mum did what she had to do.

In the Harrigan household if you were naughty you were disciplined, often with a 'Get to your room', which had the desired effect because I hated being grounded; I wanted to be outside playing, not cooped up in my room. But every now and then the smack was used for an immediate result. As we grew older the smack was replaced with 'the strap', one of Dad's old leather belts that would hang on the back of the laundry door. I still clearly remember Mum saying 'Get me that strap' on many occasions. This was usually enough to stop us doing whatever was annoying.

We feared the strap, especially when dished out by Dad. It certainly kept us in check. Often when we were in trouble Greg and I would lie in our beds (we shared a room) and talk, waiting for Dad to arrive home. We'd hear the front door open and we'd go quiet. We could barely hear Mum and Dad talking, but we knew what was being said. Then we'd hear it, the footsteps coming down the hall towards our bedroom, our door flying open and the deep voice of Dad saying either 'William get out here' or 'Gregory get out here', depending on who was in trouble.

Dad would take us to the lounge room where he would recite the incident as described by Mum and ask for our response.

Usually it was 'I'm sorry, Dad, I won't do it again'.

Dad would say, 'You bloody won't want to.' Then, bang, the strap was dished out. How many times and how hard would depend on what you had done wrong.

The strap made an appearance many times at meals when Dad was away, but was rarely used. One of the rules at the table, which could never be breached, was 'no food to be left on your plate'. Many times I watched my beans, peas and brussel sprouts go cold. I'd whinge and whine about not wanting to eat them, but there was no leaving the table until they were gone. Often we'd still be sitting there half an hour later, crying and choking on a mouthful of cold greens. As we grew older, we got smarter. Greg loved brussel sprouts and Di and I hated them. When Mum wasn't looking there'd always be a quick sleight of hand. If Greg had nothing to trade on his plate he would hold us to ransom and collect later in some way.

But back to the discipline. I hear many people argue the reasons for and against smacking children. I am for it when done in the appropriate way, which means when it is done with a force that delivers the desired affect. Enough to sting and make you think twice about doing wrong again. This was how it was done in our household and it worked, although we still did things that meant we'd cop it again. But we knew the consequences and accepted the responsibility that went with it. The discipline was character building and I wouldn't have had it any other way.

game of life

Soccer, not Rugby League, was my first sporting love. As a kid, I'd spend hours kicking my ball against a little brick wall outside our weatherboard cottage trying to finetune my skills for a sport that was dismissed throughout Sydney as 'wog-ball'. I did get to play soccer for one year during my primary school days when I captained the school B grade side in fifth class. Occasionally I was called up as a sub for the A side and I thought it was great, not because I was in the As, but because I got to wear the flash jersey.

My dream to become the new Pele or George Best was sidetracked one autumn afternoon in 1966 when a group of neighbourhood kids ran from house to house grabbing recruits for the newly-formed Canley Heights Sports and Social Club Rugby League team. I can still see the gang: Rodney Denham with Mark and Steven Smith leading the group, Kelvin Beazley,

Glen Hughes and a couple of others huddled behind them. They were smiling from ear to ear.

'You've gotta be in it, Will,' they pleaded when I hesitated. 'We wanna stick together . . . c'mon, join up!'

I was reluctant because Rugby League had never entered my head; soccer was my dream. I can remember looking up at my mother, seated on the verandah watching the scene with a smile, but when I asked her for some guidance she said the call was mine. Mum always encouraged me to make my own decisions— maybe that's where I received my grounding. Within minutes the soccer ball was left behind as I joined the group on its race to the house of the next 'volunteer', Brett Gasnier, a distant relation to Rugby League immortal, Reg Gasnier.

Rich in spirit but short on skill, Canley Heights Sports and Social Club had a less than glorious introduction to the Greatest Game of All. In those early days all the junior football was played at McCredie Park at Guildford. We were excited to be playing and it felt great wearing my oversized jersey and shorts with the sponge pads you put in the purpose-made pockets on the side. It didn't matter that we were flogged every week, we just wanted to put our gear on and feel special every Saturday morning. Which was a good thing because it took us three long winters to score our first try!

I remember that morning at Whitlam Oval on the Hume Highway at Liverpool well because I scored the try. It was more luck than anything else: like any good hooker, I chased a kick over the line and when I opened my eyes I realised I'd landed on the ball. A TRY! You beauty, what a moment . . . the parents who'd faithfully followed us about the district danced on the sidelines while we hugged each other. It was magic stuff.

When I think of those days, what stands out most is the parents' behaviour, even though we copped some terrible hidings, they only ever encouraged us. It didn't matter if we were beaten; their chief concern was we tried our best and enjoyed ourselves. Unlike nowadays when some parents yell threats at the referee, and even kids from the opposition side, the only thing I ever heard from our sidelines was encouragement and praise. We were lucky. Our mothers and fathers taught us that shaking hands with the opposition after the game was an important part of Rugby League; we were also instructed to thank the referee for his contribution and we'd shake one another's hands to acknowledge our team effort. It was simple stuff, but the sportsmanship we learnt back then placed us on the right path.

In 1970 I left the Canley Heights Sports and Social Club team to join a club my father helped form—the Canley Heights Dragons—and I was the first player to chalk up a hundred games in the red-and-black battle colours. I was still playing hooker but I also had a go at every position in the back line. As I got older my coach Geoff McKenry wanted me out on the wing because of my speed, but my heart was in the scrum as hooker. Mr McKenry eventually put me back to hooker but he'd always shake his head and mutter about the fact that his quickest player was packing down in the scrum.

One of my most treasured childhood memories of playing football was when my primary school played Cabramatta West in the 1972 grand final. Their gun player was Steve Ella, who in later life found fame with Parramatta, New South Wales and Australia—his career highlight was scoring the most tries on the undefeated 1982 Kangaroos tour of Great Britain and France. Our sole tactic for the title decider was to shut Ella down— and we stuck to him like superglue. The Cabramatta West kids were cocky before kick off because of their strike weapon, but through sheer determination, we managed to wipe the smiles off their faces. We stopped Ella and we stopped them. We won 6–3.

The more I played Rugby League, the more I became entrenched in the game. In 1975, aged fifteen, I volunteered for the coaching job of the Dragons under-7s. In the pre-'mini' and 'mod' footy days, kids played on a full-sized field, so I spent plenty of time on the field directing traffic, wiping snotty noses and hoping the kids on my team would catch the ball. It was a lot of fun—and coaching the kids forced me to show responsibility, learn to communicate, get organised and think a lot more about the rules of the game.

So when I look back I'm glad I *did* get to play some soccer in primary school, but all my life I have been well and truly bitten by the Rugby League bug.

Although, if someone had told me back then that I was going to make my mark in life by blowing a whistle and keeping players back onside, I would've thought they were crackers.

school sport

Our parents believed that encouraging us to participate in a team sport would help us develop the right attitude for life—it's something I've followed with my own boys.

Growing up in the '60s and '70s there were no playstations or videos and I wasn't a bookworm, so for me it was the outdoors. As well as the games of cricket or footy down at the local park, I'd ride my bike and skateboard around the streets. Although we didn't just ride; we'd race. We were always racing and competing against each other. At one stage I even organised a kind of 'Street Olympics' with races and medals for the local kids.

Rugby League, however, was *the* sport we'd love to play. We'd play it on our front lawns, on the road and down at Peterlee Park. They were wild and woolly matches; there were even times when a kid would dive for a try and smash headfirst into the little fences that separated our houses. While we'd suffer cuts and bruises, we always seemed to recover in time to play the next afternoon. I'm certain those scratch games put me on course to become a referee because even back then I'd enforce the rules of the game no matter what: I once sent my brother Greg off in a front lawn game, even though he was playing on my side, because he coathangered an opponent.

By the age of fifteen I was getting out of bed at 7 a.m. and running around the streets before school. Mum was the taxi driver ferrying me to swimming, cubs, footy and karate training during both summer and winter. Greg reckons the karate started my confidence, from which I've never looked back.

At school, sport was my priority and I participated in every sport I could. If I was given a dollar for every teacher's comment on my report card which said I spent far too much time on footy and swimming, I'd be very well off. A few of my teachers, like Ron Cheers and Ross Smith, even took me aside for a quiet talk, but I didn't take their advice and I paid a mighty price later on.

Nevertheless, one of my fondest memories at Fairvale was playing Rugby Union for the school side. I remember the day we played the Ella brothers—the royal family of Rah Rah—on our back oval and it was ugly! Mark, Gary and Glen Ella gave a glimpse of what they were set to do to the world's best Rugby nations when they combined to spank us during Matraville High's 96–3 cakewalk. Whenever we had the ball our fullback kicked it downtown, but the Ella boys would step and weave their way through our attempted defence and dazzle us with their class and grace. The loss was a blow to our school's collective pride.

Despite that humiliation, my Rugby Union team joined Fairvale's softball and netball teams on a tour to New Zealand in 1977 and it took a concerted school effort to get us on the plane. We held school dances, film nights, bottle drives, raffles and even delivered telephone books to raise the $18 700 to cover our expenses. The day before we crossed the Tasman Sea, the forty footballers, netballers and softballers did a lap of honour around the quadrangle, and I felt a great sense of achievement to be applauded by our schoolmates.

Unfortunately, our Rugby tour wasn't so crash hot . . . we lost each of our four games, but it was a tremendous experience for a bunch of Westies. We had snow fights; visited the bubbling pots of muddy glue at Rotorua; heard our schoolmate David Cazalet (who has since found fame as one of the world's best Elvis impersonators) sing in the Waitomo Caves; and we played bruising Kiwi Rugby teams. Some of our members fell in love on that trip and there were a few people walking down the aisle years later.

My school house team was called Alpha, we wore green and pushed ourselves in inter-school cross country races, which saw us wade through the Green Valley creek; we dived headfirst into swimming carnivals; and gave sweat and blood in basketball, soccer and League tournaments against the Beta, Delta and Gamma outfits.

I won Alpha's Sportsman of the Year award three years running and winning those trophies made me want to strive even harder. In my final year I won the inaugural Fairvale High Sportsman of the Year award in 1977, which meant I was the best sportsman in the whole school.

the start of my road map

I always wanted to be a pilot. Even now I still take my two-year-old son Jed out to the airport to watch the planes take off and land. Growing up I would build model war planes and play with them, except that the wheels or the delicate machine guns on the wings would snap off during play. My dad would try to impress on me that they were models and should be looked at but not played with. When Dad and Mum weren't around I would take the broken planes out the back, tie string around one wing, pour a little petrol over the end of the other wing, light it and start swinging it around over my head, pretending that it had been shot down in a dogfight. When the whole thing was ablaze, I would let the rope go and watch the burning plane plummet to the ground. Young Jed now has model airplanes hanging from his ceiling, but if any go missing I will make sure he can't get to the petrol can.

Heading into fifth form I took 3 unit maths, physics and chemistry, which I would need if I was to become a pilot. What a disaster! In my half-yearly exams I scored twenty-five out of a hundred for physics and sixteen for chemistry, and in maths I struggled so badly I knew I would have to drop back to 2 unit. I hadn't put enough effort into these subjects for two reasons: first I was too busy concentrating on my sport and, secondly, I didn't like them.

I remember in physics we were given a practical problem where we had a one metre long ruler, a marble and a cup. We had the ruler at a certain angle and we had to roll the marble down the ruler, across the desk and land it in the cup. We had to work out where to place the cup by using a maths formula, but I didn't waste any time. I put the ruler up, rolled the marble down, watched where it hit the ground and put my cup there and yelled out to the teacher that I had finished.

He came over and said, 'Let's see it'.

I rolled my marble down and it landed perfectly in the cup.

'Well done, Bill,' he said. 'Now show me how you came to this result?' He looked over to my book, searching for the mathematical answer.

I said, 'You won't find it in there, sir, I just did it the easy way and had a practice run and watched where the marble landed.'

That pretty much sums up how I went in physics.

I approached the school to change subjects at the end of Year 11, but they wouldn't allow it; they said I would be too far behind. I had two options: to leave school and join the navy, which I considered a genuine option because maybe I could become a pilot through the service; or go to technical college and finish my HSC. At tech I could do the HSC in the same time-frame, as they complete Year 11 and 12 in one year by cutting out the extra work.

I approached Mum and Dad and said that I wanted to leave school and join the navy. My dad said straight out 'No'; I would be going back to school and finishing my HSC. This caused a little unrest in the Harrigan household, but I knew there was no way I was ever going to win—when Dad says no he means no. An old mate of Dad's offered me a job with one of the big brickworks in Sydney, but I was still met with an abrupt no from Dad. So I had no choice and I enrolled at Liverpool Tech.

Dad arranged for me to go and work in a factory making pre-fabricated homes for two weeks prior to Christmas. At the time, I thought Dad was just helping me get a bit of pocket money, but I later realised his rationale. My job involved dipping window frames in an oil dip and then stacking them onto a pallet, which meant that I had oil all over my arms, dripping on my shirt and splashing all over me. I worked alongside one of the older fellas who was sawing timber. I took the cuts and stacked them, so that by the end of the day I'd have sawdust clinging to the oil. The pay wasn't real flash, but it involved a lot of hard yakka, so it seemed as though I was working a forty-hour week for next to nothing. At the end of the two weeks I was offered an apprenticeship, but I didn't even have to ask Dad about this one—I knocked it back.

So back to tech I went. I replaced 3 unit maths with 2 unit and commerce, and general studies replaced physics and chemistry. The tech environment was a whole new experience with freedom, responsibility and a completely different social impact. It was so different to school; here I was sitting in a class with people I'd never seen before, all wearing casual clothes and covering a range of ages spanning some forty years. The strict discipline of the school classroom had gone and everything was free and easy. I soon came to terms with it and started to enjoy talking to the older people, listening to their stories about their families, life experiences and the reason why they came back to do their Higher School Certificate.

I still didn't dedicate myself a hundred per cent to doing my HSC though. I used to do night work in a Target supermarket on a Thursday night, not finishing until around midnight or 2 a.m. So I would drive to tech on the Friday morning, park my car, jump into the back of my stationwagon, which was decked out with a bed and curtains, and go to sleep, missing the first and second periods. On other days, I would head off to the South Coast beaches with my new mates. But, despite all of that, I completed my HSC in 1978, which was the same year I would have completed it at

Fairvale High. Even so, my dream of becoming a pilot was over, so I decided to follow in the footsteps of my dad and become a cop.

I often wonder, 'Where would I be now?' had I taken just one different turn in life. One decision can have an amazing impact on your whole life. Where would I be had I been allowed to work in the brickworks? What would I be doing now? Married? Kids? The questions can go on and on, but, as you'll see, I do have a theory.

starting out

I was conscripted into refereeing way back in 1976 when Fairvale High's physical education teacher, Ross Smith, committed the school to a New South Wales Rugby League program aimed at recruiting schoolboys for the refereeing ranks. The game's hierarchy obviously saw there was a need to inject more young blood into the junior association and, to their credit, they were proactive in doing something about it. They were sending a representative to schools around the Sydney metropolitan region to give groups of kids a weekly lecture on the rules of the game, and after four weeks the students would sit for a test to gain their refereeing ticket.

There was panic in the Fairvale staffroom on the Monday before the lectures were set to start because *no one* had volunteered for the course. Determined to save his school from major embarrassment in the eyes of the NSWRL, Mr Smith took matters into his own hands and called in five senior members from the footy team—Brett Lees, Mark and Steve Smith, Brett Gasnier and me—and 'congratulated' us for agreeing to do the course.

It sounded about as much fun as a kick in the bum, and when we told him there was no way we intended to fall for that, he blackmailed us! He said that if we didn't embrace the idea of becoming an accredited referee, we'd be picking splinters out of our backsides after sitting on the reserves bench for the five weeks it would've taken to do the course. So we attended the lectures and I passed the exam for my schoolboy's referee ticket.

Big deal! The day I received my ticket, I threw it in my dressing-table's top drawer and forgot all about it.

Then one evening in 1977, everything changed. Dad's drinking hole, the El Cortez, had entered a team into the Fairfield pub competition, which was made up of teams such as the Brown Jug pub, the Kookaburra Hotel and so on. The league wasn't affiliated to the Parramatta juniors or the NSWRL, it was a private competition consisting of blokes who were woulda-beens, coulda-beens, shoulda-beens and has-beens. They were wild and woolly, and they needed a referee.

What sealed the deal for me was the pay: twenty dollars a game, two games a weekend. That mightn't sound like much now, but when you compared it to the fifty dollars a week a first year apprentice made in 1977, it was a huge earn for a schoolkid.

I had to work for it, though. I refereed a rough group of blokes who'd swill beer from a keg before going out on the field for kick off and, when I blew the whistle for half-time, they'd make a beeline back to the keg. Sometimes the alcohol fumes were so strong, you could've made the scrum explode by striking a match! And with the grog monster kicking about in their bellies, some of them would give it to me. In their eyes, I was just a kid and they'd try to intimidate me by getting in my face, challenging my decisions and swearing at me. I quickly learnt to stand on my own two feet and I'm certain it was a combination of the lessons learnt from those matches, and my police training, which galvanised me for the worst that the likes of Steve Roach and Mario Fenech could throw my way when I broke into first grade nine years later.

I'll always remember being told by a bruiser covered in tattoos that he was going to belt the tripe out of me after the match because I sent him off for foul play. He looked fearsome, but the funny thing about that particular encounter is fear didn't enter my head. I put his words behind me, figuring that whatever was going to happen to me after the match could wait, and I focused on refereeing the game to the best of my ability. Within seconds of the match finishing, the rough nut came at me, but instead of shaping up for a fight, he stuck his hand out, shook my hand and complimented me on not backing down when he put the acid on me.

One thing I found about the pub competition was that after full-time the blokes who'd put it on me during the game were happy to leave any grief on the field. While they might not have always been happy with me, they at least had the good grace to let it go. Perhaps the reason they refused to take it any further was because the boys were aware of my 'minders' on the sideline. Every weekend, without fail, my mum and my girlfriend, Fiona, would come down to the ground armed with umbrellas. They carried them as weapons and, had they been needed, the girls would've charged in swinging.

The toughest part of the job was collecting my pay—I had to get ten dollars from each team. The winners were never a problem, they'd even have the cash waiting for me, but the losing team . . . it was like pulling teeth out of a mule, especially if they were dark about my performance. They'd growl and curse, but eventually they always paid.

The Fairfield pub comp taught me a lot about having the courage of my convictions. If I didn't collect the money after the game, I didn't get paid; if I had backed down when those old hardheads challenged my authority as the ref, I couldn't have returned the following weekend because they'd have no respect for me. It was a challenge and it developed into a passion; I looked forward to getting out in the middle and controlling the shots. I also liked the fact people acknowledged I did a good job, and word of my potential soon reached the head of the Parramatta Junior Referees' Association, Kevin Jeffes.

Kevin introduced himself to me after a game and invited me to join his group's ranks because he said I had ability. He suggested it would be in my best interest to join an association affiliated to the NSWRL because it would allow me to further myself. Although, if I agreed to referee 'official' footy, I would have to turn my back on the pub league because it wasn't sanctioned by the NSWRL.

After plenty of soul-searching I quit the Fairfield pub comp. But after kissing my hefty wage goodbye in exchange for the two dollars a game I would earn in the Parramatta juniors, I was shocked to learn that Kevin and his son Kelvin wasted no time in filling my vacancy in the pub league. Kevin could referee these games because he was an 'inactive' ref and his boy wasn't refereeing in the juniors. Maybe they needed the money but I'd like to think it was just meant to be.

As a member of the Parramatta Junior Referees' Association I looked after the little kids of a Saturday morning and then ran the lines for 'C' grade of a Sunday. When I turned eighteen I had to sit for my international ticket—and in a few short years it became my passport to a new world and a book's worth of magnificent experiences. I don't think I'll ever be able to thank my old PE teacher Ross Smith enough for unwittingly putting me on track for a career which has never been dull.

the sultans of surf

My teenage years were carefree days spent with new-found friends from Liverpool Tech—a pack of ratbags who quickly became my close mates as we all enjoyed surfing, footy and the same bands. We'd use our free periods from tech to scoot down the South Coast to catch waves at Coalcliff.

On one of our surfing safaris, cruising along, singing the 'Sultans of Swing' from a Dire Straits album, we baptised ourselves the 'Sultans of Surf' and the name stuck. It might sound corny nowadays, but we took the name and what it meant seriously—we had navy blue and white T-shirts made up with 'Sultans of Surf' emblazoned across the back and our initials or nicknames printed on the front. We wore them everywhere. They were on our backs in a car crash that should've wiped us out, and they were scrunched up on the sand of a

North Coast beach when I thought for certain a shark was going to take one of us . . .

The original Sultans were John ('Boong'), Ian ('Fruity') and yours truly ('Werris'). In time we added another two bodies to our tight-knit group—one of my police colleagues, Marty Brown, and my younger brother, Greg. We were rough and ready, we'd drink too much and get into blues. We had some huge nights on the drink; and some hazy memories when we woke up in the beach car park ready to surf away a hangover.

These days it seems the trips I remember most are the ones we almost didn't return from . . . like the day we went surfing up north at McCawley's Headland, opposite the Big Banana at Coffs Harbour. The beach was deserted and the waves were pumping at a healthy four foot. I remember one particular wave, on which Boong peeled right and I went left, for what were easily the rides of the session. We paddled back towards Fruity who was clapping, which was our way of acknowledging a good ride . . . and that's when we spotted it.

A fin, *a big bloody fin*, cruising about twenty-five metres behind Fruity. My initial hope—it was a prayer actually—was it belonged to a playful dolphin. I sat up on my board and looked long and hard to try and identify it—it *was* a shark.

A mixture of panic and adrenaline gripped both Boong and I as we started screaming and waving at our mate to get the hell back to shore. At first he thought we were waving at him, so he waved back at us happily, but then he must've heard us scream

'SHARK!' because suddenly Fruity started paddling like a madman—I reckon he would've beaten the then formidable East German rowing team on this particular occasion!

I took that as my tip to get moving too, and at that moment a wave picked Boong and I up and carried us towards the shore. Neither of us tried to stand up, we clung on to our boards and hoped the wave would be strong enough to carry us all the way in. I didn't dare get off my surfboard until I felt its fins dig deep into the sand. Finally, I rolled off the surfboard, exhausted, but relieved to be safe. Then I jumped to my feet to see what had happened to Fruity.

After a few frantic seconds I spotted him. Thankfully he was on the wave behind us—screaming all the way back to shore.

That was enough for us. We called it a day and headed back to our digs at the local caravan park where we cracked open a bottle of bourbon to calm the nerves.

Sharks weren't the only danger for the Sultans: cars were literally time bombs. In 1979, Boong and I bought brand new Datsun 200B SXs; they were the car for Westie kids to own back then. In true Sultans of Surf style I bought a white one and Boong got a blue one to match our T-shirts. The cars were our pride and joy—we polished them so much I'm still amazed we didn't rub the paint off! Not long after purchasing our 'wheels' Boong, Marty and I set off on a road trip to attend the bucks' night of my best mate from Fairvale

High. He'd moved up the coast so it was a long drive and we took it in turns.

I drove the first leg in Boong's car and then Boong took control of the wheel. I was stuffed and welcomed sleep. I remember waking briefly and asking Boong if he was okay.

'No worries, Will, go back to sleep!'

Boong seemed fine, so I drifted straight back to sleep.

BAAAANNNNGGGG! Suddenly the Sultans had rocketed off the road at one hundred kilometres an hour and steamrolled one of those white marker posts. The car then tilted at a thirty-degree angle as we started to move further away from the road and deeper into the scrub. I screamed at Boong to do something, but he was out cold. I can recall everything in slow motion . . . speeding towards some trees at a frightening rate of knots . . . hearing the car rushing at great speed . . . the loud noise of gravel underneath the car . . . frantically reaching out for the steering wheel and turning it to an extreme right . . .

A split-second after I managed to spin the steering wheel we slammed into a tree; on impact we bounced off it like a pinball, and the car went spinning until it eventually ground to a halt. The tyres sounded as if they were ripping in the dirt and gravel in their desperate attempt to answer the brakes' call for them to halt. The dust kicked up by the Datsun's terrifying dance was blinding and I had no idea where we were. But we were alive . . . or rather, I knew *I* was alive.

I checked on Boong. He was dazed, but he managed to ask what had happened and when he realised how close we'd come to death he broke down. Marty was in the back of the car moaning and groaning. The poor bugger was asleep with his head leaning on the back passenger door when everything went terribly wrong. Incredibly, the force of the impact was taken about a foot from where his head had rested. I still can't believe he escaped with only a bad headache.

A truckie who had witnessed the accident raced over to our car; expecting to find a car full of dead bodies. 'You blokes are the luckiest bastards about,' he said.

I don't know if it was the shark or the car crash which made me appreciate we Sultans weren't bulletproof. We were close because of the experiences we shared during our youth, but those incidents helped make us mates for life. It is because of those near misses that I have no hesitation in saying the late teens and early twenties are the most dangerous years of a male's life. Enjoying that period of your life is easy, but surviving it—that's the challenge.

worth the weight

Days after completing my Higher School Certificate I applied to join the New South Wales Police Force. My father accompanied me to police headquarters in College Street and waited outside as I completed the recruitment exam, which consisted of a spelling and comprehension test and then a physical. Back then the police placed an emphasis on brawn, brawn . . . and even more brawn. Sometimes, I hear old-timers lament that police officers no longer look like police officers because in 'the good old days' applicants had to measure up in more ways than one. To walk the thin blue line you had to stand five feet, nine and a half inches (176.5 centimetres); boast a chest that expanded to forty inches (102 centimetres); and then hit the scales at eleven stone seven (73 kilograms).

The scales were my downfall . . . I was a stone (6 kilograms) too light. I can still recall the sergeant in command—he had a big, fat gut hanging over his belt and he looked amazed that anyone could be too light.

'Go home and beef up, son, then we'll accept you,' he said as the belly rumbled in delight at the thought of another counter lunch.

He looked like an expert on the subject of packing on the pounds so I asked him what the secret was. His tip: drink stout.

'That'll make more of a man of you,' he said with a chuckle. 'Give your girl a bit extra to hang on to!'

I didn't drink beer back then, I couldn't stand the taste of the stuff, so the thought of swallowing stout was about as attractive as sculling a schooner of sump oil.

As soon as Dad found out I'd flunked the exam because of my weight, he dragged me to the Remington building in Liverpool Street, home to the various detective squads. Dad sought out an old mate of his, Superintendent Watson, who was then one of the state's top cops. As my father explained my predicament to Watson, a distinguished gentleman entered the office, and both Dad and Watson stood bolt upright to acknowledge his presence. I followed their lead, which was a good thing because the man was Police Commissioner Merv Wood. What bowled me over most about the meeting was realising my father was on friendly terms with him.

Before leaving, Commissioner Wood pointed at me and said tongue in cheek to Dad, 'Make sure the doc gets a bottle of scotch within a fortnight, Bill.'

For the next fourteen days I stopped training; pigged out on food; and drank gallons of Guinness—I remember my first sip of the stuff, it was putrid! I persevered though and drank two cartons of it over the next two weeks.

Two weeks later I was back at College Street on the scales in front of the same jelly-bellied 'sarge'. I looked down at the setting on the scales and I could've cried because I was still three pounds (over a kilogram) too light! I looked at the sergeant and begged him to give a skinny bloke a break.

'I've tried hard,' I said. 'I did what you said and drank stout; I feel like I've swallowed a pig and I'm not training . . . please, you have to take me.'

He grinned, patted his gut slowly and said, 'Don't worry, son, by the time you reach my rank you'll look like the rest of us!'

Stepping off those scales was the beginning of a fulfilling career that saw me placed in some movie-like situations. And, while I laughed at the sergeant's crack about growing a gut (I didn't have any intention of carrying a police-issued stomach around), I would like to thank him for his tip to drink stout. I developed a taste for Guinness and I've been drinking it ever since. In 1994, I spent an afternoon at the Guinness factory: now *that* was sheer delight.

ghost shift

I believe in ghosts. To be more precise, I believe the old Pyrmont police station is haunted.

Not long after graduating from the police academy I was stationed at Pyrmont as a probationary constable and, forget the criminal landscape of the area, the first thing I was told when I reported for duty was about the old sergeant who still called the place home years after being killed in a car crash. I thought the cops were pulling my leg, but as I quickly discovered, things definitely went bump in the night.

Pyrmont was a completely different suburb back then to how it is now. There was no Darling Harbour, no Star City, no Channel Ten, no radio stations, no trendy inner city housing developments, no Anzac Bridge or coffee shops. It was a tough neck of the woods, home to a cell's worth of petty criminals and just as many hard heads. The part that was scary was after dark when the station was manned by one officer, while another two patrolled the streets in the paddy wagon; it was spine-tingling; stuff. Nothing was more frightening than being stuck in the cop shop on your 'Pat Malone' on the ghost shift.

There'd often be noises, like the bang of an object crashing to the floor. Closer inspection would reveal something like the charge book or diary had fallen off the desk, but there was *never* a logical reason for it happening. I even saw rulers fly across the room.

One night, a few minutes after the other two officers left to patrol the streets, I thought I'd start my shift with a nice hot cup of coffee, so I walked down the hallway to the back, opened the kitchen door and . . . *bloody hell*! I was confronted by a ghostly figure wearing a policeman's hat! I nearly had a heart attack—I slammed the door shut, sprinted back to the front of the station and barricaded myself behind the counter.

After allowing my heart rate to settle down, I composed myself enough to confront the supernatural sergeant, man to ghost. I retraced my steps slowly; gripped the doorknob tentatively; took a deep breath and in one frantic motion I opened the door.

The demon that'd terrified the tripe out of me was nothing more than a bloody mop with a police cap plonked on top of it. I bagged myself for being so stupid and cursed my two colleagues for a great joke.

no honeymoon

I had my fair share of girlfriends; my brother Greg reckons I was insecure because I was always spending my money to keep a steady girlfriend. It's true—after going out with a girl for three months I'd spend thirty dollars on a friendship ring, and that was big money way back then.

When I was nineteen I bought more than a friendship ring for my seventeen-year-old girlfriend Lee: we got married. You don't have to be a mathematical genius to work it out—I was married in May 1980 and my eldest son Matthew was born in November.

I'd just bought an old Morris car with a motor mechanic friend of mine, Kelvin Beazley. We planned on doing the vehicle up and having it as our muck around car. We were working on it one afternoon when my mum phoned me at Kelvin's place and told me to ring Lee straightaway.

I called Lee. She was very upset and said she needed to see me now. I told her I was working on the car and I would be down later.

Lee said, 'No, you need to come now.' I went back outside and told Kelvin I had to go, but I would be back soon.

I never did get back there that day and we never got to work on the car again either. My life changed dramatically after that phone call. I went from a carefree, easygoing teenager who loved to surf, play sport and had a new career and money in my pocket, to an adult who needed to grow up and accept the highest level of responsibility known to man: fatherhood.

When I arrived at Lee's place, her dad, John, was sitting in his chair in the lounge room.

I said, 'G'day, John.'

He just grunted and said, 'They're in there' and pointed over his shoulder.

I walked through the house to Lee's bedroom where I saw Lee and her mum, Denise, sitting on the bed crying together.

I said 'Hi' to both of them and Denise gave me a filthy look and left Lee and I alone. Lee struggled to talk through the tears but eventually got it out that she was pregnant. It took a second to sink in as I sat beside Lee giving her a hug. We said nothing for several minutes.

Finally I said, 'What do you think we should do? Obviously there are a number of options.' My first thought was that we were way too young so we would have to consider an abortion. I knew this was the wrong option, but, for some reason, it was the first thought that entered my mind. Looking back, I know I was scared and not ready to settle down. I was looking forward to a trip I had planned to the USA and, in my heart, I was still a kid who just wanted to hang out with my Westie mates and hit the beaches along the coast.

Lee said no straightaway, her mum and dad were strict Catholics and would never allow her to have an abortion.

I eventually left Lee with her mum and said that I had to go home and tell my mum and dad, but I'd be back later that evening. Before leaving Lee's house, John asked me what I proposed to do about the situation.

'What do you mean?' I replied.

'Well, if you don't marry her,' he said, 'don't think you are just going to come around here whenever you like to see the baby. You either do the right thing or get out of our lives.'

I went home and told Mum—she had guessed something major was up after the phone call she had received earlier. Mum took it a lot better than I thought, but it was telling Dad that I was worried about.

Dad got home early from work that day around 5.30 p.m., which seemed like fate to me. Whatever he had planned for that afternoon was put on hold. He told me to 'Jump in the car' and we headed straight to the Kookaburra Hotel in Canley Vale. We had a couple of beers and talked for some time. It was no longer father to son; it was man to man. Dad gave me plenty of advice, laid out the options and said a lot, but he always fell short of making the decision for me. In a way, I was hoping he would. John's comments were foremost in my mind and I told Dad 'I don't think I can have a baby and not be a part of its life'. I would be sneaking around the corner from Lee's house trying to get a glimpse of my son or daughter. But, almost in the same breath, I knew I was too young and not ready. It was decision time and it was at this precise moment I felt myself really grow from a young boy to a man.

I married Lee in a quiet family wedding. I was just completing my first year as a probationary constable in the police force. Lee and I moved into her garage, which her father and I had converted into two rooms.

I worked hard, grabbing as much overtime as I could, and I took on a second job at the Hayden Cinema in Penrith, working there at least a couple of nights a week and most of my holidays. I concentrated on earning as much as I could to get us out of the garage as quick as possible.

Back in 1980 you couldn't just buy a home like you do today. To secure a loan you had to be with a bank for a number of years with consistent savings. I could not secure a loan with the Advance Bank, who I had been saving with since 1976, so we missed out on a house in the new estate of St Clair, located some fifteen kilometres east of Penrith. Around the same time Landcom, a government agency, was about to release more land in the same area. Lee and I registered in the ballot, which was how you bought a block of land back then. From memory there were about a hundred blocks available and about four or five hundred people registered. Lee and I were drawn out and our seventh choice was still available. The land cost us $17 000. I had saved $7 000 and the Rural Bank allowed us to borrow the remaining $10 000. We paid the loan off in quick time so the Rural Bank approved a further loan to build a house. We chose a Masterton house and commenced building, but things in the home were strained.

Around the three-month mark in my marriage, I had gone home to Mum and had a heart to heart. I had told Mum that things weren't working out, I was too young and I thought I had made the wrong decision. Mum talked for a while but her message was strong: 'You made your bed now you sleep in it'. Mum has often said she regretted saying that and probably should have taken me back then because of the drama and trauma that followed.

Lee's family were pretty set in their ways of living, week in, week out. John would work his plumbing business during the week; they would go to their caravan on weekends at Windang on the south coast; they weren't into sport and they rarely went out except for church on a Sunday morning. This was in complete contrast to the Harrigan way of life.

After Matthew was born and we had been married for almost two years, Lee put pressure on me to stop playing police football on a Wednesday afternoon, to stop refereeing and to give up working at the cinema. I thought this last request strange because I was working to earn extra money so we could build a home.

I have always been athletic and involved in sport so I didn't want to give up playing footy with the cops, and I couldn't give up refereeing because I'd recently been told I could go places with it. After a number of discussions, and some heated arguments, I offered a compromise. I said that I would stop playing football, I would give up the second job, but I needed to keep refereeing. I knew I could never forgive myself if I didn't take it as far as I could. I would hate to be watching the footy one day with my son, wondering whether or not I could have made it.

So I stopped playing footy and gave notice at the cinema. On the Friday night I gave notice, I came home to find my clothes and belongings packed up in bags and boxes sitting outside our garage. I walked inside and woke Lee up and asked what was going on.

Lee simply said: 'Give up refereeing or it is over.'

I told Lee I'd just resigned from the cinema, and she knew I'd stopped playing footy, but it wasn't enough. So I told Lee I'd sleep there that night, but I would be leaving in the morning.

At 8 a.m. I rang Mum, told her of the situation and asked if she could bring her car down to help me grab all my stuff. Leaving wasn't a pleasant experience and the final word from Lee was: 'I don't want anything from you and I don't want you in our lives.'

I replied, 'I will be paying maintenance and I will be seeing Matthew.' I didn't have access to Matthew over the next couple of weeks, but I did open a bank account and started depositing maintenance.

My first experience in the family law court some years later was a poor one. The judge acknowledged my wife's application and gave me access to my son for four hours on a Sunday afternoon between 1 p.m. and 5 p.m., knowing very well that I refereed on a Sunday afternoon at 3 p.m. I was furious, but my solicitor said to go with it for a couple of months and then we would reapply. I sacked my solicitor and then went back to court representing myself. A more receptive judge granted me weekend access, even though this was vigorously opposed by Lee. The judge also asked if I'd considered holiday access, although Matthew was still some two years away from school. Half the school holidays were granted.

Things were bitter between Lee and myself until she met her current husband who helped settle everything down. Although we are not close friends, we get on well these days. Unfortunately we were just kids, forced to take on a responsibility we weren't ready for. Despite the odds being overwhelmingly stacked against us, we tried to make a go of it, but it wasn't meant to be. I have no regrets about the path my life took because my world would be so much poorer without Matthew.

juggling

As a referee with the New South Wales Rugby League I was meant to hang around after refereeing third grade in case I was needed to help out in the second or first grade matches; but often I had to rush off back to my next police shift. Sometimes it was difficult just managing to turn up for refereeing.

Once I became a copper there was no incentive for me to try to make a mark in Rugby League—or any other sport, for that matter. I suppose the hierarchy feared they'd have a force devoting too much time and energy to their outside interests, at the expense of their police work. Unless you entered the force as a footballer, like Paul Sironen or Mal Cochrane, you didn't get a look in. While those blokes still had to go on duty after a match, there was an understanding from up top to ensure their rosters allowed them time to train and play.

My roster sergeant at Central Police Station was a real yachtie, so I was forever struggling to get time off on a weekend to referee. Had I been in training for the Sydney to Hobart or the America's Cup I'd have been sweet, but I guess the old sea dog couldn't see the sense in a bloke wanting to run around a football park blowing a whistle at twenty-six footballers.

I was constantly juggling my refereeing with my police work and working around shifts. I volunteered for the dreaded seven day night shift every three weeks. This gave me a rostered weekend off, a weekend of night shift (getting to bed at 8 a.m. and up at midday to referee at 3 p.m.) and a weekend of having to juggle my shifts. I can thank a good mate, Lex Booth, for helping out here. Lex would show up early or stay back late to cover my shifts for me while I refereed. I would make it up to him by filling in for him during the week. Without Lex's help I'd probably never have made the grade as a ref.

The Parramatta juniors didn't appreciate how tough it could be either. I remember at one stage when I was having difficulty making myself available for a few matches an official suggested that I be given the flick. Thankfully, he was howled down.

It was during this period of my life that I failed to turn up for a game—for the first and last time. It was the morning my first marriage ended and I was meant to run the line for a Jersey Flegg game. But I was feeling shattered and certainly not in the right frame of mind to help control a footy game. My attempts to contact someone in charge and inform them I wouldn't be showing up failed, so there were plenty of angry officials cursing me when I didn't report for duty. The only thing that saved my career was that I'd left messages all around the place and, on hearing of my situation, the association took the view I'd at least attempted to contact them. But I never did get appointed to another Flegg game again.

Despite that incident, I knew I was establishing a reputation as a good referee. Even so, I hadn't considered a career in refereeing and I hadn't really set my mind to being one of the eight referees who controlled first grade; I was still young and keen to enjoy myself.

That all changed when a member from the referees' advisory panel approached me after a game. He thought I'd performed tremendously. He had controlled a few first grade games and he was adamant I had the ability to reach the top. The words he uttered that afternoon really hit home, 'You've got the ability to go all the way. It's up to you.'

I clung to his words because they gave me direction, especially when my desire was being tested because of the problems I was experiencing juggling shifts or thinking about my failed marriage and my son. Ultimately, I appreciated he was right; it was up to *me*.

stage door tavern

One of my most memorable police experiences, although not a pleasurable one, occurred in 1981—just fifteen months into the job—when the old Stage Door Tavern was shut down and a mob decided they'd wreck the joint.

It quickly degenerated into a riot and the police were called in to try and help restore calm . . . but it was bedlam. Of the forty officers there that night, only a dozen were armed with batons and shields; the rest of us had to fend for ourselves.

The mob bombarded us with bottles and flagons and, it was frightening with the glass smashing all around me. Because I was young and inexperienced, I was having second thoughts about being there. One officer standing near me was smashed in the head by a flagon and it opened his melon up. His blood poured onto the street and the sight of him holding his head only seemed to excite the crowd as they cheered and rained more missiles upon us. They realised that if they threw their missiles high enough, we wouldn't spot them in the dark until they were upon us.

The rabble moved behind our lines into Belmore Park and raided the flowerbeds to chuck large river stones at us. My mates and I copped an absolute flogging. As the police casualties mounted, one of the bosses finally gave the order for us to charge, and it was on.

We cops screamed through the park and the mob dispersed at a rapid pace. Many of the rioters ran onto the train platforms at Central Station and, in their blind terror, they bolted onto the railway lines to try and escape the boys in blue. It was pointless because we were so hyped up we chased them down and gave them a belting. We were angry and the drill was to whack anyone we caught across the knees to immobilise them . . . there would have been a few would-be tough guys limping like old men the following morning.

I know some people will have a fit at the thought of a burly cop dishing out some retribution, but we'd been showered with glass and stones, our mates had been badly hurt and those of us who'd escaped being hit put it down to luck rather than evasive skill. I was surprised we had to wait so long for the order to retaliate.

The wash-up to the Stage Door Tavern drama was the police hierarchy decided to form a new branch— a riot squad—which would be on call twenty-four hours a day to counter any sort of civil disturbance. They called it the Tactical Response Group and I remember the government deemed it such a dangerous job that married blokes needed a declaration signed by their wife, while single cops needed their parents' consent to join the unit. The reason I remember is because I volunteered to be in the inaugural group.

fitness drill

The job specifications for the new Tactical Response Group (TRG) required you to be physically fit and the job description demanded you remain that way by training daily. What a job. After two years in the normal police force, I couldn't get my application in fast enough.

When I joined the TRG we trained hard—we had to. In the TRG you weren't only training for yourself, your fellow officers were depending on you. When you were in the middle of a critical situation—about to bust through a door, take on a group of rioters or abseil down a building—you needed to know that your colleagues were fit and capable of backing you up. You placed your life in their hands each day.

To be a member of the TRG we had to pass a course which involved drill, physical fitness, unarmed combat, riot control, baton training and we also had to master our weapons, including the .870 Remington shotgun. The weapon became a part of us and we had to be able to strip and then reassemble it blindfolded under 'stress' in a matter of seconds. Mistakes, mishaps and laziness weren't tolerated: *everything* had to be one hundred per cent.

Every three months we were subjected to testing sessions. There were three tests: a five kilometre run, an agility course where you had to carry a shotgun, and a sit-up test. To score full marks you needed three hundred points. For the five kilometre run you had to finish in eighteen minutes or less to score one hundred points. Every ten seconds thereafter you would lose a point. It was the same for the agility course, for every second over the allocated time you dropped a point. To score one hundred in the sit-ups you had to do fifty-five in a set time, every one short cost you a point. We had a pass mark and anyone who failed to achieve the mark was made inactive. My goal was to get three hundred every time—a perfect one hundred per cent— and I did. I thrived on the hard work; I just lived to train hard.

Occasionally we'd train at the army's commando compound in Mosman where, among a host of things, Special Air Service (SAS) officers taught us unarmed combat and how to temporarily disarm a person using a wristlock, which wouldn't quite break their bones but would exert enough pain to render them powerless.

The commandos also pushed us beyond our limits with such exercises as the log run: a nightmare drill.

We were divided into four teams of four and each group had to carry a railway sleeper down through the scrub, into the water and then climb back up the hilly terrain. If one team-mate dropped out through exhaustion, it was left to the other three to finish the job. If another dropped off, the remaining two had to continue. If one more dropped out the last bloke standing would have had a hell of a job. But that never happened—everyone stuck at it, you'd die before you'd let your team-mates down.

We TRG members expected our mates to dig deep and encourage us to lift ourselves with comments like: 'Come on, mate, come on you can do it' . . . 'Don't give up, you bludger!' . . . 'Not much longer!' and a few other R-rated ones. Such spirit built a strong sense of much-needed camaraderie.

Our days at the army base would last from 6 a.m. until 10 p.m. and they'd end with a few beers in the mess and a trip to the barracks for a sleep. But we never slept long. On occasions when we least expected it, around 2.30 a.m. the army officers and TRG instructors would crash the doors open, bang garbage bins and direct us to the parade ground. We'd be given a scenario (like a riot) and we'd have to click in and react immediately.

It was hard—mentally and physically—but those exercises rammed home the importance discipline and professionalism played in an elite unit such as the TRG. It also drummed into us the value of good teamwork and the need to encourage the bloke next to us to push beyond his comfort zone.

I never underestimate the importance the TRG has had on my life. The training, the drill, the discipline and the camaraderie has contributed to who I am and what I have achieved. Money couldn't buy that and I wouldn't trade it anyway.

the upstart

There were two ways into the ranks of the New South Wales graded referees: by making it into the rep squad and refereeing SG Ball, Harold Matthews and Jersey Flegg games; or through invitation. Trialling for grade meant training with the referees who controlled the third, second and first grade games.

I received an invitation to trial for grade in 1983 after my performance in the 1982 Parramatta juniors grand final.

There I was, a raw 22-year-old referee about to mix it with the big guns including, Kevin Roberts, John Gocher, Mick Stone and Martin Weekes, to name a few, and a squad of around sixty. We had a training session at Redfern Oval and I upset them from the outset—is that a surprise?—and to this day I don't regret my actions.

Eric Cox, then the director of referees, addressed the squad and introduced Ken Boothroyd, the St

George conditioner who was to train us over the next six weeks. Back in those days we only trained together for the six Tuesdays prior to the competition—after that, you were on your own. For a lot of the blokes that Tuesday was probably the only training they did. The refs weren't overly fit, but they didn't need to be; the game was nowhere near as fast, nor as professional as it is today.

Ken took us through a warm-up and stretch, and outlined the program for the session. Compared to today's programs it was a snack. Ken said he wanted us to run flat out for two four-hundred-metre laps with a three minute break between each run. He stressed he wanted to see some effort as well.

It was a stinking hot day but his instructions seemed simple enough so when he lined us up and yelled 'GO!' I bolted.

I finished out of breath and looked behind me to see the others a distant one hundred and fifty metres behind me, running together like a flock of old sheep.

During our three minute recovery time Mark Holton, a colleague from the Parramatta district referees, approached me. He appeared agitated and hissed, 'What the hell are you doing? You've just upset the whole lot of them . . . they're all talking about you!'

Mark suggested I drop back to the pack and not show the big names up, but I didn't want any part of that. I told him the conditioner demanded some effort and that was exactly what I intended to give.

As we lined up for our second four hundred metre sprint I could feel the mob's eyes burning holes into me. But when we were told to go, I flew. I told myself they could all bite my dust and choke. Except for three or four others who were trialling, the rest were already graded and didn't need to impress.

Again I finished a long way ahead and I was receiving a lot of disgruntled looks. This time Holton and Graham Robertson, also of Parramatta district, both confronted me to lay down the law. 'Mate, all those blokes are bagging you,' they said pointing at the big names in unison. 'They're asking who the hell you think you are? Take it easy and fall back with the pack.'

I told them there was no way I would do that. 'They're already in grade,' I said, 'and I want to make it. That means impressing the right people.'

Naturally, my attitude wasn't well received but the incident set my benchmark because *every time* we trained, I led from the front. And I have ever since . . .

Years later, I heard Greg McCallum address a referees' seminar where he said the referees' professional approach to training and fitness these days was attributable to Bill Harrigan.

'Bill became the prototype referee because of his fitness,' McCallum said, 'and I realised back then that I needed to change my approach to training to come through the challenge. It was a wake-up call.'

Looking back, I'm certain many other blokes would have been bullied into slowing down and conforming with the pack mentality. But I had an immense self-belief and pride in myself which stemmed from growing up under my father's influence and being a member of the TRG. If anything, the other referees' attitude made me believe my tougher approach could elevate me to the top. And, as I left Redfern Oval that day, disillusioned and disappointed, I backed myself to do just that.

reviews

At all grade levels, except first grade, a written performance review is undertaken after every game. The report dissects the game into areas such as ten metres, rucks and general control. A rating is given in each area, ranging from very good, good, pass and fail. The referee is handed this document and it's discussed with the reviewer before the referee leaves the ground. The reviews are used as part of the promotional system.

In 1984, I approached the referees' boss at the time, Eric Cox, when I thought the referees' advisory panel wasn't marking my performances correctly.

I was twenty-four and refereeing third grade at the time. It was the last round before the semi-finals and I thought I was finished for the year because the game's top six referees would control the first, second and third grade finals, so I decided to speak up about the advisory board reports I'd received, which I thought were way off beam.

Arthur Neville, who was on the referees' advisory board, had written a report three weeks earlier, picking me up on a forward pass and marking me down because he said it set up a match-winning try for the Magpies. To this day I maintain he was wrong. I can remember the pass he zeroed in on because it was an inside short pass. I was right on top of it and I knew it was sweet, but Arthur was unhappy. I took exception and can remember saying: 'With all respect, Arthur, the grandstand you're sitting in doesn't run parallel to the ground; you're one hundred metres away from the action and you're at the back of a grandstand. I was right beside it and the pass was good.' We argued about it for a while, until I shut up and copped it.

The following week I received a terrible review when my gut feeling told me I'd performed well. Then, the week before the semi-finals, I was at Belmore and the reviewer, Ray O'Donnell, bashed my performance. I was insulted—based on what he'd noted he couldn't have been watching the same game.

As the refs' boss, Eric Cox always said anyone was welcome to talk to him about a refereeing problem face to face, man to man, and we weren't to worry about recriminations.

Eric was at Belmore that day, so after reading O'Donnell's report, I decided to take him up on his word, and, in hindsight, I could've started with a better comment because I saw the steam coming out of big

Eric's ears before I'd even finished my opening sentence. The 'conversation' went something like this:

> *Me* (holding up my report paper): Eric, can I talk to you man to man. Ray O'Donnell has watched the wrong game today; this report can't be based on my game.
>
> *Eric* (blood pressure rising): How dare you, son, how dare you. This man comes to these games eight hours a day writing reports on you referees and YOU have the temerity to say HE watched the wrong game and YOU disagree with his report! With an attitude like that, son, you won't have much of a career . . .

As Eric ranted and raved about my right to question someone of O'Donnell's standing in the game, I regretted taking up his invitation for the face to face chat.

Later that night I realised there were recriminations when the referees' coach Jack Danzey phoned me at home to talk about what had happened. He agreed I'd refereed much better than the report suggested, but I learnt an invaluable lesson about holding my tongue. It turned out Eric had my name pencilled in to do a third grade semi-final, which was unheard of. It had never happened before because, as I mentioned, the top six refs were appointed those games . . . but my outburst had cost me. So much for no recriminations.

Unbeknown to me, Eric had big wraps on me and he was prepared to back it up with a semi-final even though there were some twelve to fifteen referees in front of me.

As a veteran, I stress upon the young blokes coming through the ranks that when they're given a review they might not agree with, they're better off to cop it sweet because you risk losing too much by getting the powerbrokers offside. Some of the older referees have better tales than mine, with missed opportunities and even lost careers, and, although times have changed, a young referee still needs to have his wits about him.

motivations

At the beginning of every year the *Daily Telegraph* published a lift-out guide for the Rugby League season ahead. In 1985 I watched the top grade whistleblowers pose for a group shot—all of them running towards the photographer. They were the cream of the crop and I vowed my melon would be among them the following year.

I wanted to make first grade and I set being in that photograph—being one of the best referees in the country—as my goal. I knuckled down and trained harder. When I wanted to slacken off, I thought of that photo and what it represented, and that helped me put in the hard yards.

Sometime later, I attended a seminar where the NSWRL referees' boss Denis Braybrook said it took over two thousand candidates for them to find the eight referees who controlled the top grade competition.

Even if you made it as a grade referee, it was more likely you would fail than pass and very few referees—even those who made the eight—would ever taste a grand final or a State of Origin.

I was hooked and I decided there and then that I'd become the game's best referee and control a grand final. I vowed nothing, not lousy shifts at work or personal problems, would prevent me from making it.

I put in the hard yakka by lifting my game and by the next season I was in that group photograph for the *Daily Telegraph*. I wasn't quite in the centre of the front row, but I was on my way.

the happy hooker

I'm often reluctant to talk about my football playing career because I think anyone who does that when they didn't play the game at any great level runs the risk of being bracketed a 'woulda-been, coulda-been or shoulda-been.

I played in the Parramatta juniors and my father was told by a Canterbury official I had the skills to play first grade but would need to work hard to actually make it. When I entered the police force, trying to make grade football was practically impossible, so I competed in the police competition which consisted of teams from cop shops all over Sydney. The games were rough old encounters, with violence accepted as part and parcel of the game. From 1979 I played for Central, Liverpool, Darlinghurst (known the following year as Darlo/TRG) and finally Waverley.

The Darlo/TRG was undoubtedly the best mob I played with. We annihilated our opposition, not because we were a particularly gifted bunch of footballers, but because we were super fit. The normal cops would turn up, bash the tripe out of one another and then return to work to walk the beat—injuries permitting. They were nowhere near as fit as us though, so during a game when they faded through exhaustion, we lifted to another level. No surprise then that we won the premiership title at our first attempt.

My favourite playing position was still hooker. I liked the involvement the hooker had back in the days when the scrums were a lot more competitive. The hooker, also known as the rake, had to win the ball, defend, play dummy half and marker, be creative and, best of all, he had plenty of support in the size and brawn of his forwards.

I never modelled my game on anyone but I played the game in much the same vein as Steve and Kerrod Walters did. I liked to dash from dummy half and make up to ten to fifteen metres with each burst. Another Waltersesque quality was my tendency to score tries from dummy half when we were close to the opposition's line. I'd just dive low, towards the defender's feet, and burrow over the line.

Playing in games between different cop shops, such as Liverpool and Newtown stations, was like participating in a blood feud. In one of my first games I saw my drill instructor from the academy, Senior Constable Brown, and figured he would look after me—what a mistake. In the first two scrums Browny punched me fair in the guts.

'Why the hell are you hitting me?' I tried to reason.

'Shut up,' was his grizzled reply. 'We're playing football now.'

I realised Browny would keep hitting me until full-time, so the next scrum I got in first and hit Browny. Then it was on with all the players joining in.

When the ref restored calm and called us out, I smiled at Browny with his nose leaking claret and said, 'I'm playing footy, too.'

nz tour

In my police Rugby League career I played for the New South Wales representative side for years against the best teams from the fire brigade, armed services and the Federal police. While those games were tremendously intense (partly because my younger brother Greg was the Feds' hooker) our tours to New Zealand in 1983 and 1985 were the highlights of my playing career.

I was thrilled to be on the tour in 1983, especially since I had beaten former Manly first grade hooker, Charlie Haggett, for the rake's position in the side. We were to play three games on the tour against New Zealand sides.

We won our first game against Otahu in pouring rain; the field was a bog. From there we travelled north to Whangarei in the Bay of Islands. The footy field doubled as a cow paddock and we found out the locals had walked the field earlier and removed any hard cow patties but the fresh ones were still out there. During the game we weren't scared of getting tackled just where we landed. We won the game and the locals treated us to a traditional Maori hangi (a feast) to finish off a great day.

Our third game, and the reason for being there, was our test match against the Auckland police. It was as tough as any test match I've since refereed. We won the game but we were left sore and sorry with former New Zealand test prop Lindsay Proctor, a veteran of eleven tests, leading the way and doing most of the damage.

In 1985 we won convincingly against Otahu, this time on a dry track. The second game organised fell through, so a friendly against a few locals was played at Ponsonby in Auckland.

I asked if I could referee as it would be my first chance to referee off Australian soil. I was refereeing reserve grade in Australia at that stage, so for all I knew it might have been my only chance. The game was played in good spirit and I had plenty of fun refereeing my team-mates who were quick to point out my mistakes. Sledging was A plus.

Our third game was a rematch of the test against the Auckland Police which we had won in 1983. The Kiwis were confident and looking to take the cup away from us. They came out fighting—and I mean fighting. Headhigh tackles were par for the course. Our young team were successfully put off our game.

Midway through the second half they were up 18–6 and we'd had enough of being bashed around the head: it was time to retaliate. The game had already had its moments, but now it turned nasty. The crazy thing was we knew we'd be on the turps with these guys after the game—laughing, singing and swapping stories.

The referee was New Zealand's top international referee, Denis Hale. Denis was in trouble and he knew it. The game had deteriorated; it wouldn't have mattered who was in charge, it was impossible to control two teams of cops when they wanted to fight. The only way order would be restored was if both teams agreed to it.

Denis was experienced enough to see this, and called me out at a stoppage in play. Although I still hadn't made it to first grade, Denis knew I was a New South Wales grade referee.

Denis said something like, 'Billy, can you help me out and get the boys to play footy and stop the niggle and fighting?'

No referee wants to be remembered for losing control of a match, be it at schoolboy or international level.

'Denis,' I said, 'you help me out first. We are getting smashed. They are taking our heads off. I'm a player right now, so unless you do something about it, you're on your own.'

During this break Auckland made a replacement and a young twenty-year-old rookie took to the field: Don Mann, from the well-known Rugby League family, currently the event manager for the New Zealand Warriors. Don was on the field no longer than five minutes when he came in to make a tackle and, sure enough, up around the head he went. As my team-mates began to charge into the fray, the shrill of the whistle stopped us and Denis sent Don to the sin-bin for ten minutes.

As Don left the field, I looked over to Denis and neither of us had to say a word. I turned to our players and said, 'He's kept his end of the bargain—now we concentrate on playing footy.'

With twenty minutes still left on the clock we knuckled down and played our normal game without fear of being smashed and the tries came. It was soon 18-all. With six minutes left on the clock we were on the attack in Auckland's twenty. One of our forwards carted the ball up and hit the defensive line hard, coming down a metre short of the line. I took up my usual position in dummy half and gave all indications for a quick pass. Instead I scooped the ball up and staying close to the ground dived forward between the marker's legs scoring a four-pointer right beneath him. We converted and it was enough to keep the cup in Australia, finishing the game 24–18.

It wasn't long after that we were all drinking together and getting along like long-lost brothers.

Of course the playing was never the best part of the tours—we got up to all sorts of pranks off the field. In 1985 we shared one of our hotels with a team of netballers. Naturally the boys were tremendously excited and it didn't take long for little parties to start all over the hotel, once the bar shut and people moved on, including myself and a lovely netballer. I decided it would be a great lark to see who had ended up with whom, plus I had been the victim of a couple of pranks during the tour so I thought it was time to get my own back. As any of the other first grade referees will tell you, if you get me with a prank, I'll get you back *harder*.

So I triggered the fire alarm and had a great giggle as the girl and I looked down from the warmth of our window at everyone gathering on the freezing street below. Some of the netballers were wearing footy jerseys or our training T-shirts, and not much else.

But it was an event on our 1983 tour that was the real killer. One of my team-mates and I picked up two girls who took us on a romantic drive in their Mini Minor. Unfortunately though, it was a rainy night and we lost control of the mini down a hill and smashed into a tree. The car was so small we all had trouble squeezing out, especially the girl who was driving who was stuck against the steering wheel. Seeing as we all survived, we went back to the girls' place to celebrate and my mate immediately headed off to the bedroom with his girl. The other girl grabbed me for some action too.

Now, I hadn't really planned on staying the night because she wasn't my type but I thought, 'What the hell?' and we went for it. I was pleased to hear her enjoying the experience and didn't even mind when she started screaming at the end.

'Hell,' I said, 'you really enjoyed that, didn't you?'

'No,' she said, sitting up, 'I think I broke my ribs on the steering wheel.'

perfect match

One of the most popular television shows in the '80s was *Perfect Match*. Hosted by Greg Evans, Debbie Newsome and Dexter, a computer done up to look like a sci-fi robot. People tuned in of a weeknight to see three contestants use their wit, charm and humour to try and win a date at an exotic location such as the Whitsundays, Fiji or Bali. Sometimes it was pathetic television, other times it was hilarious and on other occasions it could be romantic, though that was the exception rather than the norm.

While the idea of going on a nationally televised dating show might sound embarrassing nowadays, back then it was something special. Rather than being ribbed for appearing to be desperate and dateless, people would be impressed someone had been on the program. 'Ohhhh, you've been on *Perfect Match*? What was it like? Is Debbie Newsome a spunk? Is Greg Evans cool? Does Dexter the robot really compute the figures?'

So when Channel Ten advertised for contestants, I chucked my hat in the ring and after a few telephone calls I was invited to attend an audition in which I was sized up, asked to fill out a compatibility form and to then talk about my interests, hobbies and childhood.

Time ticked by and I'd met a girl from Brisbane, Sue, who I was seeing. I'd almost forgotten about *Perfect Match* when I received a phone call from one of the show's producers inviting me on. Sue didn't mind me going on the show for a bit of a laugh, so about three weeks later I was on the set competing with two other blokes for the attention of a girl named Wendy. It was without doubt one of the most nerve-racking moments of my life, particularly when my ego kicked in. I didn't want to be one of the two blokes who missed out—a loser—so I used some of my best lines; though, in hindsight they were pretty poor.

Wendy picked me and, in a move which still embarrasses me, I celebrated my victory by doing an Elvis-like dance. Poor old Greg Evans didn't know what had hit him and I think he managed to slip in something like 'Wow, this boy's excited!'

Wendy and I had a seventy-five per cent compatibility rating, which made us the perfect match. Our prize was a trip to Bali! I was over the moon because I loved Bali, so even if things didn't click between Wendy and me, I'd still have a good time.

Wendy and I met our chaperone at Sydney International Airport and there was another couple going with us. I wore shorts and a T-shirt and carried an overnight bag with pretty much the same kind of clobber in it. Wendy had a suitcase and one of the other winners turned up with a suitcase, a suit bag and a carry bag.

'Where are you off too, mate?' I asked. 'A six week tour of Europe?'

Nope, he was off to Bali and had packed his best disco gear . . . unfortunately for him his first lesson on that island in the sun was thongs and shorts were the go over there.

Wendy and I hit it off. She was a good sort in every respect and we had a free and easy time and enjoyed one another's company. She was smart too, because before we landed in Bali we made a pact that no matter if we got on well or loathed one another we'd play it up to the max to get back onto the show and win a prize. If we liked each other, we'd pretend to be in the first throes of love and, if we didn't, Wendy and I would make it clear people had better keep any knives and scissors out of our reach!

So we got along and on our return we oozed lovey-dovey and, as a result, found ourselves on the *Perfect Match* couch talking about one another in glowing terms. I won a leather jacket for my trouble while Wendy was given a fur coat.

When I watched the show, however, I realised storm clouds would be brewing in Brisbane. I had pre-warned Sue about our plan to get back on the show and win a prize but when I saw the show I realised we were *too* convincing. I had my arm hugged around Wendy while her hand was on my leg—I shuddered to think what Sue would be thinking as she watched.

I used to catch a bus from Sydney to Brisbane on my days off and scrimp and scrape to catch the occasional flight to see Sue. After realising how filthy she would be after seeing the program I broke the budget and hopped on a plane first thing the following morning. I was armed with a dozen roses, a book full of heartfelt explanations and the thought to duck as soon as she opened the door just in case she threw a haymaker.

run for your life

Easter 1985, I'd taken the weekend off from refereeing in the lower grades to attend the Bathurst bike races, but it wasn't a pleasure trip. I was on police duty, and by the end of the long weekend I'd lost a tooth, been knocked senseless by a bit of rubble and suffered nerve damage in my big toe. But my injuries were minor compared to some others.

The horrific events included a fellow TRG officer and I sprinting for our lives from a crazed mob wanting to kick us to death; another officer drawing his revolver as a maniac knocked him to the ground and then shaped up to spear him through the chest with a metal pole; cops being knocked cold by house bricks; and TRG members being set ablaze from direct hits by Molotov cocktails—for eight long hours an army of four thousand feral barbarians surrounded the police compound, bombarding it with bottles and rubble and taunting us to come out and fight.

Ironically, when we were first called into action I figured it would be a bit of fun. The police media unit, who were on hand to film the sequence of events, even filmed me belting out an Elvis song as I kitted up for battle! I wasn't alone in that regard though, because, to a man, the TRG was happy to be called in to action. We'd spent weeks preparing, based on intelligence that had been gathered during the Bathurst dramas of 1983 when police and revellers at the 1983 Australian Motorcycle Grand Prix clashed violently. We'd practised our drills in an area the authorities had marked out on the parade ground to represent the police compound—we knew where we had to go and how we'd need to aim up—and we'd set up a base camp in an old building halfway down the racetrack.

Yet, *nothing* braced us for the scene we viewed from our bus as we neared the top of Mount Panorama. Thousands of people had surrounded the police compound and they were out of control—throwing Molotov cocktails, house bricks, burning toilet rolls and bottles at the dozen or so police officers trapped in the compound. The mob had started as a drunken rabble that had decided it would be a bit of fun to rock the coppers, but then they'd been reinforced by more people who started screaming and yelling insults at the police and it didn't take long for them to be whipped into a frenzy, intoxicated by the atmosphere and the copious amounts of grog they'd consumed. It became a full-scale riot and the police in the besieged compound were in danger of serious injury—or worse.

We entered the compound from the racetrack, charged off the bus and rushed out the front gate to get amongst the mob and disperse them. They ran back as we formed up in our four lines of twelve, surrounding the front of the compound—and that's when the mud hit the fan. The mob quickly regrouped and starting pelting us with anything they could get their hands on!

I was Team Two's 'fireman' armed with a shield and fire extinguisher. I also wore a canvas vest, which held another fire extinguisher and a blanket to smother the flames. My job was to roam behind line two, trying to spot the 'incomings', rushing towards where I thought they would land, and then putting them out. The officers would try to ward off the fire bombs with their shields, but if they were set alight they were drilled to stand still and wait for me to put them out—and that took a heck of a lot of discipline because it's terrifying to see yourself enveloped by flames. When I'd put the officer out I'd sometimes have to turn the extinguisher on myself and douse the flames now engulfing my clothes. One guy broke ranks. He was hit, set alight, panicked and then ran in blind terror. You can see me on the old news footage bolting after him yelling 'Stop! Stop! Stop!' But the poor bugger was spooked and kept going. I eventually caught up with him and doused the flames before too much damage was done, but as the night progressed the situation became a lot more dangerous, and a constant stream of police were being carted to the ambulance post for treatment.

I copped it about an hour and a half into the riot when a rock smashed me right in the mouth. It knocked my tooth out and I hit the deck unconscious. My mates carried me into the compound and, when I regained my senses, it was like being in a MASH unit because bodies were strewn everywhere. One bloke had copped a full house brick in the knee and he was stuffed, another had blood pouring out of a gash on his head, and other officers were being bandaged up. The mob had demolished a brick canteen to arm themselves with a new supply of ammunition—big, dirty, brown house bricks—and, as a Channel Ten reporter noted, they were throwing them with the intention of hurting policemen. They'd howl and cheer at the sight of a copper falling and being carried out of the firing line for treatment.

TRG personnel were wearing ice hockey leg pads to protect us from the rocks they threw at our shins, but as general duty police joined our line to fill the holes left by the injured, they became easy targets. The rioters soon gelled that the cops dressed in normal uniform were minus the hockey pads and missiles were directed at their legs. It was a relentless barrage and police were going down at a rapid pace with leg injuries. Imagine your leg being hit with half a brick, a river stone the size of your hand or a stubbie thrown at full force. Police were falling constantly and our lines were straining. After regaining consciousness I was sent straight back into the fray, armed with a baton and shield.

My parents, Joy and William Harrigan, on their wedding day in 1959.

Me, my dad, my sister Dianne and my brother Greg out the front of our Housing Commission house in Canley Heights.

ABOVE
On the front lawn at Canley Heights which saw a lot of action—football games, soccer and cricket.

RIGHT
I was so excited about wearing my first football jersey for the Canley Heights team, even if it was way too big.

The Canley Heights Rugby League team. We weren't the best team, but we loved to play. I'm in the second row, on the far right.

The Fairvale High Rugby Union team, taken in 1977. Ross Smith, the teacher who made me sit for my refereeing ticket, is on the far right. I'm in the top row, third from the left.

I'd just started refereeing in the Parramatta juniors when this photo was taken. I had no idea refereeing would become a major part of my life.

Graduating from the Redfern Barracks in 1979 as a fresh-faced constable.

A Westie car for a Westie boy: my white Sultans of Surf Datsun 200BSX.

I spent a lot of time mucking around in my youth, but it didn't take long for me to gain some responsibilities and smarten up.

I joined the elite TRG (Tactical Response Group) police unit in 1981. It was demanding, adrenaline-pumping work. In 1985 we went into the Bathurst bike riots in full riot gear and still got knocked about.

Rugby League Week

ABOVE
I hadn't had any formal training when I spoke to this kid, a Souths fan who wanted to jump off a highrise in the centre of Sydney. I copped some criticism from the experts for sitting so close to him and placing myself in danger, but I talked the kid down.

Fairfax Picture Library

BELOW
The full TRG kit: gas masks, bulletproof vests and loaded shotguns. This is what I was wearing when I nearly had my head blown off.

Me and Matt Moss when we both still worked in the TRG. Eventually the pressures of the job, and Matt's shooting, wore me out and I moved to the Witness Security Unit.

News Limited

I was fired up and can vividly recall one grub who'd urinate into a bottle and then lob it at us, his piss spraying our line. Then, egged on by the mob, he'd raise his hands in triumph and gee us up with a stupid dance. He angered me and my mate George Thompson and we promised ourselves the next time we were given the order to charge we'd target him for special attention. The bloke had stumbled and fallen just as the order was given and we both chased after him . . . I would've been an arm's-length away from him when the whistle for us to fall back and regroup was blown. George and I, however, ignored it. We followed him deeper into the camp sites, a bad mistake because we'd charged blindly into enemy territory. Both of us became painfully aware of our precarious position when someone rallied the retreating masses by yelling 'There's only two of them!'. They turned on us and, judging by the looks on their faces, we weren't just going to cop a flogging, they were going to kill us.

I yelled to George, 'We gotta run, mate' and we bolted—hurdling tent ropes, side-stepping camp sites and doing our best to avoid the lynching mob that was hot on our heels. As we tore up the hill I could see George and I were surrounded and I didn't know how we were going to escape.

Yet, as George and I prepared for our last stand, a mate back on the line, Des Hansen, yelled to the officer in charge that two men were missing and the TRG went into overdrive. The boys charged back to rescue us and the mob stopped, turned and fled from the ensuing well-aimed baton strokes. We were saved. As I returned to the line I realised I'd broken the TRG's standard of discipline—I'd ignored the whistle because a bloke had got the better of me. I was disappointed in myself. It was my one slip-up, and I was to ensure throughout the rest of my police career that I'd never do that again—it had placed a lot of good blokes at risk and had almost cost me my life.

Other battles raged. The Channel Seven car was torched outside the compound, destroying thousands of dollars worth of television gear. Another police officer was belted across the back by a star metal picket fence post and when he looked up the bloke who'd dropped him was poised to spear him through the chest. Fortunately a team of coppers saved him.

As the night wore on, we started to get the upper hand. When we charged forward any rioter slow to move was smashed across the knees and left writhing on the ground for the arrest team to collect. The blokes who were so brave in front of their mates went to water when dragged into the police compound to have their photographs taken. You could have asked them to tap-dance naked and they would've done it without question.

Some people complained innocent citizens were beaten by our batons. My response is that innocent people wouldn't have been there because every fifteen minutes our commander read out a declaration warning them the police would soon be taking forceful action to clear the area. We won the battle but the bleeding hearts said the TRG had lived up to our nickname as 'Terribly Rough Guys'.

All of that was lost on me when we were finally stood down in the early hours. Back at our accommodation some ripped into a few cans of beer and swapped war stories, but I was too sore so I went off to soak in a bath. While reflecting on the night I don't mind admitting I shed a tear—we had been bashed from pillar to post and placed in life-threatening situations on a number of occasions. After I got out of the bath, I managed three sips of a beer and then fell into a coma-like sleep. I was shattered. We went back out the next night and, while it was hairy, we'd restored calm. We'd done our job.

debut

Two aspects I vividly recall about my first grade debut on 19 May 1986 are the pace and intensity of the game between Western Suburbs and Cronulla—and what rattled me most of all as I trudged off Lidcombe Oval was knowing both sides were 'cellar dwellers'; at the time they were both languishing near the bottom of the premiership ladder!

In the days leading up to the game, however, it didn't matter to me where the teams were in the competition, because I had made it. I was in first grade and I was buzzing. I also had my first representative appointment, City–Country under-19s, the day before the big game. It was a good game in Newcastle, but I couldn't hide my excitement on the bus trip home as I counted down the hours till my first grade debut.

At twenty-five years of age I was given my call-up by Denis Braybrook, a referees' boss who I'll long remember as someone who wasn't scared to give young blood a go. Over the next couple of months he also promoted David O'Keefe, Phil Cooley and, later, Greg Boyd who became the youngest referee in first grade, clocking in his debut a couple of months younger than me. Phil Cooley ended up the most successful of that trio, but our rise allowed younger referees to believe they too might get the nod if they performed consistently. In the late '80s it was a part of the refs' culture that the older blokes had the next best thing to a mortgage on the top grade berths, and we basically waited for them to retire.

Phil's top grade career suffered in the wake of a bitter South Sydney–Parramatta match. He was dropped for his performance in that match; and it didn't help Cooley's cause that his decision to sin-bin Peter 'Mr Clean' Sterling for the one and only time of his career was later found to be the wrong call. (Though we've all made mistakes.) Phil was dropped, but he justified Braybrook's belief that he was made of the right stuff by making it back to first grade. Years later Phil reinvented himself as a touch judge—he went on to become one of the best first grade touchies the game has ever had.

While Braybrook gave us our chance, he also helped prepare us for our big moment; for the nine weeks before my promotion I spent up to an hour and a half a week going through my match videos with Denis, looking at various aspects of my game. It didn't dawn on me until the fourth video session that he was helping to brace me for my call-up.

A stickler for positioning, Denis gave the impression that reading the play was half the battle . . . and he was spot-on. The only problem was in first grade it was speed reading. For instance, in reserves when the defending team made a tackle the referee had time to watch the tackle get completed; wait for the player to get up and play the ball; scan to ensure the five metres was being maintained; watch the play the ball be completed and see the dummy half get the ball; take another 'squiz' that the defending team was onside and watch the first receiver take the ball.

When I ran onto the paddock at Lidcombe Oval as part of a first grade game it was a whole different atmosphere. The players were bigger, the crowd was pumped up and I felt like I'd grown in stature—I was a part of the *real* thing. It was like when a supporting band leaves the stage and the headline band comes on, suddenly the atmosphere reaches a new level, and everything seems huge.

The game itself was so much faster. I quickly learnt there wasn't enough time to check the five metres and return to the play the ball because it had usually been completed. If I took my eyes off the play the ball I could miss a loose ball and then have to decide whether it was dropped or knocked out. My strategy was to use my peripheral vision to keep check of the five metres. In that first game I could only manage to specifically check the five metres twice out of each set of six tackles.

Initially, it was a mental and physical battle to keep up with the play. I can still recall looking up at the scoreboard clock and refusing to believe we were only in the sixty-fifth minute, because I was out on my feet. With fifteen minutes to go my body felt as though I'd been through a reserve grade game *and more*! But I hung in, desperate not to allow fatigue to contribute to a mistake that would blemish my performance.

Most of the game was a blur, but I remember looking at the scoreboard, keeping a close eye on the scrums and not thinking twice about sin-binning Wests hooker, Alan Fallah. I also remember feeling a sense of achievement as I walked off the ground only to be spat on by some idiot as I entered the tunnel.

The game was played at a cracking pace and I slept well that night, but I couldn't help wonder what the hell it would be like to control a Parramatta–Manly match. A contest between the two top sides at the time was bound to be even faster.

One humorous moment amid the helter-skelter of my top grade debut occurred when I pinged Magpies prop Lee Crooks for a high tackle. He tried to explain something to me, but for the life of me I couldn't understand a word he said. A Great Britain international, Crooks boasted a broad Castleford accent, so he might as well have spoken Swahili to me because his English was impossible to decipher. Despite my waving him away, Lee stood his ground and continued to say whatever it was he had on his mind and wave his arms around. I gave him a third opportunity to return to his team but the big man had dug his heels in and repeated whatever it was again. Frustrated that I couldn't understand him, I started to think about my next move when Maggies forward Ian Schubert came to my rescue by grabbing Crooks by his collar and dragging him away.

'Bill,' he said. 'I've just returned from an off-season in England. Would you like me to interpret for you?' I nodded my head and, with a grin, Schubert said, 'He said "Sorry mate, I won't do that again!"'

My first grade debut had initiated a fair bit of publicity and on the Monday morning a picture with me sin-binning Alan Fallah (who went on to join the referees' ranks and was my touch judge in the 2001 State of Origin series) and the headline 'Cop this, said referee' made the front page of the *Daily Telegraph*. A full story appeared on page four with the headline 'Tough cop Bill makes debut as ref' and in the sports pages it read 'Debutante first grade referee Bill Harrigan kept the game flowing in a match dotted with frequent sweeping backline play'.

It was the first time I hit the headlines, but it wouldn't be the last.

on the rails

When I was in the TRG my greatest fear was copping a bullet in the guts during a building entry, but I never imagined a State Rail train would come close to cleaning me up.

During a siege, my mate Matt Moss and I were ordered to secure the rear of a building just in case the bad guys made a run for it. It was right on dusk and the light was fading quickly. We scaled fences and ran through backyards to get into position but we knew we were taking too long. The easiest way to get to the rear of the premises was to run along the railway line.

After running some sixty metres along the railway line we were closing in on the rear of the target premises. Our focus was on the location and keeping our movements covert. We were moving slowly and in a crouched position with Matty in front. He stopped, turned towards the house, then said to me, 'This is the house, Willy.'

I looked at the house and turned to Matt and began to say 'Yeah that's it' but only yeah came out because after that I yelled, 'Train!' When I looked at Matt I saw a silver State Rail train coming around the bend towards us at great speed.

There was no time to think, only react. I dived for the safety of the embankment with Matt following immediately behind. As we hit the deck the train screamed past, missing us by centimetres. By the time the train and its wind drag had passed us we realised how close we'd come to being smashed. The adrenaline was pumping and a surreal feeling engulfed both of us. Matt and I just looked at one another and laughed like madmen. We must have laid there for a good couple of minutes rolling around joking about our near miss.

I can't imagine what the poor train driver thought when he saw two blokes armed with shotguns, dressed in flak jackets and helmets dive to avoid his train! Fortunately for Matt and me our reflexes didn't let us down when it really mattered.

new kid on the block

It only took a few weeks after I refereed my first top grade match in 1986 to gain a reputation throughout Rugby League circles for being an arrogant bastard. It didn't worry me in the slightest. If anything, I wore that tag as a badge of honour because it meant the players realised they couldn't intimidate me with their constant insults and sledging. And, believe me, I got plenty!

My initiation saw me cop it from the likes of Ross Conlon, Steve Roach, Gavin Miller, David Hatch, Steve Mortimer, Phil Gould, Mario Fenech, Craig Coleman, Michael Pobjie and Neil Baker to name a few. They tried hard to sniff out any ounce of fear I may have had, but found nothing. After all, my job as a TRG police officer had placed me in life-threatening situations, so even though blokes like Mario looked fearsome when they were all revved up and ranting like madmen, they didn't compare to the hoodlums who hurled house bricks and Molotov cocktails at my colleagues and I during the 1985 Bathurst Bike riots.

I not only took my baptism of fire in my stride, but I also gave back as good as I got. Players soon branded me 'unapproachable' and accused me of being 'schoolteacher-like'. Just like schoolyard bullies it turned out the blokes who could give it out, couldn't take it, and I was amused to hear some of them complain about being spoken to in a 'derogative manner'.

It's nice to see some guys have mellowed with age; take Steve 'Turvey' Mortimer for instance. During the Bulldogs' salary cap crisis in 2002, Turvey, in his role as the club's interim Chief Executive Officer, came across as a man in total control of a dicey situation. While his supporters demanded the Bulldogs take the NRL to court for stripping them of their premiership points, Mortimer appealed for calm. His leadership under pressure was first class and I admired the way he handled a tough time.

As a young referee trying to earn my stripes, however, Mortimer was a nightmare. I guess Turvey figured I'd wilt under pressure in that first season because he'd get in my face and bag my rulings by snarling insults like 'wimp' and 'kid'. He'd also say other things, suggesting I knew nothing about the game. It was a challenge all right, but rather than make me crumble, his comments galvanised my determination to stamp my authority on the game—and I did.

When I recall my rookie season I feel grateful to have been born with a thick hide, otherwise I'd have cried myself to sleep. I was being slammed by blokes I admired as a footy fan, but the trick to surviving was to never treat anything they said as personal. I saw through their method; it was simply gamesmanship— they wanted to pull the wool over the eyes of a referee they thought was young and vulnerable. I won't deny it was a testing time, but I'm proud to say that in that first year I never left any field feeling as if so-and-so had got the better of me.

I will, however, admit there were times when I could have handled some situations differently—like the way I spoke to particular players—but I attribute that to inexperience. I think it was important for me back in '86 to realise Mortimer and his kind hadn't succeeded in putting dirt on me or making me doubt myself. I was happy to think I'd put them in their place by giving it back to them; they learnt I couldn't be bullied.

My priority in the early days of my first grade career was to earn the players' respect; not their friendship. Even though I am now mates with a few players, I realised from the outset it was stupid to think you could ever be one of the boys, because the worlds of footballers and referees are poles apart. I fought hard to earn their respect, but the mistake I made in the early days was trying to demand it. For instance, if they gave me a gobful I'd order them to cease talking to me like that. If they bent over to pull up their socks as I warned them about an illegal play, I'd bark at them to stand upright because I saw that action as a sign of contempt.

'Stuff you,' I'd think. 'Look me in the eye like a man.' As the years rolled by, I learnt from my mistakes and my attitude changed. The players judged me on my week-to-week effort and eventually I earned the respect I craved. I think they appreciated I was a consummate professional because I was fit, I had a playing background, I backed my ability and I refused to take any rubbish from them.

Refereeing also became easier with time because as the blokes who had attempted to ride roughshod over me retired, they were replaced by young guns who'd grown up watching me referee the big games. They came into the game giving me respect because of the status I already held. My job with these new players was to give them good reasons to keep respecting me. I would say earning the respect of the players is one of my greatest achievements as a whistleblower, and I can assure you it isn't something I take lightly because respect can be lost in the blink of an eye . . .

Even though I remember my first couple of seasons as a hard slog which tested my desire to continue, I learned plenty about handling pressure-cooker situations and deflecting abusive comments. I appreciate my good fortune to have had a police background because the discipline, the self-esteem and the pride that was drilled into me from my days as a cadet at the old Redfern barracks gave me a huge advantage over other young referees.

I was shocked in the early days of the Super League war in 1995 when the ARL made a public appeal for the players to go easy on the young, inexperienced ARL referees they had to install after we'd been stood down. They were carved up like a roast dinner and from all reports the experience rattled them.

I had no intention of handing them a tissue to dry their eyes. I prefer the philosophy which says through the fires of a furnace are forged men of steel. But referees' boss Mick Stone tried to give them a helping hand by urging the players to go easy and help nurse them along. I didn't agree with Mick on this matter. I think he should have instructed the referees to realise they were in charge and needed to have the courage of their convictions. If they lacked conviction then I believe Mick should have suggested they do something else with their weekends.

When Ricky Stuart read Stone's appeal he didn't know what to do and took time out to phone me. Now, let me tell you, Ricky Stuart knew how to get under a referee's skin . . . he'd do everything but belt you over the head with a baseball bat! But when he phoned to ask whether he should tone the attitude down I said, '*No*'. My response shocked him because he was expecting me to suggest he put on the kid gloves, but that wouldn't have been fair to him, his team, the supporters and, believe it or not, the refs, because the game would have been played under a false climate. I simply asked whether he ever went easy on me. When he replied in the negative, I told Ricky he'd answered his own question.

trash talk

I've seen just about the worst things that can possibly occur on the football field: eye gouging, kicking 'n' stomping, broken limbs and gashes several centimetres deep. I've been on hand to either send the player off or place him on report for his cheap, nasty shot. Some of the things I've witnessed have left me stunned, but the single event that *disgusted* me most was a sledge directed towards renowned hot head, Mario Fenech.

This particular comment wasn't just another sledge; it was the lowest form of trash talk imaginable. It was cruel, cowardly and crass and occurred during a 1986 Monday night footy game between South Sydney and Canterbury at Belmore. I've recently spoken with Mario and he denies it happened but I know what I heard.

Mario had a hair-trigger temper and opposing players, such as Balmain's Benny Elias, would bait him at every opportunity. They knew Mario's blood would boil in response to the simplest insult and he'd react without thinking. More often than not that meant throwing a volley of wild haymakers and copping the wrath of firstly the referee, and then his coach. The amazing thing was everyone knew what his opponent's tactics were all about, but Mario couldn't help himself.

When people think of Mario, they think of his explosive temper, which is unfortunate because he had a lot of ability and he could certainly play.

It was obvious from the kick off that the Warren Ryan coached Bulldogs had targeted Mario for extra attention—the game was like a street fight and, as usual, Fenech was in the thick of it. By full-time I'd sin-binned him twice . . . but I actually felt bad about that because he had been sent into overdrive by one hell of a low blow.

During a scrum a Bulldogs forward baited Mario with a deliberate personal comment. It was a repulsive remark directed at the tragic death of Mario's brother. Mario came out swinging; he threw bombs and at the time my chief concern was he'd have killed a Canterbury player had he landed one on them. In the thick of the battle his jumper was pulled over his head but he just tore the red-and-green fabric off and threw it to the ground, like a gladiator.

The brawl was about to get right out of hand and, when my touchies and I managed to separate the two teams, I sin-binned Mario. I had to maintain law and order on the field, but I couldn't blame him for reacting violently. I was so outraged by what I'd heard I swear, had I been a hundred per cent sure at the time of *who* the offender was, I'd have had no hesitation in sending him off. And had Mario dealt with him—in South Sydney style—outside the dressing shed then it would've been the Canterbury forward's look out.

Sixteen years on I'm pretty sure I know who the Canterbury bloke was. His comment was said in poor taste—it still amazes me to think he even dared utter it—but it was said a long time ago and I'd like to think he would agree it was the comment of a young and silly man. I hope he now regrets the entire incident.

That example aside, most sledging on the footy field is harmless stuff where players say such things as 'They're a bunch of cats, smash 'em' . . . 'Is that the best you've got? My mother hits harder' and so on. Real hurtful, eh? There's a huge amount of bravado involved in Rugby League and a lot of what is said and done in the heat of the moment is just show; in most cases there's very little malice.

These days swapping insults seems to have replaced trading blows to gain an advantage. When I first refereed grade football the scrum was still dangerous— a steaming, humid mass of human flesh wrestling to win the ball by hook or by crook. It was a tinder box and a fiery temper could cause the whole thing to explode. In those days props would fight tooth and nail for the loosehead and one trick they'd learned (the hard way) was to drop their head as they packed in and to then raise it quickly to ram their opponent square on the snout or cheek. That would send the other front rower over the edge and he would start throwing punches—and *bang*, *bang*, *bang* it would be on from there.

The rule changes to 'sanitise' scrums over the years have taken a lot of the aggro out of them and these days there's very little push and shove. I've noticed any fights that might arise from scrums last an average of two or maybe three punches before the fighter is shepherded away by a few mates. It's a matter of punch, punch, and be pulled away . . . There aren't too many scoring shots and, if you ask me, most of it is about 'front'. For the most part, footballers aren't boxers, and who on earth can blame them for not wanting to get caught up in that? Rugby League is already tough enough without the extra pepper.

injured pride

I hung my playing boots up at the end of the 1986 season after I'd established myself as a first grade referee. I'd worked hard to make the grade and was concerned about the threat of an injury.

Yet, while I wanted to focus on refereeing, it wasn't long before my brain felt like mush.

My father could sense my frustration and I turned to him for advice. He thought I had become too robot-like.

'You're starting to do everything they're telling you,' he growled. 'Go back and do what it was that got you into the top grade in the first place.'

I took the tip to heart because I knew Dad was right. I was refereeing with a confused state of mind and needed to fix it. I thought about it and it hit me— I was playing police footy when I made the top grade, so I made a decision to return to the field as a player.

Obviously my desire to play again and potentially expose myself to any number of injuries didn't impress the NSWRL referees' boss Denis Braybrook. While he was unhappy about my request, he listened to my reasons before offering just one piece of advice. 'God help you, Harrigan,' he said. 'God help you if I get a call telling me you can't referee because you've injured yourself.'

With those words ringing in my ears, I returned to the playing arena. It was short-lived because only six weeks later, I took a terrible knock on my knee—it was a doozey! The knee swelled up like a balloon and I hobbled about like an old man. It hurt every time I tried to move and after a while a deep bruising set in. I was in trouble and I had three and a half days to recover and fulfil my weekend duties.

I knew I couldn't call Denis—I loathed the idea of hearing him and others say 'we told you so'. And I really believed him when he said there'd be hell to pay if I was injured. I feared being dropped to reserve grade—or worse.

I had to recover, and quick. The only course of action available to me was to take a leaf out of the great Ray Price's book of pain relief, and ice it. Price was legendary in the '80s for his ability to recover from knocks. To follow his lead I had to be up every second hour during the night to whack a bag of ice on the knee to try and reduce the amount of bruising and swelling. It was in the cold of winter and you'll appreciate why *that* was hell in itself! I beat the physiotherapist to his office the following morning and we worked on the knee every day just so I could get back on the paddock.

By match day I was seventy-five per cent fit—just enough to allow me to get by. My biggest fear during the match was knowing that if I had to break into a sprint there was no way I could do it. I paced myself and jogged through the eighty minutes and headed straight home to whack more ice on my knee.

I repeated the Ray Price care of injury technique for the next forty-eight hours. Denis never did find out about the injury and I was back at full pace the following weekend. But it was enough of a scare for me to hang up the boots once and for all.

souths jumper

During one afternoon shift in my police work, my partner and I responded to a radio call to all units that there was a 'jumper' perched on a high-rise building on the corner of Bathurst and Castlereagh Streets, Sydney.

After taking the elevator and then racing up the stairwell I found myself one on one with a young kid who wanted to end it all. At that stage in my career, apart from talking to fired up forwards on the Rugby League field, I had no formal counselling or negotiator training to speak of, but there was no time to wait for the experts to arrive. I had to act immediately and learn on the job.

I asked the kid what his name was and why he wanted to jump. I was worried the wrong words could send him over the edge, but I had to back myself and believe I could talk him down.

It didn't take too long to establish a relationship with the young man (I'll call him 'Bob') because he was desperate to talk to someone, *anyone*, and in no time at all he was spilling his guts to me.

Bob was an extremely lonely person who felt as if no one really cared about him. He'd just broken up with his girlfriend, had no family and no mates to talk to . . . all Bob had was himself and he couldn't see the point of going on.

I listened and offered what I thought was common sense advice and plenty of understanding because I sensed that's what he craved. We developed a bond and by the time the police negotiators arrived they decided it would be a mistake to replace me; a decision I took as a mighty vote of confidence.

What they didn't approve of, however, was the way I had straddled the building with a leg dangling over either side. I had done that because when I first arrived Bob had his back to me and I realised that to have any chance of gaining his trust I had to make direct eye contact with him. That would have been impossible if I had stood behind him, which is the correct police procedure when dealing with a jumper.

I was later given a gentle kick up the bum because the experts said that if Bob had lunged at me he might have dragged me down with him. I copped their criticism, but I had considered that scenario when I first sat down and I made sure there was plenty of room between us. I even had an escape route ready if he tried something stupid—I planned to simply flop to my left-hand side and fall onto the roof.

It was clear that the Hollywood cop approach of grabbing the jumper and dragging him back to safety wasn't an option because, had it failed, I might have spooked the kid into jumping.

Several times Bob scared me by standing upright on the ledge, which would've only been a foot wide. His knees were trembling and he was so wobbly I felt certain he'd tumble over the side if he was hit by a sudden gust of wind. Each time he stood I encouraged him to sit back down to have another cigarette and continue chatting with me. Thankfully he listened, but each time he finished the cigarette he'd jump up again.

Apart from trying to talk him down my biggest problem was the spectators who'd gathered on the street below. They thought it was a great lark and, in a move that sickened me, some of them chanted for the kid to jump—'Jump . . . Jump . . . Jump!'—and I could see it was playing on his mind.

Bob was desperate for people to like him and I feared he might decide to impress them with a swan dive. I told him over and over again to forget them and to listen only to me, but their din became so great that I relayed a message for the cops on the ground to force the mob back out of earshot. I hoped they booted any idiot who was yelling up their backside.

I'd been on the ledge for about an hour and a half and realised time was fast running out—things seemed to be getting towards the point of no return. Bob was getting agitated and, with very little else left to talk about, I brought up footy.

It turned out Bob was a keen Souths man and I shared a secret by telling him they were my team when I was a kid. I told him my memories of such red-and-green legends as Bob McCarthy, Ron Coote, Paul Sait, John Sattler and Eric Simms.

As we spoke about the game, his eyes flickered and Bob said, 'You seem to know what you're talking about.'

I told him that I should because I was a first grade referee.

Bob said, 'Harrigan, right?'

To picture the scene now is almost laughable—there was this bloke wanting to plunge to his death debating the merits of the differential penalty, and other rules, to a whistleblower trying to save his life! We spoke about what it was like to referee first grade and what the superstars were like. When I was convinced I'd won his confidence, I insisted he come down and work his problems out with people who could help him.

I can't tell you how relieved I was when he took my tip and stepped back off the wall to the safety of the roof. As he was taken by paramedics to the psychiatric ward for treatment, I felt this incredible surge of fulfilment that I'd saved his life—yet, I also felt this terrible sense of pity that loneliness could drive a young bloke with his life in front of him to such an extreme.

bob fulton

One secret to Bob Fulton's success as a Rugby League coach was his ability to intimidate his opponents by any means available. Bob's teams reflected his competitive nature because there was a genuine meanness to most things they did. Everything was geared to intimidate and aggravate and put their opponents off their game—and that included the referee.

From my spot on the paddock it was obvious Fulton-coached teams had orders to openly argue with the referee. On most occasions they'd question every penalty with such queries as: 'What did you award that one for?' 'The penalty count is 7–1, ref, that's not fair. What are we doing wrong?' I'd only cop it for so long before I would dismiss them with a wave of my hand and shout, 'Not now, not now'.

My action of waving captains away had clubs complaining to the League and the media that Bill

Harrigan was 'unapproachable' and 'too arrogant' to deal with. But the reason I'd say 'Not now' to Paul Vautin or Geoff Toovey or other captains was because I knew they were deliberately trying to hinder the flow of play. I knew the question was a ruse to allow their team to have a breather and to fix their defensive line if I had awarded their opposition a penalty. Vautin, Fulton's first premiership-winning captain, confirmed Bozo's 'unsettle the ref' tactic in his biography *Fatty*: 'Bozo used to send a runner on for me to tell the ref the penalty count is 10–1 against us. I'd say: "Is it?" and he'd say: "No, but the ref won't know that".'

Current Sydney Roosters coach Ricky Stuart, who played under Fulton on the 1994 Kangaroo tour of Great Britain and France, also confirmed Bob's preoccupation with having his players place the referee under extra pressure: 'He liked his players to keep up in the referee's ear looking for an advantage. It might get you a penalty here or there, which can make all the difference.'

Fulton definitely liked his mind games, and in between ringing journalists to berate them about what he considered pot shots at his Sea Eagles, he took great delight in giving it to referees. I was on top of his list for a while and nothing seemed to help endear me to a man acknowledged alongside Reg Gasnier, John Raper, Clive Churchill, Graeme Langlands and Wally Lewis as a Rugby League Immortal. But there was a litany of other referees too, and he went hell for leather in his campaign to shake up the whistleblowers and have them fall into his way of thinking. He shared a few of his thoughts on the world's international referees from the 1990s with the *Courier Mail*:

Alain Sablayrolles (France): *'He couldn't referee at all.'*

Kevin Allot (England): *'It was like something out of Fawlty Towers . . .'*

John Holdsworth (England): *'He was running around like he has a wooden leg. He's as old as me.'*

But it was Bob's comments to me when we first crossed paths at Cronulla's home ground in 1987 that everyone remembers. It was loathe at first sight when he took offence to the 12–4 penalty count against his team and my sin-binning Des Hasler for repeated feed-the-scrum infringements. Vautin was instructed by the team's runner to advise me Fulton would be lodging an official complaint about my performance after the game. It was water off a duck's back and I think I said 'As good as gold' before ordering Vautin to play on.

At full-time Bob was waiting in the tunnel and he gave me a serve as I made my way back to the referees' dressing-room. Bob was furious about losing the game and having Des Hasler sin-binned and he pointed the finger at me. As I walked past him in the tunnel he let me know, in no uncertain terms, what he thought of my performance and how he blamed me for the loss. He finished his verbal spray with 'I hope you get run over by a truck. A cement truck.' Later he repeated this comment to the press, 'I'd hope he gets hit by a cement truck on the way home . . .'

While it's a laugh for me these days, the 'cement truck' episode did affect me and it scarred my family for a long time. It was only my second year in first grade, I was twenty-seven and suddenly my family and I were under intense media scrutiny. It took a toll, but it also made me stand up and be counted. It was a huge learning curve for me in how to handle public life, criticism, media interviews and the unfortunate personal abuse.

The NSWRL fined Fulton $1000, but I think the worst decision the hierarchy made was not appointing me to a Manly game for fourteen weeks. While the amount of media attention rattled me, I would have refereed Fulton's Sea Eagles the following week if it had been possible, but instead the NSWRL allowed him to think he had it over me and the other refs. He probably thought he had manipulated the League in his favour. And as it turned out Manly didn't lose another penalty count for fourteen weeks: $1000 well spent.

I have a clear memory of my next Manly game, which was at Brookvale Oval, their home ground, and how Fatty Vautin came over and said something along the lines of: 'Billy, the penalty count is 11–1 against us.'

'I don't care what the penalty count is,' I replied.

He pointed over my head to a cement truck parked in the top car park and said, 'Well, Bozo has the cement truck.'

I couldn't help but smile.

I never felt intimidated at all throughout the match, even though the crowd gave me extra attention. I was told at the end of the game Manly had narrowly lost the penalty count—for the first time since I had refereed them last. I hadn't even given it a second thought, I just gave them the penalties if they were warranted.

The Fulton experience made me a supporter of the NRL's ban on coaches bagging referees in the media. It is important people are told if they've stuffed up, but there are appropriate channels. I can't see any point in dragging the game through the mud. When a coach gives a referee a mouthful of abuse it's front page news one day, back page the next and inside the newspaper the following five days. Every referee cops constructive criticism and the $10 000 fine for bringing the game into disrepute has saved Rugby League millions of dollars worth of negative publicity.

These days Bob and I get on okay; perhaps he has mellowed in his old age because he has given me a few wraps as a radio commentator. Or maybe it's because the pressure of winning placed on a coach is no longer there. But I'll always keep an eye out for any speeding cement trucks whenever I'm crossing a road in Manly.

handling abuse

There's nothing in the referee's textbook that prepares a young whistleblower for an angry mob baying for his blood. It's one thing to be abused by players on the field, but handling abuse from the crowd is another matter. If you happen to get bailed up by aggressive fans it can be terrifying; you expect the worst. I would understand if someone lost it while they were trapped in such a situation.

My introduction to first grade refereeing ended with me being spat upon by an irate Western Suburbs fan at Lidcombe Oval and it took all my levels of discipline not to retaliate. Because I wore a referee's uniform, the slob thought he had the right to spit on me.

It wasn't the first time I'd been on the ugly side of refereeing. During my time in the Parramatta juniors

I was forced to lock myself in a dressing-room while an angry mob screamed at me to face them. They wanted to lynch me because they weren't happy with my performance; adding to the nightmare was the knowledge that my mother was witnessing the madness. All she could do to help was park the family car as close as possible to the area where the crowd was milled around, to allow me some chance of escaping if I made a break for it.

With the crowd wanting to tear me apart I decided to drop anchor in the dressing-room and I bunkered down. I knew it was best to ride the storm out, and by the time I decided to leave my bunker only a few people remained, their blood cooled. As I walked past them, I kept my head held high and there was barely a murmur directed my way.

If you want to make the cut as an NRL referee you need to be fit, have a sharp mind, possess a complete understanding of the rules, have confidence in your decisions and be able to get yourself into the right position to make a call—but that's all worthless if you don't develop a tough attitude quick smart. If you took every negative comment personally, you'd be chewed up and spat out of the game—I've seen it happen.

There was a time when incidents such as the 'cement truck' comment really rattled me, but I have learnt to take the very worst Rugby League can throw at me with a simple shrug of my shoulders and a shake of my head. While it took me some time to reach that mindset, nowadays cutting comments, ignorant abuse, unfair questions, finger-pointing and smart-alec remarks go straight over my head.

My Achilles heel, however, is my family. They're the ones who get hurt by comments from people who don't know the real me. I tell them to ignore it all, but it cuts them deeply and they feel guilty for not retaliating in some way . . . they don't need to get into fights with halfwits.

In the early days Mum and Dad had to bite their tongues whenever they heard supporters yell their hateful comments out at me. I'm glad neither of them ever reacted as I'd hate for them to give the mongrels the satisfaction of knowing their comments had hit a raw nerve. Nevertheless, the abuse does hurt them— no parent likes to hear awful things said about one of their children.

To their credit though, they've never allowed that to stop them from going out to the grounds and supporting me. They are members of Aussie Stadium and one tactic they employed to stem the tide of abuse I'd received from a group of nearby Roosters supporters was to introduce me to them. Mum figured if they saw for themselves the kind of man I am, then it would help, and it has worked.

My sister Di simply shakes her head in disbelief at the stupidity of some people's comments. My brother Greg, who lives in Queensland now, still fires up occasionally, but, as a bloke who decked a family of brothers after one of them insulted our mother, that's just my little brother.

As my profile in refereeing grew, so did the level of abuse I received and, later in my career, even my children came under fire, and things really got tough.

Abuse and negative media attention do make you question your desire to referee and, as society's sense of respect continues to plummet, life is only going to get harder for the men and women out in the middle.

gaining a profile

When I decided to become a full-time referee, I certainly didn't think about the notoriety that accompanies the job. I made my debut just before my twenty-sixth birthday and I was quickly accelerated into a completely different world, and it was mind-boggling. Suddenly I found myself becoming the focal point of conversation. Family, friends, workmates and even strangers would ask questions about the games, my opinion on League matters and what it's like to referee first grade. Media interest soon followed my rise to first grade: television stations were doing profile stories on the new kid on the block, newspapers wrote articles and wanted interviews, and radio commentators were full of praise during games—like Peter Peters on Radio 2GB in 1986, who said, 'This kid is going places'.

As the years rolled on, and my profile grew, so did the media interviews and the outside opportunities. I found myself being asked to speak at charity functions, lunches, dinners and referees' meetings. This was a whole new ball game for me, and one I found very daunting to begin with.

My very first exposure to this type of function was at a St George referees' meeting held in the League's club, which I had been invited to with Mick Stone soon after my first grade debut. I had no idea I would be called upon to address the meeting, I thought I was going along with Mick as a guest, to mingle and have a feed. Their president, John Gocher, asked Mick to say a few words and, as a seasoned veteran would, Mick jumped up and starting 'shooting the bull'. He relayed funny stories, spoke seriously about refereeing and gave the younger members an insight into first grade. He finished and sat down, then, to my horror, John introduced me. A cold shudder whizzed through my body and all I could do was stand there and apologise about not being able to talk to them. I told them I wasn't prepared, Mick was better at this and had covered everything anyway. It was a lame excuse. We were presented with a tie and pin and thanked for attending. I had no trouble talking to the fellows when the meeting was over but, as for that standing up in front, no way.

Walking back to our cars, Mick said, 'Billy, you're in first grade now and there are going to be a lot more nights like tonight coming at you. You have to learn to get up in front of the crowd and talk with confidence. You've got it on the field, now you have to get it off the field.' Mick suggested practising and taking every opportunity that came my way.

I took his advice and in 1989 I had my first big speaking gig. I'd been invited to be the special-guest presenter and speaker at the Group One Rugby League awards night in Casino, New South Wales. It was a traumatic, nerve-racking experience. I had worried about it for weeks and, moments before taking to the stage in front of hundreds of people, I went wobbly at the knees. I experienced the same sensation eighteen months later when I was about to run on to the field before my first State of Origin.

When I got onto the stage, my nerves were racing and my voice was shaky. The spotlight was on me and it was so bright I couldn't see anything out in front of me. I had my notes, but I'd lost control. I took a couple of deep breaths and thought: I have to take control here. So I asked for the spotlight to be turned down and the house lights to be switched on; this put me back in touch with the audience. I could see their faces and interact with them. I apologised to them and told them it was my first big gig in front of a large audience, and then I began my speech. The speech went well and I got better as I went through it. It was a daunting experience, but I learnt a lot from it and my advice to young referees now is: when you get up, do your best and learn from each experience, but never apologise for getting up and having a go.

laughs all round

You mightn't realise it when we're out in the middle maintaining the rules, but referees do have a good sense of humour. It's mainly shared amongst ourselves though, because if a player ever dared to say the kind of things we say to one another, he'd be binned— because we *really* stick the knife in! All with a smile, of course.

In the early 1990s Greg McCallum would do things at training that no one would be allowed to get away with nowadays. While the rest of the squad did sprint training, Greg would do his trademark slow laps around Lidcombe Oval. Greg did his own thing and in his own time, so 'doing a McCallum' became short for a referee doing what best suited him.

Tony Maksoud copped plenty of stick about his steel-wool-like hair and the amount of time he'd spend before a game wrestling his comb through it. And then there was Dennis Spagarino. He was born with a nose

Concorde would be proud of, and he got plenty of stick about that. He retaliated one day, too. I was one of the worst stirrers, so Dennis, a mechanic by trade, did something to my motorbike at training so it wouldn't start. He thought it was hilarious, until I got him in a wristlock and frogmarched him into the car park. He squarked like a captured bird and denied tampering with the bike, but I wasn't backing off with the pain until he got it started for me.

Apart from his refereeing exploits, Mick Stone was also famous for owning a powder blue tuxedo he brought out once a year to wear to the Rothmans Medal. No one else would have even worn it to a mud fight, but few people had the heart to tell Mick how ordinary it looked. The Salvation Army op shop in Newtown threw it into the incinerator the day he donated it to them.

As you can gather, our brand of humour is quite cruel; though on one occasion we received the help of Mrs Stone and Mrs Roberts to really carve their husbands up. It was our last training session of the season sometime in the late '80s and Matt Hewitt, Tony Kelly and I—the young turks—decided to have a laugh at the older brigade's expense. On this particular night we turned up late and when the squad was out on the field limbering up we ran out impersonating the older blokes.

I had combed half a tonne of talcum powder through my hair so it looked grey, whacked bandages over my knees, and, thanks to his wife, I wore Kevin Roberts'

State of Origin friendly jersey, which had ROBERTS emblazoned across it. Kelly took off Mick Stone by shoving a cushion up Mick's Origin jumper to give the impression he had a gut (he already had the balding head and he too ran like a broken-down racehorse). Hewitt pretended to be Spagarino's clone by whacking a large nose on his melon! The really pleasing thing about the entire exercise was Mick, Kevin and Dennis saw the humour in it and they wet themselves. The following year they got us back, bigger and better, when the three of them turned out mimicking us.

I have no doubt the fact refs can laugh at jokes, and accepting being lampooned helps makes us an even stronger unit. My only advice to the boys is to *never* touch my motorbike!

a grand achievement

There are plenty of people involved in Rugby League who rate a grand final as the pinnacle of any player's career, and their prestige is rammed home when I realise some of our game's greatest players—such as Wally Lewis, Wayne Pearce, Steve Rogers and Andrew Ettingshausen—finished their illustrious careers without ever winning a premiership. They would more than likely confess that elusive title is the great void in their footballing lives.

Referees are the same. We view a grand final appointment as the jewel in a career's crown. Controlling the grand final is an honour—an experience we can hang our hats on long after we've hung up the whistle.

Nevertheless, it is a tough task to get a crack at refereeing the game's biggest day because there's so many blokes pushing for just one berth. Because of that, merely being named the grand final referee is seen as the be all and end all for whistleblowers.

It confirms your status as Rugby League's number one referee and that means, while the players have to slog their guts out to decide who'll win the crown, the ref is a winner long before the ball is even kicked off.

Only a fool would bask in that feeling of glory, however, because a substandard performance will dampen your grand final appointment and have a severe negative impact on your career.

I've chalked up ten grand finals—a record I never envisaged as a rookie ref. In those days I figured Darcy Lawler's record of seven could never be eclipsed, but thankfully I was wrong.

As a tribute to the blokes who've gone before me I have compiled a roll of honour for the referees who've controlled the last twenty-seven grand finals. It shows how tough a job it is to be given the nod because in all those years only eight individuals have received their call to arms.

Grand Final Referees' Roll of Honour 1978–2003

1978	Greg Hartley
1979	Greg Hartley
1980	Greg Hartley
1981	Greg Hartley
1982	John Gocher
1983	Kevin Roberts
1984	Kevin Roberts
1985	Kevin Roberts
1986	Mick Stone
1987	Mick Stone
1988	Mick Stone

1989 ....William Harrigan
1990 ....William Harrigan
1991 ....William Harrigan
1992 ....Greg McCallum
1993 ....Greg McCallum
1994 ....Greg McCallum
1995 ....Eddie Ward
1996 ....David Manson
1997 ....David Manson (ARL)
1997 ....William Harrigan (SL)
1998 ....William Harrigan
1999 ....William Harrigan
2000 ....William Harrigan
2001 ....William Harrigan
2002 ....William Harrigan
2003 ....William Harrigan

Some of my most rewarding career moments have
occurred on what used to be called the last Sunday
in September. While I haven't written about each
grand final in this book, I've included the most
memorable ones.

grand final 1989

In 2002, a panel of Sydney journalists voted the 1989 game between the Canberra Raiders and the Balmain Tigers as the greatest grand final of all time. A genuine thriller forced into twenty minutes of extra time, I have no hesitation in nominating this as the highlight of my career for three reasons: it was a great game of football; it was my first grand final of any kind in grade football; and I was the youngest referee to ever officiate a first grade grand final.

The Raiders were the underdogs against a red-hot Balmain outfit containing the likes of Wayne Pearce, Ben Elias, Steve 'Blocker' Roach, Paul Sironen, Gary Freeman, and Garry 'Jimmy' Jack. Apart from boasting a great team, the Tigers were the sentimental favourites, with all of Sydney willing them on to win their first premiership since Peter Provan led the black 'n' golds to victory in 1969.

As it panned out, Balmain could have and *should have* wrapped the match up, but there were a couple of bad breaks that went against them: Benny Elias's field goal attempt missing the mark by a few agonising centimetres; 'Mr Reliable' Garry Jack failing to defuse a bomb cleanly at full-time; the penalty (which I stand by) against Bruce McGuire for using Walters to obstruct defenders; and coach Warren Ryan deciding to replace big guns Paul Sironen and Steve Roach too early in the game. While Ryan had no idea the game would go into extra time, the two big men would have given the Tigers size and strength in the vital twenty minutes of extra time. Jack's fumble of a Chris O'Sullivan bomb with ninety seconds left on the clock in normal time was a cruel blow because Laurie Daley managed to flick it away with a miracle pass to John Ferguson who breezed past James Grant, Benny Elias and Mick Neil to score the try which set the Raiders up for a draw— and a crack at extra time.

Over the years there has been plenty written about Balmain's defeat, but that detracts from a brilliant effort by the Raiders. A few flashes of that match which go through my mind include Mal Meninga's desperate ankle tap to bring Mick Neil down five metres from the Raiders' line and Tim Brasher regathering a Freeman chip-kick only to be halted by a last gasp tackle by Gary Belcher.

I'm told after the game Steve Roach hurled a tirade of foul-mouthed abuse at me and it was only through the intervention of Pearce that he didn't take it further.

I didn't hear Blocker nor did I see him storming in my direction giving me a gobful. All I can say is, I'm glad nothing happened because it would've destroyed a great day in Rugby League history.

Canberra defeated Balmain 19–14
Crowd: 40 500

copping it sweet

A week after controlling the grand final acknowledged as the game's greatest, I was sent to the far west of New South Wales with the Tactical Response Group to help maintain law and order during the annual Aboriginal Rugby League Knockout, but, even way past the black stump, I found it's impossible to escape the politics of refereeing.

The Aboriginal Rugby League Knockout is a great footy festival and, because it also has the potential to bring communities together, I'm a huge supporter of the tournament. Unfortunately in the years leading up to 1989, the knockouts had been marred by violent and drunken behaviour. The hosts of that year's competition, Walgett—home of the St George Dragons winger, Ricky Walford—were determined not to have their town turned upside-down by a rioting mob, so they requested a strong police presence. As a result a four-man team from my unit, TRG South, was sent to help reinforce the twenty-man-strong TRG West.

I'd been on the turps pretty hard after the grand final, celebrating the highlight of my refereeing career so far, and I was a bit fuzzy around the edges during our journey to the outback town. On arriving, however, I was pleasantly surprised to learn TRG South had been allocated the 'soft' shift, meaning we patrolled from 8 a.m until 6 p.m. 'Soft' because during those hours, most of the people were either playing footy, or out at the ground cheering on their mates.

Everyone was extremely well-behaved on our first shift, so we planned the next day's shift differently. We commenced the shift with a walk through town and a round of coffees. Afterwards we took a drive around and then went off to a dam about ten minutes out of town. We set a couple of yabby lines before returning for another. It was now about 11 a.m., so off we went to check the yabby lines. Fortunately we caught a few, threw them in the bucket and headed for the river. Shirts off, we tossed the fishing lines in the hope our yabby bait would hook a big Murray cod. An hour later we were heading back to town with a couple of fish, ready for another circuit of town before lunch. The afternoon was spent patrolling and watching footy. We knocked off at dinner time and the Rescue Squad cooks had our fish ready and waiting when we got back to our digs. After dinner, we waved off TRG West and headed to the local RSL for more celebrating.

As word spread that the grand final referee was in town, people starting treating me like a celebrity. I signed autographs, posed for photos and answered a million questions about footy. The RSL manager was obviously a fan because every time I offered the money for my order, the bar staff wouldn't take it. The RSL was so generous my colleagues wanted me to go up to the bar to 'buy' each round, but I refused to exploit the country people's hospitality.

Everyone wanted to talk football—including my superiors: the regional superintendent, the boss of TRG West and the local inspector. They thought it would be a brilliant publicity stunt if I refereed the knockout's grand final and, in their own unique way, they made it clear I was expected to say yes.

They summoned me back to headquarters from the RSL and I think they got more than they'd bargained for when they asked if I had any problems with their request because I'd had a bellyful of beer.

'Yeah, I do have a few problems,' I snapped. 'Firstly, I've just refereed the grand final and I'm still on a high, the adrenaline is still running and I'd be flat out to referee another game. Secondly, I have no gear and third, and most importantly, the local blokes have been competing against one another to referee this grand final. They've been working their butts off and I don't think they'd feel too good about having a blow-in take the glory.'

You'd think that would be the end of the matter, but the brass wouldn't give up. They said they could easily solve the issue about my having no gear, by providing me with some, and they were certain the local whistleblowers would be happy to step aside. They arranged for me to have dinner to meet the area's top two referees, who I was told were happy for me to do the decider. I went along and it was a set-up!

Apart from the two whistleblowers, the table was crammed with an Aboriginal elder, the top cops and a member of the local referees' advisory board. It was crystal clear they wanted me to control the grand final. The two referees even said they were happy for me to referee the final because they could take notes, learn from watching me live and check my positioning. But it was absolute rubbish, I could tell they were hurting and I felt sorry for them.

I followed one of them to the men's room and, free from the hierarchy, I asked for his honest opinion. I said, 'Mate, if I was in your shoes I'd be dirty about a blow-in coming and getting the big gig. How do you feel?'

The bushie looked me straight in the eye and said, 'You've summed it up, Bill, that's exactly how we feel.'

That did it for me. I returned to the table and told the group I'd made my decision and wouldn't be refereeing. The cops were filthy, the Aboriginal elder made his disappointment painfully clear but from the corner of my eye I'm sure I saw a flicker of a smile on the faces of the two referees.

'There is a correct procedure for these things,' I said. 'The local referee association should write a letter to mine so the other refs are fully aware that I am coming . . . alleviating any potential problems like this.'

Everyone agreed with this course of action but the organisers asked if I would be their guest, sign autographs and say a few words before the grand final. I replied I'd be only too happy to, and the dinner was quickly wrapped up.

The next morning my team and I were told not to worry about starting our shift but to grab our gear and head back to Sydney. The lame excuse was that because there had been no trouble we would not be needed on the last day. This was finals day and it was their way of punishing me. There was no mention of me being a guest, which was a shame, because I would have happily paid the admission price to mingle with the supporters and watch how the local referee handled the grand final.

the ultimate test

J ust like any player worth his salt, most top grade referees dream of running out onto the test arena. It doesn't matter if it is Papua New Guinea taking on France in Port Moresby, or Australia versus England, to be appointed to an international is a pinnacle to strive for, an experience that very few achieve.

While I have been thrilled to referee grand finals and State of Origin matches, few things throughout my Rugby League career have matched gaining my spurs during the 1990 New Zealand–Great Britain series in the Land of the Long White Cloud. Unfortunately, by the end of that first match I couldn't have cared less if I never refereed an international again because it was eighty of the most frustrating minutes I've ever experienced.

That disappointment aside, I have been fortunate to referee all five major League-playing nations in their own countries and, at the time of writing this book, I have refereed more than twenty-five internationals, of which twenty-two have been tests. While I haven't enjoyed all the games I've controlled, I have gained a lifetime's worth of treasured memories.

debut test 1990

I was ecstatic about my first appointment to referee the second test between New Zealand and Great Britain at Mount Smart Stadium, Auckland, in 1990. At the time, Australian referees couldn't referee an Australian game, so it was the best possible game to referee at test level. I felt a wave of satisfaction and euphoria rush through me when I realised I was about to represent Australia.

It turned out to be a major disappointment. I remember coming off the ground at the end of the match, walking into the dressing-room, turning to my touch judges and saying, 'If this is test football they can shove it . . . '

The Brits had whinged and whined their way through the game, and I had to repeatedly penalise them for being offside and holding down the tackled player. The contentious Parramatta–Newcastle match of 2002 had nothing on this. Yet I didn't sin-bin anyone because it was my first test match and I was a little overawed. Lions captain Mike Gregory grizzled about every call that went against his mob and I walked off frustrated at half-time. My test debut had developed into a game I wanted nothing to do with.

During the break, the Lions manager, Maurice Lindsay, knocked on the dressing-room door demanding to talk to me. At first I barred him saying I don't see anyone during the break, but I had a change of heart hoping that we might be able to talk and set the stage for a better second half. It turned out his troops weren't happy with me, either, but I explained I was refereeing the test the same way I would any Winfield Cup match in Sydney because it was the only way I knew. My tip for him was to tell his men the penalties would cease once his players got back onside, stopped holding the tackled player down and quit giving me a gobful.

There was a slight improvement during the second half, but not enough to make the game a Rugby League spectacle.

While the Poms whinged all the way, the team that deserved to give me an earbashing was the Kiwis because when I reviewed the match on video, I felt sick in the guts to see Martin Offiah had scored a fifty metre try off a short forward pass. I was deadset mortified and I still feel crook when I think of it. No one picked it at the time, but on the video it stuck out like anything.

I also refereed the third and deciding test in the series between New Zealand and Great Britain, this time in Christchurch. I remember the game for two significant reasons.

The first was a display of absolute passion by the Kiwi captain, Hugh McGahan, when a scuffle broke out sending players from both teams charging in to swap blows. After I restored the peace my touchie, a bloke named Baxter, said he was unsure of who the instigator was but he thought it was more than likely a Kiwi. I penalised the New Zealanders and, with Baxter's words ringing in his ears, McGahan stalked over to him and snarled, 'Don't you know where you come from you so-and-so?'

The second incident happened when Martin Offiah sprinted sixty metres to cross the Kiwi line and when he angled towards the posts I caught up with him and followed him across the tryline. There wasn't a Kiwi defender in sight and I put my whistle towards my lips as I waited for him to ground the ball.

He *dropped* it!

It was embarrassing, and adding to Offiah's woes was the amount of abuse he copped from his own men—they spent the rest of the match directing four-letter words at him. He'd dropped it while shaping up for a fancy post-try celebration and I reckon at that point he'd have loved for the earth to have opened up and swallowed him whole.

Second test: Great Britain defeated New Zealand 16–14
Third test: New Zealand defeated Great Britain 21–18

thought police

Despite the difficulties I encountered during my debut test at Mount Smart Stadium, one classic incident did make me smile. (I've replaced what was really said with the word 'idiot'.)

During the game, as the penalty count was mounting against the Poms, I packed a scrum down and a Pommie second rower tunnelled through the scrum and tried to headbutt the Kiwi hooker. He missed but the hooker saw this as an opportunity to pretend he was butted. He threw himself back out of the scrum, holding his head and yelling 'Billy, he headbutted me!'

'He missed,' I said, waving him away. 'Get back in there.' I nudged the second rower and said, 'Cut that out.'

Within seconds the second rower was at it again and we went through the same scenario. I blew the whistle and stopped play, calling out the English second rower and his captain. I told the captain what had happened and that the only reason the second rower hadn't been sent off was because he missed. Then I added that I'd had a gutful and I'd start getting rid of blokes if it kept up.

The captain said, 'You've had a gutful! Well, we've had a gutful of you.'

For that comment I advanced the penalty by ten metres.

He stormed towards me to vent his displeasure at this latest penalty. While he was angry, he was a smart guy who realised he needed to choose his words carefully to avoid being dismissed.

'Bill,' he growled. 'Can I ask you one more thing?'

Against my better judgment, I said, 'If you must.'

'If I was to call you an *idiot* what would you do?' He asked.

I said, 'I'd send you straight off.'

'Okay,' he continued, 'if I was to *think* you were an *idiot*, what would you do?'

'Nothing,' I replied. 'How could I know what you're thinking?'

With that I saw a flicker of a smile cross his broad face before he said, 'Well, in that case, Bill, I think you're an effing *idiot*!'

As he ran back into position I could do nothing except to enjoy the joke and have a laugh. He'd got me.

grandmother of a hiding

One of the most gutless attacks I witnessed as a police officer occurred on the steps of the Supreme Court when an elderly woman—she would've been in her sixties—was knocked to the ground during a free-for-all between two rival ethnic factions.

My TRG colleague Steve Walsh and I had been briefed about a potentially volatile case being heard at the Supreme Court so we were told to include a couple of stops there during our patrol. We were sitting in on the proceedings when a sheriff's officer of the court came and told us there was a rowdy group building up outside the court foyer. On our arrival in the foyer we were greeted by a Mexican stand-off between two different groups—they weren't swapping blows, there was just plenty of shouting and a lot of chest beating. For a few brief moments it felt as if I was refereeing the footy: I was in amongst the sweaty scrum yelling

'Get out of it . . . get out of it, you' as I kept them an arm's length away from one another.

And then it was on. One of them smacked another in the mouth and in a split-second there was a volley of punches, kicks, open-handed slaps and shoves. Steve and I took that as the hint to call for backup while we did our best to keep the combatants apart until the reinforcements arrived.

In the middle of the brawl stood an old grandmotherly type, dressed in a veil, and she looked terrified. I saw her get crunched and when she crashed to the deck the young blokes charged in and gave her a kicking—and I mean a *kicking*!

I saw red—it was a coward's act—so I grabbed my baton and rushed in swinging. I flayed into the pathetic 'heroes', and to protect the old woman from further harm, I straddled her and swung wildly at the mob surrounding her. I collected a few of them, too. Some of the people I hit may have been trying to assist her, but in the heat of battle I couldn't take any chances.

When more police arrived a strange phenomenon occurred: the brawlers formed an alliance and they united to turn on the cops! It looked like it was getting out of hand, so we whacked them across the knees with our batons to immobilise them and eventually we restored calm. It was difficult and we couldn't make any arrests because there were so many of them. Once you start trying to lead people away and charge them, you're out of the game.

It was nothing like Bathurst, and nowhere near as scary as a building entry with the TRG, but the incident stands out for me because after seeing that poor, old woman take a kicking . . . mate, I've seen everything.

survival lessons

I've refereed all around the Rugby League world, but no place has had the same impact on me as Papua New Guinea. Their tourism slogan 'The Land of the Unexpected' is spot-on because the place is an incredible mix of the primitive and modern worlds.

On my first trip to Papua New Guinea in 1990 I'd been assigned the two test series between the Kiwis and Kumuls (the PNG test team) and I lobbed off the plane with no idea whatsoever of the do's and don'ts of the place. Fortunately for me, Graham Ainui, the Assistant Commissioner of the PNG Police Force, met me at the airport and immediately made me feel at home. After checking into my hotel, Graham took me out on the town with some other coppers. He dragged me onto the dancefloor, sidled up to two local girls and *ordered* them to dance with us. There was no, 'Do you mind if we dance with you,' it was 'WE DANCE!'

When a fight broke out, Graham took it upon himself to restore the peace with a couple of well-aimed punches before politely returning to me as if nothing unusual had occurred. I was gobsmacked but still managed to shuffle my feet to the music. When we finally returned to the bar, I said to one of the other coppers, 'How good is this? We're out on the town, we're as drunk as skunks, we're with the Assistant Police Commissioner who has just snotted two blokes, he's made two girls dance, and he's acting as if it happens all the time! Mate, I love it!'

That was my introduction to Papua New Guinea. After that crazy night I have to thank New Zealand halfback Gary 'Wiz' Freeman for taking me under my wing and giving me some survival tips.

I was in the same hotel as the Kiwis and, even in the airconditioned lounge area, it was stinking hot, so I ordered a mineral water with enough ice to sink the *Titanic*. Just as I was about to take my first big sip, Gary ordered me to get rid of the drink. Judging by his reaction of sheer horror, you'd have thought it was poison, and, in a strange way, it was. After I'd put the glass down, he warned me the parasites in the local water and ice could put me in hospital; he also told me not to eat the salads or sliced fruit, no matter what, because the hotels and restaurants spray them with water. 'What kind of a bloody place is this?' I asked myself.

Gary was further horrified to learn that I hadn't had any inoculations, or even brought malaria tablets.

He arranged for me to see the team doctor who, after telling me I should have seen a quack weeks before leaving Australia, jabbed me with a few needles, gave me some polio drops, provided me with malaria tablets and gave me a huge supply of bottled mineral water from New Zealand. When I returned to the lounge Gary gave me a crash course on Kumul culture, or, to be more precise, surviving their excitable footy crowds.

'When you play footy in Papua New Guinea there are two things that have to happen,' he said. 'Firstly, the Kiwis thrash them, or secondly, the Kumuls have to win, otherwise we don't get out alive—and that,' he said, pointing to me, 'includes you.'

Gary's tip proved correct. In the first test at Goroka when the New Zealanders hit the 'go' button and piled on the points, the locals switched sides and started to chant and cheer for the Kiwis. Their voices were so strong it sounded more like Wellington than the middle of PNG. As soon as the game finished, the Kiwis and I were herded onto mini buses and driven straight back to the hotel. Gary was very pleased and said, 'See, Billy, I told you . . . we thrashed them, they jumped on our side and we got out of there alive.' I could do nothing except nod my head in agreement. The Kiwis won 36–4.

The second test was in Port Moresby and it was *hot*—it was like refereeing in a sauna and, to this day, I've never refereed in such oppressive conditions again. But, in League-mad PNG, a bit of heat didn't stop thousands of people from streaming into the ground and thousands more gathering outside the walls to share the atmosphere. Many more climbed the trees surrounding the ground so they'd be high enough to see the game. By kick off time the trees were full of people sitting and standing on any branch they could. The locals told me they don't call them spectators, they call them 'branch managers'. Some had trekked from the highlands to watch the game, others from the coast and to a man, woman and child they demanded a big effort from the Kumuls.

Despite the weight of expectation on them, the local players responded and hammered the New Zealanders with everything they had. While I was finding it tough in the conditions, I couldn't help but feel sorry for the Kiwis because they were dragging their feet in the heat, but, to their credit, Gary's men refused to give in. With about ten minutes remaining, New Zealand clung to a 16–10 lead, but their legs had long gone and the Papua New Guineans looked like storming home, much to the delight of the fans who were all but dancing in the outer. A punch-up erupted on the other side of the field and my touchie from Rabaul summed the situation up for me in three succinct words: 'Kiwi hit Kumul.'

Just as I was about to blow the whistle in PNG's favour, Gary ran up to me screaming 'It was self-defence, Billy . . . it was self-defence.'

I said, 'No, Gary, the report was Kiwi hit Kumul.'

'Come on, Billy, we're mates,' Gary replied, 'it was self-defence.'

Unlike Gary, who was committed to victory, I was very much aware of our surroundings because the locals could almost taste the victory and they were going berserk. 'KUMULS . . . KUMULS . . . KUMULS . . . KUMULS!' It rolled across the ground like thunder. I invited Gary to take a look at the crowd and soak the scene up. While he did this I said, 'Gary, let me tell you a story about this place. When you play footy in Papua New Guinea there are two things that have to happen or we, [indicating to him and me] don't get out of here alive. Firstly, the Kumuls have to win or second, the Kiwis have to thrash them—and you certainly don't look like doing that. So piss off! I'm with them.'

I'm sure he saw the funny side of the incident, despite the penalty going against his team, because there was a hint of a grin on Gary's face as his own advice came back to haunt him.

Despite the fact that New Zealand hung on to win 18–10, the crowd were well behaved. I signed heaps of autographs and drank about three litres of water before leaving the ground.

First test: New Zealand defeated Papua New Guinea 36–4

Second test: New Zealand defeated Papua New Guinea 18–10

stiff arm of the law

I have no idea how many blokes I've penalised for high shots throughout my career; it could be fifty or it might even be closer to a hundred . . . I haven't kept count. But I will confess to pulling off a stiff arm that makes *anything* I've seen on the footy paddock—even Les Boyd's jaw breaker on Darryl Brohman—look like kids' stuff!

Not only did I hit a bloke, but I nailed him when he had his head turned from me; the impact knocked him senseless and I reckon he saw shooting stars for at least a week. In everyday life the attack would've been considered assault, but rather than cop any flak for my action I was actually *praised* by the police brass because the bloke I ironed out was Australia's most wanted criminal at the time, who I will call Mr Wanted.

It was around the mid '80s and two elderly military enthusiasts were doing voluntary restoration work on what had been a vital part of Sydney's World War II coastal defence. They were deep in the old army bunkers and tunnels that honeycomb the cliffs at Malabar, a stone's throw away from Long Bay prison.

They were working on one of the bunkers when a 'loner' who seemed a decent kind of a bloke strolled into their camp. He had a carry bag and a rifle with him. Apparently the two fellows were concerned at first but Mr Wanted gave them an explanation they were comfortable with.

The drama started when one of the elderly men drove to the local shopping centre to buy some lunch and picked up a copy of the morning paper. I can only imagine the poor fella's hair turned a lighter shade of grey when he saw the front page plastered with a photograph of the nation's most wanted man—the same man staying at the bunker with him and his buddy! To his credit, the enthusiast was a cool customer and immediately went to the nearby Maroubra cop shop.

After hearing his story, the station's boss called in the TRG and a plan was quickly devised: my partner Buggsy and I were 'drafted' into the army's Engineer Corps. We were kitted out in full fatigues, provided with an army vehicle and given a crash course in military speak. I also learnt life in the army isn't all about shiny brass buttons and spit-polished boots because the experts said to *really* look the part, we'd have to copy what any self-respecting Diggers would do in such a situation, and turn up armed with a slab of beer.

While my partner and I did everything possible to ensure the sting would go smoothly, the mission's success really depended upon how well our informant had managed to keep it all together in what would've been a stressful situation for anyone. Our informant was instructed that on his return he'd 'remind' his mate, in full earshot of Mr Wanted, that two officers from the Engineers were dropping in later that afternoon to ensure the renovations were being done according to military specifications. This was done to make our appearance seem normal. If he'd given Mr Wanted even the slightest hint that something was afoot it could be fatal. Mr Wanted was on the run, armed and would kill if cornered.

Undercover operations are as much about theatre as they are serious police work because we had to get our role right . . . or the situation could be fatal.

When we entered the camp, I immediately spotted Mr Wanted's rifle leaning up against the entrance to the bunker. Mr Wanted was standing between it and us. While I was wary, I went into army mode and talked about the importance of ensuring the restoration work respected the army's heritage, and, to make my expertise look fair dinkum, I pointed out one or two 'flaws' in the men's work. I had no idea what the hell I was talking about, but I noticed Mr Wanted was listening to my *every* word and watching my *every* gesture. I figured he was sizing us up and when he started walking slowly towards his rifle I feared he'd twigged we weren't the real deal.

Hell! I went straight into overdrive. I thought 'Now or never, Bill' and sprinted towards him.

Mr Wanted didn't see me coming and I belted Australia's Most Wanted with the most vicious stiff arm imaginable. I cracked his head so hard it felt as if my arm had broken. The poor bastard hit the ground hard, raising a huge cloud of dust. Buggsy and I dived on top of him and secured him in handcuffs.

I didn't like doing what I did, but it had to be done . . . My job was to protect the two civilians as much as it was to arrest Mr Wanted and I couldn't take the risk that he was going for his rifle. He was transported back to the police station, where he was interviewed by detectives and later charged.

In football the hit would've seen me sidelined for at least a year, but I think it is the only time I've ever thought a stiff arm was justified . . .

deadly profession

When my TRG colleague Peter Gillam nearly blew my head off while making a film on building entries, it highlighted how dangerous it was to be a TRG officer.

When we entered a building where we suspected criminals were holed up, the adrenaline would be pumping through our bodies. After the first two officers went through the door, two more would follow them and that team of four would go through the whole building with a sweeper and a hammer man.

As two officers checked a room, the other two would leapfrog them to search the next one. Once it was deemed safe they'd yell 'Clear' and move on. The first four wouldn't stop if a door was locked or barricaded, instead the sweeper, armed with a pistol, would guard it and the hammer man would be called upon to smash his way through when the four officers returned from clearing the rest of the house. This way the TRG could clear a house in roughly seven seconds flat.

These days, two decades since my first raid, the hairs on the back of my neck still stand on end when I think about those moments just before entering a building.

TRG officers were often shot during those building entries. One of my mates, Chris Reardon, lost his thumb through 'friendly fire' because of an unfortunate stuff-up at the back door—an almighty no-no because the rule of engagement is to *never* leave a building through the back door.

The real shock, however, came in September 1985 when my mate Matt Moss, who was with me that near fatal day by the railway, was shot at point blank range during a building entry. The news left me feeling absolutely gutted. Matt was the number four officer through the door and during the search he and the boys passed a locked door opposite a main bedroom. After clearing the building they returned to the spot and Matt went through the door. The criminal they were after was sitting up in bed with his girlfriend and a child so Matt couldn't shoot, but he had the presence to jump out of the way as the bloke fired at him. His round blew a hole in Matt's arm and as Matt lay on the ground gasping for breath, the rotten dog who'd shot him immediately dropped his weapon and waved his hands in the air screaming for the police not to shoot. He claimed he thought his house had been invaded by a criminal gang.

Matt was rushed to hospital where a priest was waiting to give him the last rites. The blast had taken a huge chunk out of his tricep and Matt was drifting badly. The doctors worked around the clock to rebuild his arm; taking muscle from out of his chest and skin grafts from his backside and leg. Matt was saved and his arm was saved too, thanks to a metal contraption best described as 'scaffolding'.

The experience shook us all and Matt was laid up in hospital for months. For Mossy, the experience was even more painful because as a fit, energetic bloke he loathed being inactive.

As soon as he was discharged from hospital we headed off to South-east Asia on a three-week holiday to celebrate life, which meant we partied hard. By the end of the three weeks, the objective of letting Mossy know he was alive had been achieved.

Away from the bright lights, the music and the girls from the night clubs, Matt's shooting had really rattled me. Adding to my nervousness was the death of two Queensland TRG officers who had been the first pair through the door and were ambushed by gunmen waiting for them. The poor blokes didn't have a chance and their murders made me think long and hard about my role as the first man into a building.

Eventually, I just didn't want to go through the door first any more. I was burnt out. I spoke to my boss who agreed that I should have a six-month break from all entries. I took on the role of assisting the TRG officer in charge on the command post. The command post was a vital role: it was where the operation was run from and was full of stress and pressure. But it wasn't life threatening.

After a while at the command post, I jumped back in the saddle and returned to breaking through the doors. But another couple of years down the track I needed to take another break. I realised my days with the TRG were coming to a close, so when an opportunity arose for me to join the Special Weapons & Operations Section Witness Security Unit, I jumped at the chance. Ironically, Matt Moss took the same opportunity and transferred to the Witness Security Unit; however, he remained operational and I moved into negotiating.

I think every TRG officer experienced that feeling at some point. There is only so much high-level stress you can take. Matt Moss is as brave as they come, but he admits the first day he returned to work after the shooting was hell because he knew there was a real chance he could be killed. These days Matt works in homicide, a good cop making a difference, and he still carries shotgun pellets in his body as a reminder of the day he nearly died.

identity crisis

In 1989, I joined the Witness Security Unit, which was formed to protect the large number of witnesses who were prepared to give evidence against major criminals and crime syndicates. My job was to help provide false identities for people assisting police with crucial cases, such as Dr Victor Chang's assassination, and then to protect them. I'd had enough of the hard yakka of the TRG and I thought I'd have a bit of a break in witness protection, but I couldn't have been more wrong. I was now protecting people with contracts on their head and I realised the hitmen wouldn't give a damn about who they took out with them.

Unfortunately, ninety-five per cent of the people I dealt with were baddies who'd rolled over to help themselves. They weren't testifying against the criminals because they wanted to help, their motive was pure 'n' simple self-preservation. They'd been caught doing serious stuff and put their hands up to get the best possible result for themselves. For instance, the Chang witness spilt his guts because he was dirty about the bloodshed. As far as he knew, murdering the heart surgeon wasn't part of the deal, the gang was meant to extort money from his family and leave it at that. Regardless of their sudden conscience, it was very hard to look after scumbags you didn't even want to talk to, but it was our job and the unit worked to the best of its ability to ensure they were protected from any harm.

In the early stages of the unit's formation, it could be frustrating because we'd give the witnesses new birth certificates, a new licence and even relocate them to 'safe' areas, but we found they'd often quickly 'burn' their new identity by contacting family and friends. Eventually, after a number of bad experiences, we refined the system so they wouldn't receive the new identity and life until they had gone through the court process. Once that was completed, they would be sent off to start afresh somewhere else in Australia or overseas.

There was constant speculation in the media that criminals were being paid big bucks to roll over, but that wasn't true at all. They were paid the equivalent of social security. It was costly, in the sense that the government footed the bill to set them up in housing, but the payback was we managed to bruise—if not completely knockout—some of the 'Big Wig' operations.

Ironically, at a time when my police career demanded secrecy, some well-publicised footy controversies helped my profile as a first grade referee grow and, when I was working undercover, it became a mighty tough job to convince members of the public that I wasn't that whistleblower Bill Harrigan. Some people were so adamant I was Harrigan that I had to show them my false driver's licence and credit card as 'proof' that they had the wrong bloke.

My partner and I rehearsed a spiel that was so realistic it almost had *me* convinced I wasn't the well-known referee. It was just as well we both went to that trouble because on one job the owner of the country motel we'd booked into picked me straightaway, even though he had used my undercover credit card to pay for two rooms and he'd checked the signature against my false driver's licence.

'You know,' he started. 'You look a lot like that referee . . . what's his name? Harrigan?'

I gulped, but without missing a beat my partner went straight into character.

'Oh, not you too,' he groaned. 'You've gotta be kidding . . . is this a joke?'

The bloke looked at my partner, wondering what the hell he was talking about.

'Don't start him on that,' he ranted. 'He gets a big head and I've got to work with him. I suppose you want to buy him a beer now, like all the other jerks, and talk about footy. Good on ya, thanks very much, now he'll believe he really is that referee.'

Despite my mate's convincing act the owner looked me straight in the eye and asked, 'So, you're not him?'

To protect my cover I dismissed him with a wave of my hand and said if he wanted me to be Bill Harrigan, then I'd be him. I pointed to my licence and said my name was James Martin.

For a moment I thought we'd succeeded in fooling him, but when he finished the paperwork he said, 'Here are your keys, have a nice stay—*Bill*.' My heart sank because after failing to convince him I wasn't Bill Harrigan, I knew it would be impossible to bluff hardened criminals who can sniff bulldust from a mile away.

I bunkered down in my office from that point on, and was eventually promoted to sergeant. But, even for a deskbound sergeant, the stress of working in witness protection was incredible. I found even when I went home my mind would still be back at the office— I'd constantly ask myself if I had checked this and done that. I'd wonder if I'd given everyone the instructions for a particular case and then I'd worry if they were following them through properly. It was mental torture. The working day was also unpredictable because I could turn up to the office at 8 a.m. and be on a flight for Perth at 10.30 a.m.

Juggling my refereeing training around the awkward hours of Witness Protection duties was a huge struggle because I also doubled up as a police negotiator, which meant I was on call twenty-four hours a day. The beeper could sound at lunch time or 4 a.m. and, as a negotiator, I could be on the Sydney Harbour Bridge at 2 a.m. on the morning of a big game, trying to convince a potential jumper to climb back down.

I was conscious the players, coaches, supporters, officials and media didn't give a stuff about what I'd been up to before kick off at 3 p.m. They expected—and rightly so—that I would give them a one hundred per cent effort. But so did the jumper and his family.

Many of the controversies on the footy field are insignificant when compared to the turmoil of the people's lives I was looking after in Witness Protection. Most of them lived with the knowledge that there was a bullet with their name on it because of the deal they had made with the police. And that's much worse than worrying about a try that might have been . . .

state of origin

State of Origin. New South Wales versus Queensland. Some people reckon you don't get any better than that and I have to agree. I've refereed twenty-one, including the last twelve in a row and they're fantastic footy.

The players are playing for the pride of the colours they are wearing. They are often playing for the chance of being selected for an Australian jumper as well, but mostly it's for themselves and their team. It's eighty minutes of hard, fast footy: do or die.

I have found that refereeing these games is normally pretty easy because I can almost put my whistle in my pocket and just let the game run. The players don't try and use the spoiling tactics you see in club games; they know every penalty they give away could cost the team dearly.

I believe most supporters look forward to the State of Origin series more than they do the grand final.

Many people lose that level of emotional intensity if their team doesn't make it through to the grand final, but in State of Origin if you are from Queensland or New South Wales the emotion is there for the three games in each series. Other people usually just love it for the atmosphere, the speed and intensity. For most Rugby League supporters, State of Origin is the highlight of the season.

state of origin debut

I had my first taste of State of Origin in 1991 when I was appointed to the first game of the series played at Lang Park in Queensland. It was the Lang Park of the old days with the old stands and I am yet to see an atmosphere anywhere like it in the world.

Radio 2UE had asked me to do an interview one hour before the game. I was sitting up in the stands watching the under-17s Origin being played, but I wasn't really paying any attention to it. Thoughts about the game I was about to referee were buzzing through my head. I had drifted off into my own world; focusing on the match ahead.

When I got the wave from 2UE to come down for the interview, I stood up and nearly fell straight back down into my seat. I walked down the stairs of the grandstand towards the sideline to do the interview and I didn't think I would make it because my legs felt like jelly. It felt as if I had a swarm of dragonflies in my stomach.

I don't think I have ever felt as nervous as I was that night in my entire life—and that includes some of the threatening situations I found myself in while with the cops. I got through the interview, went to the dressing-room and starting going through the methodical procedure I do before each game. I unpack my bag and get into my shorts, socks, boots and a training shirt. I have a chinwag with the touchies and keep an eye on the clock. Half an hour prior to going out onto the field I start warming up. Sometimes I do this in the dressing-room or the corridor outside. Ten minutes before kick off I have a drink of water, throw my jersey on and put some vaseline above my eyebrows to stop sweat getting in my eyes. At the two minute call I pick up the ball and head for the tunnel.

But this was not just another game.

Finally the time came for the teams to head out onto the field and I had my first State of Origin learning experience. Some would call it a mistake, but I prefer to call it a learning experience.

The ground manager said I had to lead the teams onto the field, which was the opposite of what we did in the first grade games in the Winfield Cup competition. The ground manager gave the touchies and I the nod and we marched onto Lang Park. We were greeted with a thunderous boo and heckling that would have brought a building down. We stood out in the centre of the field ten metres from the sideline waiting for the teams. Waiting, waiting, waiting. Eventually New South Wales came out and were, naturally, booed and then Wally Lewis led the Queensland side out and the place went wild.

I said to my touch judges, 'I've just learnt a very important lesson here.'

'What's that?' One of them asked.

'You'll see if I ever referee here again,' I replied.

I did referee at Lang Park again and on that occasion when the ground manager said, 'Out you go, Bill,' I said, 'Yep, in a minute.'

'No,' he said, 'the teams are coming; out you go.'

'When the teams come out I will lead them onto the field,' I replied.

This time I waited for the Queensland team to come out of their dressing room and as they headed out to the field I walked off in front of them. When I first hit the field some of the crowd saw me and started to boo, but within two seconds they saw the Queensland side right behind me and started to cheer the roof off. As my touch judges and I walked into the middle of the field the crowd were too busy cheering for the Queensland side to worry about us. That is why I call it a learning experience.

Back to that first game. I really didn't know if I was going to be able to handle it because I was so nervous. Right up until I blew the whistle for kick off, I was a mess. I had two grand finals under my belt, but that didn't help. State of Origin was a whole different experience. As soon as I blew the whistle it was as if someone had turned the tap off. I went straight into referee mode, the dragonflies, jelly legs and sick feeling were gone. The game finished in Queenland's favour 6–4 and I rate it one of the highlights of my career.

Queensland defeated New South Wales 6–4
Crowd: 32 400

grand final 1991

I had refereed the 1990 grand final in which the Penrith Panthers lost to their more fancied rivals, the Canberra Raiders; but it was their 1991 grand final rematch that sticks in my mind.

Penrith second rower Mark Geyer was called a lot of things throughout his controversial career including a Hand Grenade from Hell, Towering Inferno and Rugby League Rebel. By his own admission, however, he deserved to be called a 'goose' for being sin-binned on Rugby League's biggest day for abusing touch judge Martin Weekes.

Mark exploded like a two-bob fire cracker in the forty-ninth minute after Paul Smith had grounded the ball for what I thought was a fair try, but I was forced to deny it when Weekes reported Raiders back Mark Bell had been punched in a tackle during the lead up to the try. Mark saw red and let fly with gutter talk so I binned him for ten minutes. I'd had a gutful of Mark by that stage because he'd been putting dirt on me all game.

Mark, for all his faults, was a nice guy off the field and he could *really* play when he kept his mouth shut. When he returned to the field he turned the grand final in Penrith's favour with two efforts he's described as flukes, but others have deemed magic.

With ten minutes remaining, Mark off-loaded the ball around Canberra's Steve Walters' body and found Brad Fittler. At twenty, Freddie had already stamped his authority on the premiership season and the Panthers' chances of victory had increased significantly when he returned ahead of schedule from an appendix operation to take the field. With the coolness that was to be the trademark of his remarkable career, he linked up with Brad Izzard who surged up the field to score the try which equalled the score 12-all. Greg Alexander's goal allowed them to hit the lead.

Then, with two minutes remaining, Mark helped end it when he chopped down a short dropout by Scott Gale. He found Royce Simmons and allowed the Panthers skipper to seal the premiership victory in his last game for Penrith . . . it was a great Rugby League moment as Simmons, with the ball tucked under the wrong arm, beat Canberra's test fullback Gary Belcher in a mad rush to the tryline. The Panthers had broken their premiership drought and with the Winfield Cup in his hands Royce promised to shout everyone a beer.

Penrith defeated Canberra 19–12
Crowd: 41 815

test match politics

It's no secret that Great Britain has never enjoyed playing under my style of refereeing—a fact that frequently exposes the politics of international Rugby League where deals and trade-offs are as much a part of the game as tries and scrums.

The method of appointing referees to internationals has changed many times throughout my career, but it always seems to be political. Usually, each country nominates three referees, normally their top three, to the international panel. The two competing countries then choose a referee from the list—one who is not from either of the competing countries. This is so a neutral referee is chosen, which I've always found ironic as referees and officials are *always* supposed to be neutral. The touch judges, however, are appointed from the home nation.

These names are then usually used like pawns in a chess game. For instance, one delegation might say they won't consider Australian Bill Harrigan as long as the other doesn't nominate Englishman Russell Smith because they don't appreciate his style. Then they might say, 'We won't use Australian Tim Mander if you flick Englishman Bob Connolly.' It's tit for tat and they keep counting out referees until they find two whistleblowers they like. It's a flawed practice because it doesn't always reward the best whistleblower but selects a referee who better suits a country's playing style.

My introduction to this political arena occurred after the 1990 test series between New Zealand and Great Britain. I was told in no uncertain terms by the British chairman at the time, Bob Ashby, that I'd *never* referee in his country while he was in office.

Don Furner, the Australian referees' coach at the time, thought it was a ridiculous situation that Great Britain wouldn't want the number one referee from Australia, so he arranged a meeting in Australia between me, Bob Ashby and Maurice Lindsay, the two men who had hated my refereeing in the 1990 test series. Don asked if we could all sort things out.

Bob Ashby responded by giving the reasons why I wouldn't be given a game and discussed in detail the two tests in New Zealand.

Then it was my turn. I'd just refereed my third Australian grand final in a row and I'd been celebrating hard, so I didn't hold back. I asked Bob how he would like it if a number of players tackled him around the head, then held him down too long and finally disobeyed his instructions to get off him? I told Bob that's exactly what his players did to me—disobeyed my instructions—throughout that series.

Bob was flabbergasted but he said, 'You've got a lot of guts to talk to me like that, so I'll tell you what I'm going to do. I'm going to do you a favour and give you another chance.'

I jumped straight in saying, 'I don't want a favour. I want the job on merit or not at all.'

Three weeks later I was in England armed with my whistle.

test match 1991

My first Rugby League experience in Great Britain was at the Vetch in Wales where the Welsh national team flogged Papua New Guinea 68–0 in front of 12 000 fans. The football was free-flowing, but what really impressed me was the Welsh singing for eighty minutes . . . while it was the coldest game I have ever refereed in, the singing from the terraces lifted my spirit.

The other notable incident occurred when the score was about 28–0. PNG had the ball, but a Welsh player went for the intercept. He got a hand to it, but knocked it forward towards the PNG outside centre, who also fumbled it forward. Phil Ford the Welsh fullback, came flying through and scooped up the ball and was off down the field. I blew my whistle but I was so cold it hardly sounded. Only three of us stopped playing, the PNG captain, a Welsh forward and myself. Everybody else was off and running.

After a series of sweeping passes and dazzling play, including a long sprint by Ford, he crossed the line to a thunderous roar from the crowd.

Ford and the other players looked for me to award the try and finally spotted me ninety metres away at the other end of the field waving them back.

Ford threw his arms up gesturing 'What?'

I waved him back again, indicating the scrum signal.

Ford threw his arm up again in a dismissive wave. When he got near me he said, in his thick, Welsh accent, 'What's wrong, Bill?'

'Phil,' I said, 'we've got a double knock-on.'

He quickly said, 'I didn't see no knock-on.'

'Where I come from,' I replied, 'if the ball touches a hand and goes forward and an opposing player touches it and it goes forward it's a double knock-on and you put a scrum down.'

Ford said, 'But did you see it, Bill? Did you see how I came through and scooped up the ball, and when the fullback came at me, I passed it out to my winger— and when he was tackled from behind he got it away to another player backing up and when he was about to be tackled, he lobbed it back to me. I caught it, sprinted another forty metres in around under the posts and put it down. Where I come from if it looks that bloody good you give a try.'

Before I could say a word the PNG captain, who was still standing beside me said, 'Where I come from if he had of given a try we would have eaten him.'

Wales defeated Papua New Guinea 68–0

test match 1992

Two years after walking away from my first test appointment between the Kiwis and the Poms feeling disillusioned about test football, I was back in the fray controlling another Kiwi–Poms series. This time, the match was a cracker, living up to all my expectations.

It was close and fast with plenty of intensity, big hits and a bit of biffo, but the thing I most remember about the game was my chance to get one back on the Kiwi captain, Gary Freeman, because, even though I liked him, he'd test me to the nth degree in just about every game we crossed paths in. To his credit, Gary was smart enough to back off when he knew he'd pushed me far enough.

On this particular day a fight broke out just before half-time. I noticed Gary was receiving medical attention down at the other end of the field near the grandstand which housed the dressing-rooms. I watched as he started to leave the field and I told the players, 'No one is going anywhere until I sort this fight out.' Gary was heading to the dressing-room for an early mark and New Zealand's vice captain Brent Todd said he would stand in on Gary's behalf. I said that wasn't good enough and that I wanted Gary. An official ran into the shed and Gary came and stood outside and signalled 'What?' at me.

I waved him over and when he was about thirty metres away from me, he yelled, 'What do you want, Billy? It's half-time.'

I said, 'No, come over here.'

He walked on so I turned to Todd and the Great Britain captain and said, 'No more of that in the second half. Let's just play football.'

At this point Gary turned up beside me and said in his familiar sarcastic tone, 'What do you want, Billy?'

'Nothing, mate,' I replied, 'it's half-time—let's go take a break.' And I walked off leaving him behind me going off like a boiling kettle.

knowledge control

B elieve it or not, I'm not a control freak; but if I walk into a situation that needs to be controlled, and no one else is up to the task, I'll take the job on.

People often ask how I control a spiteful first grade match, or a player so hyped up he's ready to run through a brick wall for the good of his team. While I've benefited from refereeing Origin battles and from my police background, I believe anyone can take control of a situation, but first and foremost they need to be able to take control of themselves. This is where an individual's confidence and self-esteem kicks in. If you're confident about yourself and your ability then you'll take control of most events without even thinking about it. If you add good communication skills and knowledge you've got the lot. If you look at anyone who is at the top of their field, be it sporting or business, you'll find all four characteristics. They're in control.

While a person might get by with confidence, self-esteem and communication skills, without the last one—knowledge—they'll be found wanting. Knowledge will increase with experience and I like the old saying 'knowledge is power'.

I'm certain many of you reading this book reckon it would be easy to referee a game of footy, especially if you've loved the game all your life. If one of your mates at the pub arranged for you to referee a match tomorrow, how would you feel as you ran out onto the field? You might be confident because you've watched footy since you were a kid; you might have good self-esteem and your communication skills might be great; but if you don't have the knowledge of the rules and you have to make a split-second decision—you're in trouble. If you're wrong, your confidence will take a hit, your self-esteem will desert you and the spectators will start bagging you. Your calls and your communication skills will be worthless when the wavering tone in your voice exposes you to the players. Before you know it, you'll have lost control of the match and nothing will turn the tide back in your favour.

One thing you need to accept about control is you can only control things up until a certain point. There will always be the X-factor that is out of your control. On the footy field I can keep two teams back ten metres, I can ping blokes for lying on the tackled player for too long and I can even order the forwards to pack down the scrum a second, or third, time if the first couple of attempts are sloppy. But if a brawl erupts there's very little I can do except blow my whistle, stand back and wait till they stop swinging. I'm not going to physically drag players off one another—that would be stupid. It's the action I take after they've finished slugging it out that will determine the amount of control I will have for the rest of the match.

Once you establish control, you're in the driver's seat.

state of origin 1994

In 1992 I refereed one of Origin's grittiest matches at Lang Park when Allan Langer kicked a field goal from eighteen metres out in the dying seconds and Queensland won 5–4. I missed State of Origin in 1993, but came back in 1994.

The selection procedure of referees for State of Origin is that the visiting team select the referee— and normally they select someone from their state. So when the game was played in Queensland at Lang Park, New South Wales would select the referee, which meant that a New South Wales based referee would handle the game.

In the 1994 series Queensland broke away from this tradition. Game One was to be held in Sydney, which meant Queensland would select the referee. Seeing as I'm from New South Wales, I figured I could have a break and I'd booked a trip for Bali.

A week before I was due to fly out Mick Stone rang me and said 'Are you committed to going to Bali? Because you may want to think about not going. The whisper I am hearing is that you may be needed for Origin.'

'How can that be?' I asked. 'It's going to be a Queensland-based referee for Game One?'

'Well,' he said, 'the strong whisper I am hearing is that Queensland may pick you.'

About two days later Mick rang me and said that I had been appointed by Queensland to Game One.

This was a huge shock to everyone involved in Rugby League. Some people said it was stupidity on Queensland's behalf to give away their advantage by not having a Queensland-based referee.

My response to that was: rubbish. I am a referee, I am neutral and that is the way I will always be. The talk around town, after being appointed to Game One, was that I would probably end up being the first referee to referee the whole series. But Queensland won Game One, so New South Wales overlooked me for Game Two, which was played at the Melbourne Cricket Ground, and appointed Graham Annesley. Queensland stuck with me for Game Three.

Game One was one of those games which is replayed and talked about over and over in Origin history because Queensland snatched victory from New South Wales right on full-time. It seemed as though New South Wales had won the game and were locking the ball up while the clock was counting down. With only several seconds left on the clock Queensland received possession and had their last throw of the dice, and what a throw it was. The ball went through several hands, finishing with Mark Coyne who was tackled metres from the line, but still managed to stretch out and slam the ball right on the line. These days the try is replayed over and over and rates as the most memorable try of any Origin series. It broke the hearts of all the New South Wales players and the 40 000 strong crowd. Although New South Wales went on to win the series when they defeated Queensland in Game Two and Three.

Game One: Queensland defeated New South Wales 16–12
Crowd: 41 859
Game Three: New South Wales defeated Queensland 27–12
Crowd: 40 665

metres and yards

I copped a bucketload of abuse during the days of the five metre rule because my detractors said I'd drag the defending team back anywhere between eight to twelve metres. They condemned me for it, saying I was meddling with the rules. My view is, however, if I encouraged the authorities to introduce the ten metre rule midway through the 1993 season then I'll sleep easy, because it's made Rugby League a genuine showpiece.

When compared to today's game, the five metre rule was an absolute shocker. Under that system, Rugby League was just biff 'n' bash . . . the game was nothing more than a re-enactment of trench warfare where blokes were nailed by murderous defence.

When Warren Ryan coached Canterbury in the mid-'80s he made defence his team's main priority. He developed a defensive pattern which shut down the opposition's attack and limited their scoring opportunities. The Ryan formula was brutal stuff, but it ensured the Bulldogs premiership success. Perhaps the lowlight of that era was the only tryless grand final on record—Parramatta's 4–2 win over Canterbury in 1986.

Rugby League was well packaged in the '80s, but the actual game wasn't a spectacle by any stretch of the imagination. Sure, there were great defenders such as Dave Gillespie, Wally Fullerton Smith, Ron Gibbs and Les Davidson, but people wouldn't have continued to turn up to watch the code if it had remained dominated by defence.

The fans want to be entertained and when I took the players back a few extra yards they were—and didn't they lap the extra tries up? It was revolutionary. With extra room the ball was sent out wide via sweeping backline moves and I remember seeing the fans up on their feet and cheering! In no time at all blokes such as Andrew Ettingshausen, Steve Morris, John Ferguson, Alan McIndoe and Ricky Walford were acknowledged as 'entertainers'. The crazy thing was, they always had the ability to be just that, but the five metre rule stifled them.

Over the years I've heard people attribute Canberra's success in the late '80s and early '90s to my refereeing because it opened the field up for them. For the record, they didn't receive any special attention—I refereed the Raiders the same as everyone else. If anything, I guess they knew how to use the ball—and the extra space— better than most of their opponents. While Brisbane,

Manly, Norths and Canterbury also benefited from the rule, the Raiders seemed to handle it best. When you look at their firepower—Brett Mullins, Mal Meninga, Chicka Ferguson, Kenny Nagas, Laurie Daley and Ricky Stuart—it's not too hard to realise they deserved their tag as one of Rugby League's greatest attacking sides. Personally, I was glad they broke the Ryan-inspired mindset that the game revolved solely around defence, because everyone tried to emulate them and soon most teams were moving the ball around.

The difference between the two versions of Rugby League is reflected in the scorelines from the NSWRL premierships in the 1980s and the modern day NRL. Today's fans see a lot more tries, which translates into more excitement. I use soccer to reinforce this argument because I think the round ball game would be a lot more exciting if we saw scorelines such as 9–8 and 11–10. At the moment, a person who's paid big bucks to see an English Premier League match can miss the only goal of a game because he's turned his head or gone to the toilet at the wrong time (yes, I'm talking from personal experience).

Despite saying what I have on the ten metre rule and the need to dazzle, I don't believe Rugby League can be played at a faster pace than it is these days. A further increase in the distance between the two teams would take a lot of the intensity out of the game. Under the ten metre rule the players—and refs—have needed to get fitter *and* a lot smarter. When it was first introduced, the defenders would sprint up upon the opposition in one line, but they couldn't maintain that level of enthusiasm or fitness for eighty minutes.

Over the years there have been subtle changes made to the defensive patterns, and perhaps the most effective is the one the Roosters have employed under Ricky Stuart. Two or three defenders target the attacking players who might get the ball. They race up to tackle the ball carrier while he's in mid-flight. They're in the bloke's face before he's travelled two or three feet, and as three or four players commit themselves to the hit, their team-mates hang back a yard or two to clean up a miss or offload. The tacklers then bust a gut to get back onside and catch their breath as a team-mate takes over the rush-up. I've heard people say that this is a gang tackle style of play and shouldn't be allowed, but they're not breaking the rules. I've watched them closely and they time their run so they pass me in full flight as the ball clears the ruck. It only takes a second and a half for them to cover ten metres at that speed. It's a good tactic and it works.

As I say, it would be detrimental to the game to take the defensive line back any further, but my advice on how to counteract the Stuart approach is for the attackers to take a leaf out of Paul Sironen's old book and charge onto the ball at speed and run straight and hard or go wide fast. It's simple stuff, but at the time of writing this book everyone is looking for an answer.

naming numbers

Over the years I've been criticised by people within the game and by members of the media because they've taken exception to my calling players out by their Christian names, rather than by their numbers.

I've never been able to understand why these critics allow themselves to get so worked up by me calling, for example, Penrith forward Martin Lang 'Marty' whenever I've needed to communicate with him on the field. The players prefer to hear their name, rather than their number, when the referee needs to talk to them because we're acknowledging them as people, not mere numbers out of a *Big League* program.

When I broke into first grade in 1986 I identified the players by their number because I didn't know who they all were. I knew enough about man management to realise it would've been a mistake to call Eels great Peter Sterling out by his name and then, in the same breath, yell out for 'Parramatta's number one' to join us. The number one would have to be wondering why Sterling gets called by his name, while he's known by his number.

I started calling players by their name during Super League because of the numbering system. Super League allowed the players to pick their own number, like in American football, and that meant a player in the number eight jumper wasn't necessarily the Bulldogs prop. It didn't take off quite as Super League had hoped because the fans liked the player's position to correlate with their numbers.

In any case, I found there's a much better reaction yelling out a player's name rather than bellowing 'Number four, get back onside'. I know if someone yells out 'Bill' on the street, I'll turn around, but if they yell out 'Hey, you with the green shirt' I wouldn't respond immediately. I'd have to think and look down to see if I had a green shirt on and I'd wonder what the hell the bloke wanted before turning towards him. It's the same with players' numbers, it takes those extra few seconds to register that the referee is talking to you.

As for familiarity among the ranks, I have always believed referees have to be careful about knowing players socially. A classic case that springs to mind is Mario Fenech. I was roped into having an after-match drink with him by my father. Mum and Dad had gone to the South Sydney Leagues club after I refereed the Rabbitohs and they struck up a conversation with Mario. When I walked into the Leagues club to meet my parents, Dad called me over and I started talking to Mario. The warning bells were sounding in my head every moment I was in his company though, because I was worried people could make an issue out of a referee fraternising with a player. My mum even told Mario I was a Souths supporter growing up. And, guess what? The next time I refereed Souths, Mario played on it . . . he still brings it up today. After that incident, I told my mum and dad I'd never put myself in that position again. As a referee you can't afford to appear as if you've been compromised, and what appears to be a harmless incident can have major repercussions.

Terry Hill and I work well together on the Lowes commercials and his cruel run of injuries has meant I've only refereed him once since he joined the Wests Tigers. Even though we laugh and carry on while doing the commercials, I wouldn't treat him any differently to other players on the paddock.

There have been some blokes who I think I could've been good friends with, like Gary Freeman and Paul Sironen, but it just couldn't be. While it does deny friendships being formed, I have no doubt my approach is the only one a referee can take if he wants to remain credible.

busking

I've always maintained referees should be better paid, but the way an irate English supporter threw money at me during a 1994 match between arch rivals Leeds and Featherstone Rovers almost brought tears to my eyes. The *Daily Telegraph-Mirror* said I was 'lucky to escape serious injury'.

Greg McCallum appointed me to the match while I was in England to referee the third test of the 1994 Kangaroo tour. I thought it would be a good way to warm up for the test, but some bludger took umbrage to my awarding Leeds captain Ellery Hanley an eight point try during a spiteful encounter. I was waiting for Hanley to take his shot at goal when the sniper struck—with a pound coin that hit the bullseye.

Now, an English pound coin is a tad bigger than an Aussie two-dollar coin and they feel twice as heavy, especially when they hit you on the funny bone. The coin hit me so hard my knees immediately buckled as the pain shot up my arm. It took all my might not to show I was hurt because I didn't want the bloke to feel any satisfaction. When I looked towards the direction where the 'missile' (as it was called in the media) had been launched I saw a sea of angry Featherstone fans all baying for my blood.

They were livid because their team faced relegation after a poor season and they had reached the stage where *every* competition point counted. The eight-pointer didn't help their cause, and as the ref who awarded it, I had little chance of opening a fan club at Featherstones' home ground, Post Office Road. After being hit I moved around every time there was a break in play, just to make it a little more difficult for anyone else who wanted a crack at me.

Before the Featherstone incident I'd always told my friends and colleagues the small stadiums that allow the crowd to sit on top of the game were what made the English match day atmosphere so special. But, as I discovered, that closeness also makes it possible for them to hurl more than mere insults at the refs. As it turned out, the middle of the field was probably the safest place for me because at full-time I needed a police escort. Even though the mob had been blocked off by the law enforcers and ground wardens to allow me a safe exit the Rovers supporters, furious with losing, spat abuse at me with such insults as 'Get stuffed you Aussie convict!' and plenty more too coarse to print.

While I still stand by my decision to award Leeds an eight point try (Hanley had copped a nasty cheap shot after he'd grounded the ball to score), I understand where the Rovers fans anger stemmed from—their passion for the team. When it comes to tribalism, Pommie fans leave their Australian counterparts for dead. In Australia someone born in Balmain might support Brisbane, but in England people are much more parochial. If you're born in Wakefield, for instance, you live, breathe and eat Wakefield. Generations are brought up on stories handed down from their grandparents about on-field heroics, and Featherstone is no different. Since the club was first formed in 1902, the Rovers have won every major honour the English game has to offer, but the night I refereed them they faced the ignominy of being dropped to second division and, forget the players, they saw me as the man responsible for their club's impending disaster.

As I looked at the madness in the faces of the people yelling at me I thought of a line from former great English referee Billy Thompson, who refereed the first State of Origin match in 1980; he spoke of a mate who considered joining the whistleblower's ranks. 'I have half a mind to become a referee, Bill,' his mate said. 'Well,' was Thompson's reply, 'that's more than most of us have!' Based on my Featherstone experience, Bill's reason for never using the referee's car park reserved for him on a match day also rang true: 'They wondered why it was always vacant,' he said. 'Well, lad, there, painted in big, bleedin', black letters on a white background was the word REFEREE. I'd have needed to buy a new car *every* weekend!'

The madness didn't end with my return to the referees' dressing-room. I asked my touchies what they normally did after a match and it turned out they would go to the directors' boardroom for a drink and then kick on at a local pub. It sounded like a good plan but they were a bit concerned about the reaction I'd get after the way the match panned out. 'No worries,' I said. 'We'll go into their room with our heads held high and then go to a local pub.' I wanted to sample the local hospitality but the boys warned me I'd receive no Featherstone cheer; if anything, they feared I'd be ripped to pieces if I dared walk into any pub in the district. With that, I thought kicking my heels up in Leeds sounded a more sensible option after we'd paid our dues to the Rovers directors.

I don't know what I expected in the boardroom, but I was made to feel anything but welcome. The directors' after-match speeches to the players and sponsors were punctuated with cheap shots about me and my refereeing—and it only went downhill from there. After twenty minutes they opened the partition to allow the club's members to mingle with the players and, within seconds, I had an angry crowd gathered around me.

Two years after that fateful night I was back refereeing in northern England after being muscled out of Australia because of the ARL's decision to stand down all whistleblowers aligned to Super League. I spent some time with local ref Ray Tennant and he escorted Brian Grant and I to the Featherstone–Batley match where I was to learn the Rovers fans have elephant-like memories. Ray asked the car park attendant whether he remembered the Aussie referee who relegated his club in '94. The reply was 'That so-and-so Harrigan'. With that Ray told him I was in the car and the bloke went off like a sky rocket . . . then the bloke in the ticket office went off . . . the program seller went off . . . the old woman who sold raffle tickets went off . . . My biggest worry, as Ray threatened to broadcast my arrival over the ground's PA system, was wondering how many pound coins would be embedded in my head by the time I left Post Office Road that night.

testing times

In 1994, Mick Stone, the referees' boss at that time, informed me the selection process had changed for the forthcoming test series between Australia and Great Britain and, because the Brits had the home ground advantage, the game was to be refereed by an Australian.

This was great news for me—for the first time I had the opportunity to referee a test match involving Australia. And not just that but Australia versus Great Britain: the ultimate test match.

My joy soon turned to fear when I learnt I may miss the series because of Great Britain's ongoing dislike of my refereeing. Mick told me the Poms had baulked at the Australians nominating me. Political brokering was on again and a final compromise was reached: it was decided two referees would take part, Graham Annesley and myself, one refereeing the first two matches and the other refereeing the third test and the one-off test match against France in Béziers.

When Mick told me this I said, 'Mick you've got to go into bat for me. I really want the first two matches. Mate, I'd be happy with the first test match and give the following three to Annesley.'

I wanted that first test match because it was to be played on the hallowed turf of Wembley. I'd seen test matches, English Rugby League Challenge Cups, all the big League matches played there on TV, not to mention all the big soccer games. To referee there would be the icing on the cake.

It's a goal I've never achieved. It's one memory Graham Annesley has that I don't.

Win, lose or draw, I've come to expect the Poms will never be happy with my refereeing and I've missed out on a number of games because of it.

In 1996, I refereed the second test between New Zealand and Great Britain. New Zealand won and the Poms immediately started to blow up about my refereeing. I was told to forget the third test because they were going to give it to Steve Clark for the experience.

I was furious. Unofficially I had been appointed to the third test. I was happy for Steve but the politics angered me.

Similar events happened in 2001 when Englishman Bob Connolly and I refereed the first and second games of the Australia versus Great Britain test series. The countdown to the third and deciding game was a political battle worthy of Canberra or the House of Commons: the Brits didn't want me to referee the match and come hell or high water, Australia didn't want Connolly out in the middle. It became a tense and tight standoff and when the two nations failed to come to any agreement, the hierarchy decided to put both countries' names into a hat. They agreed whoever was drawn out of it would control the third test while the 'loser' would referee the one-off international between Australia and the Brits in Sydney in July 2002. Fate favoured me on that occasion and I was out in the middle for the final test, much to Britain's bitter disappointment.

With all the changes I've seen to the system of appointing referees—pulling it out of a hat has to be the best yet—it seems it always comes back to politics.

A test match is meant to be the pinnacle of a referee's career. As a referee you can work hard for it, you can be the best, but that doesn't mean you'll be chosen for the game. Your name might not even make it onto the shortlist. Imagine if the names of players were pulled out of a hat for a test match! The chance to represent your country is something you earn. Why should it be any different for a referee?

test match 1994

Refereeing an Australian test team against the old foe, Great Britain, was without doubt my greatest thrill in international football. I don't mean to take anything away from the New Zealand–Australia clashes, but when I was growing up Australia versus Great Britain were the games I remembered. Being handed the opportunity to be on the same field as the Kangaroos, who I rate pound for pound as the best football team of any code in the world, was a definite honour for a boy from Canley Heights.

Plenty was riding on the match because it was the series decider and, while the match was a straight up and down affair, it was impressive to watch the review tape and see the Aussies withstand a tough opening ten minutes in the second half. I am certain the confidence Mal Meninga's men gained from repelling raid after raid set them up for a 23–4 victory to retain the Ashes.

One of the great scandals from this match—which didn't receive too much coverage—was a senior British player allegedly confessing to Laurie Daley that the ERL had narrowed the Elland Road field in width to nullify the Kangaroos attacking ability. *If* it is true, it is a disgrace, and it didn't work anyway.

Australia defeated England 23–4

touchies' touch up

Southern France might be famous for fine wine, a delightful climate, provincial cooking, artists, breath-taking scenery, vineyards and the Riviera, but it's no place for a Rugby League referee. Legend has it that part of the French game involved players and fans chasing the whistleblower through paddocks, ponds and back alleys when his performance failed to please them. I never saw *that* happen, but I did see a different form of intimidation during the half-time break of the 1994 Kangaroos–France test at Béziers.

The Roos were 42–0 at half-time, thanks to an immaculate defence and a near perfect attacking game. Like many of the 6000-strong crowd it wouldn't have shocked me to see the boys in green and gold crack the century mark.

At half-time I was sitting in the dressing-room with my French touch judges and one of my mates when a group of blokes dressed in trench coats barged through the door. The touchies jumped straight to attention as this group stormed towards them and their leader started unloading on them in their native tongue. I don't understand French, but by the tone—and pitch—of his voice he wasn't there to exchange pleasantries. Suddenly the heavies turned on their heels and left the room, slamming the door so loudly it sounded like a gunshot, which made the touchies jump.

The touchies quickly glanced at me, then back to each other and then they bowed their heads and sat back down. The atmosphere in the room had dropped to zero.

When the touchies left to get the teams to return to the field for the second half I asked my mate, who could speak fluent French, what the hell had happened. The guts of the drama, he said, was the angry bloke was a high ranking official and he was furious with the touchies because they'd failed to do what was ordered of them. Apparently they'd been told the best way to keep the scoreboard competitive was to run in and report every Australian misdemeanour—real or imaginary—because this would help break down the Kangaroos' killer cohesion. When the touch judges told the heavy there was nothing to report he was far from impressed and ordered them to find *something*—or else.

I couldn't believe it!

Despite the underhand plan to slow down the scoring rate, Australia won the test by a record 74–0.

Australia defeated France 74–0

life and death

I shake my head in disbelief when I hear Rugby League described as a 'life and death' activity. I take my responsibility to the game seriously because I'm in a crucial position to make calls which could well decide the outcome of a grand final or State of Origin series; but life and death? Who the hell are they kidding? I've stared life and death situations straight in the eye as a Tactical Response Group police officer and negotiator and there hasn't been a football incident come within cooee!

I remember the day a bloke, who I'll call Bruce, was ready to jump off the Gap, a notorious suicide spot in Sydney's eastern suburbs. Bruce figured his life was ruined because his gymnasium business had gone belly up and his wife had walked out on him. In his tortured state of mind he believed the only way out was to jump into the ocean.

My negotiating partner, Jane, and I realised *most*— but not all—of his will to face life's challenges had deserted him. I say *most* because Bruce didn't jump straightaway, which meant he wanted someone to talk to.

So there was Bruce sitting on the edge of a windswept cliff-face—hoping I could help him find one reason to step back from the edge.

It was about ten in the morning and Bruce had given me a 2.30 p.m. deadline. If I couldn't talk him out of it by then, he'd jump. It was tough because nothing would sway him and, with every piece of logic I offered, valuable time ticked away. Forget footy, *this* was fair dinkum life or death . . .

To me, an outsider, Bruce's personal dramas didn't seem big enough to warrant ending it all. I don't deny he was under extreme stress, but I know of many people who have endured a lot worse without contemplating suicide. At the time, however, I didn't judge him, I saw him as a person who needed to be saved from himself.

There are a number of stages police negotiators must follow in a 'jumper' situation. The first is to find out about the person and work on a sympathetic line where the attending officer 'tries to understand'. In the meantime your offsiders are collating as much information as possible and relaying it to you. Depending on the jumper's state of mind—and the situation—various stages are worked through, from the sympathetic to a tougher stance where you make direct challenges to the person, but I hasten to add, such a stance can only be done by people trained for the job and only when all other stages are exhausted. You must be careful not to completely press the self-destruct button that has already been triggered in the jumper's head.

As I spoke to Bruce I asked about his likes and dislikes, his interests and hobbies. I needed to hear him say something that would allow me to relate to his life without it becoming too personal. He said nothing which struck a chord, but I could see that Bruce looked after his body and was probably a bodybuilder so I decided to attack his vanity.

'You know, Bruce, once you jump your body will spatter all over the rocks.'

His face was enveloped by a look of disbelief. It seemed he'd thought that after he drowned the water police would fish his body out of the drink intact.

He said, 'No, I'll miss the rocks and hit the water.'

'Nah, mate, your body will be ripped to shreds by the rocks. You'll be cut up, mate . . . you'll be mangled.'

I could see he started to think about the ramifications of jumping. He didn't want to mutilate the body he had spent countless hours fine-tuning with weights and strict diets.

I remained conscious of the 2.30 p.m. deadline Bruce had set, as we continued to talk, and I hammered home the idea that he'd destroy his body if he jumped. We talked for so long that I finally pointed out to him it was 3.15 p.m. and we were forty-five minutes past his deadline.

I told him that meant he didn't really want to jump. 'You don't want to go, mate. You don't want to go.'

I suggested we walk away from the scene together and, if things didn't work out, he could return another time, but he refused to budge.

Throughout this ordeal my partner Jane was constantly asking Bruce if he wanted a cup of coffee. She kept repeating that we could go for a cup of coffee and discuss his problems, even though he'd made it clear he didn't like coffee from the first offer. It was making Bruce agitated and it was starting to annoy me.

By 6 p.m. it was past the end of my shift and we weren't gaining any ground. It was time to try new negotiators with new ideas; besides we were tiring. Jane moved out and a new negotiator moved in. I did the intros and, when we were comfortable, I handed over the lead negotiations and said, 'Well, Bruce, I've been up here for hours, mate, and haven't been able to convince you to come down. I hope everything works out for you. See you later.' I then gave a debriefing to the command post situated down the road and went home hoping Bruce wouldn't jump.

My phone rang at 3 a.m. and I was told to return to the Gap. I was tired and could only think, 'Don't tell me he's still there!'

Bruce certainly was and I was back with him at 6 a.m.

The mood had changed though. Bruce had gone from sitting on the edge of the rock to standing on a little ledge. I could only see him from the waist up and I was scared that he was going to go through with his threat.

'Mate,' I said. 'What are you still doing here? You said you were going to jump by 2.30 p.m. yesterday afternoon but you didn't. You've been here all night . . . I'm telling you, Bruce, you don't want to jump. Come on, let's shoot through from here and we'll have a talk about it.'

I tried to attack his ego again. 'Bruce, in about half an hour there'll be busloads of Japanese tourists jumping off buses here. Do you really want them to take your photo and show this to their family and friends back in Tokyo?'

That's when Jane piped up with her idea of sharing a cup of coffee again. Bruce reacted badly to the invitation. He was ticked off and told Jane again he didn't drink tea or coffee. I decided to use it to my advantage. I offered to make a deal. I said if I made Jane go away and get me a cup of tea he had to climb back to his old place at the top of the cliff. He nodded his head yes, but Jane didn't want to go. I ordered her to get the cup of tea and, after she disappeared, I told Bruce he had to fulfil his end of the bargain.

As he tried to climb from his ledge back to the top of the cliff, all hell broke loose. He lost his footing and for a split-second I feared he would plunge to his death. It happened so quickly I sprung up, but it turned out Bruce was a natural-born survivor. As he was about to plummet to his death, he reached out and grabbed hold of a long runner of grass. His weight pulled the grass out of the ground, but it was strong enough to support Bruce as he dug his other arm into the dirt and rock so he could stabilise himself.

Once Bruce climbed up far enough to get most of his bodyweight above the cliff it was safe for me to grab hold of him from the back of his trousers and reef him over the ledge.

As he realised he was safe, I could see Bruce was a man of mixed emotions. He was distressed because he had almost lost his life and he was also extremely embarrassed because after he lost his grip, he wet his pants in fear. They were drenched. All I could do was assure him he'd done nothing to feel ashamed about. The good thing was that, at his moment of truth, Bruce realised he wanted to live.

The last I saw of Bruce was when we dropped him off at the Prince of Wales hospital for a psychiatric assessment. I didn't follow his case because I learnt early in my cop career that it is too emotionally draining to get involved.

Trying to talk a person down from a cliff-face when he's looking for a reason to jump is what I call life and death. Rugby League, on the other hand, is important to a lot of us, but when it is all said and done, it's just a game.

off track

Throughout my career I've had the occasional game where I know I haven't performed to the best of my ability or to the one hundred per cent rating I expect from myself. But on one occasion I was well below par, probably only refereeing at sixty per cent of my best.

The game was a Friday night match between Brisbane and Canberra in 1993. My timing was out, my decision-making wasn't as good as normal, things weren't clicking and everything felt laboured. My thoughts—my focus—were not entirely on the game.

Most people watching wouldn't have realised, but for people who knew me, and were aware of my high standards, it was clear that something was wrong.

Mick Stone, the referees' boss at the time, knew something was up and asked me what was wrong.

He could tell I'd lost a lot of weight and seemed distracted.

So I told Mick what was going on: my second wife, Carolyn, had asked for a break in our marriage. I was a shattered mess, worried about my boys and the future, and had been trying to keep it together refereeing on the weekend. Clearly I wasn't coping.

Carolyn and I had met in 1986. She'd been a fellow cop and we'd married in November 1988. In March 1990 our first son, William, was born, followed by his brother, Andrew, in April 1992.

I began juggling three jobs—family, the cops and refereeing. I had just completed three first grade finals in a row (1989, 1990 and 1991) and was ranked number one in the game. I was a sergeant in the police force and was working in the Witness Security Unit, which demanded a lot of time and responsibility. I still had to fit in my referee training and I had a wife, two kids under the age of three, and access to my eldest son, Matthew, all of whom I wanted to spend time with.

It was hectic, but I thought we were doing okay. That all came crashing down in 1993 when I came back from doing *The Men of League* calendar shoot and Carolyn told me she wasn't sure she knew what she wanted anymore. She needed a break from the marriage.

I was shocked and devastated. I went to my aunty's place and I remember lying in bed staring at the ceiling, so upset I just let the tears stream down my face.

The boys were one and three years old—too young to know what was going on, but I was worried about the impact it would have on them and their futures.

I begged Carolyn to have counselling sessions to try and resurrect the marriage and she agreed. We floundered along for a few months, but weren't getting any closer and Carolyn still couldn't decide what she wanted. I thought if Carolyn couldn't commit to me, if she couldn't tell me that she loved me, then I couldn't see any point in carrying on. So we called it quits.

Once the decision was made, I put the experience down to fate, vowed not to have any regrets and tried to get on with life.

At thirty-three, I moved back in with Mum and Dad. But it was hard. I used to have the boys on the weekend and when I dropped them back at Carolyn's I'd drive home bawling. William was only three and he used to sit at the window watching me drive off. He never understood that I had left—he just thought I was in the car driving around all the time and then, on weekends, he figured the car would stop and we'd go driving some more.

I missed my boys, so eighteen months later when Carolyn wanted to make things right I agreed and we tried to make the marriage work again . . . but there had been too much water under the bridge and too much hurt on both sides. We split up for good in December 1996.

Eventually I got my direction back and returned to concentrating on kids, footy and work, unaware that destiny was steering me towards the woman who would be the one.

bill's best team

For seventeen years my referee's badge has been an open ticket for me to enjoy the game I love up-close. I know I've deserved to be there because I've worked damned hard to be the game's best whistleblower, but I'm humbled to think I've been able to get to know some all-time legends on and off the field.

I've seen players warts 'n' all—and they're tough. I've heard what they've said under pressure; I've seen how they've played with pain; I've been blown away by their courage to run into brickwall defence; and I've witnessed their determination to tackle one hundred-kilo-plus human wrecking balls. And then they back up and do it all over again. Top grade Rugby League players are a collection of rare athletes who can handle the mental and physical strain needed to survive—and thrive—in the world's toughest contact sport.

Selecting my dream team was a mind-boggling project; hair-ripping, actually. It was hard to find that 'special' element which separated one player from the pack. For instance, to pick my halfback I had to weigh up the careers and skills of Steve Mortimer against the likes of Peter Sterling, Allan Langer, Greg Alexander, Des Hasler, Ricky Stuart, Gary Freeman, Adrian Lam, Andrew Johns, Shaun Edwards, Andy Gregory, Stacey Jones and Geoff Toovey. A mighty list, and a mighty tough ask. In the end I culled a few names, drew up a shortlist and examined what each candidate offered.

For example, Stuart wasn't only a brilliant tactician, but he also had the incredible ability to drill long, radar-like passes twenty-five metres away; Langer boasts a brilliant kick 'n' chase and he can also inspire his bigger men to lift themselves; few had Sterling's gift to read a game and set up play; Mortimer was tough and gritty; while Andrew Johns possesses a near perfect all-round game. I could have picked three complete sides of equal ability, but, if nothing else, my top thirteen will cause a lot of debate.

The players in Bill's Best Team were picked on the basis of how good they were at the peak of their careers. Translate 'peak' to mean when they played international football, State of Origin or dominated their position (be it in the Winfield Cup, Super League, the ARL or NRL).

In the case of combinations—such as second row and centres—I've placed an emphasis on how they'd complement their partner. For example, I have selected a solid defensive second rower to work in conjunction with an explosive runner.

The sportsmanship displayed out in the middle carried some sway but you'll see I've given the nod to a couple of characters who'll *never* be invited to the referees' end of season ball. The simple fact is: you can't deny class.

I've taken eras into consideration. For instance, the hooker in the modern game has little—if any—role in winning the ball. Yet, in selecting Bill's Best Team, I've pitted them against the old breed of rakes who scraped their shins fighting for the ball.

Each player has been considered in the position they played during their peak. For instance, halfbacks who became hookers in the twilight of their career have been judged as halfbacks.

Finally, the referee's decision is final. If you don't like what you read, blue about it amongst yourselves!

So, let the debate begin. Here is my best-ever team drawn from the hundreds of players I've

refereed since my rookie year in 1986 through to
season 2003:

Fullback:	Garry Jack
Winger:	Eric Grothe
Centre:	Michael Cronin
Centre:	Mal Meninga
Winger:	John Ferguson
Five-eighth:	Wally Lewis
Halfback:	Andrew Johns
Lock:	Ray Price
Second rower:	Paul Sironen
Second rower:	Gorden Tallis
Prop:	Paul Harragon
Hooker:	Steve Walters
Prop:	Steve Roach

I guess an interesting fact in my selection is
just two current players have made the cut—
Johns and Tallis. I imagine the selection which
will raise the most eyebrows is John Ferguson,
but I've explained my reasons below.

Fullback: Garry 'Jimmy' Jack (Western Suburbs,
Balmain, New South Wales and Australia)
Former Balmain forward Paul Sironen once said
of Jack: 'I was always confident when Jimmy was
on the deck because I knew, if anyone managed
to break through our line, he wouldn't only pull
'em down, but he'd smash 'em.'

I heartily agree: Garry Jack was an aggressive player who thrived on pressure. I'm aware that towards the end of his career—after he returned to the Tigers in '95 following a stint with the English club Salford—there were critics who said he'd lost it, but I'm not worried by that. At his best, Jimmy Jack was in a league of his own as a fullback, especially in the toughness stakes. He was a rock-solid defender and a number one who could break through the first line of defence. It's also true Jack wasn't blessed with the skill of Brisbane's Darren Lockyer, but the blokes I've selected up front compensate for that.

As a player for a referee to deal with, Garry didn't mind having a bit of a whinge if he wasn't happy about a call. But his role seemed to be more of a backup. If Benny Elias or Steve Roach had a dummy spit about a penalty going against the Tigers, Jimmy would ride their coat-tails and say such things as, 'Yeah, yeah, Blocker's right . . . you got it wrong. That's a shocking decision!'

The fullback contenders: Garry Jack; Colin Scott; Gary Belcher; Paul Hauff; Tim Brasher; Robbie O'Davis; Brett Mullins; Jonathon Davies; Matthew Ridge; Darren Lockyer.

Winger: Eric 'Guru' Grothe (Parramatta, New South Wales and Australia)

When big Eric made one of his trademark blockbusting runs it was like watching a plane crash. Just like an out of control aircraft, Guru took a long time to stop, and the amount of twisted wreckage he left in his wake was frightening.

I'm told the fear he instilled in his rivals contrasted with his peaceful demeanour off the field where one of his great passions was playing the guitar in pub gigs.

While plenty was made of Grothe's ability to make the hard yards, his old captain Peter Sterling remembers the Guru's defensive ability fondly in his biography *Sterlo, Story of a Champion*: 'If the other side made a bust against you, the odds were that he'd run them down . . . An unbelievable talent.'

Eric didn't concern himself too much with us whistleblowers. A free spirit, he was in his own world—and what a world—trampling over the defenders and pulling off bone-jolting hits.

The wing contenders: Eric Grothe; Dale Shearer; Kerry Boustead; John Ferguson; Les Kiss; Michael Hancock; Wendell Sailor; Mat Rogers; Alan McIndoe; Rod Wishart; Nathan Blacklock; Ricky Walford; Willie

Carne; Brett Dallas; Matt Sing; Adam MacDougall; Lote Tuqiri; Jason Robinson; Sean Hoppe; Lesley Vainikolo; Hazem El Masri; Daryl Halligan; Anthony Minichiello.

Centre: Mick 'The Crow' Cronin (Parramatta, New South Wales and Australia)

Mick Cronin was coming towards the end of his career when I broke into grade, but I'll always remember a 1985 reserve grade Mick played in because he set the place alight the afternoon he returned from an eye injury which threatened his career. The opposition was crammed with young blokes determined to make a quick name for themselves by stopping Cronin. It was a mistake. Every time they swarmed in on him, Mick just stood in their attempted tackles and slipped the ball to his partner, Brian Jackson. Jacko ran in five tries that day.

I consider myself fortunate to have refereed first grade in 1986 because it allowed me the opportunity to run on the field alongside Cronin and Ray Price in their farewell season. They remain two of the best.

Mick Cronin enjoyed the reputation as one of Rugby League's true gentlemen, and I'm pleased to say from my few on-field dealings with him, that I found the title was deserved. Like his centre partner in my dream team—big Mal—he was never a problem.

The centre contenders: Mal Meninga; Mick Cronin; Gene Miles; Kevin Iro; Michael O'Connor; Chris Mortimer; Mark McGaw; Andrew Ettingshausen; Ellery Hanley; Peter Jackson; Gary Connolly; Tony Currie; Jarrod McCracken; Gary Schofield; Paul McGregor; Mark Coyne; Steve Renouf; Terry Hill; Ryan Girdler; Jamie Lyon.

Centre: Mal 'George' Meninga (Canberra, Queensland and Australia)

Meninga possessed an incredible brute strength which put the fear of God into his opponents. I remember one game when Western Suburbs played Canberra in the late '80s that made an impression on me because it's the only time I saw Mal get angry.

The Magpies had clearly upset Mal and it reached boiling point when Meninga was about to stroll over the Wests' tryline and score. Out of the corner of his eye, he saw their fullback coming towards him and, rather than put the ball down, I watched the big man change direction and charge straight towards him. When he closed in on him, Mal reached out, grabbed the Magpies number one by his jersey, lifted him a few feet off the ground and then smashed him down into the earth. It was like watching Godzilla swat a blowfly! With that done, Mal put the ball down and collected the points.

I'd watch in awe as Mal pulverised the opposing defensive line with his bone-crunching runs. From the safety of my spot six or seven metres away from the action, I felt grateful that I didn't have to tackle him because his giant thighs were lethal weapons.

I never had any trouble refereeing Mal. Even when he questioned a decision, I found him to be a quietly spoken gentleman at all times. He was civil, respectful and professional.

Winger: John 'Chicka' Ferguson (Newtown, Easts, Canberra, New South Wales and Australia) Chicka will never be remembered as one of Rugby League's great defensive wingers, but his evasive qualities when he had the ball in his hands brought people to their feet. I don't think his defensive deficiencies create too many dramas in my team because he has two outstanding centres inside him, while 'Mr Reliable' Garry Jack is on patrol at fullback.

I could quite easily have picked Mat Rogers, Wendell Sailor, Michael Hancock or Kerry Boustead in this spot, but as a genuine football lover, I get a great kick out of seeing a sweeping backline finished off by an elegant winger; now, *that's* a breath-taking sight.

Mal Meninga was also a huge Ferguson fan saying in his book *My Game Your Game*: 'No other winger consistently evaded the first tackler as he did. He had a step off both feet and the quickest acceleration of any player I've seen.'

A quiet man, I don't think any referee heard 'boo' from John, let alone have any problem with him.

Five-eighth: Wally 'King' Lewis (Brisbane, Gold Coast, Queensland and Australia)
'The King', 'The Emperor of Lang Park', 'King Wally', the superlatives to describe Wally Lewis's greatness could fill a book. For what it is worth, I rate him as the best footballer I have ever laid eyes on. He was so special that I know the day will come when I tell my grandchildren I refereed him.

Lewis had *everything*; and while he might not have involved himself in the action quite like Andrew Johns or even Laurie Daley, he could read the game three tackles ahead of the other players. Apart from a brilliant kicking game and precision-perfect passing, Wally could also make the big hits in defence. His leadership was also without peer, I've never seen anyone who could lead by example like him.

As a player to deal with? He had a dollop of Jekyll and Hyde—although I should stress I had no real trouble with him. That said, Wally *would* let off steam when he was frustrated. He'd give some refs the evil eye, and because he knew the TV cameras were focused on him in a big game, when a penalty went against his team he would pull a face or roll his eyes to let the viewers know his exact thoughts on the call. It was how he made a point without saying a word . . . and it worked.

The five-eighth contenders: Wally Lewis; Brett Kenny; Cliff Lyons, Terry Lamb; Laurie Daley; Brad Fittler; Kevin Walters; Matthew Johns; Anthony Mundine; Trent Barrett.

Halfback: Andrew 'Joey' Johns (Newcastle, New South Wales and Australia)
One of the most spectacular things I have witnessed on the football field was Joey's boomerang conversion kick in Auckland during the 2001 season. He set up the kick just ten metres out from the tryline and ten metres in from the sideline, giving him practically no angle to work with.

When I saw how his shot started I thought he had stuffed it. The ball was travelling virtually parallel to the tryline but as it neared the posts it curved and veered to the right and sailed straight over the black dot. It took me a few seconds to regain my composure because I was genuinely stunned. I thought I had seen everything on the football field, but then I saw that!

There are some great halfbacks nipping at Johns's heels for selection in my team, but he has that special quality which makes him a fair dinkum superstar. He can play as the seventh forward when needed and I also appreciate his all-round skills and toughness. The great Ricky Stuart said of Johns: 'Joey is the complete package . . . the most complete footballer in my time.'

As a player it is very rare for Johns to lose it on the field. I'm happy to say in my experiences with him I've found the Knights captain excellent to work with.

The halfback contenders: Andrew Johns; Steve Mortimer; Mark Murray; Allan Langer; Jason Taylor; Paul Green; Peter Sterling; Greg Alexander; Des Hasler; Andy Gregory; Shaun Edwards; Ricky Stuart; Gary Freeman; Brett Kimmorley; Adrian Lam; Geoff Toovey; Stacey Jones.

Lock: Ray Price (Parramatta, New South Wales and Australia)

Even though I only refereed him in his last season of first grade, I rate Ray Price slightly ahead of Bradley Clyde as my lock. It could have gone either way because both were workhorses who were trained to keep going when others waved the white flag. Unlike Ricky Stuart, who had genuine skills, the strength of Price and Clyde was that they could take the ball up time and time again and they *always* tackled around the legs. Price received my vote on the strength of his defensive abilities. He would pick himself up off the ground and pull down *another* attacker with an almost monotonous regularity.

I am also well aware of his iron-willed dedication to ensure he made it to the ground when others might have missed a game through injury. In the '80s, the Rugby League world was alive with stories of how Price would take a bad knock in a game on a Sunday, go home, set the alarm for every two hours throughout the night to get up and ice the injury. He'd then be at training on Tuesday. Amazing stuff.

Regarded by many as a prickly character, I can only guess Ray went easy on me as a referee because I was a rookie. Unlike a few of the other

The scene that confronted the police on top of Mount Panorama during the Bathurst bike riot in 1985. For eight hours a mob of around 4000 bombarded us with bottles, bricks and Molotov cocktails, setting a car alight and injuring police officers.

Chris Seabrook, Western Advocate, Bathurst

In 1986, my first year as a first grade referee, I wasn't going to let anyone intimidate me, not even hot-headed Souths player Mario Fenech. Over the years, I've never thought twice about sin-binning a player if they infringe the rules. These days Mario and I are friends.

News Limited

I loved playing football, hooker was my favourite position and I played for several champion police teams. Eventually I had to give up playing because, as I discovered the hard way, an injury could sideline me from my refereeing duties.

Rugby League Week

After each grand final the referee is presented with a trophy from the Prime Minister, in this case Bob Hawke, in the dressing-room. This was in 1989, after the thriller between Canberra and Balmain. My son Matthew is on the right.

I was thrilled to be on the field in 1990 to referee my first test match with touch judges Steve O'Grady and Denis Hale. It was the second test between New Zealand and Britain at Mt Smart Stadium in Auckland. By half-time I never wanted to referee another test match.   New Zealand Herald

After the TRG, I worked in the Witness Security Unit and became a police negotiator, sometimes talking suicide jumpers down hours before kick off.

STATE PROTECTION GROUP
- *POLICE NEGOTIATOR* -

This is to certify that,

William James HARRIGAN

Having completed the course approved by the Academic Board, New South Wales Police Academy, over three phases and achieving the required assessment, is recorded as a graduate of the New South Wales Police Negotiator Program.

Given under our hand
and the seal of the
N.S.W. Police,
State Protection Group,
this 9th day of September, 1994.

Norman K. Hazzard
Superintendent
Commander,
State Protection Group.

Denis Clifford
Commander,
Negotiation Unit,
State Protection Group.

In 1994 with my mum and dad, receiving the National Medal given to members of the police, ambulance and fire services for fifteen years efficient service. A year later, after a lot of thought, I left the police force to referee full-time.

As a full-time referee with Super League and now with the NRL, I have been able to focus on my training and fitness levels. Being fit is about attitude: if you want something enough you'll push yourself hard to get it.

I spent a lot of time in Papua New Guinea during the Super League years. Mount Tavurvur, near the port of Rabaul, had erupted in 1994 and was still smouldering when I visited in 1996. I took this photo on the runway where I got covered in ash.

In Papua New Guinea people can't get enough of Rugby League—they're big fans of anyone associated with the game, even the referee. This was taken after a game when they mobbed me asking for autographs.

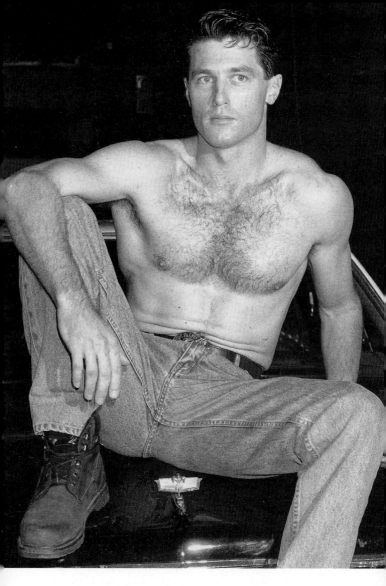

In 1994 I was asked to be in the popular *The Men of League* calendar as their 'surprise' model. Like every other bloke approached, I thought it would be a bit of fun.

Rugby League Week

veterans, Ray seemed happy enough to let me get on with the job.

The lock contenders: Ray Price; Bradley Clyde; Wayne Pearce; Bobby Lindner; Paul Langmack; Paul Vautin; Brad Mackay; Jason Smith; Billy Moore; Tawera Nikau; Jim Dymock; Adam Muir; Nik Kosef; Steve Menzies; Luke Ricketson.

Second rower: Paul 'Sirro' Sironen (Balmain, New South Wales and Australia)

Sironen remains one of the most destructive second rowers I've ever seen. He'd charge onto the ball from fifteen metres out with his legs pumping like pistons and on impact he'd skittle the defenders like nine pins.

One of my most enduring memories of the 1989 grand final between Canberra and Balmain is Balmain's English import Andy Currier's charge down the sideline. His body was outside the sideline, but his left foot was just inside touch by a matter of millimetres. He managed to get a kick away and it was chased down by big Sirro and the Tigers were on their way to a grand final try.

Just as amazing, in a game crammed with blood feuds, Paul was regarded even by his fiercest rivals as one of Rugby League's nicest blokes and he extended that demeanour to the referees.

The second row contenders: Paul Sironen; Gorden Tallis; Noel Cleal; Steve Folkes; Gavin Jones; Bryan Niebling; Trevor Gillmeister; Gavin Miller; Stephen Kearney; David Gillespie; Gary Coyne; Bruce McGuire; Mark Geyer; Andrew Gee; Gary Larson; David Fairleigh; Dean Pay; David Barnhill; David Furner; Chris McKenna; Bryan Fletcher; Daniel Gartner; Solomon Haumono; Andy Farrell.

Second rower: Gorden 'Raging Bull' Tallis (St George, Brisbane, Queensland and Australia)

His nickname Raging Bull (as in Jake La Motta, the former world middleweight boxing champion who fought as if he didn't deserve to live) says it all. I've seen him do some wonderful things on the field, and one or two dumb things as well. Though, I should add, those incidents occurred when he was young and wanted to live up to everyone else's expectations of how tough he should be.

Tallis is a once in a lifetime type of player; a player of raw aggression and sheer class. He possesses a good offload and, almost surprisingly, the big man is also blessed with a good turn of pace. Before a career-threatening neck injury in 2001, he had all the attributes required to be regarded as the world's best second rower.

Even in 2002, when he was a touch under his best form, Tallis was still the type of player who was closely marked by his opponents because they were waiting for him to cut loose and do something.

Broncos coach, Wayne Bennett, attributes Gorden's success to his will to win: 'He's an inspiration not because of his work ethic but because when he does something he does it so bloody well . . . flat-out.'

Prop: Paul 'Chief' Harragon (Newcastle, New South Wales and Australia)
I felt the full force of Harragon's powerful frame in a Newcastle–Souths match at Marathon Stadium. He charged towards the Rabbitohs' line and caught me out when he suddenly changed direction. I was trapped between Chief running at full bore and, unbeknown to me, a Souths forward had locked in to make the tackle. From my position Harragon looked extremely scary—his face twisted in determination and his legs pumping furiously.

With a collision inevitable, I braced for impact . . . and then it happened. BANG! I copped the big double whammy because as Harragon collided with me, the Souths player collected me from behind. I hit the deck like a sack of spuds, and to this day I still don't know how, but I bounced up off the deck and said to Chief, 'Get up and play the ball.' My words, however, were said through clenched teeth, and I had to do all I could not to show I was in pain.

Big, mobile and tough, Harragon was all class. He led from the front and was a natural-born leader. A hard man who never took a step back, he had the good grace to show the referees respect—even those unfortunate enough to be steamrolled by him.

The front row contenders: Steve Roach; Paul Harragon; Lee Crooks; John Lomax; Peter Tunks; Greg Dowling; Dave Brown; Ian Roberts; Jason Stevens; Brad Thorn; Shane Webcke; Martin Bella; David Boyle; Paul Osborne; Phil Daley; Sam Backo; Dan Stains; Glenn Lazarus; Paul Dunn; Peter Kelly; Mark Carroll; Rodney Howe; John Cartwright; Joe Vagana; Jason Lowrie; Martin Lang; Adrian Morely; Petero Civoniceva; Jason Ryles.

Hooker: Steve 'Boxhead' Walters (Canberra, North Queensland, Newcastle, Qld and Australia) When I picked my hooker—a position close to my heart, because it's where I played—it came down to a coin toss: Ben Elias or Steve Walters. 'Boxhead' got the call, but in terms of skills they were even in defence, attack, in the ability to run from dummy half and create opportunities and, last but not least, they were equal in hooking for the ball.

Royce Simmons wasn't far off the mark either but his being that tad slower than Benny and Steve ruled him out of contention. Kerrod Walters also came close to getting called up because I loved the way he'd dart around the field: he'd throw his head back and go for it . . . I thought he was brilliant, but his oldest brother and Benny had that little bit more to offer.

I got a kick out of refereeing Balmain and Canberra when Elias and Steve were pitted against each other because they hated each other's guts—and they let everyone know it, too! Watching them pack into a scrum was like throwing two wild cats in a bag and waiting to see which one survived. I'm certain the root to the ill-feeling between the pair stemmed from their simple desire to win the Australian jumper.

The hooker contenders: Steve Walters; Ben Elias; Kerrod Walters; Greg Conescu; Richard Swain; Jason Hetherington; Royce Simmons; Mario Fenech; Lee Jackson; Mal Cochrane; Jim Serdaris; Robbie McCormack; Danny Buderus.

Prop: Steve 'Blocker' Roach (Balmain, New South Wales and Australia)

Steve Roach spoke to referees and touch judges in a derogative, indecent manner. He would go off like a firecracker at the slightest provocation by a rival player. He had a woeful judiciary record and was the subject of a bitter stand-off between top coach Jack Gibson and the NSWRL. Gibson threatened to resign as coach of the Blues Origin side if Roach was selected in his team. All this makes Roach sound like a nasty piece of work and, in many ways, he was.

A rugged, explosive prop, Roach would bully and intimidate his opponents. Yet, like traditional front rowers of years gone by, he knew how to offload a good pass and he knew how to absorb punishment. Paul Sironen estimated seventy-five per cent of his tries were scored courtesy of a Blocker 'special' after he'd sucked in three or four defenders. Unlike Ian Roberts and Paul Harragon, he wasn't a mobile prop, but Roach did have the ability to make hard yards in attack and to nail the opposition in defence.

A tough nut, he'd risk the referee's wrath by going over the top with a high-ish tackle or a full-blooded punch to a rival's nose. While that would sometimes mean a sin-binning or conceding a penalty within striking distance of the Balmain goal posts, the trade-off for the Tigers was Blocker had his opponents walking on eggshells and few risked upsetting him.

He was a challenge for referees.

bill's best sledgers

Throughout my career, one of the questions I am most often asked by Rugby League fans is: Who was the most annoying player to referee? In writing this light-hearted chapter on Bill's Best Sledgers I mean no offence to any of the players chosen. I have selected this team on form, when they were at their best in whingeing, backchatting and questioning every decision.

Fullback: Neil Baker (Canterbury, South Sydney, Penrith)
I would hear Neil yelling abuse and whingeing about decisions constantly during a game.

He would even come out of his fullback position to get in my face when he thought it was necessary.

Winger: XXXXX
Unfortunately the best sledger on the wing is still playing, so I'm not going to name him . . . yet.

Centre: Ross Conlon (Wests, Balmain, Canterbury)
Probably a surprise inclusion for some people, but Ross was a quiet achiever. He always had an opinion and a whinge and made sure I heard it.

Centre: Mick Pobjie (Newtown, South Sydney, Balmain)
Mick never gave me a break. He questioned my decisions, backchatted and would give me a fiery spray whenever he thought it was warranted.

Winger: Michael Hancock (Brisbane)
Hated being tackled and would no sooner hit the ground then he would start kicking out and screaming about being held down. He wasn't happy and would let me know about it in no uncertain terms.

Five-eighth: Peter 'Jacko' Jackson (Canberra, Brisbane, North Sydney)

Many in the know would shake their heads at the thought of leaving out the 'King' Wally Lewis, but I had very little trouble from Wally, although I did bin him once when he played for the Gold Coast after he gave my in-goal touch judge a mouthful.

Peter Jackson was special and made this team because he had a quick wit and used it well. I binned Jacko a couple of minutes after binning Bella in the 1992 Origin game for calling me a cheat because Jacko said, 'Do you remember what Marty said? He was right.' Jacko would subtly get at you with wit, humour and sarcasm. I had to place him in my team because he still gave it to me, but I've got to respect the way he did it. It was always quick, short and precise. Good on ya, Jacko, rest in peace.

Halfback: Craig Coleman (South Sydney)

There was tremendous competition for this position between Geoff Toovey and Craig Coleman, but I had an out: Geoff spent a lot of his career in the hooking position, which allowed me to pick Geoff as hooker and Craig as halfback. Thank goodness because if Geoff hadn't played hooker I could not have split them.

I simply couldn't leave Craig out of my team: he was a pain. He never let up: whinge, bitch, backchat, complain, abuse, intimidate and he still fitted in playing—and he could play. But, jeez, he could whinge too.

Lock: David Hatch (Cronulla)
David Hatch was Cronulla's captain and he used the position for all it's worth. There has always been a perception the captain can question every ruling; but it's only a perception, it's not a rule. David used it as a rule. He questioned every decision and let you know when he disagreed. He questioned you so much he became a pain. Every time I made a decision against Cronulla when he was playing, I remember singing to myself 'Here You Come Again' by Dolly Parton.

Second rower: Gavin Miller (Wests, Cronulla, Eastern Suburbs)
Another Cronulla captain who'd spend as much time complaining as he did ripping into the opposition. I can still hear his distinctive tone.

Second rower: Martin Bella (Manly, North Sydney, Canterbury, North Queensland, Gold Coast)

Sarcastic, abusive and deliberate: if Marty had a beef, I knew about it. I had cause to send Marty to the sin-bin in a State of Origin match on his home turf, Lang Park. He called me a cheat and for that there are no second chances. I also sent Martin off for a deliberate headbutt in a local grudge match between North Sydney and Manly. He got off through inconclusive video evidence. We always seemed to be at loggerheads.

Prop: Steve Roach (Balmain)

Many people have asked me if I was the ref Blocker patted on the head when he was sent off. It wasn't me, it was Eddie Ward, but that's the way of Blocker. He would give it to everyone from the opposition players, their officials, the spectators and the referees. He addressed us with no respect nor any regard. He was made captain in a game against Newcastle because Pearce and Elias were out injured, and from the kick off he made no effort to call me by my name. He'd refer to me as 'Greg' (McCallum), 'Mick' (Stone), 'Graeme' (West) or 'Kevin' (Roberts).

Eventually, when he and Mark Sargent swapped punches, Blocker looked at me and in an attempt to get a penalty said, 'What about that, Billy?'

I smiled as I replied, 'So we do know my name, do we? Tit for tat—cop it on the chin!'

Needless to say big Blocker was furious and a verbal spray came my way.

No one was exempt. Blocker has the rare distinction of being the one and only player to be selected in both Bill's Best Team and Bill's Best Sledgers.

Hooker: Geoff Toovey (Manly)

I couldn't leave out Geoff. Fortunately he'd played as much time as hooker as he did halfback. In doing so he pushes Mario Fenech out of hooker, but again fortunately for me Mario played prop, too. Geoff was a referee's nightmare—I don't have to go into detail here. I will give Geoff the benefit of the doubt and say it was probably not in his personality to begin with, but more to do with instructions from his coach, Bob Fulton. Either way, he was a pain in the arse.

Prop: Mario Fenech (South Sydney, North Sydney)

Mario, Mario . . . Boy, didn't he give it to me and every other ref? Backchat, abuse, whingeing and the hard-done-by captain scenario. What Mario didn't know about referee/player communication you didn't need to know. I don't know how many times I binned Mario but the most memorable was the double binning in a Monday night footy game against the Bulldogs at Belmore in 1986. In saying all of this, you couldn't meet a nicer bloke off the field. I've worked with Mario at the NRL for the last five years and I've seen a totally different persona to the man I knew on the field.

All the players that made Bill's Best Sledgers could play. Some played for Australia, some their state and others held their own in the domestic competition. The majority of the team are from my early years, but that's probably because I was raw and their opportunity to intimidate me was greater. We also had no electronic technology to pick up every word spoken back then, so they could get away with more.

I've had fun thinking about the positions and the numerous players I've had to consider. No hard feelings if you made the team, I certainly haven't held any grudges and, if I could turn back the clock, I'd have you all on board again. But this time you'd all have to watch your language.

the war begins

The first rumbling I heard about a rebel Rugby League competition to be known as 'Super League' was at the Australian team's headquarters in Leeds during the 1994 Kangaroo tour of Great Britain and France. I was in the UK to referee the third test and I was with a group of journalists, playing pool, when the *Daily Telegraph*'s Peter Frilingos asked if I knew any details of the proposed competition. I didn't, but I was all ears as he and the other reporters spoke about a World Series cricket-style scenario happening in Rugby League.

At the time, the man rumoured to be bankrolling the event, Rupert Murdoch, was known as the 'King of Sport' because his satellite pay-TV network had a stranglehold on the world's most prestigious football codes. His broadcasting rights included English Premier League soccer, the NFL in America and Rugby Union throughout Australia, New Zealand and South Africa.

But it wasn't enough . . . Murdoch had a blueprint to add Australian Rugby League to his collection.

My main thought as we stood around the pool table was the amount of money that would be required to establish a rebel League competition. I calculated it would cost millions to take over the ARL. Imagine how much it would take to get the top players, coaches and officials onboard, not to mention the infrastructure . . . so I all but dismissed it from my mind.

Like all League lovers, I woke on the 1st of April 1995—April Fool's Day—to learn that News Limited, headed by former Kangaroo John Ribot, had signed up the code's biggest names with what seemed to be an open cheque book. Bradley Clyde, Laurie Daley, Ricky Stuart, Allan Langer, Andrew Ettingshausen, Steve Renouf and Matthew Ridge were among the superstars who'd pledged their allegiance to an organisation which appeared happy to reward loyalty with a massive bank account. The Murdoch-owned *Tele-Mirror* trumpeted the first salvo of what was to be a destructive and divisive war with a front page story: 'Stars Rush to Super League!' in which they listed some of the big coaching names who'd joined, like Bennett, Sheens and Anderson, and declared, 'In the past 24 hours, News Limited representatives have signed players in Sydney, Townsville, Brisbane and Canberra where many were on duty for their clubs.'

The ARL, backed by billionaire Kerry Packer, recruited Bob Fulton and Phil Gould to help plot their counterattack and, amid a flurry of cheque signing, they secured the likes of Brad Fittler, Andrew Johns and Steve Menzies.

It was an emotional time and passions ran high—players were placed under enormous pressure to sign with whichever group expressed an interest in them and, ultimately, everyone involved in the game was forced to pick a side. Numerous friendships ended in harsh words—even the great Mal Meninga was razzed by Rugby League immortal John Raper at a public meeting where Mal said he'd got nothing out of his career. The loyalists called Super League 'Super Greed' and those who signed with the Murdoch group said they were simply doing the best they could for themselves and their family.

Some of the incredible scenes included test prop Paul Harragon herding his Newcastle team-mates onto a bus and driving them to the ARL's headquarters to pledge their allegiance and cop a golden handshake; Canterbury's Jarrod McCracken, Dean Pay, Jim Dymock and Jason Smith ripping up their Super League contracts to return to the ARL; and Kerry Boustead quitting his job as the chief executive of North Queensland as a protest against the Cowboys embracing Murdoch's 'global vision'.

It wasn't just the players who were affected though, fans from various Super League aligned clubs returned their membership cards as a protest against their team jumping on the News Limited ship, and newspapers and talkback radio were full of passionate letters and calls from people lamenting what they called the loss of their game

The ARL's response to the Super League threat was over-the-top—they signed junior footballers as young as fourteen to contracts worth anywhere between $5000 and $10 000 in return for the promise they'd play for the ARL *if* they made grade.

The only people who seemed to be forgotten amid the mad rush were the referees and touch judges. And wasn't that a surprise?

the arl honey-pot

If Super League or the ARL wanted to truly boast they had the best game, it was crucial they recruited the best referees.

I was surprised at the way the war between the two parties was being fought, but I didn't really have a preference for Super League or the ARL at that stage. I was busy working as a sergeant in the police force, although I was interested to see what the two sides had planned for officials.

A few weeks into the war, the referees and other officials were called to Lidcombe Oval where Mick Stone addressed us as a group in the grandstand. Mick warned us that anyone who signed with Super League would be stood down immediately from refereeing in the ARL. He added that Phillip Street, the ARL headquarters, wanted a commitment from us, which meant we were to sign a five-year loyalty agreement before the night ended. Mick said there were solicitors waiting downstairs in the dressing-room armed with contracts, and, with a grin and a wink, he mentioned there was a 'honey-pot' for those who signed up.

On hearing that, I reckon we all started thinking of what we'd do with our cash . . . put a deposit down on a house, do renovations, purchase a new car . . . At the time we referees would earn a match appearance fee of $515, with no base salary. None of us were contracted as full-time referees; we all had full-time, often stressful, jobs outside our football schedules. We had to fit our training in around our day jobs, or rather our day jobs around our training and League commitments. We received a small training fee of about thirty dollars, but there wasn't really anything to cover us if we were injured. But now it looked as though the ARL were going to offer us a regular, annual income over five years.

My hopes were heightened after I introduced myself to one of the solicitors and he lowered his voice and said I was going to be the highest paid of all the referees.

You little ripper, I thought; I felt as if I'd won lotto. I became *really* excited.

The solicitor began to write a '5' and then a '0' on a blank part of my contract.

'You beauty,' I said, thinking of the five-figured contracts they'd been paying unknown, junior footballers who might not even end up playing grade football. They're going to pay me fifty grand, I thought. Finally I would be able to focus on refereeing and not have to worry about trying to juggle my full-time police work as well.

But the solicitor finished at $5000 and I was shocked.

'You've forgotten a zero mate,' I said pointing to the paper. 'That should be $50 000!'

I walked out, telling anyone who'd listen I wouldn't sign ... I called it a joke and the reaction from my colleagues suggested most of them were unhappy with their deals on the table, too. Some of them had been promised $3500, others $1000—for *five years* loyalty. It was almost laughable because while footballers were being paid $350 000 loyalty cash a year for five years, I was being offered $1000 a year, while others from my association were being wooed with $200 a season.

When Mick fronted us back in the grandstand he knew something was wrong and he wanted to know why we were so upset. I piped up, asking what would happen if we didn't sign that night. He said the ARL might allow us an extra day or two to think about it. When I asked what would happen if we didn't sign after that deadline, he didn't have an answer ... I think the ARL figured we would've been thrilled just to have been thought of, but they were wrong.

I jumped up and said, 'Mick, you told us there was a honey-pot but instead we were presented with a joke!' When I threatened to reveal exactly what I'd been offered, Mick and the solicitors leapt up and down, waving their hands around like crazy, because they wanted to protect the confidentiality clause.

'Bugger your clause,' I said, 'I haven't signed it.' To put the others in the picture, I told them that as an international standard referee I'd been offered half the amount of money the ARL had offered schoolkids! With that the boys knew I was offered $5000. I think only eleven blokes—mainly touchies—signed up that night.

The rest of us decided to wait for something better.

joining the new league

I n the lead-up to the ARL meeting and loyalty offer at Lidcombe Oval, Mick Stone had asked me on a couple of occasions if I'd signed with Super League, and I could look him in the eye and say 'No'. What Mick failed to ask was whether I was *negotiating* with Super League . . . had Mick asked me that, I would have told him the truth: yes, I was.

When the Super League war started, my manager at the time told me that I'd be worth a telephone number-like figure to Super League. While I liked what he said, I'd proposed to Steve Clark and Graham Annesley that if we banded together, and fronted John Ribot with my manager representing us, we would be in a position to negotiate a better deal as a group.

The ARL had done nothing to increase the offer they'd made us at Lidcombe Oval, so as a group we referees were in limbo. Eventually, fellow whistleblower Brian Grant opened the lines of communications with

Ribot, by phoning to ask whether anyone in the Super League bunker had spoken about the referees. Ribot made it clear he was keen to talk to me, Steve and Graham but said he refused to deal with my manager. It was a mess and we were being treated like pawns.

When we finally met Ribot in the Holiday Inn at Coogee we learnt Super League's vision for referees was to pay twelve blokes $50 000 each. Unfortunately though, Super League had shown a surprising lack of foresight because nothing was mentioned about developing the referees' structure, a training program or even junior development. Ribot and his advisors figured their commitment to refereeing would be nothing more than having twelve blokes out on the field, blowing their whistle. After we explained why that approach was misguided, Ribot decided he needed more time to think about what Super League could do for the referees.

In the meantime, lower grade players were being paid between $100 000 and $200 000 a year to help boost the ranks of the two warring parties.

I had no experience of negotiating a business deal and, without my manager, I was feeling the pressure. Mick Stone was still occasionally asking if I had signed with Super League. Ribot needed a decision and placed an offer on the table that he said was his best. I knew I had to move quickly, so I accepted Ribot's offer of a $65 000 salary, a fully serviced car, a mobile phone, $1000 a match and bonuses for representative and finals games. I felt like I had sold myself short, knowing what my manager had thought I'd get, but it was better than my pay packet from the cops and I was keen to referee full-time.

Knowing signing the contract had ended my ARL career I picked the match I intended to bail out on and I bought tickets for my family to watch my swansong in the establishment's ranks. The game between Cronulla and Balmain at Shark Park was nothing to write home about—it was one of the most atrocious games I've ever controlled—so I waited another week before revealing my hand to Stone and the ARL. I was appointed the 1994 grand final replay—Canterbury versus Canberra—the following weekend and it was an absolute cracker. After those final eighty minutes, I told the ARL where my allegiance was and they showed me the door.

It wasn't until January 1996, when Steve Clark and I started work in the Super League office, that the full ramifications of the pay packets we had accepted really hit us. Since we weren't refereeing, Clarky and I were being used as office clerks, typing into a database the amounts of money shelled out on players we hadn't even heard of—and my jaw dropped with each figure. The Penrith reserve graders, for instance, had signed for anywhere between $80 000 to $200 000! It was incredible, and while we whistleblowers were on a better wicket than when we were with the ARL, I couldn't help but believe we'd been let down badly.

Sometimes, through sheer disbelief, I'd yell out to Clark (who sat only three tables away), 'Hey, Steve, do you know Joe Bloggs who plays for North Queensland?' When he'd answer 'No', I'd tell him Joe Bloggs was on $180 000 per season for three years. We could do nothing except look at one another and shake our heads.

The more numbers I punched into the terminal, the more disillusioned I became.

With Super League, however, we fared much better than our ARL counterparts. When I think of the ARL offers it seems amazing to think some referees who were approached to sign up with Super League knocked the offer back cold. After Ribot signed Steve Clark, Graham Annesley, Tim Mander and me, we still needed to sign one more. We sought out Greg McCallum in England where he was working as their referees' boss, but he declined; Eddie Ward admitted he only had one season left in him and he thought he'd get the big matches in the ARL when we left—and he was right, Eddie refereed the 1995 grand final; Dave Manson was also targeted, but he stuffed up his chance by trying to play the Super League and ARL off against one another. Eventually Brian Grant, who was originally signed on as the refs' coordinator, was given the gig. We also signed a lot of good, young up and coming referees such as Steve Chiddy, Darren Gocher and Steve Carroll. By the end of the raid, I thought Super League's promise to deliver the best Rugby League had to offer rang true because, apart from everything else, they'd signed the game's top referees which ensured their games would at least be well controlled.

Even the ARL would have to agree they used referees in first grade who'd never have gone within a cooee of a top grade gig, had it not been for their desperate circumstances. When all is said and done, the ARL could have prevented that from happening. The main reason they lost us was because their honey-pot was as enticing as a bucket of prawns in the sun.

severed ties

One of the worst aspects about the Super League war was the strain it placed on previously firm friendships. Referees who'd been mates were divided by an 'us' against 'them' mentality: the bloke who helped guide me into grade, Kevin Jeffes from the Parramatta referees' association, refused to talk to me; a touchie was caught lying about the way we Super League recruits went about out business; and when an old-time official heard Graham Annesley was going to a barbecue at Chris Ward's house the official refused to go . . . and on the madness went. The scars of that time still haven't fully healed.

The incident that left me reeling most was when Eric Cox blasted me at Kogarah Oval the week after I was stood down from the ARL for signing a Super League deal. Eric had helped nurture me as a young referee by giving me an occasional kick up the backside when he thought I needed to be put in my place, and by praising me for a job well done when it was warranted. Like Mick Stone, I was in Eric's stable and that meant he had helped me out in so many ways that I couldn't even begin to thank him.

At Kogarah Oval, I was heading into the referee's room to wish my old colleague Paul McBlane all the best. I saw Eric outside the door and I offered him my hand, which he reluctantly took in a wet fish handshake. He mumbled, 'G'day'—at least I thought it was g'day— and I figured the only reason Coxy forced himself to do that was because people were watching us.

When I came out of the referees' room I saw Eric talking to the St George doorman and I turned to look out the tunnel towards the footy field. Then I heard someone yell out a barrage of foul language that would've made a wharfie blush. I turned around and saw Eric pointing at me. His face was beetroot red and he ripped into me.

'You're not welcome! You're a Super League low life! Where's your loyalty? You so-and-so . . . get out of here.' Eric made it painfully clear he thought my ties with Murdoch's camp meant I didn't deserve to be at an ARL game . . . and I was rattled.

I tried to tell Eric we were still friends, but that notion was quickly shot down. 'You've lost the plot, Eric,' I said after another barrage. 'I thought I was in your stable!' And *that* set him off—he screamed I was no mate of his and for me to 'rack off'.

I was working for ABC radio that day and when I told the commentators about the exchange they sent their sideline eye down to interview Eric. It was sad because he battered me on a national radio program saying: 'Listen . . . listen . . . I fought in World War II and we had to dig into the trenches. We fought for this country and people like him don't deserve to live in this country that we fought for in the trenches. He's a disgrace.' His words cut deep, but the one thing I have always admired about Eric is he calls a spade a spade. Unlike many other people I've come across in life, he'll say what he thinks to your face and I respect that.

While I was upset with what he said to me in the tunnel and on radio, I think I can understand what triggered the outbursts. Eric fought in World War II as a member of the Royal Australian Navy and I believe he saw my defection as a sign of betrayal. In reality, I was just making the most of an opportunity to improve my life.

Over the years Eric and I have had our flare-ups, but he has done way too much for my career and development for me to hold a grudge. Eric is Eric, he's a hardhead who can become blinded by emotion, but I also know he has a good heart. I'm well aware of the amount of charity work he does and how generous he is with his time for any member of the referees' association who seeks his guidance. Eric now works for the NRL and will tell you he has only one allegiance: to the game of Rugby League. It doesn't matter whether you were ARL or Super League, unlike some others, Eric has moved on and left the past behind him.

Last year at the referees' Life Members night, Eric was acknowledged for his service to referees and his recently received OAM (Medal of the Order of Australia). Mick Stone spoke and mentioned how he and I were from Eric's stable, but we had both been in, then out of it, in and out, in and out, but he thought we were in it at the moment.

I know I'm in Eric's stable and I'm glad to be there. I have a lot I owe Eric for, from the nurturing of my career in the earlier days to the endless advice and help ever since. When Super League and the ARL joined forces in 1998 to form the NRL, Eric and I picked up from where we left off.

hard times

O f all my family members, my eldest son, Matthew, has had the hardest time because of my career. He was bullied at high school by older kids who realised who his father was. Their taunts and insults made his school days a misery.

It all came to a head during the Super League days when everyone seemed to have an opinion on the state of play. More often than not, those Rugby League identities who took the big bucks were branded 'mercenaries' and 'pariahs'. When I was stood down from the ARL's ranks after agreeing to terms with News Limited, it became open season on Matthew in the playground.

The kids started chanting '*Paxton . . . Paxton . . . Paxton*' at Matthew in the playground, on the bus and in the schoolroom. (The Paxton chant was after a family who'd been smashed on Channel Nine's *A Current Affair* because they were said to prefer living on the dole rather than taking jobs handed to them on a platter.) It was sheer misery for Matthew. I remember trying to tell him that if I was a 'Paxton' then I was being paid plenty of money not to work, but that didn't make things easier for him. He was living every schoolkid's nightmare every day.

When I was a kid my father had made me stand up and fight the kid who'd bullied me for my lunch, but I didn't want to put Matthew in that situation. He was finding life tough enough without that pressure. My advice was not to feel as if he had to defend me, instead I'd prefer for him to walk away from a fight. And *walk*, the poor kid did. A mob would wait for him at the bus stop to give him heaps about being Bill Harrigan's son, so Matt would get off the bus kilometres before his stop and then walk home alone with his torment.

The situation finally erupted the day an older kid encouraged a student of Matthew's age to fight him. The kid threw a punch and Matt responded. While Matt broke his hand on the kid's head, the punch was enough to end the fight. It also sent out a warning to the other kids what they could expect if they picked on him. But because his school had a strict no-fighting policy, Matthew and his assailant were suspended for three days.

I was furious. Matt didn't deserve to be punished— he was the victim—it was those other cowards who should've been given a boot up the backside. So I approached the Brother in charge of the school and let him know how I felt. By the end of our meeting I had not only made it clear that I thought the school had failed to protect Matthew from the bullies, but I made sure the older kid was suspended for encouraging the fight to start in the first place.

Unfortunately that wasn't the last occasion Matthew suffered as a result of my career. In 2002 the organisers of the Australian Sports Commission's 'Fair Go for Officials' asked me to speak at a forum aimed to tackle the level of abuse against referees and umpires. I thought it would be a straightforward talk; however, I actually found myself having to choke back tears when I stood in front of the audience. My emotions overwhelmed me when I recalled a phone call Matthew, who was then nineteen, took on *his* mobile phone the day of a semi-final involving the Sydney Roosters. An anonymous caller told Matthew: 'I've got your number and I know where you live—if he doesn't look after us [the Roosters] today he's dead.' Matthew was rattled and when I remembered the impact it had on him I found it hard to speak to the group. I realised just how tough a time Matthew endured because of my refereeing.

One of my other sons, Will, also copped a bit of a rough time at school and his mother, my second wife, Carolyn, phoned to say he was hurting badly. Will had told her he wished his father was anyone other than Bill Harrigan. On hearing that, I demanded she put Will on the phone and, rather than mollycoddle him, I took the gloves off and ripped into him.

'How dare you think that!' I barked. 'If you really think it is so hard being Bill Harrigan's son then don't come out to the football with me. Don't go into the dressing-rooms to meet the players and get their autographs . . . don't come out onto the field after the grand final and kick the game ball around . . . and forget State of Origin. You're in a privileged position, Will, and you should be proud your father is Bill Harrigan. Think, mate, about what you're saying.'

I allowed Will to sleep on those comments and he phoned to apologise the next day. I accepted his apology, but I felt sad when I put the receiver back down. I couldn't believe Will would be ashamed to be my son. He'd always worshipped the ground I walked on. I didn't hold it against him though, because I know the playground is a tough place—children can be the masters of hurting one another. I should point out that it wasn't my aim to hurt Will when I took him to task, I just wanted him to realise his old man had been through a lot to allow him and his brothers to enjoy experiences most kids would give their front teeth for.

My message hit home, too. After the next grand final I controlled, Will and his brother Andrew were again out on Telstra Stadium kicking the game ball around in front of 80 000 people. I caught his attention and yelled out, 'Hey, Will, are you happy your father is Bill Harrigan now?' I'm rapt to report his smile said it all.

transition time

I was excited about Super League. Finally I could referee full-time and it was an opportunity to referee an international competition with the best teams. It was set to be challenging, exciting work with new technology and new levels of fitness.

After the ARL sacked the Super League signees we became a little concerned about our skill level diminishing. It would be almost twelve months before the Super League competition would commence and we knew we had to keep refereeing or we'd go rusty.

We rang schools and offered our services, but none were prepared to give us games because they were worried about the repercussions from the NSWRL. It was a difficult time for everyone in Rugby League in Australia. All we wanted to do was referee, but we couldn't. Not in Australia anyway.

To keep up our refereeing skills four of the full-time referees aligned to Super League—Tim Mander, Steve

Clark, Brian Grant and myself—discussed our options and thought, 'Why not referee in New Zealand and Papua New Guinea?' Both countries had signed with Super League and it was a win-win situation for all involved: we would get to referee which would be good for us as individuals, it was good for Super League's investment in us as referees, and an opportunity for New Zealand and PNG to use us while we were over there.

The idea got the green light, so we soon found ourselves travelling to PNG one weekend and New Zealand another. We didn't just go to Auckland or Port Moresby either, we could end up anywhere in the country. In New Zealand there were teams from all the major areas playing in the Lion Red Cup competition and in PNG it was the Pepsi Cup. I'd arrive in Auckland on a Friday night and catch a flight the next morning to the province I was refereeing in, such as Hawkes Bay or Taranaki. I'd meet with the local referees and they always had something set up in addition to the game, whether it was a seminar ready to start or going off to watch a couple of them run around the park refereeing. Saturday evening usually meant a dinner with the refs and their partners.

It was a real buzz refereeing in those countries. They issued me with their referees' uniform and treated me no different to the locals when it came to being assessed and appointed to games. The games were played with a different air about them and I never had any trouble from the players. People in those remote areas were excited to see someone they'd seen on the television, even the spectators were supportive. For me, refereeing in remote areas of countries I had hardly given a second thought to was a thrilling experience.

When the courts intervened and prevented Super League from kicking off in 1996 we continued travelling to New Zealand and PNG. This time it wasn't so demanding because on 1 January 1996 we all commenced full-time employment with Super League. Up until then I had been flying home every weekend and heading straight back into the Witness Protection Unit. Now, for the first time ever, I had some time off.

I played golf, went to the movies, became a house dad and trained harder. The training harder doesn't sound like much of a break, but it was. It was the first time I'd been able to train and then go home, relax and recover. Before then I'd always fit my training session around work or refereeing.

I started a training group with Ian Hamilton, 'Hammo', who is now one of my best mates. We started training together doing plenty of running and boxing. We ripped into it six days a week and soon we had guys lining up to join in. For the next three months we had a core group of six and we trained hard. The group has grown over the years and we still train together every Tuesday, Wednesday, Friday and Saturday morning.

After a couple of trips refereeing in New Zealand and PNG in early '96, I thought 'Why not England?'

Greg McCallum was the English referees' boss at the time and welcomed the idea of having us over there.

There was no cost to them and Greg started us at the bottom saying we would have to earn our place like anyone else. We were only too happy with this because we were looking for game time, no matter what grade.

We went over in pairs. I teamed up with Brian Grant. Tim Mander and Steve Clark were to change over with us in six weeks time. I quickly climbed the ladder and made Super League, the English first grade, within three weeks. Some of the refs were ticked off because it meant someone had to stand aside. I can sympathise with them, but I didn't just get slotted in, I had to work for it. The referee who was swapped out each week still got the match payment so it was some consolation.

I worked hard and was rewarded with a European Cup match: England versus France. It was the first time I had refereed with the new technology, a video referee. England were piling the tries on and I still hadn't used the video ref.

Russell Smith, one of Britain's top referees, was my standby and ran the water for me. During one drink break after a try, he said, 'Bill, you know you have the video to check tries. I'm not trying to tell you how to do your job, but it's there if you need it.'

I said, 'Thanks, mate, I know, but I haven't needed it yet.'

Soon after, England crossed the line again but they lost the ball and knocked on. I was about to blow the whistle and head to the twenty-metre line for a tap-restart when I thought—use the video. I figured I may as well use it and get some practice in. I blew time-off by raising both arms above my head and then I drew the outline of a square indicating I wanted the video ref to check the try. It was my first time calling for the video ref and I drew a *huge* square.

The result was what I expected, 'NO TRY'; twenty metre restart.

The next time England scored, Russell ran out to give me my drink and, while I was taking a gulp, he said, 'Bill, you know when I said use the video . . . I meant the video, not the bloody cinema.' I choked on the water with laughter.

I stayed over in England for a while longer and refereed the European Cup final in Wales at Cardiff Arms Park too. The English referees were angry I'd won the final over them, but it was there for the taking.

Super League finally kicked off in 1997 after the initial pro-ARL court verdict was overturned and Super league won the right to start its own competition. The competition comprised former ARL teams Auckland, Brisbane, Canberra, Canterbury, Cronulla, North Queensland, Penrith, Perth and two new teams, the Adelaide Rams and the Hunter Mariners. The teams also all played in the World Club Challenge.

We were full-time referees, with new technology and training programs to ensure we could keep up with the players.

swarmed

I've copped a barrage of abuse in the name of refereeing, but nothing has scared me quite like the day thousands of fans stormed onto the field after I'd controlled a 1995 Pepsi Cup game in Papua New Guinea between arch rivals Mount Hagen and Chimbu.

My appointment coincided with a hairy time in PNG—the escalating crime and mob violence had forced the authorities to enforce a curfew to try and curb the problems. Fortunately I was only there for the weekend on this occasion.

Referees in PNG have a pretty tough lot in life at the best of times because they live in fear of getting a hiding if they fail to please the majority, and a kicking if they anger the minority. If they manage to escape punishment, then it's likely one of their family members will be bashed senseless instead. During my trips to PNG I've met refs who've had black eyes and fat lips as a result of players and supporters venting their fury.

One whistleblower even confessed that whenever he had to make a tough call against his village team he 'ignored' it because he genuinely feared he and his family could be killed in retribution. At first I thought the ref was geeing me up, but the look in his eyes confirmed he was fair dinkum. Rather than lecture him about the integrity of our position, I felt a deep sense of sympathy for him. 'Well, you do what you have to do,' was all I could think to say.

The Mount Hagen and Chimbu teams were blood rivals and, with the game being played in Mount Hagen, it was painfully obvious the locals expected their team to win. My commitment to honouring and upholding the game's rules was tested in the final few minutes, when, after trailing 30–28, the home team went for broke and unleashed a spectacular backline move which proved too good for the Chimbu defensive line. Unfortunately, I knew the final pass was forward. So I did what I had to do: pulled them up and packed down a scrum. The mood in the outer turned ugly. They were howling . . . and, even though I don't speak pidgin, I knew they weren't throwing compliments my way!

When the full-time siren sounded I was horrified to see the Mount Hagen supporters race onto the pitch. They jumped over the fence and swarmed towards me like angry wasps! I could hear them chanting something but I couldn't make it out . . . my only thought was to sprint towards the tiny grandstand where the PNGRL officials were sitting.

The mob were moving in on me at an alarming rate—I could feel their collective hot breath beating down on my neck. I thought they wanted to harm me, so I decided to take a few down with me! In my panic I started hitting out with my elbows to keep the ones moving in on me from the side at bay. The cops could see my predicament and moved in, laying into the crowd with pick handles, whips, sticks and canes. Amid the violence two blokes grabbed me around the thighs and I yelled for help. But I soon realised they didn't want to harm me . . . they wanted to chair me off the paddock. They wanted to honour me! I started laughing because the people who I'd thought wanted to belt the tripe out of me were merely trying to pat me on the back.

I screamed at the coppers who were still laying into the crowd to 'Stop it!'. For the first time, I could hear the chant that had rung out around the ground since the full-time siren and it made me smile: 'BILL-EE . . . BILL-EE . . . BILL-EE . . . BILL-EE!' It echoed around the valleys and mountains. Perhaps it was just sheer relief, but, as I sat on those shoulders, a feeling of euphoria washed over me.

Forget grand finals, State of Origins and test matches—I was experiencing my most memorable Rugby League moment and I lapped it up. The singing and chanting, the sight of people waving at me, the two bruisers chairing me off on that incredible day in 1995 is still vivid in my mind now.

The ground didn't have a dressing-room so I was placed gently onto the back of a table-top truck and driven back to the hotel. I felt a bit like the Pope in his Pope-mobile as the driver negotiated the winding, muddy track that doubled as a road. People jogged alongside the vehicle for miles wanting to shake hands, yell compliments and shout questions about the Aussie game. It was a magic moment and after I returned to my hotel and showered I took time out to savour it. I think I wore a massive smile for the rest of the week.

scott of antarctic,
harrigan of rabaul

During their respective Rugby League careers, Steve Roach and Mark Geyer were both frequently described by the media as 'volcanoes' because they'd go off if someone dared to bait them during a game. I saw them erupt a few times and it wasn't pretty. Their eyes rolled, their mouths foamed, snot sprayed out of their noses, the veins in their neck stuck out and their bodies deadset trembled with rage . . . then I had to stand between them and the bloke they wanted to flog. All part of the referee's job!

In 1996, I didn't spare a thought for either Blocker or Mark when I stood a stone's throw away from the still smouldering Mount Tavurvur, near the port of Rabaul in PNG. Tavurvur made international headlines in late 1994 when it blew its stack and forced the people in Rabaul to flee. As the bleak pictures of paradise destroyed were televised on the evening news, I felt sad for the townspeople of Rabaul.

I had been to Rabaul a few years earlier and I remembered the place as a lush, tropical wilderness famous for snorkelling, boat trips and a beautiful golf course. I wasn't only taken with the beauty of the place, but I was enchanted by the footy-mad locals who were proud to call former Queensland halfback Adrian Lam one of their own; they wore the achievements of the 'Kumul Kid' like a badge of honour. I also visited the old World War II sites and saw where the Japanese navy established their submarine base, along with the hospitals and storage areas they set up in the cave systems that honeycomb the hills. Crashed Japanese bombers dotted the jungle and, as an Australian, I paused to think of the thousands of diggers who were either killed or captured at Rabaul when the Japanese launched their invasion.

In 1996, when I returned to Rabaul to referee in the Pepsi Cup, I listened to locals talk of their frightening ordeal during the eruption—how Tavurvur's explosions produced plumes that rose three kilometres above the cone while boulders were hurled half a kilometre towards the bay. I arrived late at night and I thought it was raining, but I soon realised the 'raindrops' were actually dust and pumice still spitting out from the volcano!

Sunrise revealed the full extent of the eruption and the devastation left me gobsmacked. It was as if a giant had just trampled over Rabaul and then ground it into the dirt with the heel of his boot. I explored the island and was sad to see the once beautiful rainforests and lush golf course were buried under tonnes of ash. Rabaul looked like a moonscape.

The only thing that appeared truly alive was Mount Tavurvur. The ocean bubbled at the base of the volcano like a massive witch's cauldron, while great clouds of ash and steam billowed from Tavurvur's mouth. Like any tourist, I wanted to get a photograph of the source of such destruction so I drove out to the old runway, which was the closest point. The runway was covered in metres of packed ash—it was like being on snow.

I parked my car next to an old abandoned Cessna aircraft at the end of the runway next to the harbour and started to click away. I was now a stone's throw away from Tavurvur and looked on in wonder at its power and size. Suddenly strong winds hit and stirred the sleeping ground cover of ash into a frenzy. In a matter of seconds I found myself trapped in a blizzard of dust and volcanic dirt. It was hard to breathe and I could see less than four metres in front of me. I made it back to my car safely enough, but I felt like the ill-fated explorer Scott of the Antarctic because I couldn't fix my bearings in the ash storm to turn the car and get back to the road. I sat there for about twenty minutes and began to feel pressured. Numerous thoughts raced through my mind: firstly, the ash storm wasn't going to stop for quite a while; secondly, I had to be at the airport later that afternoon to fly out; thirdly, I was worried if I drove too far either way I'd end up in the drink. I tried to think of a way out and then common sense clicked in.

I decided to retrace my steps. I knew I parked facing the volcano beside the plane so if I could slowly turn the vehicle 180 degrees I should come across my original tyre tracks, if they weren't already covered. I had the car door slightly ajar and watched the ground while I turned. It was a scary feeling but luckily they were there, faint, but still there. I followed the tracks until I hit the road, which also was nerve-racking because it was still hard to see and any traffic using the main road wouldn't expect a vehicle coming off the runway. With Mount Tavurvur bubbling and burping behind me, I made my way out and decided that dealing with the likes of fired-up players like Mark Geyer and Steve Roach wasn't such an ordeal after all . . .

super fit

Aside from the technological innovations it introduced, one of the great things Super League did was to lift the standards of refereeing, especially the referees' fitness.

The Super League administration were partly able to do this because they made refereeing a full-time career. This allowed referees to devote time to our physical fitness, focus on our games and look at ways of improving and expanding our skills and abilities. Once again I had fallen into a career where you were required to, and paid to, maintain a high level of fitness—and I loved it.

Super League had signed referees and touch judges from all over Australia and New Zealand, so weekly group-training sessions were logistically impossible. To overcome the tyranny of distance we received rigid programs and were told to train on our own. We then gathered every six weeks and underwent a series of gut-busting tests to see who had worked and who had been loafing.

The tests involved an endurance run, after which we would have a sprint recovery and then an agility test where we had to run backwards, forwards and sideways to replicate what we did on the field. We then endured more sprints; a sit and reach flexibility test and then the dreaded beep test which sorted out the men from the rest. The session normally took about an hour and a half and by the end of it we were exhausted.

I treated the session as a challenge and made it my aim to smash the individual records every time I turned up . . . and, more often than not, I did just that. One of my most satisfying moments was the dreaded endurance run which took a little over seven minutes. My first goal was to go sub-seven. The third session I broke the barrier and, as I improved my fitness, I managed to get my time down to 6:51. But I started to believe I would never get it beyond 6:50 because, no matter how hard I tried, I couldn't get past that time.

Steve Clark provided me with the motivation to crash beyond that barrier. Clarkey had spent several serious months on his fitness. He had appointed a personal trainer and, by the end of it, his improvements were obvious. On this particular day he turned up to training to have a crack at me and I welcomed the challenge.

The new look Clarkey was beside me from the word 'Go'. I'm usually out on my own from the first turn around the corner post, but Clarkey was pushing the pace. When I couldn't shake him I thought to myself, 'Crikey, he's improved'. The first lap was a cracker and Clarkey and I had opened up a lead never seen before. But Steve started to drop off. He'd failed to pace himself and obviously had run on belief rather than condition. He soon ran out of steam and I think he finished in fifth place.

He'd pushed me so hard in the first half of the run I dug deep and thought, 'Here's a chance to bust the 6:50 mark'. I knew the time had to be good if I maintained the pace: I finished in 6:36.

I could hardly breathe. I couldn't get enough oxygen in and I started to panic. I have never hurt so much physically at any time in my life as I did at that moment.

Was it worth it? *Absolutely*.

big brother

When Super League unveiled the video replay to adjudicate on suspect tries in 1997, there was a mixed reaction to its introduction. Some supporters applauded it as a massive breakthrough because they figured it would signal the end of tries being wrongly awarded because a touchie or referee had stuffed up. On the flipside, however, the traditionalists saw it as yet another modern-day intrusion on their grand old game. They feared the replay system would lead to unwelcome breaks in play as the video referee viewed the vision from a number of angles, which would penalise the team that had the roll on.

In the inaugural year of Rugby League's technological age I was considered a rebel because I seldom went to the video referee. A graduate of the old school, I was still happy to live and die by my own decisions and only use the video when I had doubt.

John Ribot, the boss of Super League, had other ideas and called me into his office for a chat. During our meeting he made it crystal clear that he was concerned at my failure to make full use of the available technology.

After hearing his gripe I explained that I didn't know we were obliged to use the video referee. 'My understanding,' I said, 'was when in doubt, yell out to the man upstairs' and I did when I had doubt about the decision.

I guess Ribot appreciated there was no point telling me bulldust because he took time out to explain the facts of life—and rule number one was that the video replay was like a television commercial during a game. When there was doubt surrounding a try, going to the video ref meant everyone's eyes honed in on the big screen at the ground, waiting for Big Brother to press the green button for a 'TRY' or the red for 'NO TRY'. Sony Playstation had bought the rights to sponsor the video referee, which guaranteed them a captivated audience for anywhere between thirty seconds to two minutes. The message was loud and clear: the video referee was all about business and sport. I took the tip and, in my next match, I ensured our sponsor was well looked after by going to it on *five* occasions.

I drove poor old video ref John Gocher crazy—at one stage, with a huge smile on my face, I referred a try to John even though there was nothing wrong with it. When John asked what could possibly have been wrong with that one, I said there could've been a problem with an obstruction during the lead-up to the four-pointer. The replay showed the try scorer went under the posts from five metres out without a hand being laid on him. Watching it on the screen was embarrassing, but I don't think there was any problem about oversaturation because I didn't hear a peep of complaint from Ribot about that effort.

While Super League is long gone, the pressure to look after the sponsors associated with the video referee remains. Before the 2002 Kiwi–Aussie test I was told the match sponsor was on a user-pay contract and only had to pay its fee to the NZRL if their logo appeared on the video referee screen. It was another case of commercial reality, so I knew what had to be done and, at the first possible opportunity, I went to the man upstairs, then, just to make sure the Kiwi League would get their cash, I did it again in the second half.

I know the practice might sound wrong to some people, but this is one of the realities of the modern world. Businesses need to make cash—movie producers sell product placement to help fund their blockbusters; television and radio stations survive on commercials; footy jumpers are sponsored; the NRL has sold the goal post crossbar to an advertiser; cricket bats are seen as legitimate advertising billboards; and there're even sponsorship signs in hospitals and schools. As long as the advertising commitments don't interfere with the outcome of the match then we'll have to learn to tolerate them. Sending decisions up to the video ref doesn't alter the integrity of the game. If anything it ensures the right decision is made.

During the 2002 season, Barry Gomersall called for the video referee system to be canned. The Grasshopper figured 'Big Brother' had taken the human element out of the game. 'They're not game to make decisions any more,' he told *Rugby League Week*. 'We've got far too many stoppages.'

As someone who has refereed under Big Brother, I disagree. The video referee has become an accepted part of the game. Standing out in the middle, I can feel the crowd's collective anticipation when they lock their eyes on the screen and wait. It's captivating.

I sometimes wonder how many decisions we got wrong back before the video ref was introduced. Calls were often made based on gut feelings, or sometimes just in the hope you got it right. You've seen them every weekend: the one where the corner post is taken out as the ball is planted, the 'Did he touch or not?' scenario and the classic, 'Was it grounded properly?'. Now that the game is covered so much more by media and the expectations of players and supporters to get it right have increased, the video referee is a blessing.

Like everybody else, I used to think 'How hard could it be to make a decision in the box?' People have this idea that the video ref is sitting in his box, drinking a glass of chardonnay and relaxing. He's not. I found that out in season 2003 when the NRL decided to use the full-time referees as video referees as well. Give me the footy field any day.

The video referee sweats when making a decision and, when the call goes up, he's placed under an enormous amount of pressure because time is of the essence. He's conscious that the game has to keep moving and he faces numerous frustrations in the hot seat because he can't just hit buttons to see the vision he wants to see, he relies on the television director to cue up the tape and then he must view the incident from every available angle. Sometimes he's doing this while the crowd slow handclaps to try and hurry him along. That pressure can lead to the wrong call being made.

Most times, however, the video ref gets it right. I don't think the players and fans mind the stoppage in play, so long as the end result is correct. I don't think they'd even mind if it took two minutes to ensure the call is spot-on.

At the moment the video ref is only used when a try is in doubt and for acts of foul play, but I think we need to widen the video ref's scope to help clarify a few other grey areas, such as stealing the ball. Stealing the ball can be one of the toughest calls a ref must make during a game. When the ball is lost in a one on one encounter, it's straightforward enough, but when it's two defenders in on the one man, questions race through your mind: 'Did the ball carrier drop it or was he given a bit of a nudge? Was the ball knocked out of his hands by a big hit? Did the attacking player lose control when he climbed to his feet to play the ball? Did the second man in reef the ball out of his hands?' Just the messy nature of a tackle can make it impossible for the ref to view what happened, so it's a perfect scenario to get the video referee involved.

Now, someone like Gomersall might say that will slow the play down, but, it would be like a speed camera on the roads—it would keep most players honest. After being caught out by the video referee we'd see the penalties awarded for stealing the ball decrease rapidly because the footballers would realise they'd be caught out. And the video referee would allow the right decision to be made.

I can live with the powers that be not using the video ref for stealing the ball, but I think it's an absolute necessity when two or more players contest a loose ball and it goes dead in-goal. Who made it dead? This is a huge decision because a team is going to take either a line drop-out or a twenty metre tap. If they're wrongly given a line drop-out they have the attacking team straight back in their face, putting them under more pressure to defend, rather than being deep in their opposition's territory after their tap-kick. A classic example was in the 2002 finals series between Cronulla and St George–Illawarra when the ball went dead in-goal and the touch judge gave me a call that later proved wrong. If we'd had Big Brother check the video, we wouldn't have made that mistake and the Sharks would have been attacking the line for another set of six tackles.

I've often been criticised by the media for not using the video referee a lot, but that's because I work hard to make sure I'm in the right position to make a call and I back my judgment. When there is doubt though, I'm all for Big Brother.

super league origin 1997

In 1997, under the banner of Super League, a tri-series was played between Queensland, New South Wales and New Zealand. It was Super League's answer to the State of Origin and the series was to be played with each team playing each other once and the two top sides playing in a final. Before the series started the referee appointments were decided and it was to be one game each to Graham Annesley, Steve Clark and myself. The best performance would be appointed to the final.

I refereed the match between New South Wales and Queensland, who ended up making it to the final to be played at ANZ Stadium, as did I. The final was one of the highlights of my career, after the full eighty minutes, it was a draw. After twenty minutes of extra time, it was still drawn. At this stage, the rule was to toss a coin and then go into a further period of extra time until someone scored.

I summoned both captains, Laurie Daley from New South Wales and Alfie Langer from Queensland, to the centre of the field for a coin toss. Most of the players, including Laurie Daley, were unaware of the rule regarding extra time and were a little confused about what was to happen next. When he got to where Alf and I were standing Laurie said, 'What's happening, Billy?'

I said, 'We have to do another coin toss.'

'What is this one for?' he asked.

Before I could reply, Alfie looked straight at him and in his nonchalant way said, 'Whoever wins the toss wins the game.'

Laurie looked from Alf to me, back to Alf and back to me with an exasperated look on his face and finally said, 'Fair dinkum?'

I jumped on the bandwagon, 'Yeah, that's right, Laurie, whoever wins this toss wins the game.'

Laurie looked straight at me and said, 'You are kidding.'

'No, he isn't,' Alf said seriously. 'What do you want? Heads or tails?'

Alf tossed the coin. Laurie called, but he still couldn't believe he could lose the game on a coin toss.

Before anything could be said I told Laurie, 'We weren't being fair dinkum, you've won the toss. Queensland will kick to you. Which way do you want to run?'

The game went for a further three minutes, then Noel Goldthorpe popped a field goal, ending the game in New South Wales's favour. The first thing I thought about before the ball had even landed on the ground was 'Get the ball'. I quickly blew full-time and said to my touchie through my communication gear 'Get the ball'. The touchie ran over, got the ball and brought it back to me and I held onto that ball as though it was a part of me. It is now one of many in my collection, but one I cherish most of all.

New South Wales defeated Queensland 23–22
Crowd: 35 570

super league grand final 1997

Super League's one and only grand final was famous for being the first title decider played outside Sydney; for being the first grand final to be played at night; and for boasting the biggest grand final crowd in twenty years. They spared no expense on the build-up to the game with a full-scale street parade and sensational entertainment.

There were many from the old school who considered the match in Brisbane a Mickey Mouse affair, but I certainly didn't share their opinion because, apart from hosting some of the game's best players in either competition it also represented my first appearance in a title decider since 1991.

The players were dead keen to win the title, Andrew Ettingshausen hosing down suggestions that it was only half a premiership because he was desperate to add some silverware to the Sharks' threadbare trophy cabinet. The Sharks, however, were never in the hunt. After a tough opening twenty minutes the Broncos cut loose to lead 10–2 at half-time and from there, there was no looking back.

Brisbane defeated Cronulla 26–8
Crowd: 58 912

fate

I've argued and debated about my beliefs in fate many times over the years. It was a great topic to get into while working twelve-hour shifts in the Witness Security Unit. A couple of the women in the unit agreed with me to a certain point, but couldn't go along with my whole philosophy. They believed in fate, but also believed you could change your destiny. I agree, but I believe you only change your destiny because you were meant to.

Here is how I see it. You are born on a certain day at a certain time because it was meant to be. You will die on a certain day at a certain time because that is also meant to be. Everything you do between these times you are meant to do. This is the part where I lose many people because they believe they have the power to change things by the decisions they make along the way. I don't completely disagree with this, but I take it a step higher, and say you make these decisions because you were always going to. It's in your plan.

Why did Pete's shotgun blast miss me by centimetres? Why didn't the sultans hit the tree head-on at over one hundred kilometres per hour? Fate.

Let me relate a story to you, which is a true story told to me by a sergeant when I was in the TRG. My friend, Sarge, was with his partner filling up his car at a petrol station. A friend of theirs rolled in to fill up at the bowser beside them. They hadn't seen each other for some five or ten years and they asked their friend to stay and have coffee with them. He um'd and ah'd, finally said okay but then changed his mind and said no, he'd better get going. What's the hurry, they said, it'll only add on fifteen or so minutes. The friend had made up his mind and said no, he'd get going. They exchanged numbers and promised to catch up soon. Sarge and his partner had coffee and left some twenty minutes later. An hour and a half down the road they were held up by an accident involving a truck and car. The driver of the car died in the crash. It was their friend.

For months on end my sergeant kept torturing himself, wishing he had made the guy stay with them. 'If only he had stayed with us for that cup of coffee, he'd be alive today,' was his great lament. While it's a fair regret, Sarge had no control over what was about to happen to that bloke, and neither did he.

Over the years I've found accepting fate has made life easier for me because I can accept decisions, change and personal heartache better than most. It's still shattering when I lose a loved one or someone close to me, but I feel a sense of calm in knowing it was their time. Their number was up. It has helped me put life into perspective.

If I do something stupid and think 'Why did you do that, you idiot?' I simply say to myself 'Because you were meant to'. I then get on with fixing it. This philosophy goes hand in hand with my attitude to seek out the positives when a negative interrupts my life. If you don't do this already, try it. Wherever there is a negative—no matter how big or shattering—you will find a positive. Concentrate on the positive and you'll find it will grow. It will help you get through whatever impact the negative has on your life.

Let me give you a couple of examples from different moments in my life. When my grandparents Tom and Thelma Shepherd retired, they headed north to Port Macquarie to enjoy the warmer climate. They were six hours away and we rarely saw them because of the distance. In 1991 my pop passed away as a result of asbestos poisoning. It was shattering for the family and this earth is worse off for his passing. But I accepted the tragedy a lot easier because of my belief in fate and I went in search of the positive. What good could there possibly be in the passing of this great man, my pop? I knew I would miss him dearly so how could there be a positive? But it's always there.

The positive eventually surfaced sometime later when my mum and uncle convinced my grandma it was time to move closer to my mum. Grandma moved to Sydney and is now only a half-hour drive from my place. Grandma is ninety-two and has slowed down over the last eighteen months but she's still fighting fit. I get to see her more and she gets to spend time with my sons, her great-grandchildren.

On a smaller scale, when I was stood down in 2002 after the Newcastle versus Parramatta game, the positive was having the weekend off, catching up with my mate and taking a motorbike ride.

Looking back on all the heartache I've gone through with my two broken marriages and the devastating impact that had, not only on my life, but my boys as well, it has been a shattering negative. Yet out of this negative came the biggest positive: the chance to meet the woman who changed it all, Lesley.

heaven sent

To meet my wife, Lesley, in the way I did reaffirmed
my belief in fate.

It was 1997 and I was living in a four-bedroom
house with my eldest son, Matthew, and two of my
close friends and training mates, Ian Hamilton and
Scott Thomas. Ian was in the same situation as me
with a recent marriage bust-up and access to his three
daughters every second weekend. I had access to my
other boys, Will and Andrew, on the same weekend,
so it was a little hectic when they all turned up.

I was working full-time for Super League so my
week revolved around training, preparing for my game,
relaxing and spending quality time with my boys when
they came over. I had to travel a fair bit on the weekends
with my Super League commitments, so my time was
pretty well taken up.

One day Hammo said a friend of ours had scored
us an invite to an Ansett flight attendants party in a

house at Caringbah. I wasn't too keen to go because I wouldn't know anyone and I was refereeing at Penrith on the Sunday afternoon. We'd been invited so we could meet girls, but with two marriages already behind me, I just wasn't interested. Hammo was keen to meet new women and begged me to go with him. Eventually I agreed, but insisted I would be leaving before 10.30 p.m. because I was refereeing the following day.

We were to meet a girl by the name of Madonna two houses down from the party who would get us in. Madonna wasn't comfortable taking two strangers in and I wasn't comfortable going in with a stranger, but it turned out Madonna and I had trained with the same group of people at the Bondi Diggers club, so it was okay.

Once we were inside, Madonna left Ian and me while she went and mingled with her friends. After about an hour standing on our own I felt uncomfortable and ready to decamp. Hammo asked me to hang around a little longer, but I told him I was bored; I couldn't drink any more mineral water and I felt I was hanging around like a stale bottle of grog. I was about to leave when Madonna came back and dragged us over to meet a few people.

We were introduced to a group of four ladies, one of whom was wearing a beret and long boots: Lesley. One of the ladies asked me if I was the football ref and I said, 'No, but I have been told I look like him.'

Lesley obviously had no idea who I was because after the introductions she called me Ian while we all chatted away. But, as it turned out, I had bought my jet ski from her ex-boyfriend, so she figured out I was Bill Harrigan, even though she had no idea who Bill Harrigan was, or what he looked like.

Not much later I left Hammo at the party and headed home to get some rest.

In the following weeks Hammo started dating Madonna and each time he came home from a date he would say, 'Do you remember Lesley from the party? She said to pass on her regards.' Madonna was doing the same with Lesley, although neither Lesley nor I were sending messages.

Madonna and Hammo organised a small dinner party to continue their matchmaking plans but Lesley refused to attend if she was being lined up with anyone. Madonna told her that she wasn't trying to line her up with anyone and Bill would not be there. Hammo told me Lesley would be there, but I told him I still wasn't ready to date anyone.

I turned up late with my two boys, Will and Andrew, after being at a family get-together. Lesley was very annoyed with Madonna, but neither Hammo nor Madonna were deterred and they kept passing on messages.

Eventually, I rang Lesley and I enjoyed talking with her. I called a couple more times and a day of sailing was organised. I hated sailing but I knew Lesley enjoyed it. Some months later, Lesley told me she only went sailing that day because she knew I had gone to the trouble of organising it, even though I had mentioned to her I hated it. After an agonising day on the water for me and an enjoyable one for Lesley, Hammo and Madonna joined us for dinner.

We agreed to telephone each other and over the next month we spoke on about twenty occasions, but our work commitments made it impossible to meet up and go out. Lesley constantly travelled interstate as a hostess while I was flat out with the demands of refereeing. We got to know each other pretty well as a result of our extended phone calls and we eventually had a night out together at Tawera Nikau's restaurant in Cronulla, Zulu's. (Nikau was a first grade forward for Cronulla and Melbourne Storm.)

For our next date Lesley invited me over for dinner, but I couldn't make it early enough so I said I would come over later and we could watch a classic all-time favourite movie of mine, *The Gunfight at the O.K.Corral*. Lesley agreed and sitting on opposite ends of the lounge through the three-hour epic was our second date. We still laugh about it.

Our friendship grew over the next couple of months into a relationship and it's the greatest thing that has ever happened to me alongside the births of my children.

Some months later Lesley was looking for a new place to live and the house that I was living in was more like the Brady Bunch since Hammo and Scotty had moved out and two other friends, Jenny and her three boys and Debbie and her daughter, had moved in. I thought it was time for me to move on, so I suggested Lesley and I get a place together.

Lesley was keen but she was very concerned about how her parents might take it. Her mum and dad were from the old school, both in their late seventies, and Lesley didn't want to disappoint them. As the only child, Lesley is her mother and father's pride and joy so when we'd decided to move in together I asked for their permission first. While her dad, Les, wasn't too keen on the idea he gave it the green light, but Lesley's mum, Jean, was more to the point. She just said, 'It's okay with me, but if you do *anything* to hurt my daughter I will cut your balls off.'

I was stunned and shocked at the blunt statement, but I think Jean was just as shocked it had slipped out of her mouth. It was so out of character. We brought the story up many times though and Jean, highly embarrassed by it, still had a laugh. Jean's probably cursing me now with a smile on her face while she watches over us from above.

When I met Lesley, Jean had fought off cancer twice and had a heart condition, and I watched on sadly as her health slowly deteriorated.

After living with Lesley for a couple of months I knew we were meant for each other, it felt like a match made in heaven. From informal discussions I had with Lesley I knew she felt the same way and we would eventually marry. The discussions also revolved around how we would get married and, to my surprise, Lesley said she was not into the church and all the trimmings and wouldn't care if we just shot through to an island for a holiday and did it while we were there.

Lesley and I decided to have a baby before we married because, at thirty-seven and forty, we weren't getting any younger and, more importantly, we wanted Jean to have some quality time with her grandchild while she still could.

I know both sets of parents would've preferred us to have gone down the traditional route, but they all understood our motive and gave us their blessing. My genuine wish for Lesley's mum to spend time with at least one grandchild came true when Jed was born on 28 March 2001. Thankfully Jean was given the chance to watch Jed grow from a baby to a little boy walking around and she cherished the seventeen months she had with him. Jean remained very witty—the larrikin her family told me she was—right to her last day.

Meeting Lesley and having Jed together was a huge positive at a time when I least expected it. To find a person so beautiful in heart and soul, looks, character and personality changed my life and made me a very happy man. The positive has had an impact on my boys as well, giving them a lady (we don't like the term stepmum) who loves them as her own and has had an impact on their formative years.

But that was meant to be, wasn't it?

my boys

My personal life has been like a rollercoaster ride with plenty of ups and downs, but it's a ride I'd do over and over again if it meant the same result: my boys.

My eldest son, Matthew, is twenty-three this year. I would have liked to have spent more time with Matty and been able to have had more of an influence on his life while he was growing up, but it wasn't to be. In saying that though, my ex-wife Lee and her second husband, Colin, did a good job raising him.

I saw Matthew every second weekend, Saturday morning till Sunday night, so it was difficult to have that much of an impact on his life, but no matter where I was I made sure I saw him. Sometimes that meant travelling a long distance, but I would dedicate the weekend to him. We'd play on the beach, hit the swings in the local parks, kick a ball around and go on adventures.

If I was refereeing, my mum would come to the game as well and babysit him while I was on the ground. Back then I was still refereeing the Parramatta juniors, and first grade only consisted of Sydney teams so there was little travelling. Matty loved to sing this song:

> *Just me and my dad*
> *What a good time we had*
> *We went out in the woods*
> *And it really was good*
> *Just my dad and me*
> *We're good company*
> *What a wonderful fun time we had*
> *Just me and my dad*

We'd make up new verses and if we sang it once we sang it a thousand times during the thousands of kilometres we drove together. Lee used to complain, and it was a legitimate complaint, that Matty was hard to deal with when he returned from a weekend with me because he would be on a high after two days full of attention.

You can't blame a dad who sees his son or daughter for less than forty-eight hours every fortnight for wanting to spend the time they do have totally with their kids. This is the reason why I support equal access for the non-custodial parent, which is predominantly the father. I know there are issues and circumstances, which differ in every case, but for many like me it would be a godsend because it would allow the father to have more influence in his child's life.

It's been a little easier with my two boys from my second marriage, Will and Andrew, because I've lived close to them. I've also had extra access to them—having them from Friday nights to Sunday and also every Wednesday night as well. Even so, I'd still like to have more time as, unlike Matthew having a stepdad, there has been no other male dominant in their lives and I believe it's important.

All the boys have been into sport, but I've never pushed them one way or another, I've always said 'I don't care what sport you play during summer and winter as long as you play something'. They all started off playing soccer and I remember one cold May morning watching Matty play soccer for Hoxton Park in the under-7s. It was my birthday and Matty scored his first goal. He looked over to me with a smile as big as a Cheshire cat and it brought a tear to my eye.

Will and Andrew moved on from soccer to Rugby League around the age of ten. Matty used to play tennis in summer, but the other two played baseball and I had a dabble at coaching Will for a couple of years when they had no coach. But I enjoy standing back and watching them play more because I can concentrate on them.

As well as playing sport, they've all had to spend their fair share of time being dragged to the footy with me, even when I know they weren't real impressed with having to go.

I've included them in my career, getting them out onto the field and they're always in the dressing-rooms chasing their heroes' autographs. Heaps of the players know them by their first names and enjoy having a chat to them when they're around.

Matty still enjoys reminiscing and looking at the photos of the 1997 Super League grand final when he made the journey to Brisbane with Lesley, my mum and me. I'd lined it up for Matty to run my water bottle for me. He experienced the atmosphere of the changerooms and then dressing in his tracksuit and referees' jersey. Next thing, he was waving to his Nan and Lesley from the middle of the field in a grand final.

Will and Andrew also got their chance to run my water during a game at Cronulla. On one occasion Will was on his way to give me a drink after a try was scored and got sidetracked when the Broncos goal kicker said, 'Hey little fellow, you got a drink for me?' Will said, 'Yes', forgot about me and gave my drink to his Broncos star.

Unfortunately, in recent years the NRL has had to stop kids being on the field due to insurance and liable injury issues. But my boys still hit the dressing-rooms, chase autographs and are the envy of their schoolmates. I'm glad they've had this opportunity because they've also had to endure a lot of schoolyard bullying because of who their dad is.

It's taken plenty of juggling throughout the years fitting in the boys' sport, my footy, access from two families and now looking after little Jed, who is just two years old. I couldn't have done it without the help of my parents and, in the later years, Lesley.

These days, thanks to a full-time refereeing contract, I'm able to care for Jed all day on Thursdays and Fridays, while Lesley works at her shop. Jed loves planes and motorbikes so sometimes we go to the airport and watch the planes then drive to a Harley bike shop and look at the bikes. Some of the owners let Jed climb on the bikes and he pretends to ride them with all the sound effects. I just stand back and watch him—it's hilarious. Spending all day with him I get to read his books, watch his videos and teach him things, like colours and counting. Being older and more mature, I enjoy my time with Jed immensely.

I look at all of my boys now and realise how quickly they're growing up. Matt's an adult getting on with his own life, even though I still see him as one of my little boys. I wonder how much impact I've had on their lives. It's been different with each one, from the two days a fortnight with Matty, the little extra time with Will and Andrew to the twenty-four-seven with Jed. Even though I've tried to spend as much time as possible with each of them, it would have been great to have been able to spend time with the other three as I do now with Jed.

Every Wednesday night I have a big dinner. Matt takes a night off from his work as a chef, I have Will and Andrew for the night and Jed loves having his older brothers around.

At least one night every week I've got all the family together—and that's better than any lotto win.

manly mayhem

My appointment to referee the opening match of the 1998 season between Manly and Brisbane at ANZ Stadium was a great honour, representing the official reunification of the code under the NRL's banner. As a game between a team from the Super League competition (the Broncos) and the ARL (the Sea Eagles) it was a huge game for the supporters and followers of the game who had been devastated by the 'war'.

Yet, behind the scenes, the game's hierarchy had serious concerns about the way Manly would behave in the spotlight. Under the ARL administration, Bob Fulton's Sea Eagles had developed a reputation for riding roughshod over the inexperienced referees who'd been conscripted to control the ARL Optus Cup matches when they weren't ready for either the step-up in class or the pressure. The administrators of the new NRL didn't want their showpiece game to degenerate into a shoddy display of Manly's trademark sledging and niggling.

In the lead-up to the Broncos match I was advised by the NRL's referees' boss Mick Stone to watch a few Manly tapes as part of my 'homework' because I hadn't refereed them for three years.

One incident which left me speechless was when Manly's skipper Geoff Toovey 'went' for referee Paul Simpkins—it was like watching a Doberman attack a defenceless creature. Toovey wasn't happy with a call and he let Simpkins know it. He snarled at him and then, to emphasise his displeasure, he started poking his finger towards Simpkins' chest.

I was stunned Paul allowed Toovey to get away with that kind of behaviour. Even when I started in grade I always demanded respect from the players. Paul's response to Toovey's attack left me shaking my head in even further disbelief. Paul stepped back. *He stepped back.* I guess he wanted to give himself room, but he may as well have waved the white flag. Toovey was immediately on the front foot and stepped forward, poking at him again. Rather than make a stand, Paul *again* retreated. And guess what? Toovey stepped forward and was into him a *third* time. The Manly skipper had achieved his goal, he'd established his dominance over the whistleblower and, by doing so, he had diminished the referee's authority. I know Paul learnt a valuable lesson that day.

Personally, I have no problem with players trying to exert their authority, because the way a referee responds to such a challenge is a test of his character—and mettle. I vowed that type of situation wouldn't happen with me in charge and that promise pleased Mick Stone. He said he never wanted to see that type of behaviour by a player *or* referee ever again. My hours of homework also identified three areas in the Manly camp that needed watching: Toovey, centre Terry Hill and backrower Nik Kosef. When I relayed that information to Mick he threw John Hopoate's name into the mix as a potential troublemaker too. I identified a couple of potential troublemakers from the Brisbane side too and with that Mick and I were happy with the preparations.

The game started off like an absolute cracker. There was a great atmosphere with a whopping crowd of 40 000 and it felt good to be on the field as part of one competition again. The NRL had taken on a lot of Super League's innovations and I felt in control.

It was about ten minutes into the game, when Geoff Toovey and I crossed swords. He gave me a gobful after I awarded Brisbane a penalty, so I marched him ten metres. He didn't like that and was in my face in much the same vein as he'd been with Simpkins, minus the finger poking. Channel Nine forgot to turn down my microphone during Toovey's four-lettered tirade so everyone around the country, including young kids, could hear the almighty spray he was giving me. It was frustrating because he refused to listen to reason and, as he continued to unload on me, I thought 'Stuff this for a joke' and binned him for ten minutes.

Toovey's outburst, and my reaction, set the pace for the rest of the game—the Manly blokes believed they were being hard done by and they let me know it in no uncertain terms. They focused on backchatting me rather than tackling their Brisbane opponents and by full-time they'd lost the penalty count 17–6 and the match 22–6.

Toovey, as captain, let his blokes down on this occasion because he seemed to make a self-declared war with me his main priority on the field. I had always admired his playing style: he'd tackle his heart out, he'd run the ball up like a forward, he'd play on in pain when others would have called it a day and then he'd inspire his team-mates to push themselves when they seemed to have no fuel left in their tank. He was a pain in every referee's backside with the way he carried on but, pound for pound, he was one of the toughest players I ever refereed.

Yet, as much as I admired his spirit, he lost me momentarily on that particular Brisbane night because in the seventy-ninth minute when I sent John Hopoate off for using abusive and offensive language to describe my performance, Toovey chipped in with 'What's this favouritism, Bill? What's going on?' And then he said, 'One competition, Bill.'

I interpreted his comments to infer I was favouring Brisbane because the Broncos were a Super League team and I had Super League ties. I have never tolerated my integrity being questioned, so I told Toovey he could join his winger in the dressing shed. Toovey left cursing my name.

As you'd expect, coach Fulton backed his man to the hilt and told the press Toovey was entitled to query decisions and didn't deserve to be punished by the referee. 'There were times when some of my players might have overstepped the mark with the referee,' said Fulton. 'But in Toovey's case, I don't believe that happened because he is entitled, as captain, to question decisions.' While Fulton said players couldn't win with me in charge, the referees' fraternity did enjoy a victory that night when he realised the lopsided penalty count meant his team's reign as bully boys would no longer be tolerated. As Fulton said, 'If my players are having too much to say on the field, then obviously I will have to do something about that.'

My word he had to . . .

(While Hopoate was suspended for two matches by the judiciary for contrary conduct, Toovey escaped further punishment even though he was found guilty on the same charge.)

samson's hair

Of the numerous controversies that have plagued me throughout my career, the one that still amazes me is the time I copped it for letting my hair grow long. The media went to town; the mob in the outer blasted me; players called me Fabio or Tom Cruise behind my back; the newspapers started to label me a sex symbol; my Super League, and later NRL colleagues, hammered me; my mother even wrote me a note asking me to get it cut; and people such as the celebrated publicist Max Markson figured I was hoping to reinvent my image in the hope it would increase my bank balance *and* satisfy my ego.

My reason for allowing my hair to grow south was simply because, after seventeen years of being forced to have a short back and sides as a member of the police force, I decided to let it go. When it became a media issue, Super League referee co-ordinator Graham Annesley asked me to go to the barber, but there was nothing in my contract about the length of my hair, so I allowed my mop to flow free. And, jeez, it irritated people.

I remember one lump of a bloke, a Canberra supporter, who made a point of letting me know what he thought of my hairstyle during a Raiders–Bulldogs match at Belmore. Every time I was at the top end of the ground, he'd rest his gut on the fence and scream out, 'Harrigan, you idiot! Get a haircut you idiot' (I've replaced the word he actually used with 'idiot'.) This joker was at it all game and I'd had a gutful of it so on one occasion, as I turned to run out to the twenty metre line, I said quietly to myself, 'Ah, why don't you go and get . . .' My triumph was short-lived though because my video ref, John Gocher, was in my ear yelling, 'Billy! Billy! You've just gone over Foxtel!' I'd forgotten I was wired up for the TV audience and there was nowhere for me to hide.

The hair affair really blew up when Manly coach Bob Fulton laid into me after Manly lost the opening match of the 1998 season to the Broncos. His team was penalised 17–6 during their loss, and a bitter Bobby Fulton made it clear he despised my refereeing *and* my new look. 'The game has got to get rid of him unless he changes his ways,' Fulton told the *Sunday Telegraph*. 'He thinks he's bigger than the game and more important than the players. Have a look at his hair—he's the biggest lair in the game . . .'

The comedian Brian Doyle seized on Fulton's ill feeling and added a joke to his routine. 'Fulton actually likes Harrigan,' Doyle would tell club crowds. 'Sent him a present . . . a microwave oven. Told him it was a hair dryer.' FootyTab also jumped on the bandwagon with a newspaper advertisement based on Bob's beef. 'FOOTY TAB PAYS OUT NO MATTER HOW LONG YOUR HAIR IS!' it screamed in bold type. 'This week pick the margin has jackpotted and any footy fan could win. We don't care if your shorts are too tight or if you pose nude for the odd calendar . . . '

I got a smile out of that, but at the time I thought Fulton was out of line when he got personal. I told the *Telegraph* he'd lost the plot—and those three words were enough for the Sea Eagles to want me fined $10 000. The thing that really annoyed me was my kids copped the brunt of it at school. I had a seventeen-year-old getting into fights and two others aged six and eight who couldn't understand why people hated their father.

I figured the reason for Fulton's outburst was because he was under pressure. Someone had stood up to his team and he'd lost the plot. Now the NRL was looking to slap a $10 000 fine on him and people were criticising him for making his attack on me personal. Fulton threatened to sue former Origin referee Barry Gomersall for his comments on the Footy Show when he said it was one of the 'lowest acts' he'd seen and Fulton should apologise.

At the height of 'hair-gate' *The Sydney Morning Herald* digitally altered a photograph to show me sporting a bald look, a Mohawk, curly hair, a crew cut and my long locks. 'Harrigan's long locks irritate old-timers,' wrote Roy Masters. 'One of his nicknames is "Tom Cruise", although he says I am the only person who calls him this to his face.'

My mother had had enough. She wrote me a letter that pretty much said, 'Enough is enough, get your hair cut so it looks neat and tidy.' I figured Mum knew best, but a phone call from Andrew Denton, at that time radio station 2MMM's morning host, hastened my decision to get my hair cut. Andrew said he'd pay a few thousand bucks to the charity of my choice if I had my hair cut 'live' on his program. I said yes and it was set down for that Friday. On the Monday night Andrew told someone his plan and the following morning *The Footy Show* contacted the NRL because the Subway sandwich franchise had offered $20 000 for me to get clipped live on *The Footy Show*. I initially refused because I'd given Denton my word, but after discussing it with Andrew he appreciated the $20 000 could do a lot of good for the Children's Hospital. He asked me not to commit till he got back to me later that day. I received a call from Andrew on the Tuesday afternoon and he said I'd get a new offer from *The Footy Show* and I should take it.

He was right—the offer was raised to $25 000 and I accepted the deal. Andrew Denton confessed that he rang someone at Channel Nine and said he was willing to match the $20 000 because he wanted my haircut to be on his radio show. Andrew told me he didn't have that sort of money but he told them he did it to get square with them for pinching his idea. I thought it was a good get and a better deal for me on behalf of the Randwick Children's Hospital.

The haircut was a major event with *The Footy Show* dressing me in trendy new gear, providing fashion expert Charlotte Dawson to host the segment and allowing me to have my own hairdresser. I heard it was one of *The Footy Show's* biggest television audiences, but I still can't fathom why. It was only long hair and look at the hairdos running around on the field in 2003! Anyway, in the end Rugby League's most talked about hair hit the floor and was swept into a dustpan, and the Children's Hospital received $25 000. Good stuff.

wired for sound

Geoff Toovey and I rarely saw eye to eye on any subject, but I wholeheartedly agreed with him when the former Manly captain called on the game's hierarchy to stop wiring referees for sound.

Toovey, dubbed the 'world's smallest volcano' because of his penchant to blow up when the pressure got to him, expressed his view after being caught out giving me an almighty spray punctuated by blue language during a live telecast. 'Do we really need them?' he said of the microphone in 1998. 'I reckon things that are said on the field during games should stay there and not be released for public consumption.'

He was right on the mark because the television and radio microphones have only added extra stress and pressure on the players—and sometimes refs—

because we all have to watch our tongues. It isn't always easy for people to show restraint in a sport like Rugby League. It's passionate and blokes, including the nice guys, will scream before thinking about what they're saying. Yet, during live television and radio calls, foul language is piped uncensored into the lounge rooms for millions of people to hear and we're talking about gutter language, too . . . it isn't the kind of thing I want my sons to hear from blokes they might see as role models.

While players and refs would love to see the microphones destroyed, it will never happen because the television executives love it. They call it 'eavesdropping' because their director can use what the ref is saying to a player during a crucial moment as part of their broadcast.

After the Toovey incident the boss of Channel Nine sport, Gary Burns, brushed it off as an incident hardly worth mentioning. 'We did not have one complaint,' he told the *Daily Telegraph*. Burns even admitted Channel Nine turns the volume *up* whenever it appears as if something controversial is about to happen. He also said, 'There is the possibility the odd swear word will creep in. We are prepared to wear that and we think the public will understand.' Burns justified the microphones by saying they would help to take some of the 'mystery' out of referee decisions, but I don't think it has helped all that much. Even when they hear our explanations people still bag out the referee.

The first time we really used microphones was when the NSWRL gave touch judges new communication gear. They had a microphone placed on top of their flags with a button they'd push to talk. The referee had an earpiece and a receiver but no microphone, so he could hear what they were saying but he couldn't respond.

I was refereeing a pre-season country carnival game in Bega where Illawarra were playing Canberra on a very hot February day. Canberra had just scored and Mal Meninga was setting up his shot for goal. My two touchies were positioned behind the posts.

Suddenly I heard static in my earpiece followed by, 'Hey Bettsy, twenty-metre line, three rows back, blonde hair, purple boob tube.'

There was more static in my ear and then, 'Oh yeah—good spotting, Kev.'

I looked at the pair of them and saw where they were looking. I thought I'd have a look myself and they were right. Sitting there larger than life was a very good-looking blonde lady with a big purple boob tube. She had certainly caught our attention but I couldn't respond to the boys.

Suddenly I heard Meninga's boot striking the ball and swung my head back to watch his kick.

The ball was heading straight for the posts and the touchies were still looking at the blonde-haired lady. Their attention was brought back to the kick when it almost struck them in the head. Up went their flags and I awarded the goal.

One of the first blokes I needed to pull into line about the danger the ref's microphone could do to a player's reputation was Brisbane five-eighth Kevin Walters during a match against Melbourne. The Storm's lock Tawera Nikau ran the ball up, but the pass to him was forward and I pulled it up. Out of the corner of my eye I saw Andrew Gee had lined Nikau up for a big hit but, after blowing my whistle, I took my eye off the ball.

Next thing I knew, my touch judge was on the field yelling 'Billy I'm here . . . Billy I'm here.' I thought he was in about the forward pass but it turned out Nikau had whacked Gee in the jaw with his elbow when they came into contact. I asked Gee to show me his gob and, on inspection, I could see his teeth had been pushed back and there was also some blood trickling down.

As I placed Nikau on report and awarded the Broncos a penalty, I heard someone yell from my right 'How would you like your teeth pushed back!' The comment was punctuated by foul language and I saw it was Walters with a huge grin on his melon. He was having a joke with me, as was his way, but rather than coming across to the viewers as a joke I realised it would've sounded like a threat so I gave him a cold stare and put my finger up to my lips as a sign for Kevvy to shut up.

After the Broncos scored a try a couple of minutes later Walters, Langer and Tallis stopped during their walk back towards their positions and Kevin asked why the heck I carried on like a good sort when he was only having a joke. I covered the microphone, lowered my voice and told him how the players needed to be careful what they said on the field when they were close to the whistleblower because *everything* could be heard on Foxtel and Optus. He was genuinely shocked and apologised for what had happened.

Tallis, however, seemed intrigued by what I had just revealed. 'You mean the commentators can hear everything we say?' he asked. When I nodded in the affirmative Gorden put his mouth down towards the microphone and bellowed a 'cheerio' to the callers: 'How the fxxx are you all going up there?' I reckon the director would've had a heart attack!

There were other classics broadcast over the air, including the time when Paul McBlane called Jim Dymock out after a punch-up. After the touchie made his report on the incident, McBlane said with deadly seriousness, 'You've just heard what the touch judge said. He claims you hit him.'

Now, rather than show the hint of any remorse, Dymock displayed a great pride in his handiwork: 'Yeah, I did,' he said triumphantly. 'I belted him, go ask him!'

My mate Tim Mander gets my blue ribbon for the time he couldn't quite spit out the word 'abdomen' after a dust-up. 'You whacked him in the abdi-om . . . er, abdemo . . . ah, *guts*. You hit him in the guts!'

I'll admit classic moments like these can be very funny but sometimes it's a bleeping pain in the bleep!

stuff-ups

It should go without saying I treat any mistake I make on the field seriously. Even after seventeen years at the top, my reaction to watching a video review and learning I stuffed something up is the same as when I was a fresh-faced rookie. I *still* feel hot flushes, my guts *still* turn and I *still* ask myself how the hell could I get that particular ruling wrong? When I finally settle down and accept I can't change what happened on the paddock, I try and find out why I got it wrong. Sometimes I'll phone the player involved to apologise. That might sound like an easy way out to some people, but calling a player to admit I've made a mistake isn't easy.

The first bloke I ever needed to say sorry to was Brisbane winger Willie Carne. I can remember the incident as if it happened five minutes ago: the Broncos were playing Newcastle and they'd introduced a new attacking ploy in which the halfback or five-eighth would chipkick over the defensive line out wide to give their speedsters—Carne or Michael Hancock—a crack at a loose ball. During this particular game Willie regathered the ball and was tryline bound, but I was certain he was half a metre offside so I awarded the Knights a penalty. Willie was far from impressed with my ruling, but, as one of Rugby League's nice guys, he resisted the urge to let fly with a barrage of abuse. All he said was, 'I was onside, Billy, I was deadset onside.'

Needless to say, I didn't believe him but I promised to buy him a ten dollar lottery ticket if my video review of the match proved I was wrong. I thought it was a safe bet, but when I watched the 'eaglecam' tape (a wide angle view of the game) my jaw dropped: the eaglecam proved Willie was half a metre *onside*. I eventually went to bed, but it was a restless sleep because I felt lousy. All I could think about was my error and how it should have been a try. The next day I made an interstate call to Willie to offer a wholehearted apology. He accepted my message graciously and, despite his initial reluctance, he later took the ten bucks to buy a lottery ticket.

Whenever I've made a mistake like that I go through a long and detailed checklist of what could have gone wrong, but I have found, rather than beat myself up, it's far more beneficial to learn from an error to ensure it isn't repeated. A comforting philosophy I've formed over the last seventeen years is that the first time you make a certain blunder it can be put down to the learning process, but do it a second time and it's a fair dinkum mistake.

My earliest learning process in first grade was to never, *ever* watch a 'bomb' go up into the sky. It was my fourth or fifth big match and I drew the blue ribbon game between Balmain and Parramatta. I think I received the nod because both Mick Stone and Kevin Roberts were sick; nevertheless, I was excited because 28 000 fans had packed Parramatta Stadium and I was refereeing the likes of Peter Sterling, Ray Price, Mick Cronin, Brett Kenny, Eric Grothe, Wayne Pearce, Benny Elias and Steve Roach. It was the stuff every young referee's dreams are made of and I wanted to make a huge impression with everyone, but one simple mistake nearly blemished the whole experience. When Balmain kicked a bomb high into the air, my eyes followed the ball into the sun and I was dazzled—I couldn't see a damn thing! Eric Grothe had regathered the ball and started on one of his classic kick return chargers when his momentum came to a sudden halt with a blast from my whistle. I was out of whack from my dose of the sun and the quick spinning of my head. I had blown my whistle because I thought something was wrong with the play, but nothing was. Confusion reigned, but no one was more put out than me. I even asked myself 'What are you doing?' as I called for a scrum to pack down. When a bemused Peter Sterling asked what Grothe had done wrong, I struggled for an answer. I couldn't give him one so I just stared dumbly at him.

So I'd stuffed up, but I've made sure to never repeat that error and if I'm at a referee's coaching clinic in Papua New Guinea, Townsville or England, I make a point of seeing how the refs react to a bomb going up. If they look into the sky I tell them about my Parramatta Stadium experience and explain they needn't watch the ball because it will eventually come down. I stress they should instead be more concerned with what is happening at ground level. They should scan the field to ensure all the players are onside; look at the wingers and fullback because their reaction will give them an idea of where the ball will land and then they should run into position. While those steps might appear simple, I only developed my bomb formula of scan, look, run, position because I made an embarrassing mistake in my rookie season.

There is a lighter side to making a mistake and sometimes you can do nothing but accept you've goosed yourself. I had one such experience in a 1991 pre-season match when Brisbane played Penrith at Broken Hill. In hindsight I should have blamed the red outback dust getting in my eyes for what occurred, but it all happened too quickly. One of the Walters boys, it might've been Kevin, was wrestling with a few defenders so I yelled 'HELD—play the ball!' I then looked to my right to check the five metres and, lo and behold, I turned around and saw Walters was still running. I blew a penalty in Penrith's favour and all the players—even the Panthers—looked at me as if to say what the hell is going on? I walked towards a flabbergastered Walters to mark the spot of the penalty.

Walters said, 'What was that for?'

'I told you to play the ball,' I replied.

Then I heard a voice from five metres away say 'I did'.

I looked towards the voice to see Walters standing exactly where I told him to play the ball. The penny dropped—and how! I realised Kevin had played the ball and his twin brother Kerrod (they're the spitting image) had scooped the ball up and sprinted from dummy half.

When Allan Langer queried my decision, I attempted to cover my tracks by saying Walters hadn't played the ball properly. Alf, however, was too smart for that and he scoffed, 'Bulldust, you got 'em mixed up . . . you got 'em mixed up.' And with that he then called me 'Grasshopper', as if he'd mistaken me for Barry Gomersall. All I could do was smile. Alfie had caught me out.

The postscript to this story is that even to this day the Walters boys and Allan Langer still call me 'Barry' (Gomersall) or 'Greg' (McCallum) to remind me of my mistake at Broken Hill. If nothing else, I guess that proves no one forgets a ref's mistake no matter how big—or small—it might be.

the firm

On 28 April 1998 I received a letter from Graham Annesley, the National Rugby League's chief operating manager, which emphasised that refereeing is now a job bound by industrial relations laws. That means, in terms of being an employee of the NRL, I am no different to a bloke working on a factory production line or a clerk in an office. This was rammed home in no uncertain terms when I received an official 'warning' because the hierarchy wasn't happy with some things I'd done. There were several matters that had combined to put a black mark next to my name and resulted in a letter from Graham identifying my misdemeanours.

- Public comments relating to an NRL coach (Fulton)
- Unauthorised media appearances (which I dispute)
- Public comments on NRL related issues

- Personal management company intervening in standard employer/employee related manners
- Lack of accountability for full-time duties

The letter went on to provide clear directions the organisation required me to comply with. Failure to comply would result in my employment being terminated.

Fair enough. But I still don't know what Graham thought I got up to during the week, because up to that point my whole life was devoted to living, eating, breathing and sleeping Rugby League refereeing. Obviously I was shattered to be given an official reprimand and threatened with the sack. I felt as if I'd been kicked square in the guts. I thought I'd been a good employee: I was happy to help out at charities, I went beyond the call of duty to promote refereeing at junior clinics or conferences and last, but not least, I was performing where it mattered most—on the paddock.

I started to think about chucking refereeing in and it's a huge possibility I would have given it up without the advice of my wife, Lesley.

Lesley suggested I treat refereeing as I would any other job and, by taking her tip, I think she saved my professional sanity. She had seen what kind of toll the constant criticism from outside and within the NRL had done to me. I was irritable and starting to become negative, but under Lesley's suggestion life became a lot brighter. I concentrated only on my game and didn't worry about any other match played during the weekend, unless it was one we really wanted to watch together.

But my new approach went further: I no longer read the newspapers' sports pages; I didn't listen to the sport reports on the television or radio; and I didn't go out of my way to talk football when we went out.

Not talking about football was hard though, because people want to ask questions and talk footy and I believe in my position I need to accommodate them. It's a part of my job to enhance and promote footy but, more importantly, I need to answer everyone to feel comfortable about myself. I'm not the sort of person to fob someone off because I'm tired of the same question.

I have learnt over the years that the thirtieth person who asks a particular question is entitled to the same response as the first person that asked it. The thirtieth person is not aware I've answered the same question twenty-nine times so they need to hear it answered with enthusiasm as if it was the first time answered. I want the thirtieth person to go away and say, 'Hey, that Bill Harrigan is okay'; not 'that Bill Harrigan is a so-and-so'. Over the years I've seen some personalities behave non committally with fans away from the cameras. They mustn't realise the damage they do; word of mouth is a very powerful thing.

Back to Lesley's advice, I followed other people's approach to work in that once they clocked off from the factory floor they went home and forgot all about it. I followed suit, so if I refereed on a Friday night, we didn't live football on the Saturday or Sunday. Instead Lesley and I went out and enjoyed family weekends—taking walks by the ocean or going out on picnics. I no longer lived six games of football a weekend and, by doing so, I felt an intense pressure lift from my shoulders. I began to enjoy life and work again because I found I couldn't wait to get my kit bag and go to work on a weekend. My on-field results spoke for themselves because people—and the comments came from people in the know, not me—started to say how well I was refereeing.

While I didn't appreciate Graham's letter of warning, and I know why he had to send it, I look back now and I see it as something which not only forced me to redefine what was important in my life but it also helped me to regain my groove as a referee. Thanks, Graham.

the rent's not free

I have no doubt the NRL will wipe its hands of the idea of full-time referees when Steve Clark, Tim Mander and I eventually retire, and that's disappointing. The decision will be purely financial.

At the moment, the hierarchy sees much greater value in spreading its referees' budget across the board to help develop referees, rather than plough most of it into the pockets of a handful of people. I appreciate their point, but it isn't as if they're overseeing an amateur sport like discus throwing or archery which has no money in the bank. The League has sponsorship deals worth millions and they could use a larger slice of the money pie both to develop refereeing at the grassroots and to look after the whistleblowers who've made the cut. After all, it's great motivation for the younger referees coming through the ranks to see that there is a possibility of a full-time career. But the NRL sees reverting to part-timers as the way to go so it's what will happen in the future.

Relying on part-time referees also flies in the face of the League's desire for the game to be seen as a showcase on the global stage. To help achieve that aim the NRL needs a corps of professional referees dedicated to living, breathing and studying the game; understanding the idiosyncrasies of the individual teams; conducting seminars and junior coaching clinics; and preparing themselves mentally and physically for refereeing. While the refs will always give their best, the NRL simply won't get the level of commitment I speak of if blokes are forced to juggle their outside profession, family life and the well-known demands of whistleblowing. I know that even if the League embraced professional refs there'd still be errors made in the heat of the moment, but they'd be minimal compared to the current set-up because Rugby League would be policed by a group of blokes whose professional priority is refereeing and not trying to maintain an outside job as well.

I know full-time refereeing works and has helped make Rugby League a much better spectacle for the fans at the ground and the ever growing television audience. Some people will say I'm being selfish and looking after my bank balance, but the beauty of full-time refereeing is it has relieved the few of us contracted to the NRL of the outside problems that can affect an individual's performance on match day. We're free of work demands; we're paid to maintain a high standard of fitness; we focus on the demands of our trade; we can get our injuries treated properly; and we get to spend time with our families. Basically, come kick off time on a weekend, we have room in our heads to concentrate on the game. Our minds are completely at the ground, not back at the office wondering about order forms that needed to be filled out or dealing with customer complaints.

There's also the financial demands of the day job as opposed to the referee's rewards, and I look towards Paul Simpkins to champion my cause. Paul is a member of the New South Wales Police Force, but to be free for his NRL duties during the winter he works part-time, three days a week. Unfortunately, he'll have to continue to do so for as long as his refereeing days last. It isn't easy to work part-time in the police because they only have a limited number of positions available. If, at the end of a season, he applied for a full-time spot to alleviate his financial shortfall during summer he'd need to apply *again* for part-time work and there's a genuine chance it won't be available during the football season. Having tried to work my refereeing career around police duties allows me to appreciate how much easier Paul's life would be if the NRL put him on the payroll as a full-time employee.

The referees have to be at our headquarters on a Monday and Tuesday for video reviews and then we have compulsory training every Monday, Tuesday and Thursday until the evening. Game day could be Friday night, Saturday night or Sunday afternoon, and it's not just in Sydney, it's wherever the game is played—a referee could be flying to Auckland for a Saturday game. We only find out about the games on the Monday afternoon or Tuesday morning, so you can't really plan ahead. This doesn't include what referees might do in their own time, like time in the gym or reviewing game videos at home.

Despite their efforts, part-timers don't receive a contract or any extra cash for training. They are given $1600 a first grade match and $400 for the video reviews, and, while that might sound like a fortune, it doesn't add up to enough for a bloke raising a family or paying off a mortgage to chuck in his day job. If they miss a game through poor performance part-timers don't get anything. Touch judges are on an even worse deal and, while everyone has to work their way up from the bottom, the first division whistleblowers are paid very little for their time and efforts.

When Super League approached me to sign a contract I thought long and hard about leaving the police force because I'd spent almost eighteen years building up a career through the ranks and, at the time of my offer, I still had a twenty-year career path in front of me. To sign on meant throwing that away to take up a job with a limited life span and it was a downright scary decision, but ultimately I grabbed it on the condition it was a five-year deal.

Despite having an uncertain future after my refereeing days I have no regrets about my decision. I also like to think Rugby League has benefited from having the likes of me, Steve Clark and Tim Mander focusing on our craft. The big question now facing the code is whether the NRL administration places a monetary value on such professionalism?

sharing the load

I have no doubt most referees, and I'm one of them, would prefer to be left as the sole whistleblower on the field. We have our own style, our own way of positioning ourselves during a game and our individual interpretations of the rules. The NRL, however, has touted the idea of using two referees to control a game due to the increasing pace of the modern game and the demands on the referee.

The idea of two referees was first raised in 1987 when I was involved in a trial match between South Sydney and Eastern Suburbs where we had two referees on the field. I had the whistle and Dennis Spagarino had a flag. My role was to stand over the rucks and Dennis would go back the five metres (which would now be ten).

This model is still thrown up today as a possible method of refereeing, but the problem with it was that it took my creative style, reading and positioning out of the game. It was like running a six cylinder car on four. Dennis marked the five metres, but even back then I liked to get the players back seven or eight metres to open it up. I felt the game was cramped and it knocked me around physically because I had to get to every ruck, which is just not possible over eighty minutes. I didn't feel like I had complete control during the game either, because I couldn't police the five metres properly.

One of the major problems with this model occurred when I was following the ball out of the Souths backline, they had an overlap and there was the distinct possibility a try was on. I could hear Dennis behind me yelling, 'Billy, Billy, they're offside!' I quickly looked over my shoulder at him and he was chasing me with his flag up so I blew the whistle and stopped play.

'What have you got, Dennis?' I asked.

He said, 'Easts were offside over here' and pointed the other way, opposite to the ball movement.

Shattered, I had to go over and penalise Easts on the other side of the field. Souths got the penalty, but the advantage play would have been the better option because they would probably have scored over the other side of the field.

This was new to us and Dennis was only doing the job he was told to do: keep them back the five or raise the flag and tell the ref if they're not. He did this and it felt like my option to play the advantage rule was restricted. My ability to keep the game flowing was obstructed.

After that experience, I decided that if the NRL were thinking about using two referees I might be able to help. I spent a bit of time thinking about a model and then practised and refined it with former first grade halfback Perry Haddock in his Oz Tag competition. I was so keen on it I provided the NRL with a blueprint.

In 2001 the NRL again experimented with the idea of using two referees for matches involving teams not in contention for the finals.

The first of two trials took place in round 22 when Steve Clark and Shayne Hayne tried an 'interchange' system in the North Queensland–Canberra match at Townsville. Their brief was to simply rest on the sideline whenever they needed a break. In all, the timekeepers noted Clark was on for fifty-two minutes and Hayne the remaining twenty-eight. The experiment met with the approval of both teams, but the League figured it was hard to gauge whether or not the venture was a success because it was a meaningless match!

My observation is that there are a couple of problems with the interchange plan. Firstly, the referee risks pulling a muscle when he returns to the field because his body will go cold during the break and it takes a while to warm up when he's called back into the fray. Secondly, both teams have to contend with each ref stamping his own authority on the match when he is on the field. That means that a defender might be able to lie longer on a tackled opponent when one ref is on the field, and then get pulled up for it when the other ref comes on; one whistleblower might go half a metre further back than the other when he enforces the ten metres, and so on.

A second trial took place in round 25 between Penrith and the Wests Tigers at the Panthers' home ground. I took particular interest in the way Tony Archer and Steve Richards handled themselves because *this* was my plan: two referees officiating simultaneously, controlling the game as they normally would. One in the action, controls the defensive team, and the other trails behind the attacking team waiting his turn to rejoin the fray. The referee controlling the defensive side is the head referee and the only one who can blow the whistle. In the event of a changeover the ref who stood behind the attacking team now moves up to become the head referee and controls the defensive team. The other referee drops back behind the now attacking team and becomes another pair of eyes. It's that simple!

Tim Mander and I had trialled the system in a schoolboys' game where it worked a treat. We walked off the paddock feeling so much fresher than refereeing on our own and I thought I'd come up with a winner.

What I liked about the plan was it remained as close as possible to the current refereeing set-up. I normally control the match from the defensive team's side of play so I can police the ten metres. When there's a changeover I sprint twenty metres to get the other side back the ten metres. Under my proposed system, that sprint is removed once and for all because, as soon as there's a changeover, I back off and move behind the attacking side's line. Apart from being saved from that sprint, the 'rest' also allows me some downtime to switch off for a few moments—I'm not policing the ten metres, I'm not barking orders at the players and I'm not worried about the tackle count. I'm watching the football and, if needed, I could even be called upon to help the other ref rule on something like a stolen ball. The beauty of this system is, rather than having to concentrate fully for eighty minutes, the ref gets roughly half of that in downtime. That has to be good.

The other advantage of my plan is, unlike the interchange system, both sides get their fair go of both whistleblowers' styles, ruling out complaints about one referee's ten being half a metre more than anothers, or one ref allowing the defenders to lie on the tackled man for a second longer than another. This happens because every three or four sets of possession the referees start looking for an opportunity to switch teams at a scrum or line dropout or some other stoppage in play. The other plus for the NRL is that under my model the referees could back up and officiate another match on a weekend. Tim Mander and I, for example, could referee the Friday night game and then turn out for a Sunday match.

Unfortunately the trial at Penrith Park was written off, the authorities deemed it confusing for the referees, the players and the spectators . . . but that was due to the fact Archer and Richards were given scant instructions before the game. They'd never seen the model before, they'd never used it, let alone trialled it, and they were given about ten minutes worth of instructions before being sent out onto the field not really knowing what the hell was going on.

In hindsight, the NRL would've served the idea better to have introduced the refs to it through schoolboy football before trialling it in a first grade match, because the whistleblowers needed time to become proficient at it. I was disappointed to hear it get ripped apart; it should've been a rip-roaring success because it *does* work.

Whether the League eventually adopts my model, the interchange system or a third plan remains to be seen. No matter which one they eventually run with, referees will still make mistakes and be accused of getting it wrong. Regardless of that, the two refs system will achieve one important goal—it'll take eighty minutes of abnormal tension and stress off the man in the middle.

I'd rather be alone in the middle, but if there are going to be two referees, let's get it right.

grand final 1998

The final I refereed the week before the grand final, between Parramatta and Canterbury, should've been the grand final. It was action-packed. The Bulldogs fought back at the death by scoring an incredible eighteen points in eleven minutes to force the game into extra time. Eels fullback Paul Carige kicked the ball back to the Bulldogs with only seconds remaining and to his horror Craig Polla-Mounter snapped a field goal from forty-six metres out—and it never looked as if it was going to miss the mark.

Even so, my touch judges and I weren't a hundred per cent sure it had scraped over or not, so I 'broke the rules' and asked the video referee to make the call. The reason I say I broke the rules was because there was a policy in place which said video refs didn't have the power to rule on one-pointers, but this was an exceptional circumstance because the call would determine whether the Bulldogs went through immediately to the grand final or if they needed to play an extra twenty minutes.

The video referee studied the shot long and hard and eventually came to the conclusion that the ball had sneaked under the crossbar. The Dogs were condemned to that extra twenty minutes and, even though they won, I'm certain it affected them a week later in the grand final.

As for the grand final itself, it was a one-sided affair with Wayne Bennett's Broncos winning seven tries to two. Incredibly, they clawed their way back from trailing the Dogs 12–10 at half-time.

The victory went a long way to prove the Broncos were a world-class outfit and there were even calls from some sections of the media that, based on the way they'd ripped Canterbury apart, the Broncos' Super League title should have counted as a full premiership.

Brisbane defeated Canterbury 38–12
Crowd: 40 857

bash the ref

It takes a certain toughness to survive as a referee, especially nowadays when elite Rugby League referees are allocated security guards to escort them from the car park to the dressing-room, onto the field and then back to their car. The security procedures were introduced in 1998 after Steve Clark was spat upon and had some liquid substance thrown over him by an irate St George supporter at Kogarah Oval and was then followed to his car. The same weekend I was jostled by a group of Souths supporters outside the Sydney Football Stadium following a match against Brisbane.

The incident at the SFS happened as I waited for my wife Lesley. Before I knew it I was surrounded by a gang of wild-eyed Rabbitohs fans who blamed me for their team's loss. It started off as verbal abuse with them calling me a 'cheat' and so on, just as it appeared to become physical some referee colleagues and Stadium security charged in to keep the group away from me. What was really disturbing was the reason I had to wait for Lesley—she had been holed up amongst the Rabbitoh army and reduced to tears by their behaviour and taunts of 'Kill Harrigan!'

Lesley was given a brutal initiation into Rugby League's 'hate the referee' culture when she sat in a corporate box at a game. You'd think a corporate box would be a civilised spot to watch a game of footy from—they serve fine wines, canapés, gourmet food and even dessert—but Lesley found an extra course was the dirt they dished out about me with 'maggot', 'dog' and 'scumbag' being some of the terms of endearment.

Lesley wasn't a Rugby League supporter then and, after the match, I was astonished to see a look of fear and genuine disbelief in her eyes. It was also obvious she'd been crying and I was disgusted to learn it was all a result of the insulting things she'd heard said about me.

When we first started dating, Lesley copped it a lot from people who couldn't understand why she would date Bill Harrigan. When she was still working as a flight attendant, a baggage handler in Brisbane got stuck into her all the time about how 'Bill is a cheat'. Eventually Lesley arranged for him to meet me after a game and, to this day, he rings me to wish me the best before a big game.

It isn't easy for Lesley sitting in the stands during a game listening to people abuse me. It hurts her deeply, especially when she has Jed or my other boys, Matthew, Andrew and Will, with her, but over the years she's hardened to it, even though she refuses to accept it is a part of the business I'm in.

Twenty years ago when I first started refereeing, I would hear, 'Get 'em back, you maggot', or 'You're blind! Where's your guide dog?'. As a referee, I could cop that, but nowadays I get, 'You f***ing dog. I'll kill you! I know where you live. I know where your family is.'

Things are getting worse. Just recently a Gold Coast referee retaliated after being assaulted and Steve Clark was abused before a first grade game with the comment, 'How's your missus? I hope she rots with cancer.'

Lesley recently bore the brunt of another barrage of abuse after I refereed the St George–Illawarra 18–16 victory over the Rabbitohs at the Sydney Cricket Ground.

The Rabbitohs lost after I ruled their skipper Bryan Fletcher scored a try via a double movement with only seven minutes left on the clock. The video referee looked at the incident and couldn't make a ruling, so I followed my original thought and blew a penalty for the double movement. The Dragons held on and Souths continued to languish among the premiership's cellar dwellers.

It was a disappointing end to the first game of Rugby League played on the hallowed field since 1999. As I walked off the field I sneaked a quick peak at the spot where I sat as a kid when I watched a couple of SCG matches involving the Rabbitohs and remembered what it was like to follow them during their last golden era.

Souths think I hate them, but, my mother intends to bail up their old president George Piggins one day to show him a photo taken of me when I was a kid dressed in the red and green battle colours.

As I walked off the ground on this particular afternoon, I copped plenty of abuse, missiles were thrown at me and even a member elbowed me and had to be dragged away by security. Meanwhile, up in the stands, the people who had thrown missiles at me were in Lesley's face giving her a gobful until they were eventually restrained by the security officers.

It shouldn't be like that.

Even so, referees at my level are a lot better off than whistleblowers in the juniors or out on the local park—at least we have security.

mr jones

In 1998 breakfast radio king Alan Jones started a legal fight with me when he implied I was biased during an interview with the then NRL boss Neil Whittaker. He asked Whittaker, 'Is there a kind of bias out there which is a hangover from the ARL–Super League days and what are you doing about it?' His comments were broadcast to up to 250 000 people and they heard him suggest I favoured former Super League teams.

The end result of his broadcast was I suffered a humiliating backlash. Strangers in the street questioned my fairness and integrity. A bloke in the local Woolworths store called me a cheat. Almost a year after Jones made his comments I refereed a Souths–Brisbane match only to have a Rabbitohs fan barge into me by bumping his chest into mine and snarling, 'Jonesy was right, you are a fxxxing cheat!' Also, a lot of comments from my peers, such as 'How many condos do you have in Brisbane?' cut to the bone. They may have been said in a joking manner but the message behind the words angered me. It was an affront and, apart from my integrity and sense of honour, Alan Jones had also attacked my credibility along with my professional reputation.

I immediately commenced legal action against Jones. It wasn't something I did lightly; I was concerned he would fight and I had a lot to lose. After all, his radio show still rewrites ratings records. He was Oxford University educated, he penned speeches for former prime minster Malcolm Fraser and, such is his power of influence, people maintain he can change government policy with a few well-directed phone calls and faxes. Despite this, he had questioned my reputation and I intended to defend it at whatever cost.

I have taken similar action against Peter Peters and Greg Hartley, when they were commentators for 2GB in 1987. They also questioned my integrity so I employed a solicitor and ended up settling out of court. It was never about the money, it was about preserving and defending my integrity. Peters and Hartley were also meant to apologise on air for their comments as part of the reconciliation. Peters interviewed me and as he wrapped up the conversation he said something like, 'Well, that's Bill Harrigan, and he's a ref with a future.' There was no apology for the insult and when I walked out of the commentary box I was furious. After that I vowed I would always protect my integrity.

I decided upon legal action when it became obvious Alan Jones had no intention of retracting what he'd said. I've said it before, but a referee's integrity is of paramount importance—without his credibility intact he has nothing.

Jones, who coached the Wallabies and the Balmain Rugby League team, had armed himself with an eight-page document which, he said, proved I had awarded fifty per cent more penalties to ex-Super League teams than former ARL-aligned sides.

He argued in the New South Wales Supreme Court that his comments were defensible as comment. He presented these facts from the 1998 season: when I refereed Brisbane in four matches the Broncos received thirty-three penalties to the opposition's fourteen; when I didn't referee them, Brisbane scored seventy-two points in five games with one hundred against.

It wasn't much to hang a legal case on, but Alan was adamant the sample of statistics wasn't too small. He did concede that before and after his allegation he'd made comments that I was one of the games 'best referees', but he argued that didn't mean I wasn't biased during the '98 season.

In the court transcript he said: 'Before the [Super League] war began, Bill was our best referee. In 1998, when so-called "peace" was declared, my view was and [is] amplified by the figures, that Bill was not on Rugby League's side but the side of Super League.'

He maintained he'd raised the issue of my penalty count because he hoped it would help me handle the 1998 finals with a greater degree of 'objectivity'.

My own feeling was Alan could have been more objective by interviewing me and putting his questions to me, but he told the court he spoke to Neil Whittaker because he was the only person who could handle the 'situation'.

On the matter of my refereeing, I pressed the point that there was much more to judging a referee than cold, hard statistics. You can't rely on the final score and penalty count as the sole indicators for a referee's performance. The game has too many variables and situations to consider before judging a referee. For instance, penalties are given for various reasons—some are mandatory, others are at the referee's discretion.

The judge agreed and in her summing up of the case on 27 July 2001 Acting Justice Jane Matthews said: 'The allegation of bias . . . is a very serious one to make against a referee, particularly a referee of Mr Harrigan's prominence.' She also agreed I was upset because I pride myself on my integrity and that it was 'highly probable' my personal and professional reputation had been diminished in the minds of a large sector of Jones's audience. Acting Justice Matthews awarded me a total of $90 000 costs.

I was happy it was over because, even when you know you're in the right, legal action is a draining process.

To his credit, Alan offered his hand and wished me the best in the up-and-coming Origin game as he left the court. It was a far cry from the pitched battle he had just been fighting to prove my 'overwhelming bias' and how unfit he thought I was for the job back in '98.

I accepted the gesture for what it was—fair and sportsmanlike. Alan has got on with his life as one of Australia's leading radio broadcasters keeping everyone from politicians to sports administrators on their toes—and I applaud that.

I hope he appreciates I have kicked on with my own career as a Rugby League referee who values his integrity enough to fight a legal battle.

Hopefully there are no hard feelings.

care for kids

While the people who bag me, make crank calls, scream abuse from the outer and write poison-pen letters about my refereeing have made a definite *negative* impact on my life, they pale into insignificance when I compare them to the *positive* influence a group of special kids had on me throughout 1999.

I crossed paths with these amazing children when I volunteered to spend a few hours each Tuesday with them as part of the Captain Starlight program, which is dedicated to doing all it can to bring a smile to kids in their time of need.

Many of these boys and girls were fighting terrible illnesses, such as cancer or leukaemia, and their struggle taught me there's a lot more to life than worrying about people who feel their team was unfairly penalised, or that my ten metres looked more like eleven. The parents and the hospital volunteers who dote over these kids also taught me plenty about inner strength, compassion and commitment

I decided I'd spend my time with the kids reading stories because my kids had always loved story time at our place each evening—I'd make it theatrical by exaggerating the monsters' noises and tickling them at certain points in the story. I figured I could spread that kind of cheer around at the Prince of Wales children's hospital too. There was no publicity or media for 'Referee Bill's Story Time', I just wanted it to be the kids and me.

I'd turn up and read a book to the kids in the Starlight room, which would be broadcast to the kids in their rooms if they couldn't make it out of bed. I'd put my jersey on, read a number of stories for an hour or so and then I'd ask questions relating to the stories and a footy question to finish off. The correct answers would receive something I'd taken along as a prize, like caps and miniature balls. There were times when I'd look at their innocent faces and I would come close to losing it. On my way out, I'd visit some of the kids in their beds.

I learnt not to ask kids about their fellow patients the hard way. Sometimes when I'd enter a ward and see an empty bed I'd ask whether the kid had gone home. But they hadn't been discharged . . . they'd died . . . and being told that by another kid who was battling to stay alive was tough. Sometimes the children would request certain books for the following Tuesday and when I'd turn up . . . the child who'd wanted *Blinky*

Bill or the kid who'd asked for *The Magic Pudding* had left us.

I would be churning inside but somehow I managed to keep it together. Referee Bill would pull on his jersey, hand out a stack of footballs and other memorabilia and then read his stories. I learnt to be careful in the way I spoke to the children and tried not to say things like 'I hope to see you next week', because the chances were they mightn't have been there next week, some were fighting to see the night out. So my farewell was geared towards offering the children some hope. I'd say 'Well, that's the end of Referee Bill's Story Time. I hope to see you next week . . . no, I don't . . . I hope you're all better and gone home.' With that, I would close the book, walk out of the hospital—out of sight of the children—and try to hold back the tears. On some occasions I'd bawl all the way back to the NRL offices in Moore Park.

Even now, years later, I still choke up when I speak about those kids. The longer I stuck it out the harder it was to turn up because I'd be badly affected by it. I couldn't help it. How could you not get involved or be deeply affected by such suffering? I think I took it even harder seeing those kids and thinking of my own boys who were the same age. My wife, Lesley, thought I should stop going because I was forming attachments and it was breaking my heart.

There was one boy, Steve, whom I became close to. It was a hell of a rollercoaster ride because one day I'd hear he was swimming and doing real well so I'd drop my guard and think he was going to be all right, and then suddenly he'd be back in hospital with little hope of seeing the next morning. There was nothing I could do except hope he would pull through and wonder how on earth his parents coped. As it turned out, Steve *always* pulled through and I was over the moon when he lived out his Starlight Foundation wish to visit the US Navy's Top Gun school for fighter pilots. That was a triumph. Steve and his family eventually moved out to the deep west of New South Wales, and it's long been my hope that he's living a rich, fulfilling and loving life.

Eventually Referee Bill's Story Time stopped in 2000. I justified it to myself because the new NRL referees' bosses wanted us to be at the office early each Tuesday morning so I couldn't do the reading. Although I could have gone on a Wednesday or Thursday—I just couldn't put myself through the emotional grinder again.

To this day my actions still haunt me. I wish I had told the Starlight people that it was too overwhelming for me on some occasions and I'd start again after a break.

I help indirectly these days by participating in charities for the kids' hospitals and research institutes— I was the MC for the 2003 Star Ball for Starlight—but I can't speak highly enough of the doctors, nurses, hospital staff and volunteers who work the kids wards, day after day. They are the heroes.

grand final 1999

'll remember this game until the day I die, and not just for the atmosphere generated by the world-record crowd of 107 000 spectators in the Stadium that was to host the 2000 Sydney Olympics. The game itself was a cracker; a match of two completely different halves with the Dragons dominating in the first forty minutes before being overwhelmed in the second. The Storm, spearheaded by four-times grand final winner Glenn Lazarus and rampaging Tawera Nikau turned the tide and the Dragons were soon battening down the hatches.

Anthony Mundine, who quit football the following season to try and win a world boxing title, had the chance to give the Dragons a greater lead but the ball was knocked out of his hands as he tried to ground it for a try. From my position in the middle, I saw that as the moment the Storm realised they could win.

But the reason I'll remember this game is because I had to deliver what many called the Rugby League 'call of the millennium' after Melbourne Storm's Brett Kimmorley chipkicked across the field to winger Craig Smith. St George–Illawarra centre Jamie Ainscough responded to the challenge by flooring his Storm opponent with a high shot in the Dragons' in-goal area and it sent Smith into Disneyland. Both men landed in a crumpled heap on the ground, and I can remember seeing the ball tumble out from the mess.

My touch judge, Col White, screamed for me to 'CHECK IT OUT, BILLY! CHECK IT OUT!' I blew time-out and told Col to tell me exactly what he'd seen before I sent the message to the man upstairs—the video ref. At this stage many people at the ground, including my touchies, thought I would call a penalty try but I was actually considering whether this could be an eight point try. It needed to be clarified whether Smith had lost the ball due to an act of foul play. Had he been subjected to an act of foul play while scoring a try?

Col said Smith had been hit high but he wasn't aware of the impact point, nor could he say for certain if Smith had grounded the ball. Based on Col's report I sent a message to the video referee, Chris Ward, asking him to check whether the Melbourne Storm player had been deprived from scoring as a result of an act of foul play (in the shape of a high shot).

With a premiership riding on his call Chris studied the video replay for what seemed to be an eternity—though my concern wasn't the time it took for him to make a decision, I was more worried about getting it right.

I watched the vision replayed over and over on the big screen and, as far as I was concerned, it was obvious Smith had dropped the ball as a result of being hit in the head by Ainscough. Chris and I were in constant contact throughout the process and I could hear him discussing his predicament with Tim Mander and Ian Smith who were sitting in the box with him.

Tim said, 'No doubt it's not a try, but I don't think you can say that.'

Chris replied, 'That's an impossibility, I'm not going for a . . .' Chris stopped in mid-sentence as they viewed the incident from another angle that showed the reality of the situation. From the first angle they had viewed they weren't going to entertain a penalty try, but after viewing the second replay, reality struck. Penalty try.

After a number of replays, I said, 'Chris, talk to me.'

Chris said, 'Billy, I reckon he would have scored if he had not been hit in the head, and it was an illegal hit. Therefore a big call . . . it's going to be a penalty try.'

With that, I awarded a penalty try and I can still see the looks of disbelief on the Dragons' faces as they realised what had happened. Matt Geyer booted the goal and the Storm won by two points.

In the aftermath of the Storm's victory there were numerous rumblings of a conspiracy theory, of me giving the Storm a leg-up because of their Super League ties, but I handled the game fairly and squarely . . . Jamie Ainscough hit Craig Smith, not me! There are still some old Dragons who claim I robbed them but I know in their hearts they realise the decision made that fateful afternoon was the correct one and the only one possible.

Melbourne defeated St George–Illawarra 20–18
Crowd: 107 558

darcy lawler

The late Darcy Thomas Elgan Lawler is remembered in Rugby League folklore as the referee who ruled the roost during the golden era of Gasnier, Holman, Raper, Kelly and Churchill. Former referees' boss Eric Cox nominated the one time milkman from beachside Maroubra as the greatest whistleblower he ever saw. 'A champion at a time the game was as hard and demanding as it has ever been,' he said. 'A man of great authority on the field.' On the surface I agree Lawler's career record justifies such an opinion. From 1948 to 1963 he established a record by refereeing seven grand finals. A huge effort.

When I equalled Darcy's record of seven grand finals in 2000, I realised I might be on the verge of obtaining my goal to be the best referee ever.

On the Wednesday night before a grand final, the referees have a dinner where life members are toasted and relive past memories with each other and the current referees. I'm embarrassed to say that on this night in 2000 I thought it was time to meet the great Darcy Lawler, so I turned to Mick Stone and said, 'Which one is Darcy Lawler? I want to say g'day.'

Mick replied, 'You're a bit late, Billy, he died years ago.'

I felt like a bloody idiot.

The man they called the legend. The man I set out to beat—and I didn't even know he'd passed on. Nor could I have recognised him had he been alive. Not good.

Worse was still to come as I found out an ugly shadow of doubt has settled over Lawler's career. People, such as former Western Suburbs hard man Noel Kelly, put their name—and reputation—on the line to confirm that the old rumours that Darcy Lawler would manipulate some matches were true. Reading Kelly's testimony in the official South Sydney Juniors history book *The Juniors: The Best for the Best* in September 2002 left me reeling. It was a terrible kick in the guts.

My initial reaction was to dismiss it as nonsense, but I stepped back and looked at the facts. The Juniors would never have printed such a statement if there was no truth to it. After all, Lawler was the club's secretary–manager for twenty-seven years. Secondly, the person who relayed Kelly's belief was respected sportswriter Ian Heads, and from my dealings with 'Headsy' I believe he's far too credible a person to allow such a statement to go unchallenged.

Heads gave Kelly's account of the 1963 grand final, the famous mud bath between St George and Wests which produced the well-known 'gladiator' photo of Norm Provan and Arthur Summons embracing after the Dragon's victory which the Winfield Cup was based on. It would seem the stench that followed that game had nothing to do with the stink from the Sydney Cricket Ground slush.

According to Kelly, fellow Magpie Jack Gibson told him before the match: '"Mate, we can't win . . . Darcy has backed them [St George]. Gibson has independently confirmed the story, nominating the go-between who "put Darcy's money on".' St George won the grand final 8–3. Kelly continued: 'I will never forget Darcy Lawler for what he did that day. I have no doubt we were robbed.'

I wish I had never seen that allegation. It rams home the fact that *every* referee must keep his nose clean because no one gets away with even a whiff of controversy. You can't allow yourself to be compromised because, when you die, one of the few things you leave behind is your name, and nothing is worth losing that for.

I have never been approached by anyone offering a bribe. I have never heard of it happening in my era, either. If I was approached I wouldn't hesitate to tell the person offering the bribe to get lost and then I'd report them to the appropriate authorities. My integrity can never be bought. I live by it and I protect it. It's the only thing in life that can never be taken from me.

You can only give it away yourself and, if you do, you can never get it back completely. It's worth protecting.

I have been 'leant on' twice while overseas refereeing test matches. When I controlled the Wales–PNG match in Cardiff in 1991, a Welsh official approached me before kick off.

'This is a very important game for Wales, Bill,' he said. 'It's our first game since 1984 . . . we need to do *really* well.'

I said, 'I'm sure it's important for PNG too.'

'You don't understand,' he replied. 'Wales is a Rugby stronghold and for League to emerge we need to do well tonight.'

'This sounds like a pre-match pep talk you should be giving to the players, not me.' I could see where the conversation was headed and wanted no part of it. I told the Welshman his team would do well if they played well. Then I left him to stew in his own juice.

The second incident occurred in France in the lead-up to an Australia–France test. This time a French journalist tried to emphasise how important it was for *his* country to do well. He told me that he could arrange a spread in a French modelling magazine for me, provided France did well against the Kangaroos. He continued gibbering, and while his English was terrible, the message was all too crystal clear for my liking, so I told him to beat it.

My way to deal with both incidents was to nip the conversations in the bud and walk away—it simply isn't worth listening to such rubbish.

As for Darcy, he was the referee referred to as the legend, the one I wanted to eclipse. I still believe Lawler's list of on-field achievements is something every referee should aspire to, but his lamentable legacy—a questionable reputation as a referee who could be bought—has gutted me. I just wish I'd never heard about it and I still hope it's not true.

head games

I've always subtly and professionally used mind games to keep ahead of the field, but I copped some of my own in 2001.

It started in the half-time break of the Bulldogs–Parramatta game at Telstra Stadium in round twenty-three. I'd just finished talking to my touchies about the first half and I pointed out I probably needed to keep an eye on the Bulldogs around the rucks and the ten metres. They, along with my video referee, Chris Ward, agreed.

Then Peter Louis and Brian Grant, the referees' coaches at the time, walked in and Granty said, 'How's it going?'

I said, 'Good, we were just talking about the rucks and ten.'

Louis then jumped in and gave me a spray about the lack of action against Parramatta. He believed they were the problem around the rucks and ten metres.

The dressing-down he gave me left not just me gobsmacked, but the touchies and Chris as well. I'd never experienced anything like it as a referee. It was a half-time talk some coaches might give their players after a poor first half, but we had had a good half and we all agreed about the Bulldogs. So how come the coach saw it a different way?

I didn't appreciate Peter's comments at all and, when he left the room, I spent the next couple of minutes composing myself to take on the second half. *I* knew what I had to do and wasn't going to be intimidated by the half-time chat. But it was hard not to think about Peter's outburst: was it fair dinkum or was he playing head games?

There had been a couple of other occasions in the preceding weeks when I had wondered where Louis and Grant were coming from. In particular, they had grilled me about some decisions in my first game of the semis and I felt like I was in the witness box. When I approached them about it, after explaining my actions, Granty said they agreed with me. I scoffed and asked what the hell was that earlier grilling all about then. Granty said, 'Just keeping the discussion interesting.' I could see a pattern forming and thought to myself: mind games are being played here or I'm being set up for a fall.

I have never taken my status as the game's top referee for granted—as the referee who controls the grand final—I realised a long time ago it's something that is way too easy to lose. An NRL referee is at the mercy of someone else's decision as to who gets the nod for the big games, and who gets left behind. While I have accepted that much of my destiny is out of my hands, I've always aimed to make any decision for a big game an easy one by refereeing myself into the appointment.

Throughout the 2001 finals series, however, there was a concerted push for Paul Simpkins to referee the grand final. I came under a lot of media pressure as Simpkins gained widespread support to knock me off my pedestal. There was a genuine move to build him up and he was performing.

I wasn't happy about the way Louis and Grant tried to make me feel insecure during the final series and, well after the season was over, I let Granty know it. I told him I didn't think Paul was refereeing as well as they'd made out to the press. And he agreed!

Granty said Paul was refereeing well, but he was concerned about me going into the semis thinking I had the grand final wrapped up, so they had decided to try and shake me up. The aim, said Grant, was to drag me back to the other blokes' level.

When I heard that I was infuriated. If Paul Simpkins was messing with my head I'd say fair enough, but I couldn't believe my coaches would do that. Surely, as the coach, you would want the best possible performance from all your referees—meaning you'd push everyone forwards, not backwards. I couldn't understand their logic when a referee's performance reflects on all referees and the NRL, and I made it painfully clear that as coaches it was wrong to mess with one of your team's thoughts.

Granty, calling me by the nickname the other referees have given me, finished off by saying, 'King, you perform best when placed under pressure and you didn't let us down.'

letters from the edge

If you want to see passion, get a Papua New Guinean local talking about Rugby League—they can't get enough of it! I reckon anyone with a Rugby League profile of any sort has, at some time, received a letter from a PNG fan pledging everything from lifelong friendship to their ardent support. Their passion shines through in each of the letters I've received from Port Moresby and beyond. I find such sentiments a far cry from a poison-pen letter by a Broncos supporter who is dirty about their team being on the wrong end of a penalty count, or the rantings of a Souths supporter hoping all refs rot in hell!

A trademark of the Papua New Guinean letters is the way the author butters you up for one hell of an ask in the final paragraph. I received one such letter from Benny of Boroko in 2001. Accompanying his note was a beautifully carved wooden eagle and the carefully printed words in his letter were the kind every whistleblower wants to read about himself with such gems as my being the 'best referee in the world'. *But* there was a motive.

> *Dearest Bill Hurgan* [sic],
> *I use to admire your ways of referee. I am one of your supporters in PNG in all games you reff* [sic]. *All games you reff* [sic] *such as club games, State of Origion* [sic] *and like this one, Kumuls vs Kangaroos. I am always at the back of your support. This is my privilege to see you live in PNG reffing* [sic] *Kumuls and Kangaroos. I rate you the best referee in the whole world. With that I present you with this Eagle. I am your best friend and I'm requesting you for the old jerseys. Old Kangaroos jerseys from 1–13. Old jersey one each from all the clubs in Australia.*
> *Yours faithfully,*
> *Benny*

It's amazing how much power the Benny's of that part of the world think I wield. While I couldn't provide the set of used Australian jumpers or the jersey from each NRL club as he'd requested, I did send him a token—and full marks for trying.

Brisbane Broncos big forward Gorden 'Raging Bull' Tallis and I haven't always seen eye to eye, we've had several run-ins and plenty of controversies. But the 'feud' between us is more of a media beat-up than any real dislike on our part.

News Limited

Sending Manly captain Geoff Toovey off to the sin-bin in the opening match of the new NRL in 1998.

News Limited

Bob Fulton is well-known for telling the media that he hoped I would be run over by a cement truck back in 1987 when we first crossed paths. After his Manly team's loss in 1998 he had a go at my refereeing and my hairstyle, calling me a 'lair'.

News Limited

We referees are a pretty close bunch, even though we train hard against each other. This photo was taken during the early Super League days. Left to right: Tim 'Pinhead' Mander, Brian Grant, Steve Clark and me.

The media have often criticised my profile, branding me 'arrogant' and 'Hollywood', but if I can use my name to help others, then I will. In 2003 I sang as part of the Westmead Children's Hospital fundraiser and dressed up in full Kiss make-up.

Happy Medium Photo Co

Referees get abused and threatened all the time, but it's nice to know that when I referee at Townsville I have a few fans in the crowd.

ABOVE
People always want to know which team I supported as a child. Ironically, Souths supporters think I have it in for them.

RIGHT
Me and my three eldest boys: Will (on top), Matthew and Andrew.

TOP
My wife, Lesley. Meeting Lesley reaffirmed my belief in fate—she's given me strength and love when others have been lining up to put the boot in.

BOTTOM
Holding my youngest son, Jed, just after his birth, with his older brother Andrew.

TOP

In the 1997 grand final my eldest son, Matthew, ran my water for me. He experienced the atmosphere of the dressing-room and on the ground in front of over 58 000 people.

BOTTOM

All of my boys are involved in the game and visit the dressing-rooms to talk to their favourite players and get autographs. This is my youngest son, Jed, sitting on Gorden Tallis's lap after the Brisbane–Parramatta game in round seven, 2003.

When Lesley and I got married I wanted everything to be perfect: and it was, although she had no idea what was about to happen that day.

the gould league

When he isn't under the pressure of coaching, Phil 'Gus' Gould is one of the game's great ambassadors: he's thoughtful, forthright and a tremendous observer of the game at all levels. If he criticises the referees, it is normally constructive, and, it has even heartened me on quite a few occasions to see he's gone into bat for the whistleblowers when others have appeared hell bent on ripping us apart.

But Gus hasn't always been so ambivalent—there was a time when he seemed to think he was above the game and he would do his utmost to bully the refs. Like me, Gus has strong views and if he believes in something he'll refuse to back down, even when there's a crowd of people yelling at him to sit down and shut up. Our clashes throughout his playing and coaching career were often a bitter battle because we are both strong-willed men and neither of us would take a backward step.

Our first run-in occurred in a 1986 Monday night footy game between Souths and Wests at the Sydney Cricket Ground, back when Gus was playing for Souths and I was still a young referee. I had sin-binned him for an indiscretion, but he refused to go. He just stood there glaring at me in disbelief. I wasn't in the mood to entertain him.

'You can go NOW!' I barked. 'If you don't go, we don't play—it doesn't worry me at all.'

Gus knew I was serious and he finally turned on his heels and stormed back towards the Rabbitohs' dressing-room.

'Who does that guy think he is?' I said under my breath.

Our next bout occurred in Perth, when Gus coached the 1989 Canterbury Bulldogs side. Plenty was at stake because the match was effectively a sudden-death semi-final that had arrived a month early for the Dogs and Canberra. As the first ever NSWRL game played on the West Coast there was intense interest in the clash. Over 20 000 people turned up to watch and it was beamed back live to Sydney by Channel Nine. Viewers watched Canterbury play with their trademark determination and they even lead at one stage, 14–6. But the Raiders rallied and two late tries allowed Canberra to surge home, 18–14.

The Dogs' season was over and Gus blamed me for the defeat. For a man who has often been described by his players and fans as a cool and calculated character, his emotions definitely got the better of him this day because he stormed down to the referees' dressing-room, barged through the door and unloaded on me.

Gus was red-faced and yelled, 'You cost me the game! You hurt my players—come and look what you've done to my players because they're broken-hearted, some are even crying.'

Gus had overstepped the mark, but rather than becoming involved in a slanging match—or worse— I told him to leave before he did something he might later regret.

Gus refused to leave and continued to abuse me. I remained calm and warned him that, like me, he was answerable to the League for any charge of misconduct. Yet again, Gus refused to take the tip. Instead he ripped off his tie and said he was talking to me as a man, not a member of the League, and again he challenged me to see the effect the loss had on his players, which he wrongly attributed to my refereeing.

'Come and see what you've done!' he screamed.

I remained firm, ordering him to beat it.

In the end someone dragged him out of my face, but I could hear him continue to rant and rave outside my dressing-room. It was emotional behaviour and I thought long and hard about what action I'd take.

I walked back to the hotel from the ground with my touchies, Col Jones and Col White. The Bulldogs were staying in the same hotel and arrived in their bus as we approached the hotel. One of my touchies wanted to wait outside while the players disembarked and headed to their rooms. I refused and said, 'We're walking straight in fellas.'

As we waited to get into the lift, the players entered the foyer and made their way towards us. The same touch judge wanted to wait and get into another elevator, but I refused.

'No way,' I fumed. 'We're going to get in with them and we're going to hold our heads up high because we've done nothing wrong.'

So, we were crammed into the middle of the Bulldogs pack and the atmosphere, as you might imagine, was icy cold. It wouldn't have taken much for it to erupt into an ugly situation. Fortunately though, one of the players made a one-line remark, which cracked everyone up, especially me, and we all left the lift laughing.

Even so, I was still in the frame of mind to report Gus to the NSWRL for gross misconduct. The following morning, however, Gus approached me at breakfast and said while he still didn't agree with some of my rulings, he was terribly sorry for the manner in which he'd behaved. I accepted his apology and decided not to take the matter any further.

Gus and I locked horns again in 1994 at Cronulla's home ground.

Gus, then coach of Penrith, was sitting on the reserves bench close to the play and as the game progressed he became infuriated, yelling out to me that the penalty count was lopsided. When I heard him direct foul language at me I asked my touch judge to confirm if Gus had said what I thought he had. He had, so I walked over towards Gould and said 'No more, be quiet'.

When Penrith was awarded a penalty he recommenced his tirade: 'At least we'll get the chance to practise one tap-kick move!' I later learned that was the Panthers' first penalty in seventy-three minutes, but it didn't excuse his behaviour. Gus had left me with no alternative except to call time-off and order him to leave the field.

'If you want to yell abuse at me, get behind the fence and join the others,' I said. But, in a scene reminiscent of our first meeting at the SCG in 1986 and then the Perth dressing-room, Gus shrugged his shoulders and said he wouldn't leave.

It was developing into a Mexican standoff so I warned him the game wouldn't start until he left. *Again*, he refused to leave, even though the crowd was booing and hissing him. It took the intervention of Panthers skipper John Cartwright to convince Gus to do the right thing and leave. Although, when Gus departed, he played the clown by pretending to return to the sideline and then, to the jeers of the disbelieving mob, he jumped outside the fence. His sideshow must've looked just as ridiculous to the television audience.

It was bad, *really bad*, and I had no hesitation in filing a report that opened a huge can of worms for the NSWRL. The press photographers captured Gould clapping me off the field which added even further drama to the situation. It seemed so childish, but, as in Perth, Gould blamed me for his team's 32–0 loss. Increasing his fury was my having sin-binned two of his men.

As a result of the Shark Park madness, NSWRL boss John Quayle dragged Phil and me into to his office in Phillip Street to sort out the mess. Quayle was faced with the unpalatable situation where the New South Wales Origin coach and one of the code's top referees were at loggerheads. He spoke to us individually and then together. But he faced a dilemma: did he back the coach or the referee, because Gould refused to admit to anything and I refused to back down. I pointed out that I had a touch judge as my witness, but Gould, a former law student, countered saying he had people from the reserves bench prepared to back him up. It was a stalemate, and the NSWRL didn't need the grief.

In the end, the NSWRL brokered a deal described by some as 'diplomacy' but in reality it wasn't. Basically I withdrew my complaint; Penrith was fined $4000 for the comments and Gus apologised. In Quayle's presence, Gus and I agreed for the best interest of Rugby League to publicly shake hands and get on with life. The entire matter was swept under the carpet within minutes of our agreeing to their terms, though, to this day Gus maintains he didn't say what I accused him of, while I'm still adamant he did yell abuse at me. We had a press conference, which was a joke really because neither of us wanted to be there and deep down neither

Gus nor I really believed it when we said everything was 'fine'.

I should stress Gus and I get on well now; perhaps we've mellowed with age.

I know Gus views referees and touch judges differently these days after having had first-hand experience as a touchie. In 2002 Gus donned the referee's uniform and ran the line in the pre-season charity shield match, Souths versus Saints. It was done as part of a story for Channel Nine's *The Footy Show*. As a commentator and critic of referees and touch judges, Gus decided to see it from our point of view. It was a case of put up or shut up; Gus chose to put up.

He had to attend referees' training and I spent sessions with him preparing him for his debut. We covered rules, positioning, communication and more training. After a couple of weeks and a practical session refereeing a practice game at the Sydney Roosters' training, he was ready.

Gus only got to run the line in the charity shield game, but the desired effect was achieved. He acknowledged it was a lot harder than he thought and it changed his views on referees and touchies. The story came across very well and I was surprised by the amount of positive feedback. Gus is still critical on a referee's performance if it's warranted—sometimes he has to be in his role as a commentator—but there is a new-found respect.

he's only the referee

Whenever I speak at a sportsman's dinner or charity bash I put a diner in the hot seat to highlight the pressure we refs are under when making a split-second decision on the run.

I ask the unsuspecting diner to tell me something about the person at the other end of the room whom I'm pointing at. While that might sound simple enough, it isn't because there's always a mass of people and tables, the light is dim and waiters might even be moving about serving dessert, or the view of the person I single out might be partially obstructed by another person at his table. At the same time I get someone else to stand on a chair behind my guinea pig and they enjoy an uninterrupted view of the surroundings. When they're arranged I ask, 'What colour wine is the man I'm pointing at drinking and how full is his wine glass? Tell me NOW!'

I watch the poor diner at ground level crane his neck and move his head from side to side in his struggle to spot the bloke. On the other hand, the person standing on the chair has no problem: 'Glass of white, Bill . . . half full.' The person from the elevated position makes it look so easy, the other guests must think the bloke in his seat has hit the turps too fast. He hasn't, he's just helped me explain why radio commentators pick up forward passes referees sometimes miss.

It proves the commentator has a distinct, stress-free advantage from his elevated spot in an air-conditioned box. It also highlights the pressure we whistleblowers endure because, unlike the commentator, the referee must keep a tackle count, enforce the ten metres and keep an eye out for any illegal play. He also has players yapping in his ear, his line of vision is often obstructed by footballers from both sides and, as the game wears on, he might even be tired. But if he misses one dodgy pass the armchair critics see red! 'Who is that moron,' they scream breathlessly. 'What a joke . . . the ref's a disgrace! Is he blind?' The reaction is always the same: *attack, attack, attack.*

The critics and commentators don't seem to understand that, while they enjoy an uninterrupted view of the game, the referee does not. They seem to think we see the game from their angle.

People must accept mistakes will always be made through human error. They should also appreciate the really good referees minimise those mistakes because they know how to get into position to make decisions and they work damn hard to get there.

Sadly, a lot of people who commentate and report on the game don't seem to appreciate the level of work we do. What consumes a huge chunk of air time on weekend talkback radio, and then acres of newspaper space the following day, is how the whistleblower stuffed up, but there's hardly any mention of the player who missed the tackle to let the try in.

I used to get upset with my father because he'd listen to the radio and then relay what the likes of Ray Hadley or Warren Ryan and Johnny Gibbs had said about my performance—even though I'd told him I didn't care and didn't want to know. I rarely read the papers these days because, as far as referees are concerned, it's mainly negative.

There's a definite culture throughout Rugby League of 'Oh well, he's *only* the referee'. And I've seen this attitude from players, commentators, spectators and, most worryingly, the parents of my kids' team-mates. It's an attitude that desperately needs to change because the day is fast approaching when the refs are going to say at 3 p.m. on a match day, 'Forget this, I don't need this grief . . . I'm going home. See you later.'

Perhaps that's what's needed to make the critics finally appreciate that the whistleblower is an important part of the game and he should be afforded respect.

In 2002 a young ref controlled my son's team in the Cronulla competition. He was doing his best, but that wasn't good enough for the father of one of my son's team-mates. He went berserk and tore strips off the young referee . . . It was ugly and he was genuinely shocked when I told him to put a cork in it. 'This bloke's costing *our* team,' he whined. 'He's hurting *our* team.'

That didn't wash with me—I saw a referee trying to do a tough job so I told him to stop picking on the kid and let him control the game.

I don't watch refereeing through rose-tinted glasses either. I readily accept not every referee is great, but not every footballer is a star, either. The difference is that the referee at any level is the whipping boy. Whenever Darren Lockyer, Gorden Tallis, Andrew Johns, Brad Fittler and Braith Anasta have poor games it hardly rates a mention in the media. If the referee makes a blunder he's belted from pillar to post and his right to be out in the middle is questioned.

There are some excellent reporters and commentators who know the game backwards, but some people consider themselves experts when they clearly aren't and never will be. They survive because they have been to plenty of games and know how to throw a match report together by going to a press conference and listening to what the coaches say.

The media bashings used to get under my skin and upset me, but these days my reaction when a referee cops a serve is to ask myself a few things about the critic: Who is the reporter/commentator? Which team does he support? Did he have a bet on the game? Did he play much park footy? Was he influenced by what the coaches had to say after the match? How often does he bag the referees? *Has he ever refereed?*

While I concede there'll always be room for improvement from the referees, the fact is Australia boasts the best Rugby League whistleblowers in the world. No matter where else you might look—New Zealand, England, France, Papua New Guinea, Russia, Lebanon, the United States or even Morocco—there's none better. But I also know that fact gets lost amid the media bashings and the intense scrutiny of bar stool experts. Unless everybody works to remove the 'he's only the ref' attitude, the day will come when there won't be any more referees.

parra-battered

Referees live and die by their decisions and I was *buried* the night I sent four Parramatta players to the sin-bin in their round seventeen match against Newcastle in July 2002.

The Knights had played the Eels at Parramatta Stadium just three weeks earlier and had eventually dominated and rolled right over the top of the Eels. Result—a win for Joey Johns and the Knights. I knew this would be fresh in Brian Smith's mind and he would be planning to prevent Newcastle from a repeat performance, just like any other coach would.

I made sure I went into the game—as I always do— fully prepared. I always study teams before matches, look at their players and their idiosyncrasies. It's my 'homework' and I've been doing it for seventeen years. It allows me to be proactive, rather than reactive and it's why I've been able to let games flow and keep penalties to a minimum.

At the coin toss I rarely say anything to the captains except 'enjoy yourself fellas', but on this occasion I advised them to take the tip and not lie all over the tackled player. Both sides started out fine but, as Newcastle started to get a roll on, Parramatta went back to slowing the play the ball down. I went into proactive mode straightaway and started warning players on the run not to hold down the tackled player or slow the play the ball. I was yelling myself hoarse trying to make them get off the tackled player.

The Eels refused to listen to me and I can vividly recall a Parramatta player expressing his fury at being 5–0 down in the penalty count, but like his team-mates, he refused to acknowledge *why* they were on the receiving end. Even after I advised him the tally could get worse if they didn't get off the tackled player quicker, they still persisted.

Eventually I whistled up a couple of penalties against Parramatta for holding the player down. I continued to warn them on the run and I warned their stand-in captain, Daniel Wagon, after a Parramatta try. The Eels still persisted with their tactics so I called time-out and gave the team an official warning. I warned them a third time because they obviously didn't understand my message. I even gave them leeway after the half-time break by penalising them twice rather than using the bin . . . but, rather than make the most of my leniency, the Eels continued with the holding down and spoiling tactics. I heard a Parramatta player yell to his team-mates 'keep doing it' and that did me.

I'd had a gutful and in the fifty-fifth minute I binned Michael Buettner. 'You won't cop the warning, have a spell,' I said.

Three minutes later Nathan Hindmarsh did exactly the same thing and I binned him. Captain Nathan Cayless challenged my decision. 'I was warning them every time you were off the field,' I gasped in disbelief [Cayless had been on the interchange]. 'I gave an extra two penalties after half-time to get your act together. You were doing it on purpose.'

I thought my words were fair and reasonable, but Cayless took exception to my tone—the tone of a frustrated man. He said, 'I'm talking to you with respect, how are you talking to me? You are talking down to me.'

I said, 'I'm talking to you in the same way you're talking to me.' With that I waved him away.

Five minutes later Adam Dykes joined the queue and I couldn't help but wonder whether the Eels wanted to be penalised out of contention. 'You get out,' I said pointing to the sideline. 'You won't learn will you?'

Then the final insult occurred in the seventy-third minute with Buettner giving my touchie a spray when Newcastle's Mark Hughes scored the match-winning try. 'He's wearing the same shirt I am,' I fumed while pointing to the touchie. 'And you've given him a gobful. That's unacceptable, have another ten.' Buettner stormed off back to the sin-bin as Dykes ran back on.

It was twenty minutes of madness . . . and twenty minutes I hope I never have to go through again.

People have suggested my decision to use the bin was about ego, but that's way off the mark. I simply had a job to do—to keep the rucks clear and keep the game moving—had Parramatta heeded my warnings they wouldn't have lost four men to the bin. They probably would've won the game. On the flipside, had I not policed the rucks and penalised Parramatta, Newcastle would have been complaining—and rightly so.

I walked off the field feeling as if I'd passed a serious test, and I was heartened by the number of NRL officials who wanted to praise me for the courage of my convictions. Referees' boss, Peter Louis, came into the dressing-room and said something like, 'Well done, Billy. It's about time someone stood up to them, they've been doing it for too long.'

The funny thing is I'd been through a tougher experience in my rookie season when I sent off a player and binned five others in a match between Manly and Norths at North Sydney Oval. While there was a definite reaction back then, it lacked the intensity of Brian Smith's response at the post-match press conference for the Parramatta–Newcastle game. He brought up Bob Fulton's old 'cement truck' sentiments and from what I read and heard he was convinced his team had done nothing wrong: 'Bill Harrigan is a mighty, mighty fine referee, he's been without doubt the best referee I've seen on a consistent basis but everybody's seen what happened tonight and I think you can understand what my view might be tonight.'

Eels chief executive, Dennis Fitzgerald joined in saying the NRL should put me 'through an anger management course'.

Knights coach Michael Hagan's opinion differed. He suggested I could have pinged someone earlier. Hagan told the *Sunday Telegraph*, 'Full marks to Bill because he was courageous enough to continue on when it was clear they hadn't taken his advice to get off the tackled player quicker.'

In the aftermath of the match, however, his words didn't seem to have the same impact as Smith's and the barrage of criticism from the media and talkback callers.

Hundreds of Parramatta supporters and so-called Rugby League fans rang in to complain about how I robbed the Eels of premiership points. The television news and football shows showed constant replays of me sending the four players to the bin and supporters were whipped into a frenzy.

I can understand why that happened . . . when you watch the television coverage of a game you get a close shot of the tackle but as the players hit the ground the director changes to a long, wide shot and you lose the reality of the ruck. You fail to see the player being held down by a defender holding onto his jumper; you don't see the same guy struggle to get off the ground and then be pulled back; or the spoiling tactic of a hand on the ball.

I watched the TV coverage of that game and it didn't give you a real feel for what was happening out in the middle. It's only when a penalty is given or the commentator specifically asks for a replay that they show an up-close, slow motion shot of the ruck. If you could watch the game again and see all the rucks from the same tight shot, you'd soon see what was frustrating the Newcastle players and me.

Brian Smith took the extraordinary step of writing a column in the *Australian* newspaper demanding an apology from me for publicly suggesting that they intended to slow the play the ball down. The NRL set up a meeting between Brian and I, in which David Gallop, the NRL chief executive, and Graham Annesley tried to broker a peaceful resolution; but it wasn't working.

In the end I asked if Brian and I could sort it out on our own. We had to avoid a major incident—a high profile coach suing the number one referee whilst both were still active was a no-win situation for the NRL or the game. Imagine the repercussions—they wouldn't have been able to appoint me to Parramatta games and it would have been a real mess. Forty-five minutes later Brian and I shook hands and the meeting was over.

A week after the game I attended a Parramatta training session, which Brian Smith and I agreed would be a worthwhile exercise. The intention was to mingle with the players and let them see me go through the hard yakka with them. The players would be able to talk to me and ask questions, if they wanted to, while training in an informal way. However, it ended up being a media circus and looked like a publicity stunt. It was unfortunate the meeting wasn't kept quiet because I thought it was worthwhile and achieved a great deal.

the whipping boy

Even with time, the aftermath of the Newcastle–Parramatta game of 2002 has left a bitter taste in my mouth that won't go away. It was one of the darkest moments in my career when the NRL stood me down for the weekend.

My use of the sin-bin on four separate occasions to punish the Eels when they refused to listen to me, put my name in the headlines for weeks on end, and, even now, a year down the track, I'm often asked at parties, the shopping centre and even my local coffee shop, for my thoughts on that incredible night. While I copped plenty of flak from the media, the Eels and their army of supporters, I was pleasantly surprised by the amount of support I received—people flooded my office with e-mails and faxes telling me to keep my chin up because I'd done the right thing.

I wasn't prepared for what happened next.

I was called to Graham Annesley's office so I could be officially informed that I was being stood down from the following weekend's round. It was only the third time in my career I'd been dropped from first grade, and it bruised my pride.

I continue to think that *if* the NRL believed I'd stuffed up, then they should've kicked me in the pants, pointed out *where* my game had fallen down and then appointed me to a first grade game of lesser importance as punishment.

Graham said the NRL's decision to drop me was to take pressure off me, but I disagree; it actually placed me under greater scrutiny. Instead of giving me room to breathe, their decision made me a media target throughout the week and my return match was under the spotlight.

Before the meeting ended, Graham asked me a question which still rattles me: 'Did you ever think of the big picture?'

My reaction was, 'Huh, what do you mean?'

He continued, 'The game. Did you ever think about the repercussions on the game?'

I replied, 'Do you mean was I asking myself what will this mean to the game—the "big picture"—if I blow a penalty or send a player to the sin-bin? The answer to that Graham is NO!'

I told Graham that when a whistleblower is on the field the big picture looks after itself; he referees the game to the best of his ability and with integrity.

Imagine what would happen if *every* referee stopped and thought about the so-called big picture before he blew his whistle during the match? What kind of games would the fans see then?

In 2003, I was appointed to the return match played at Parramatta Stadium and I knew the previous year's encounter was always going to be a media issue. Channel Nine dwelled on the sin-binnings and drama of the previous season, and when I watched the review tape I noticed how they commented (in the early stages of the match) that Parramatta had already received more penalties—two—than they did in an entire eighty minutes of action twelve months earlier. They kept at it throughout the match, but I got through it unscathed.

Although I've moved on, the fallout from the Eels' sin-binning in 2002 will go down as one of my greatest disappointments.

odd man out

In the lead-up to the 2002 grand final all hell broke loose at the NRL's headquarters when a betting agency advertised it would take bets on the amount of penalties I'd award in the decider.

The bookmakers capitalised on the hullabaloo that followed the 8–2 penalty count in favour of the Sydney Roosters against Brisbane in the preliminary final and their action left NRL chief operating officer Graham Annesley fuming. He labelled the move a 'cheap publicity stunt' and told the media: 'I think it's outrageous and a disgrace . . . to take bets on something like penalties which is solely at the discretion of the referee.'

I didn't give the matter a second thought at the time because week in, week out, I trudge off the paddock with no idea how many penalties I've dished out during the game. It's a statistic I'm not interested in. There have even been times when I've had to ask someone in the referees' dressing-room for the final score.

There's way too much happening during the eighty minutes—such as keeping players back ten metres, looking out for forward passes and knock-ons, watching for high or illegal tackles, communicating with the players, running all over the field to get in the best position—to worry about statistics.

I've since thought about the move for a gambling agency to take money on penalties and I agree it shouldn't be allowed. People would always wonder whether a referee had money on himself to blow, for example, ten penalties to three. It wouldn't be hard to do—if *that* was in a bloke's nature. In an extreme case, high rollers, or even the underworld, could make a lot of cash if a referee was to 'listen' to them, and a referee could have his—or his family's—life threatened if he refused to play ball.

Even without such a betting procedure in place, we're already having our integrity constantly questioned. After the Broncos–Roosters 2002 preliminary final, punters north of the border figured I'd penalised their team out of a grand final berth.

I didn't know it took until the sixty-ninth minute before Bennett's men received their first penalty of the game. Why would I? If someone had asked me when I first blew the whistle in the Broncos' favour I'd have guessed it was midway in the first half.

The fact they were pinged so heavily was their own fault. They refused to listen to me when I continually told them to get back the ten metres. As I said after the game, I worked my butt off to try and get the message through to them. If you watch a tape of the game you'll see I waved my hands around to try and get their attention, as well as yelling at the Brisbane players by their names to get back onside. Those efforts were to no avail because they refused to listen.

Broncos skipper Gorden Tallis told Australian Associated Press journalist Wayne Heming he thought I was inconsistent. 'As a player that is all you want,' said Tallis. 'You don't want anything else but consistency. On Saturday night I don't believe he was . . . it's as simple as that.'

I don't know how Gorden reads the word 'consistency'. I would think if a referee was constantly picking up my team on offside infringements then I'd consider two things. One, my team is *consistently* breaking the rules and two the referee is *consistently* picking us up on it. So, as captain, I would be barking at my team to get onside and give the referee no cause to penalise us.

Tallis was quoted in the *Daily Telegraph* saying of the Roosters' effort: 'They must have the boss of the NRL or somebody really high up in the NRL or God looking on them.'

They didn't need, nor did they have, anyone looking after them. Instead I suggest their coach has them playing disciplined football. As a referee, you get teams working with you as the Roosters did in this game. If one of their number was in front of me he kept right out of the play and throughout the match they fought to get back onside. My memory of that match is that the blokes in red, white and blue played disciplined football, the Broncos did not. In previous years the Broncos were very disciplined and did exactly what the Roosters did.

What grated on me after that match was the assumption from people in (and out of) the Broncos camp that penalty counts should finish either dead level or, at least, close to it. It's a terrible mindset because penalties are used to punish teams—and players —who infringe the rules. No team is entitled to be awarded a penalty because their opponents have had a run of penalties.

If you don't want a lopsided penalty count, you stay back ten metres and keep out of the way if you're offside, you get out of the rucks without interfering with the play the ball and you don't do anything stupid that will bring a penalty. You play disciplined football. It's pretty simple stuff. Yet, Brisbane didn't comprehend it.

The last time I looked in the rule book there was no mention of a whistleblower being obliged to 'square up' in the event of one team enjoying a rush of penalties.

twelve in a row

In 1998 Super League and the ARL came back together to form the NRL and again we were back to the good old days of the State of Origin. In 1998 I took a clean sweep of the series by being appointed to all three games.

In 1999 I was appointed to the first game at Lang Park, but at the end of the game the New South Wales coach Wayne Pearce and some of his officials were not happy with my performance so I was not nominated for Game Two. Mick Stone told me that New South Wales had a problem with my policing of the ten metres, however, if the series went to a decider for the third game I would be back in. I watched New South Wales win Game Two and gave a silent cheer because this meant Game Three was the decider and I would be back in.

But, as often happens when you don't have control of a decision, things can change. And so it did on this occasion with Steve Clark being reappointed to Game Three in Queensland. Although I was very disappointed I copped it on the chin and looked to my belief that these things are meant to happen.

Over the next four years, I dominated the 2000, 2001, 2002 and 2003 series by being appointed to all the games. In doing so, I passed the previous State of Origin record holder, David Manson, who had refereed ten games. I also hold the record for the most Origins in a row—twelve. Officially I have refereed twenty-one State of Origins but my tally is twenty-three because I include the two games that I refereed in the Super League tri-series, after all, they were New South Wales versus Queensland.

In the first game of the 2000 State of Origin series there was some controversy when New South Wales had the ball and two players dropped it. I was standing right on the spot and my touch judges and I believed the ball went backwards so we called play on. Gorden Tallis challenged my decision, screaming out that there were knock-ons. I said, 'No, there weren't—play on.'

Play proceeded down the field and all the way down Gorden never let up about the knock-ons. Finally I said, 'Just shut up and get on with playing.'

'You've had an absolute shocker, Billy,' Gorden replied. 'You're even worse than *that* ref.'

'You're going to the bin for that,' I said.

Meanwhile Ryan Girdler had scored for New South Wales in the corner and I awarded the try. Afterwards,

I turned, looking for Tallis to sin-bin him over his running comments down the field.

Gorden seemed to know he was in strife and must have thought he had nothing to lose so he let rip with the now infamous comment, 'You're a fxxxing cheat.'

The comment was heard by TV and radio listeners and I waved him off, 'I won't cop that from anyone, Gordie . . . get off.'

We stood toe to toe with me directing Gorden to go and Gorden standing his ground. Finally he walked.

The next time I saw Gorden was in the dressing-rooms when he apologised for his comment, although he still believed there was a knock-on. I accepted his apology and said I would look at the incident.

The next day I viewed the video with the other fourteen referees employed by the NRL. Some angles of the television replay tended to show that there was a knock-on, yet other angles were inconclusive. When I asked, 'Who believes there was a knock-on?' all of the referees put their hands up. When I asked if they thought the first touch was a knock-on, half put their hands up. And when I asked who believed the second touch was a knock-on the other half put their hands up. So I found myself in a situation where fourteen referees were divided over which particular incident was a knock-on and no one believed there were two knock-ons.

To this day, I have still not conceded that there was a knock-on. I have certainly told people that, as a group, the other refs believe there was at least one knock-on, but because it was not unanimous I still must go with what I believe—that neither touch was a knock-on.

State of Origin returned to Suncorp Stadium, formerly the cauldron Lang Park, for the first game in 2003. A new stadium, capacity crowd and both sides fired up after the third game draw of 2002. This game always had the makings of being a ripper and the players didn't let anybody down. It was fast, intense and the hits were brutal. New South Wales scraped home after a very entertaining game, which has been rated as one of the best Origins ever. I agree. It was one of the best I have refereed.

One of my most memorable Origin moments from this period was off the field. On the day of a State of Origin game it was common practice for the president of the referees' association or the referees' boss to make a short speech and then issue the embroidered State of Origin jerseys to the match officials for that game about an hour before kick off.

In 2002, just after I learnt I would be controlling the game, Brian Grant told me I was responsible for getting the shorts and socks for the touchies and myself for the first Origin game. I took them out of a box in his office and thought nothing more about it.

On game day, about an hour before the game, I gave the boys their shorts and socks and we all dressed in our own time, putting on our training T-shirts, which is common practice. As kick off time approached I started wondering when our jerseys would be issued.

About ten minutes out from kick off I said, 'Who's giving us our jerseys?'

Darren Gocher said, 'What do you mean? Granty said you've got 'em.'

'No I haven't,' I said.

We kept pacing around the room, keeping warm with only minutes to go, when Darren said, 'Stop mucking around, Billy, and get the jerseys out.'

I said, 'Look at me Goch and read my lips: I . . . don't . . . have . . . the . . . jerseys.'

I grabbed my mobile and rang Granty who was now up in the video box. 'Granty,' I asked, 'who's got the so-and-so jerseys?'

'You've got them,' he said.

'Pig's arse I do.'

With that Granty came down and burst into the room saying, 'You're joking. I told you to get them out of the box. They were in there with the shorts and socks.'

To this day both Granty and I agree to disagree on this point. I've done a lot of Origins and the jerseys were always presented in the shed, fully embroidered.

In the end, we decided to use the jerseys worn by the officials in the earlier game which was the under-19s State of Origin. They had different badges and didn't have one of our major sponsors on them, and they were sweaty and dirty, but they had to do.

It wasn't anywhere near the best pre-match preparation I've experienced but I can sit back and laugh about it now.

grand final 2002

I refereed the 2000 and 2001 grand finals, each played with gusto and courage, and I was on hand as Brisbane and Newcastle did their victory laps around Telstra Stadium.

In 2002, the New Zealand Warriors made it into the grand final and, for the first time, there was a real threat that the premiership trophy would be leaving Australia. It was up to Brad 'Freddie' Fittler's Sydney Roosters to stop the foreign charge.

The game was another hard-fought battle which will be remembered for the legal hit on Brad Fittler by interchange player Richard Villasanti. When Villasanti drove his head straight into Fittler's melon while Freddie tried to regather a loose ball, it proved to be a rallying call for the Roosters. The sight of Fittler being hauled off to have a nasty head gash treated angered the tricolours and the Roosters muscled up. I'm sure the 80 000-strong crowd and worldwide television audience of a few million felt a collective shudder when they saw Roosters tough nut Adrian Morely crunch Villasanti with a hard, but fair, get-square soon after.

The Roosters had made it to the grand final partly thanks to a solid defensive strategy and this game was no different. They tackled hard and the Warriors had no answers.

The 2002 grand final was a special milestone for me because it was my *sixth* consecutive title decider, equalling the record set by Darcy Lawler between 1956 and 1961. It was also my ninth grand final . . . extending my record run.

I set goals at the beginning of every year, with my ultimate goal in 2003 being to be appointed to the grand final. Fate played its part and the 2003 grand final was my record-breaking seventh consecutive grand final and tenth grand final overall . . . and I'd like to think that, like Lawler, that figure will take a lot of beating.

Sydney Roosters defeated New Zealand Warriors 30–8
Crowd: 80 130

brassed off

At the beginning of the 2003 season I was in the Kiwi city of Invercargill to referee a pre-season trial between the New Zealand Warriors and Penrith.

Even though I was only there for a night I remember Invercargill as a pretty place with heritage buildings, hospitable people and beautiful scenery. The other town 'feature' which has made a lifelong impression was their local brass band which entertained the crowd before the match.

In the NRL, I don't bother to check the field before calling time-on because I have a television director give me the nod to start the game. In Invercargill I knew there was no TV coverage and no director, so I blew my whistle, the ball was kicked off and within seconds the game was in full swing with big hits and quick passes along the backline.

Meanwhile, something else had caught the crowd's attention. According to Penrith's operation's manager,

Peter Mulholland, the scene before kick off went something like this.

The Panthers trainer, Paul Watson, expressed his concern when he saw I was about to start the game. 'Someone should tell Billy the brass band is still on the field . . . he's not going to start the game is he?'

Peter paid tribute to my professionalism by saying, 'Don't be stupid. Of course he won't.' Just as he finished his sentence I blew time-on!

When the play was almost on top of the troupe, Peter and the Panthers bench thought it was a real hoot to see the looks of horror on each band member's face! They gripped their trumpets and tubas for grim life when they saw one hundred-kilo-plus giants charging towards them. What Peter found even funnier was that when they beat their hasty retreat none of them broke rank, or even missed a step as they *marched* off the field with military precision! Apparently the last member just stepped off the field as the play trampled over what had been their spot.

Peter filled me in on the details after the game, and, even though the band had been exposed to considerable risk, I couldn't help but burst out laughing at the image he painted.

To this day what really has me stuffed is the fact I didn't see them . . . I was so focused on the game I didn't even notice the band as we passed them when they left the field!

utilising the limelight

The media have often labelled me 'Hollywood' because they think I court the limelight. But, as far as the other referees and people who know me are concerned, Hollywood is not my name. In the early '80s the media always used to call former first grade referee Greg Hartley 'Hollywood' then they started transferring the name to me. But there's only one Hollywood, and that's Hartley.

In the early days, I hated the media attention and I used to turn down interviews all the time so I could concentrate on refereeing. Since then I've done plenty of media with appearances on TV, radio talkback, magazine stories and newspaper articles. My mum kept a scrapbook when I first started, and over the last ten years I've kept up with the numerous cuttings and magazines stories. I'm glad my mum started it and I'm even happier I've kept it going. I look forward to my retirement when I might pull out the scrapbooks and relive the memories with my kids and grandchildren later on. They are a picture of my career—the good and the bad—I've kept them all.

The media really got stuck into me when I appeared in *The Men of League* calendar in 1994. It wasn't the first time I'd appeared in a calendar, I'd been Mr August in *The Sons of Beaches* in 1986 for a bit of a laugh and some extra bucks. I was thrilled to be asked to appear in *The Men of League* calendar because I saw it as a massive breakthrough for referees—we were finally being seen as a part of the game and its marketing.

During the Super League days, when we were stood down from refereeing, I also did some work as an extra on shows like *Australia's Most Wanted* to earn some extra cash. These days one of my regular gigs is to make a fool out of myself with ex-footballers like Paul Sironen and Terry Hill on Lowes ads. Mick Stone says he cringes whenever he sees the ads, but they've been hugely successful and a lot of fun.

I'm often asked the effect the limelight has on me and how I handle it. It wasn't easy to start with and I did take it to heart. My immediate family and close friends used to surround me with love and support to get me through some of the rough times. As the years passed, the roles reversed as I became used to media attention and I started to feel sorry for my family, relatives and friends because they would cop as much stick as me. The examples are endless and, to me, that's the disappointing part of my high profile.

Nevertheless, the positive side of the recognition far outweighs the negative. My profile has enabled me to open doors for myself, my family and other people. For myself, I've been able to go places, meet people and see and do things I obviously wouldn't have had the chance to do. A quick example was in New Zealand last year. The local referees' association chipped in for a number of their members to look after me for a couple of days. This included dining out, drinking, sightseeing and playing a round of golf, followed by a 10 000 foot tandem parachute jump. The parachute jump was kept quiet till we got to the airfield because they didn't want me to chicken out. It was great and I really enjoyed and appreciated it. They didn't get the reaction they were hoping for though, which was to see terror written all over my face, because fortunately for me, a couple of years earlier I did a course and jumped from 10 000 feet solo.

Despite the people who are willing to bag me at every opportunity, I have a lot of fans too. Women come up to me and say, 'I only watch football when you're refereeing'. A lot of them write to me as well, as do young kids and junior referees. Once I made a woman's day when her friends asked me to surprise her by opening the car door on her wedding day. It completely suprised her and she didn't believe it was me at all.

For other people, I've been able to use my profile to help charities and people in need. The time I give and the list of functions I've attended is large, but I do it because I can help people and that makes me feel good. I look forward to the day when I have more time and can lend a little more help.

I've given a couple of my jerseys to charities because refs' strips are pretty rare and can go for a lot of money. The most memorable was the jersey I wore during the 2001 season, which I had all the captains in the finals series sign and then I had it framed with a photo of the skippers holding the Telstra Cup. I donated the whole thing to the Westmead Children's Hospital fundraiser and it sold for $3500.

Despite what people think, I am quite shy by nature and I was terrified at the beginning of the 2003 footy season when I got up to sing in front of about eight hundred people for the Westmead Children's Hospital. It was billed as 'A Night with the Stars' and a handful of personalities like Jeannie Little, Wayne Pearce and John Raper took to the stage with an eight-piece band and two backing singers. I was asked to have a go. I love singing in the car, the shower and sometimes even on the field, so I said yes.

But when it came time to jump up on the stage that night the wobbly legs were soon back. 'Give me a footy field any day,' I told the organiser. I sang two songs on the night, the first being 'Beth', a ballad by the rock group KISS. I went the whole hog and dressed up wearing the face paint, the wig and the accessories.

Then I took the make-up off and went back on and sang Ronan Keating's 'When you say nothing at all' as my second number. Just having the first one under my belt made the second song so much more enjoyable for me. I'd tossed the nerves and really got into the song. The night was a huge success, raising $280 000.

I also use my profile these days to actively campaign for better conditions, not only for League referees, but for all officials. I regularly speak at seminars involving officialdom. In 2002 I was invited to Wellington, New Zealand, to be special guest speaker and open the Hillary Commission, which is equivalent to Australia's National Officiating Program. I also spoke at the 'Fair Go for Officials' seminar in Sydney, where officials and players met to discuss the rising concern for officials in all sports.

I dream of the day officials will be received by their governing bodies, the media and spectators for what they are really worth. But you know what? I think I'm dreaming.

wayne bennett

O f all the great coaches from my era—Phil Gould, Graham Lowe, Warren Ryan, Chris Anderson, Tim Sheens, Brian Smith and Bob Fulton to name a few—none stands quite as tall as Brisbane's Wayne Bennett, literally or metaphorically.

We've had the occasional problem, Wayne and I, but I still can't help admire him. As Brisbane's coach he's enjoyed five grand final victories during his unprecedented sixteen years as head coach of the one club.

To outsiders, Wayne Bennett is seen as a brooder. *Sydney Morning Herald* reporter and former first grade coach Roy Masters reckons there are people who look happier than Bennett when they're vomiting. Yet, I've heard the people who matter most to him in football— his players—speak in awe of him as a fatherly figure and a friend they'd gladly bleed for. Bennett is reserved, but he still has a friendly word for my boys when they're in the changing rooms.

Wayne and I are quite similar, although I'm a little more outgoing than him. His views on self-discipline, running past the line, respect and motivation are the same as mine.

The only thing that disappoints me about Wayne is he doesn't attend the NRL coaches–referees' meetings during the off-season; instead he sends an underling to act as his ears and mouthpiece. The coaches–referees' meetings are a chance for us to talk about clarification and interpretation of the rules and to investigate and discuss avenues to improve the game. Every other coach thinks it's important enough to turn up to and the referees show up keen to contribute. I could understand if he missed one or even two meetings, but to *never* show up leaves me to assume he isn't interested.

Yet I *know* he's interested in what the whistleblowers think because, in the lead-up to the 2003 kick off, we met in Sydney without the knowledge of his players or even his club to thrash out some issues which came out of the 2001 and 2002 semi-finals.

He'd even compiled a video and asked why I awarded a penalty against his team in one instance and not against the Roosters in another.

The problem, as I explained to Wayne, was by isolating each particular incident we didn't see the penalty in its entire context. We didn't see the lead-up to it; perhaps I'd warned Brisbane four or five times about being offside or for lying over the tackled player while the Roosters might not have done it enough times to be penalised. I told Wayne his video was unfair, and, to his credit, he accepted my point and moved onto wider issues.

Since he was there to speak man to man, I didn't hold back and pointed out some areas of concern about the current Broncos outfit. I told him my observation was he'd replaced veterans who'd retired with a younger group of players who thought it was their right to abuse the referee when calls went against them. As elite athletes, they should be better disciplined than that.

Another problem I thought Bennett faced was he coaches a club that demands success because they've experienced it for years, but the field has caught up with them, and it's a tougher slog for them to win these days. They don't always take out the games they're expected to and that's frustrating to them. The Broncos' behaviour of the last two years is very unBennett like. He took my words on board and said by having a greater understanding of the problems his players were causing for referees he could do something about it. Wayne publicly supported the NRL's edict for referees to crack down on any signs of dissent from the players. 'We need to keep good people as officials and we won't keep them if they are being abused while they are doing their jobs,' he wrote in his *Courier Mail* column. 'I tell my players that if they get penalised for dissent not to look for sympathy from me.'

On the lighter side, it brought a smile to my face, as it did most people's, to see the rarely seen emotional

Wayne Bennett when his Broncos won the game in extra time against Wests Tigers under the new golden point rule. A rule Wayne was highly critical of on its introduction. It was great to see.

tallis tales

A lot has been made of the relationship between Gorden Tallis and me, especially in the media. Gorden isn't called the Raging Bull for nothing—when he gets fired up he looks like he's ready to rip your head off—but that's never bothered me on the field.

I dismissed 'Tallis-gate' as a media beat-up because Gorden and I had always had a good relationship, but then events in the Australia–New Zealand test of 2002 made me reconsider. We'd come through the send-off of the 2000 Origin series and a couple of minor altercations during competition games, but our working relationship seemed to hit rock bottom in 2002 after I sin-binned Gorden in the opening Origin match of the series. It's an act I'll forever regret, although at the time I thought Gorden did force my hand.

I'd warned Gorden, as the Queensland captain, that there were too many penalties and I'd take firmer action with the next bloke to offend. I thought my message was clear and concise, but Gorden did exactly what I'd warned him against (lying across the tackled player) in his very next tackle. I was stunned and felt as if I *had* to sin-bin Gorden because he'd appeared to defy my warning. I felt I had to back my threat with action so I waved him off the field.

I now concede it was the wrong move because the half-time break was only forty-five seconds away and I could have used that as an opportunity to speak to him again. In the wake of that sin-binning—and Queensland's loss—all hell broke loose, with Queensland Rugby League boss Ross Livermore branding me 'arrogant' and 'unapproachable' and the NRL's referees' boss Peter Louis telling the *Sydney Morning Herald* he thought I'd overreacted. 'Not for a minute am I saying Queensland lost because of Bill Harrigan, but it is concerning when players say you can't approach the ref.'

I like to make a little bit of fun about what was a mighty controversy at the time by telling people Gorden actually asked me to give him a break because he was tired. While people laugh, there is an element of truth in it because a couple of years ago Gorden *did* beg me to bin him to help him salvage some professional pride. He was playing like a 'busted' and needed time out to rally and regroup. In between breaths Gorden confessed he wasn't playing well and could use a breather.

'You're kidding,' I said, 'you'll have to do something for me to do that.' I thought it was a gee-up but Gorden was doubled over with his hands on his knees, puffing like a steam train.

I haven't told this story publicly because up until now I still don't know if Gordie was fair dinkum. But, in light of his bagging me for a wrongful sin-binning, I think it's important to say Gorden hasn't always objected to the idea of ten minutes to cool his heels and catch his breath.

Some people saw our so-called feud as a potentially serious problem for the Broncos' premiership hopes, so the club's media manager brokered a top-secret meeting between Gorden and me at my parent's house.

I waited for Gorden in the front yard and ushered him quickly out of the cab and inside before anyone could see us. I introduced him to my mum and dad and they had a chat for a while before we moved to the backroom to discuss our issues in private. It was very civil and lighthearted and, by the end of it, Gorden and I agreed we shared a mutual respect for one another and any 'problem' was more of a media build-up than an issue between us. We decided to get on with life and try not to give the media any more wood for *their* fire. We also decided not to react any differently towards one another during a game as a result of that meeting.

So our next game was 'respectful' and as I walked off the paddock I hoped the media fire could be extinguished. But I was wrong . . . terribly wrong. War broke out between us a few weeks later during the 2002 preliminary final when I refereed the Roosters and Brisbane.

During the game Gorden's men refused to listen to my calls for them to fall back ten metres and get out of the rucks. As a result they ended up on the wrong side of the penalty count. Gorden thought he and his team were being unfairly punished and he blasted me with both barrels.

It seemed as if all the old dramas, like the send-off and sin-binning in the Origin matches, were dredged up in his mind and he adopted a siege mentality. I became the enemy and, rather than focus on stopping the Roosters' momentum, he divided his time between abusing me and trying to direct his team. The Broncos lost the game and with it the chance of a grand final berth. I shook my head in disbelief at his antics, but, while I didn't stew over them, Gorden did.

Everything came to a head when I walked out for the October 2002 test between Australia and New Zealand at Westpac Stadium, Wellington. The coin toss was a test of both my patience and humility. It started when Gorden, as the Australian captain, refused to even look at me, let alone offer to shake hands. He looked towards New Zealand captain Stacey Jones as he walked to the spot outside the dressing-room for the toss. I watched the pair shake hands and then I shook hands with Stacey. Tallis was obviously still fuming about the preliminary final loss but his behaviour was not what I expected from a national team's skipper. It was insulting and I thought there was no way I'd do the coin toss until he acknowledged me. It was a matter of principle. Could you imagine if a referee did that to a captain? He'd be entitled to wonder what chance he and his team had if I couldn't be bothered to say hello.

In an attempt to lighten the mood I said, 'G'day Gordie, how's it going?'

He simply grunted, 'Good'.

I then said, 'I want to go to Queensland for a holiday . . . will they let me in?'

Another grunt, but this time he extended himself to two words: 'Not likely'.

I learned a few months later that he complained to Wayne Bennett that I made him acknowledge my presence before the test. When I spoke to Wayne he advised me that I perhaps shouldn't demand that from Gorden, but I will. I'll always demand it because like any other captain he should show the referee some respect at the coin toss. Gorden doesn't have to shake my hand if that's a problem for him; he only needs to say 'Hello'—nothing more, and nothing less.

Things didn't get any better during the game and Gorden was lucky Chris Anderson replaced him because I thought about binning him when he started ripping into me. I went against my better judgment by not sin-binning him because the last thing I wanted was for that test to be remembered as another chapter in the Harrigan–Tallis feud. Nevertheless, he tested my patience and I reacted poorly. After he complained about losing a ball I snapped at him: 'It's not my fault you can't hold the ball.'

After the game I read that Gorden vowed to never utter another word to me or mention my name. I'm not thin-skinned and I've been around long enough to accept a player mightn't be happy with me, but this time I thought, if Gorden doesn't want to talk to me, then that'll do me.

Gorden is one of the code's greatest players but he has an Achilles heel: I think he thinks referees don't like him and he treats a penalty or warning as a personal affront. I know Kangaroos coach Chris Anderson agrees. The big forward gave the impression the message had started to sink in when he told the press: 'I've got to take them [the referees] all out of my head and just get on with playing my best for the team.'

I hope he remembers his words because Gorden is nowhere near the force he can be when he's engaged in his running battles with the referees instead of focusing on the job of playing football. When things don't go right his response is to attack the referee and all those old grudges rise to the surface.

It happened to him during that test in Wellington, as *Illawarra Mercury* journalist Dave Murray noted in his match wrap-up:

'Where was the man regarded for the past four or five seasons as the most feared forward in the National Rugby League? The bloke who used to require up to three or four tacklers to stop his progress?'

I can tell Dave Murray where his man was. Gorden spent his debut as Australia's test skipper abusing me . . . as a veteran he must know that's a battle he *can't* win and it's a battle he'll *never* win. I'm often asked how I control an emotional time bomb like Gorden when he's ranting and raving. People ask if I ever feel intimidated or threatened he might cross that line of no return and have a crack at me, but the thought doesn't even cross my mind, nor would it cross Gorden's.

I have watched Gorden play up-close and personal for a number of years and it's my opinion that ever since his career-threatening neck injury he hasn't been the same player as the one who'd leave a trail of destruction behind him when he ran the ball. He's still a very good player, and occasionally the devastating Tallis appears, but not as much as he used to.

Gorden probably tells those around him that he's okay and the injury doesn't worry him, but I have my doubts. Sometimes he seems gun-shy to me and I don't blame him at all. I imagine the fear of injuring his neck must play on his mind and why wouldn't it? It's the same problem which has ended a couple of great careers including former Great Britain forward Phil Clarke and St George–Illawarra hooker Nathan Brown. It says plenty about Gorden's courage and commitment to think he's not only made it back onto the field but he still plays hard and strong.

Round 7 of the 2003 premiership saw Gorden and I cross paths for the first time since the Wellington Test when I refereed the Broncos–Eels match at Parramatta Stadium. I didn't know what to expect from Gorden at the toss, but it was as if nothing had happened between us in the past. He even cracked a joke, and I was certainly relieved. There wasn't a harsh word directed in either direction. Like me, Gorden appreciated how much easier life was not to read or hear about Harrigan and Tallis going toe to toe the day after a match.

As I showered and changed, three of my boys, Andrew, Will and little Jed, ventured into the Broncos' dressing-room to chase up their heroes' autographs. Andrew's number one player is Gorden and one of the benefits of that incident-free match was I didn't cop an earbashing from Andrew for 'picking on Gordie'. When I looked for them I found them chatting to Gorden and I took time out to capture the moment by taking a photograph of Jed sitting on the Raging Bull's lap. It was the same after this year's State of Origin games. After Game One we sat down, had a beer, a chat and a laugh. It was like old times.

There is no bad blood between us and I really do hope Gorden recaptures his magic because Rugby League needs the Raging Bull to play at one hundred kilometres per hour. I also hope Gorden finally appreciates Rugby League also needs him to tone down the tantrums and if he does that he'll find a resurgence of the popularity he once had south of the border. I like Gorden, and have a lot of respect for him, and when we've both retired I look forward to buying him a Guinness and getting to know him better.

fit for life

At forty-three, I'm proud to still be in peak physical condition. From a young boy growing up in the streets of Canley Heights to a full-time professional Rugby League referee, being fit and active has been my life.

I hear people in everyday life say they don't have the time to train or keep fit: *rubbish*. It's all about how much you want something. If you want to get fit you can find time and you can *make* time. People always say 'Oh it's easy for you because it was part of your job to keep fit', but I had to make sacrifices too.

When I was appointed in 1986–87 as driver of the TRG escort vehicle for the prison van carrying the Comancheros to Penrith court in the wake of the Milperra massacre I had to start work every morning at 6 a.m. at the TRG office and be at Long Bay Gaol by 6.30 a.m. We didn't finish until 7 p.m. each night and, after a day guarding and carting prisoners around,

I wasn't keen to train at night—so when? Most people would say the day was too long and they are too tired, but my attitude is make time not excuses so I used to set the alarm for 4.30 a.m.

I was living on Campbell Parade at Bondi Beach so the well-lit promenade became my training ground. I'd be rubbing the sleep from my eyes as I crossed the road to the nine hundred metre long promenade. After a couple of laps warm-up it was in to it. I mixed up the distances and the intensity and just charged up and down the pathway time and time again.

It was dark, lonely and on many occasions freezing, but it was also quite peaceful to run with the sound of crashing waves. It would allow me time to think clearly about where I was heading in life and where I wanted to go in refereeing. I knew other referees were home in bed and wouldn't do what I was doing and I used that knowledge to improve my mental toughness.

There were times when I could quite easily have slept through the alarm, but I found that little voice in the back of my head wouldn't allow that. I guess my getting up at an ungodly hour came down to a matter of me *wanting* to remain in peak condition.

I always looked for the chance to work up a sweat. On the occasions during the Milperra Massacre case when I got a one hour break from guard duty I'd whack on my runners and run through the streets of Penrith.

These days my body is starting to slow down. When I started refereeing first grade I earned a reputation for sprinting past some of the players who were racing for the tryline. I would beat them into the in-goal and wait for them to put the ball down, then award the try. Being so fit and quick allowed me to get into position with ease and made making the decisions easier. I still bust my gut to get in the right position, but the days of chasing and passing the players en route to the tryline have long gone. They leave me behind in their slipstream.

When I turned forty, my body seemed to take that milestone as the sign to say, 'Time to slow down, Billy boy.' Slow down I have, but I refuse to wave the white flag.

My approach to training these days is to be smarter. I've found shortcuts that stop me from burning out. Rather than hammer myself for long periods of time on the track and in the gymnasium I work out in short, intense bursts. I'm still as fit as I've ever been, and still weigh the same as I did in 1979, I've just slowed down and don't bounce back as quick. I need more recovery time.

In 2003 my weekly training program reads like this (although the training varies slightly, depending on what day I'm refereeing):

Monday	Referees' training at Telstra Stadium
	Swimming, weights and stretch
	(10–12 a.m.)
	Sprints and stretch (6–8 p.m.)

Tuesday	Boxing (6–7 a.m.) mates group since 1995
	Referees' training at Telstra Stadium Sprints (6–8 p.m.)
Wednesday	Rest day
	Mates group ride (6.30–7.30 a.m.) may join in if feeling okay
	Occasionally referee Oz Tag at Cronulla
Thursday	Referees' sprint training at Telstra (6–8 p.m.)
Friday	Beach workout soft sand and surf during summer
	Run or sprints during winter (6.30–7.15 a.m.) mates group
Saturday	Rest day
	Mates group run 5–6 kilometres (8 a.m.) join in sometimes
Sunday	Referee

Training is about attitude. Do you have a strong or weak attitude? Good or bad? A good, strong attitude will see you train hard and with enthusiasm. It will also see you train effectively, whether you're with a group or on your own. Training on your own is the hardest way to train, but with the right attitude you can do it.

If your attitude is right, your self-discipline will be right. If you're going to sprint forty metres at full pace from a standing start you go forty metres. You don't put your toe on the start line or one foot in front of the line. You don't slow down till you pass the finish. Eight out of ten people will slow down as they approach the finish. What you do in training, you do on the paddock on game day or in life. That's because it's your attitude.

I've watched refs train over the years with the majority not pushing themselves to charge past the line. I've used this in my own mental preparation, knowing my competition lack the same attitude and self-discipline I possess. I've always started behind the line, finished past the line or made the turning line, never falling short. Is it a big deal? Over a lifetime: yes. It becomes a way of life and it might only be ten metres shorter over the whole training session, but to me it's more about cheating yourself and your attitude.

So don't just think about it. Get out there and do it!

winning mentality

I hardly ever wear a shirt during training sessions because I hate the feel of a sweaty shirt clinging to my body. Obviously I rug up during the middle of winter but, other than that, it's shirt off. In the early years I copped plenty of flak from my peers, as have the young refs who have followed my lead today, but I like the other refs to see I'm proud of my body. I use it as a way of psyching out my rivals, the blokes vying with me for the title of Rugby League's top referee.

Over the years I've learnt blokes unhappy with their physique tend to hide it under T-shirts, but not me. I've worked hard to keep in good condition and I'm happy to flash the flesh. I know such an unabashed pride in how I look has made an impact on the other whistleblowers. Some of them hate it when I rip the shirt off because it reminds them of how hard I work on the training paddock and in the gym. And I know that as well as the comments they make in jest, there are some nasty words said on the quiet. But *that* works to my advantage, because, while they're left concerned about me and my training, I've got my sights set on being the best.

I rely more on mind games as I grow older and the younger referees get fitter and faster. Over the years I've lost some of my speed but I make a point of staying right on the young blokes' heels during our sprints and distance runs. Sometimes they're fifteen or twenty years younger than me, but I stick to them like glue. With each step I can almost hear their thoughts screaming above the blood pounding in their ears: 'Why the hell can't I shake him? . . . When is he going to give up? . . . The old bastard is still right behind me . . . Why doesn't he grow old somewhere else?'

As they wrestle with these thoughts, every now and then I'll pull out all stops and put one huge effort in to pounce and run past them at full pace. The sight of me sprinting from behind and breaking free close to the end of the race usually smashes their spirit and, as I soak up the victory, I can see they're trying to work out what it'll take to better me. They've seen that I can charge from behind on the training paddock and they know I'll lift when the pressure is on.

Sadly age has caught up with me and my speed and recovery time has slowed, but my endurance and determination are still there and my mental toughness is concrete.

In my pursuit for the top spot, I often listen for comments to feed off. In 2000, I was the designated driver at the Dally M awards chauffeuring Tim 'Pinhead' Mander and Brian Grant back to their hotel after the function. Granty had had a bellyful of grog and Pinhead—who was my main rival going into the final series had sipped a few reds—shocked me when he said it would be a great thrill to finish as the season's *second* best referee. I immediately picked up on what he'd said, but it was Granty who hammered Pinhead for being content to take the back seat.

'What do you mean?' he scowled. 'You should be saying you're going to knock him off the perch and that you'll referee the grand final. Bugger this rubbish about being the second best.' He tore into Tim.

Rather than getting fired up by Granty's comments, Tim said he was being realistic. He reckoned there was no way he'd beat me for the top job, but he was happy to live with the fact he was at least good enough to be rated a contender.

Now, I like Tim—he's one of my best mates—but, once I heard him say that, I knew the grand final was mine.

I think the secret to succeeding is doing what you have to and finding things to hang on to—an edge— whether it's a throwaway comment like Tim's, a rev-up or even a personal challenge.

I also consider fostering a sense of teamwork to be an important ingredient in the winning formula. Every year during the build-up to the grand final appointment, the referees in contention for the big gig are partnered up with two touch judges. In 2001, I was buddied up with Shayne Hayne and Steve Richards and the three of us worked well together. They both seemed to have the same ideas and mental toughness as me and they embraced my mentality from day one.

When we were teamed up I set the ground rules, which were a throwback to my days with the Tactical Response Group. We warmed up together; we didn't entertain outsiders before, during or after training; *and* we pushed each other when we needed encouragement during a drill.

It's probably obvious by now that I revel in working with a closeknit unit and it's always been a source of strength for me to see the rival teams look more like Brown's cows than grand final contenders as they stretched individually, mingled with members of other teams and then trained without any real conviction.

In 2001 Hayne, Richards and I were all appointed to the grand final.

Last year when the hierarchy divided the refs and touch judges into their groups of three for the finals series my 'team' from 2001 was separated, so I had to try and instil the same *esprit de corps* we had enjoyed with my two new team-mates, Darren Gocher and Gerrard 'Belgium' Sutton. (Keep an eye out for Sutton, he's a new young ref with plenty going for him—and he rips the shirt off.)

As long as we train for the grand final we don't associate with the other refs. We stretch together, stick to ourselves and push each other.

They caught on quick.

Young Sutton almost went all the way with me to the grand final with only half a season under his belt as a touchie—a great achievement in itself. But he was stood down after week two of the semis, not on performance, but in Granty's words 'lack of experience for the big one'. He would have learnt a lot and I know if he sticks with it, one day he'll be there come kick off. Steve Richards got the call-up for his second grand final on the trot. It's funny looking back to that first training session of the finals series when Richo told me it felt strange being in another team with less direction and a different attitude to mine. He said it felt like being in the race, but on a different horse. Still, he wasn't giving up and, in the end, he made it.

This might all sound like up-myself stuff, but psychology is another tool in the referee's kitbag, along with fitness, confidence, communication, positioning, knowledge of the rules and mental toughness. The art of playing mind games and intimidating your competition is one I've worked on and perfected over the years, and I'm certain it's what's helped me get to the top.

heavenly wedding

When I decided the time was right to get married to Lesley, I circled 13 December 2001 as our wedding day. I didn't think I could deny Lesley's parents, Jean and Les, from seeing her get married, so I prepared a plan and put it into motion. The only problem was I didn't mention it to Lesley or our parents.

I was appointed to the Australia–Great Britain test series in England in October and November 2001 so I knew I had to have the wedding plans in place before I left.

Step one: the ring. I rang a friend of mine, swore him to secrecy and asked him to get a ring made for me. I knew Lesley's ring size because I'd set it up with a store owner to find out for me. I used some lame excuse to get Lesley to try a ring on in his shop and I went back later to find out the size.

Just to get the ring made took a fair bit of undercover work. I knew Lesley had a picture of a ring that she loved in her jewellery box along with a set of diamond earrings that she wanted to use if she ever had the ring made. I pinched the picture and had it photocopied and placed the original back, I pinched the earrings and left their box in Lesley's jewellery box.

I kept my fingers crossed that Lesley wouldn't find them missing in the time I had taken them to the day I was to marry her. I bought a bigger diamond to match the earring diamonds and then had my friend get the ring made to match the picture. I gave him the time frame and expected it to be finished when I got back from England.

Step two: I went undercover. I met with the owner, Claude, of the Sea Level restaurant in Cronulla to arrange special music, a slap-up meal, champagne and the best seat overlooking the surf to help make what I hoped would be a special day even more memorable.

Step three: get the job done. I arranged for George Capsis, the Cronulla Sharks chaplain, to do the honours. George said he had been subjected to strange requests before but mine outdid them all. To marry a woman that didn't even know it was her wedding day would be a beauty. He said he'd love to marry us, but there was a hitch. He was concerned that he had not met Lesley and there was an application period.

So I had George come around to our place one day to discuss christening Jed. Although we talked about the christening, it was George's opportunity to meet Lesley and he asked some questions on our thoughts of marriage. He did this to satisfy himself that Lesley was open to the prospect of marrying me someday. George was satisfied with the outcome of the meeting and agreed to my request.

Happy in the knowledge that all my plans were put into place and locked away, I headed to England for the test series. When I returned I rang both our parents and my beautiful ninety-year-old grandmother, Thelma Shepherd, who got along terrifically with Jean and Les. I suggested we should get together for a Christmas lunch because Grandma was spending Christmas 2001 with Uncle Ian's family in Newcastle.

I had to push hard to get the ring finished in time and I only collected it from my mate the morning of the wedding on my way to picking up Lesley's parents.

That morning Lesley couldn't understand why I wanted to wear slacks and not my trademark jeans. I knew it would be a mistake to protest, so I whacked on my denim strides and I smiled when she dressed in a white dress, placing a flower on the front to hide her maternity bra strap.

Lesley, our parents and Grandma, thought it was a family get-together for an early Christmas celebration, but I floored them all. When Claude arrived with a bottle of champagne I said, 'We are not really here to celebrate Christmas early, we are here because I would like to ask Les and Jean for permission to ask their daughter to marry me.'

Everyone was in tears when Les and Jean said, 'Yes', and especially when I asked Lesley, 'Would you marry me anywhere, any place and any time?'

Through tears Lesley said, 'Yes.'

We toasted the moment with champagne and I couldn't help bringing up the quote from the first time I met Jean when she threatened me with what she would do if I didn't look after Lesley saying, 'Jean, I'm looking after your daughter so you can put your scissors away.' Jean broke out into laughter.

At this point I heard my dad say to Mum, 'I told you there was more to this day, Joy.'

I thought to myself, 'If only you knew what is to come.'

The meal was brought out next and Mum said, 'When do you think you will get married?'

I said, 'Probably after next footy season.'

Mum said, 'It would be lovely getting married down here on the beach if you got a day like today.'

'You know, Mum,' I said with a smile, 'you are absolutely right.'

It was now around three o'clock so I suggested we have our photograph taken outside to commemorate a special moment in all our lives. Lesley asked if we could have the snap taken at the table so Jean wouldn't have to struggle to go outside.

'No,' I said, 'we really have to go outside.' I used the excuse it was such a beautiful day and I didn't want the remnants of our meal and wine glasses in the photo, and she bought it.

With that we walked into the sunshine. The sky was blue and while the nearby surf was pounding it had nothing on my heartbeat! BOOM . . . BOOM . . . BOOM.

I carried two chairs out for Jean and my grandma and set them up in the park opposite the beach and the restaurant. Jed's godparents, Frank and Robyn, were looking after Jed for us and Frank had turned up to take some photos. I had let Frank and Robyn in on the secret that morning.

Frank took a couple of snaps of us, then I jumped out in front of everyone and said, 'I'm sorry, I've misled you again, we're not out here just for this photograph. I'd like to introduce you to Mr George Capsis.'

I looked towards the tree George was hiding behind and Lesley turned to see him come out from hiding.

Lesley looked at me and I was beginning to cry as I nodded my head in the affirmative. I said, 'I need to ask you something. Do you remember when I asked you to marry me I said, "Will you marry me anywhere, any place and any time," and you said, "Yes" so I would like to ask you . . . would right now be okay?'

There were more tears and when Lesley said 'Yes' I turned to our parents and they were all crying. Frank snapped away capturing the moments whilst George oversaw the most sacred of ceremonies.

At the end of the ceremony we went back into the restaurant to Lesley's favourite song. We signed the paperwork as Claude brought over the second chilled bottle of champagne. The packed restaurant was now aware of what was going on and congratulations were coming from left, right and centre.

Just when everything had died down and Robyn had joined us with Jed, I hit Lesley with my last surprise.

I said, 'We have to go shopping for some summer wear for you because tomorrow we're on an 8.30 a.m. flight to the Gold Coast and then transfers to Curan Cove resort on Stradbroke Island.' With that I gave Lesley the airline tickets and vouchers.

Tears flowed again and what topped it off for Lesley was I had included Jed on the honeymoon.

I rang my other boys to tell them the news and they were tickled pink for us. I did have to explain why they weren't at the wedding but they accepted my reason and were very happy for us. A couple of my close friends were put out, but after hearing my reason to keep it close and personal with our parents and my grandma, which I could not have done with other friends present, they saw it my way.

The whole day was beautiful and a memory I'll cherish for many reasons besides marrying my best friend, my lover, the person I trust with my innermost secrets, the person who listens to me without judging me and has been a steadfast supporter when others have lined up to lay the boot in. We're now husband and wife, we're confidantes and, most of all, we're happy. I love her, and without wanting to sound like a would-be Mills and Boon novelist, Lesley has given me an inner strength I'd never known before. In six years we haven't had an argument. On a couple of occasions we've disagreed and Lesley thinks they're fights but, from my previous marriages, I can say in all certainty that we haven't had a blue.

While she is no longer with us, I like to think Lesley's mother is resting easy with the knowledge I have so far fulfilled my promise to look after her daughter.

Lesley, I love you more. X

epilogue

My eldest son, Matthew, turned twenty-three in November 2003. I look at him sometimes and try to picture myself when I was his age. I shake my head in disbelief when I compare the two of us. I look at Matt and think if I was so young and raw, how did I do it? At twenty-three, I'd already been married and divorced with a three-year-old son. I'd negotiated with banks for housing loans, I'd been through the Family Court and I'd been in the police force for four years dealing with life-threatening situations.

I often wonder how I did it. It was a huge amount of responsibility to accept at nineteen. My mates were still single heading out to nightclubs, drinking, dancing and chasing girls, but I had to grow up quick.

Sometimes I think about how life would have turned out had things been different. How far would I have gone with soccer if my little mates hadn't found me that afternoon on the recruitment drive for the footy team? Where would I be if Dad hadn't forced me back to school? Would I be the CEO of the brickworks or a commander in the navy? I wonder how life would have been different if I hadn't met Lee. I would have taken off on my booked cruise on the Fairstar and who knows where I'd have gone from there and with whom. I wonder about life without refereeing and not having the great times I've experienced, friends I've met and places I've seen. I shudder at the thought of the times I nearly didn't make it: the train with Mossy, the shotgun with Pete Gillam, the tree with Boong, the Bathurst riot . . .

As I come to the twilight of my refereeing career I look back and I'm amazed by the journey I've travelled and the heights I've achieved. From my humble beginnings in the pub competition to perhaps my tenth grand final, it's been one heck of a ride.

Have you ever sat down and wondered about *your* life? It can be a very intriguing, relaxing experience. Try it.

But no matter how much we wonder, *I believe everything is meant to be.*

grand final 2003

It was Sunday evening, 7th October 2003, and the time had come for one of the most eagerly anticipated grand finals of the modern era. The media billed the game as east versus west, the rich versus the poor and the yuppies versus the fibros. The one I liked most, however, was the café lattes versus the instant coffees. Regardless of the hype, the game let no one down.

What a game to finish my career on—it was a thriller. The consensus of most people already suggests this was the greatest grand final of all time.

Penrith went into the match as underdogs against the hot favourites and current titleholders, the Roosters—but what a fairytale ending they gave all to see. The game was played at State of Origin pace. There were minimal stoppages and I issued only three penalties.

The Panthers came out fired up and played the Roosters at their own game. They rushed the line in defence and tackled in packs of three or four defenders. It was no place for the faint-hearted. Bodies were put on the line and the force of the impact on some of the crunching tackles made me flinch on occasions. Even the smallest player on the field, Preston Campbell, pulled off some of the biggest hits of the match.

Both sides had their chances and both sides dominated the game at various times but it seemed neither could put the other one away. The Roosters came oh so close when Chris Flannery lost his footing on one occasion and was stopped millimetres short of the line. I thought that if he had scored the Roosters would have gone on with it and won the game.

Another major play was the lead up to Penrith's first try. Luke Priddis scooped the ball up from dummy half and raced up the short side. The Roosters' Jason Cayless was desperately trying to get back onside but hadn't made it. I called him offside and he pulled out of the play leaving a hole for Priddis to run through and Penrith scored.

But who could ever forget the turning point of the match: THAT TACKLE BY SCOTT SATTLER. The Roosters had cleaned up a spilt ball by the Panthers, which was quickly given to winger and fast man Todd Byrne. Todd raced away with the line wide open and only a forward, Scott Sattler, chasing in cover defence. A winger against a lock forward . . . and yet Sattler made the necessary ground to bring him down—but it wasn't just about bringing him down. It was about how he did it. It was a copybook low-diving tackle that took Byrne into touch.

THAT tackle will be talked about forever and will go down in history as the best tackle ever. The jubilation on the faces of the Penrith players as they hugged and congratulated Sattler was as if he had scored the winning try. It was something very special, and just what the Panthers needed. They were never going to be beaten from there.

After full-time when people kept telling me it was a great game, constantly asking 'How good was that?', I could only shake my head and agree with them. I knew I had been involved in something special, but as a referee you don't get to enjoy it the same way the spectators do. During the game, I was too busy concentrating hard and pushing myself to the limit, and at the end I was just too fatigued to realise how great it was. I knew that would come after, when I had the chance to watch the replay.

Emotions were flying high after the game with the Panthers and their supporters celebrating wildly. The misery of defeat engulfed the Roosters but there was nobody more quietly emotional than me. I was standing on the field, waiting for the presentation with my boys there with me, and I was holding my youngest at the time, Jed. (Since then Lesley and I have given birth to another boy, Charlie James, in April 2004.)

I hugged Jed tight and a tear rolled down my face as the enormity of my thoughts hit me. I looked around the stadium and thought to myself that this may have been my last game. I soaked up the atmosphere and the moment is still fresh in my mind—I hope it remains that way forever.

Now that the dust has settled I rate the 2003 Grand Final as one of the best games I've ever been involved in, and one of my best refereeing performances. I still rate the 1989 Grand Final as the highlight of my career, probably because it was a great game of footy and it was my first grand final, but it's only a whisker in front of this one.

A month after the grand final I announced my retirement and I couldn't think of a better game to finish my career on.

with the roosters

After my retirement, in 2004 I took on a role as a technical adviser with the Sydney City Roosters coaching staff. The role has already caused controversy amongst a number of NRL coaches. Manly coach Des Hasler made a statement after the Roosters played Manly that the Roosters have an unfair advantage because I am on the coaching staff.

The Roosters are a very professional outfit and are always looking for an edge. They have set the benchmark in a number of areas over the last two years, and other clubs are now following suit. Andrew Johns was not embarrassed to admit that the Knights are copying the Roosters' defensive tactics. Also, when the Roosters recruited prolific goal kicker Daryl Halligan to improve their goal kicking, other clubs soon did the same.

Instead of suggesting an unfair advantage, why not acknowledge their initiative?

My role with the Roosters is to help the coaching staff with rules and their interpretations, and to make training as realistic as possible. The Roosters had a good discipline record with the penalty count last year, but part of my role is to improve on that again.

We have been a little disappointed by some ill-disciplined play giving away costly penalties in the first few rounds this year, but the results Ricky and I hope to achieve with my appointment will not be visible until the back end of the season. We have to slightly change a mentality, which takes time.

If Des or any NRL coach has a problem they have an opportunity to speak directly with current referees through referees' boss Robert Finch. Robert has also made the referees available to attend the training sessions of any club. Obviously it would be logistically impossible to have them attend training every week, but the opportunity is there to have them if a club feels it's necessary.

If Des or anyone else is suggesting the unfair advantage may have something to do with me being an ex-ref and that the current referees are lenient towards the Roosters—well, it's ludicrous.

those certain players

Now I'm retired, I'm like any other league spectator sitting up in the grandstands. The thing I really miss is being out in the centre. I've got the sports ears, and I tune into the referee, but it isn't the same.

Being out in the middle certainly had its advantages and gave you a completely different perspective to every other football-loving fan. It gave me the chance to see up close those special players who are, quite simply, better than anyone else at what they do.

Seeing the players in their environment—the field— is a special privilege only a referee gets the chance to experience. No television camera or microphone can capture the real atmosphere that exists out on the paddock. The difference . . . well, entering the field is a surreal feeling, like being in another world.

Every team has a certain player, a player who takes control and can turn a game in a single moment. Players like Andrew Johns, Freddie Fittler, Steve Menzies and

Gorden Tallis to name a few of the current players. It's also no fluke that most of the 'certain players' end up being captain of their team.

Out on the field, I was up close and personal to these players, privy to their talk, their moves, their hits and the jubilation they shared with their team when they scored a try.

Andrew Johns is fast approaching legendary status whilst still playing. He has it all—kicking, running, passing, defence and the razzle dazzle that no player can predict. The key factor I was privy to was his talk. I knew when he was pumped and shouting, yahooing on the big hits and encouraging his players that he was in his zone—and when he was there he could do anything.

Freddie is another player who talks the team up and then leads by example. When he's playing well, the team performs well. Who could forget the 2002 Grand Final against the Warriors when Freddie decided to take the game into his own hands midway through the second half? The rest of the team followed his lead and the result is history.

Gorden Tallis also just leads by example. He lets his big hits and his rampaging runs do the talking. He inspires his team and they step up a gear and keep Gorden's momentum going.

Steve Menzies is another inspirational leader who can change a game by a quietly spoken word to his team followed with a classic piece of play.

Then there was the best I ever saw: Wally Lewis. There was an aura about this man who could do it all. He led by example if he wanted to or just directed the team with mere words, but you knew he could change the game whenever he wanted to. He was that good.

All the players I've mentioned, and many others, have had their own way of taking control or turning a game. I don't believe it is something you can learn or develop—it's just something these 'certain players' have. Why or how is a good question, but I believe it's just a phenomenon. But, one thing's for certain, it's provided me with many special moments that few others will ever experience.

generation x

Now, more than ever, first grade footballers must be aware of their behaviour on and off the paddock because they're role models to a generation of kids who, I'm sorry to say, have no idea what the word 'respect' means.

I've watched the junior players coming through the ranks and, in my opinion, a great number of them lack character because they haven't been through a school system or society that places an emphasis on respect and pride. These days they don't have to wear a school uniform; they don't need to wear polished black leather shoes; they can get away with swearing at a teacher; they don't fear their punishment because there's no cane and detention is a meeting place for a chat; if caught they get off lightly for vandalising school property; and sport is no longer compulsory. Forget being grateful for the simple things in life, kids today demand their parents buy them label clothes and the most expensive sports shoes on the market.

On the footy field, which has long been a test of a young man's character, some of them act like spoiled brats. Their response to being tackled hard is to give the impression the world is against them and start swinging. When they're penalised for an infringement they blow up, screaming and ranting like mad men. They don't believe in the old creed that the ref's call is final; they think they can bully the ref into seeing things their way. I can only imagine the old breed that was drilled to call the referee 'sir' and to respect his decisions must hate witnessing this spectacle.

I know there're plenty of good-natured kids out there, but when I first started refereeing grade football no nineteen-year-old newcomer would ever dream of screaming, ranting and raving at me because of a decision I made. Firstly, he respected the position I held and second, his senior team-mates would've put him in his place quicksmart and his coach would most likely have dragged him off the field and then dropped him to reserve grade until he grew up.

But where does he get that characteristic from? Apart from the breakdown in society of discipline, respect and attitude, I believe kids are seeing their role models in elite sports and emulating them. When kids see their heroes like Gorden Tallis or Geoff Toovey pay out on the referee when things don't go their way, they think it's okay to do it on a Saturday morning.

It's happening in all sports and I only use league as an example because it is the sport I have been involved in. The television cameras zoom in on the ugly, twisted faces players pull, the verbal explosions and the dagger stares at the official. Their contempt at being penalised is obvious and it reinforces the belief that this is the way players should react when they don't like a decision.

Parents are also role models and have to lead the way. The way is not standing on the sideline verbally abusing an official, an official who is doing their best and providing a sport for your child to play. Remember: without officials you don't have a sport. The way is not to belittle players or the opposition with unsavory remarks or to let your children speak to you or any adult in a derogatory manner. Hand out the discipline so they know the difference between right and wrong and what will be tolerated and what won't.

As much as I would love to see it, I don't think we'll ever see a return to the days when kids respected their elders, when they had pride in wearing polished shoes to school and sweated on being picked in any of the school's sporting sides. Society has allowed that sense of discipline to slide downhill over the last twenty years and it will only be turned around if the public demands it, but it will be too hard to impose that will on kids who've never lived with it. So there will continue to be a decrease in respect, discipline and attitude, and in sport this will mean the ongoing exodus of officials— and that will be a catastrophe.

a real code of conduct

The start of the 2004 season for the NRL was a nightmare and one that sent Rugby League reeling. All the effort that went into making 2003 a year to remember was lost. Instead of riding high on the back end of one of the best years ever, it kicked off as low as it could get.

The NRL were always on the backfoot with the threat of court action over salary cap issues, rape allegations, the dress code and attitude of the Bulldogs' players whilst under investigation, the Bulldogs' drug allegation, extra time stuff-ups, the controversy over the issue of a breach notice to Brisbane for fourteen men on the field and a host of other issues.

A lot was said about the Bulldogs' Coffs Harbour episode and the allegations of rape. The rumours were many and rife as to what may or may not have happened. Everybody seemed to have an opinion as to what should happen to the Bulldogs and the players involved.

I was asked many times by media, friends and the general public as to what really happened. It was taken for granted that I would have inside knowledge because of my affiliation with Rugby League.

Well, I didn't have any inside knowledge, nor did I ask anyone if they knew what happened. I preferred not to know because that made it easy not to comment.

The only comment I did make when people discussed what they had heard or expressed their opinions on what should happen to players involved was this: I said, 'You know, unless you were there and saw what happened you really have no idea what the true story is.'

That was it. That was the extent of my input. I'd prefer to let the investigation by the police and the NRL run its course and provide the real story.

When it comes to the punishment, however, I do have a strong opinion.

And what I have to say relates not only to the Bulldogs' scandal but to Rugby League and all sports for that matter. Any criminal offence committed by any person, sportsman or otherwise, has to simply be dealt with by the police and the courts. No discussion here and certainly no sweeping under the carpet. In today's society you are accountable for your own actions and must pay the consequences for stepping outside the boundaries.

As for behaviour contrary to a code of conduct, there needs to be zero tolerance. It's unfortunate it has come to this but, with Rugby League being so high profile and experiencing so many indiscretions over the last few years, it's time to get tough.

It's only when severe penalties are put into place and enforced that the message will get across.

I'm talking huge fines, lengthy suspensions and termination of contracts. If a zero tolerance is adopted the first couple of offenders will pay dearly but it will quickly send the message to the rest to make sure they keep in line.

When the players know their ill behaviour will not be tolerated, they have no comeback if they stray from the code of conduct. An example would be that when the criminal investigation is finalised by the police into the Coffs Harbour rape allegations, regardless of the outcome, the player who brought the lady back to the hotel has to be punished.

The termination of his contract would fit the indiscretion. Too harsh? Not at all. The punishment needs to be severe because a policy was in place that no one was to bring a lady back to the team hotel. Now this player knew it and had he not brought her back the whole incident would not have happened.

Next, using a hypothetical situation, even if the lady was a willing participant the players who chose to get involved still need to be disciplined. The lady was not supposed to be there so they should not have had anything to do with her. Their punishment should be a lengthy suspension from playing, which would impact on their financial position, and increased community services. What's lengthy? Twelve weeks.

Another example, where an allegation has brought the game into disrepute in England, is happening as I write this chapter. Two English Rugby League players are under investigation for waging a bet on a game of Rugby League their team was playing in. This is in contravention to their code of conduct and they both knew it. So, if they are found guilty, the punishment should be a life ban from playing Rugby League anywhere. That sort of message should stop it from happening again.

These issues aren't isolated to Rugby League—other sports have also had their fair share of controversy involving everything from allegations of rape to gambling and taking banned substances. Fans are sick of the continuing indiscretions of some of their sporting heroes, and are demanding that stronger action be taken now.

A heavy-handed zero tolerance policy would soon straighten out everyone and the few that don't come up to speed would be weeded out. Rugby League and other sporting codes need to adopt a zero tolerance policy *now* to regain the lost credibility sport has experienced over the past couple of years.

acknowledgments

To write this book was a bigger task than I expected. I want to thank the effort and work by Daniel Lane and everybody at Hodder Headline for their professionalism, working ethic and for keeping that personal touch. In particular, a special thank you to Matthew Kelly and Deonie Fiford for their commitment and dedication. Writing this book has been an eye-opener—it's been fun and I've thoroughly enjoyed it. Thanks to everybody who has contributed to the book and played a hand in my life and got me to where I am today. A big thank you to my family, my boys and, for all of her support, my best mate, lover and wife, Lesley.

index